I
HIT

Rick Alexander

◆ FriesenPress

Suite 300 - 990 Fort St
Victoria, BC, V8V 3K2
Canada

fictionrick.ca
info@fictionrick.ca

www.friesenpress.com

ISBN
978-1-5255-7846-5 (Hardcover)
978-1-5255-7847-2 (Paperback)
978-1-5255-7848-9 (eBook)

1. FICTION, CRIME

Distributed to the trade by The Ingram Book Company

Dedication

For all those born outside the box,
looking in.

PREFACE

Occasionally people have come to me and asked, "Did you hear about so and so getting shot?" A person might also try and get me to comment on an ongoing fight between two groups, that includes deaths.

I understand gossiping can be interesting; the problem is that <u>speculation becomes evidence.</u> Investigators, on both sides of the law, will react to speculation, leading to arrests or further deaths. So I always stay neutral around such serious topics, by giving no opinion.

I've heard a lot of street gossip. People get real inventive when they're in the midst of it all. Fingers pointing, combined with agents spreading creative stories, are an investigator's main tool. I have never been one who adds to the drama.

It dawned on me in the spring of 2019 that I should write a fictional book that would have all the realistic situations that create the recipe for a blood feud. I wrote the first draft in ninety days, at approximately two thousand words a day, six days a week.

I did my best not to make the book feel like it was about any specific person or situation. This is a fictional story. No real person is depicted in these pages. This story is my participation in the gossip; I've delivered an opinion that everyone can read and openly talk about. I tried very hard to use names that haven't been in the news. It was difficult. I found there are only so many names, and so many accused. Any likeness to a name or place is due to the limited amount of names in existence.

There are no real characters in my book. Please don't ask me, "Is this character supposed to be so and so from Surrey?" Every character is fictional, just as every situation is fictional.

While writing this first book, I quickly realized that the story is too big for one book. I made notes as I wrote to create books two and three. A three-book series is the only way I can give an accurate depiction of the life that people are living while trying to survive outside the law.

I had a lot of fun writing this story. I want everyone to enjoy reading it as much as I enjoyed writing it. This is the first time I let loose and imagined, producing a complete story. So enjoy the read; and don't ask me if this is a true story!

1

Walking along the sidewalk in the upscale residential neighbourhood, Damon takes in all the actors in this theatre playing their part. The morning sun is still low over the Cascade Mountains to the east, casting a shadow across the dew-covered lawns from the houses on his left. The executive homes are endowed with glass walls on their backs to take in sunrises every morning.

All the soccer moms have their kids at school, and are out doing their daily grind, which starts around 8 a.m. in this area. A garbage truck is pulling away from the last house at the end of the street, which has only six houses within Damon's view. The sweeping road is designed to give each 6500-square-foot house a bit of privacy. The yards are well spaced, with at least 100 yards between each home. All the cars that should be here are sitting in their usual spots. On Damon's left, one neighbour's red Porsche Cayenne sits in its driveway on the right-hand side of the garage doors; it never leaves before 10 a.m. On the right-hand side of the street is a company Escalade, limo black with windows to match. This one is here until at least 5 p.m. When Damon had walked along this street at 10 p.m., the driveways were full of hundred-thousand-dollar cars, at least two at each house. Although the bills are higher, this is still a working-class neighbourhood; everyone has a place to be every day, like clockwork.

Damon is breathing in fresh air with that touch of morning dew from the light rain the night before. Damon hears the deadbolt on the house to his left side go. *Click bang.*

Damon notices a man, about forty years old, coming out the front door of the next property in a white spa-like housecoat; the man stops, bends, and grabs the newspaper that the paperboy dropped off at about 6:30 a.m. Damon bends over and gives his shoelaces a light tug. Once they're undone, he begins tying them again. He sees the man turn and reach back through the red front door, placing the newspaper on an unseen shelf or chair. The house is by far the nicest on the block, with copper gutters and tinted windows. The exterior is made of light-grey stone blocks. This gentleman is the only guy home on a weekday in this strip of houses. The only reason Spa Man is outside is to give his small Bichon, with its perfect lion haircut, a morning potty break. Damon knows he'll also grab his garbage can.

This neighbourhood has been nice to hang out in, Damon thinks as he stands and begins to walk. He moves a little slower than he would normally, if he were going somewhere. The man in the white housecoat walks towards the street to grab the garbage can. He looks at

Damon in the casual way any neighbour does at this time of day, when nobody else is around. He's waiting for the acknowledgment that anyone normal gives another in the unique privacy of an unplanned encounter.

Damon has on glasses that are only glass; he doesn't need eye correction, but he does need to cover his face. His coat is a beige high-end West Coast sport jacket, his pants the type of professional beige slack that someone well-off might think of as a casual walking pant. Damon off-handedly lifts his left hand in a dismissive but polite wave, and shines a half smile that says, "I don't want to talk to a guy in pyjamas who's collecting garbage cans."

The man in the white housecoat is almost at his garbage can, and gives the same greeting back. The man gets to his can before Damon passes by. Damon hears silence on the street. The man in the spa coat quietly calls out, "Prada, get outta there." Damon plays his part and casually looks; the dog is going into the flower garden under the front windows of the house. The man is ten feet in front of Damon, about to grab the garbage can, but the little white dog digging up the garden is disrupting the act. Damon does what any good actor does in a live theatre—improvises. He comes to a stop in mock shock, mimicking what the man is doing. The man naturally looks back at Damon with the exaggerated distressed look that some get with their pets.

Damon, laughing lightly, "Dogs eh?" He turns and walks again, which gives the man in the spa outfit the opportunity to get back to his garbage and dog duties.

The Spa Man added grabbing the garbage can to his morning routine this week. He quickly grabs the rolling can with his left hand and turns to his right, all the while keeping his eyes locked on the little dog. The white fluff-ball is wrecking the garden and getting dirty. Spa Man starts his walk back to the house. In that same moment, Damon very casually reaches into his big sport-jacket pocket, making sure not to grab the trigger on the loaded .22 calibre autoload pistol.

Damon watches the man's eyes, and his focus, turning to the dog. The man takes two steps towards the house; Damon takes two steps straight down the sidewalk, passing out of the man's peripheral vision. Damon makes a move that he has drilled at least 5,000 times. He draws his gun from his pocket without any snags between the firearm and his clothes. And in the same moment his step changes direction; he's facing the Spa Man's back. Damon levels the gun at the base of Spa Man's skull.

All is as it should be in this part of the play: no neighbours, yard workers, or any other people, and right in the middle of a busy city. He sees the spot the bullet will land. *Am I blessed?* The first shot rings, *pop*, a hit. The Spa Man's entire body tells the tale that something is seriously wrong. He looks as though he has been gripped by an electric shock, as he falls to his left. Damon shuffles a half-step closer and to the right, so he can place a second follow-up shot in the brain.

Pop

This one is a direct centre-of-the-brain hit. As the second hit lands the man is already half-way down. He hits the ground with both shots in his skull. Damon has already turned and is casually placing the gun back in his pocket, making sure to not snag the metal on his coat.

As Damon turns away, he notices the little white dog's round head sticking out of the orange daffodils, wide-eyed. The dog has never been to a gun range, and is mute with fear as it looks at the two humans; one on the ground, and one walking casually away.

SURREY, 9:22 A.M.

"911 emergency, what is the nature of your emergency?" the female operator asks in a calm, level voice.

Nancy's voice is hushed and raspy. "I think maybe… no, for sure maybe, someone was shot in the street."

"Where are you, ma'am?" the operator asks.

Nancy has her back against the wall in her master bedroom, whose window faces a row of houses with the Cascade Mountains behind them. "I'm in my room."

The operator responds back, "Are you in any danger?"

Nancy looks around the room. With a sigh of relief she says, "No, I'm alone in my house and what I heard was outside across the street."

The operator notes from the call tracing that this is an upscale area, but hasn't called in shots fired, yet. She needs a few more details. "Ma'am, what is your name and address?" Nancy answers calmly and correctly. The operator asks, "Can you describe what you saw?"

"Yes, I was outside on my master bedroom patio working on my laptop, and I heard two little bangs like Halloween. I put my computer down and stood up to look around. When I looked down the street, I saw a person lying face-down on the ground in a housecoat. Another man was walking away from him."

The operator types in "Shots fired" and sends it to police dispatch.

"I watched them for some time. The man on the ground never moved, and the other man walked away."

"What was the walking man wearing?"

Nancy stutters. "Maybe a grey jogging suit, or brown?"

The operator announces, "Nancy, the police are on their way. Can you safely look back outside and tell me what you see?"

Nancy takes her weight off of the wall, as soon as the operator asks the question she's turning to peek around the doorframe. She has left her glasses out on the deck, but she's not going to get them.

Nancy is edging her head around the corner; she sees the man in the white housecoat lying still on the ground, exactly where she last saw him. Her heart races, and she knows he's dead. "I see the man on the ground." Nancy looks along the sidewalk where she last saw the other person, but there's nothing. She looks all the way to the end of the road; there's no one anywhere. "I don't see anyone else."

SURREY, 9:23 A.M.

Damon knows the clock is ticking. He has adopted methods from numerous government and military-agency books that have been written about E/E, escape and evasion. One of the books highlighted, "The enemy has a plan to mobilize itself and capture and kill invading forces. You need to know that plan."

The main difference is the people trying to catch a hitman here in Canada aren't actually his enemy, and under no circumstances are "booby trapping, or setting up an ambush to create more chaos," options. So everything Damon has read about the proven tactics from heroic soldiers, who have the full support of their government to do their killing, needs to be edited and adjusted. He has a much harder job to ensure there are zero 'enemy' casualties during live operations. All his plans involve him being invisible and disappearing. His family has been in Canada for generations. He won't even consider harming an innocent person doing their job: planning, planning, planning.

The sidewalk is shrouded in shadows from the houses on the left, reaching halfway across the street at this time every day. Damon stays on the left side of the road to keep his body in the shadows, even though there's a direct route kitty-corner across the street to his vehicle, which is parked at the end of the block and to the right.

His heart is pounding so hard he can hardly hear his thoughts. Without moving his head, Damon's eyes are like a lizard's looking for any sudden moves. His ears are on 100 percent alert for any changes in the environment, such as an upset brother with a 12-gauge shotgun running up behind him. Or an off-duty police officer with his service dog, targeting him. *Stop it, stick to the plan you've drilled. Too many movies man, breathe in deep, breathe out, repeat.* As Damon gets to the end of the street, he's able to peer back down the road and have a good look at the scene. He resists looking around like an owl from the moment he fired the second shot, but that would be useless—and draw attention from anyone who just started to pay attention to the street. So he's always had it in the plan to look to the right as he crosses at the corner, no jaywalking.

Nothing has changed at all; the street is completely empty. The Spa Man is only a little white bump; if any new observer sees him from this distance, they won't look twice. Maybe a rock, maybe a pile of recycling?

Anyhow, his heart slows twenty-five percent after that good look back. No boogeymen armies filing out of the grey stone building to avenge their fallen leader. Damon casually looks at his watch, and sees that it's 9:23 a.m. He knows that the shots went off after 9:21, because it takes one minute and thirty-seconds to get from the front of the stone house to this spot at the opposite end and other side of the street. Damon is passing the first house on the corner, a giant blue Victorian dollhouse with white trim.

The first time-check to make sure plan A is going along as planned has gone fine. It's all by the clock after the shots ring. No time for on-the-spot thinking. If measured planning is good enough for special forces to work this way, it's gotta be good enough for a regular assassin.

Damon walks off the curb and goes around to the back of his newer-model blue Toyota Corolla. He grabs the fob in his left pocket and unlocks the car while walking. Damon gets in, puts on his seat belt, and inserts the key into the ignition. The car starts quietly.

Damon turns on the lights, shoulder checks, and pulls casually away from the curb.

Nice and slow, he reminds himself.

2

Officer Sara McDonald is parked at the Tim Hortons' on 56th Ave, located in a district of Surrey. "Shots fired," announces over her radio. Her heart races in anticipation of the maximum horror: is this the start of a school shooting? Open firefight with assault weapons between two rival drug gangs? Officer Down?

She looks at her car's information screen. "Residential shots fired, neighbour heard two small-arm rounds. A man down, and a person in a light jogging suit spotted walking away." Sara's body relaxes as she hits her duty car's lights and heads over to the scene. Sara is well-versed in residential shootings. This is Surrey, which held a record as the shooting capital of B.C a few years earlier.

As Officer Sara drives around the traffic at one of the red lights heading westbound on Highway 10, she keeps her eyes on the road like a hawk. Sara wants to floor the throttle, but nobody ever moves fast enough for a police cruiser. So she has to go around all the sleepy public who don't know about a shooting, and who probably think

13

this marked police car is after a speeder, or someone who's texting.

Sara is heading westbound on 56th in the far-right lane. She cuts left from the curb lane around the other traffic as she pulls a screeching turn onto Highway 15 southbound. Her sirens and lights have been on since she pulled out of Tim Hortons. She negotiates this driving manoeuvre while laying on her horn. Sara is seeing everything at once in the complicated highway intersection.

Sara presses the gas pedal to the floor. Her cruiser rips down the road that heads south towards the U.S. border. *It's about ten minutes to the scene, at full speed with no delays.* Sara sees an update on her screen that a second police cruiser is five minutes out. She knows this guy will wait for backup before getting out of his car. Sara keeps the pace up, 130 to 150 kilometres an hour when no cars are around, under 120 kilometres an hour when passing civilians.

Sara turns into a residential area that was developed two years ago. She remembers that each house is unique, and all with generous yards. *Fancy folks.* Sara has slowed to fifty kilometres an hour, scrutinizing every yard and vehicle that she passes. *No light jogging suits yet.*

Sara is an active Judo black belt and an award-winning shooter, both pistol and rifle. If she sees anyone wearing a light jogging suit, she'll slam on her brakes and take them down with gun drawn; if her gun gets jammed or broken, she'll physically handle them without a second thought. It's her duty; she gets paid to do this, and wants to do this part of the job.

As Sara turns left past a big blue Victorian house onto the street of the report, she sees the other cruiser parked in the middle of the road with its lights on. It has its headlights pointed at a fallen garbage can, or maybe a white bag of garbage, or some rocks. *Nope, that's the victim,* her mind races.

She grabs her radio transmission button. "When I stop this car, you get out and cover me while I look around the front of the building. Use your long gun, I'll use my sidearm."

A man's voice comes back over the radio, his voice shaky. "Okay Sara, thanks for getting here so fast." Sara knows the other officer is a good guy, and has passed physical training and the firearm course, but he has very little actual skill in combat. He's aiming for an office job and a good retirement. When they first met on the gym mats, Sara thought that a guy so fit and well put-together would be there for a fight; instead he ran right into her hip toss and had the wind knocked out of him for three minutes. Since that toss she's been taking him aside and showing him how to fight. She silently vows to teach him how to shoot better.

Sara parks her cruiser on an opposite angle to the other cruiser, facing the victim, and leaps from her car. Behind the open driver door, she draws her 9mm autoloader pistol from its holster. She quickly scans the front of the house. The front windows being tinted, she can't see inside; she guesses that no shots came from inside the home, considering the victim's housecoat and direction of fall.

Realizing these houses have vast yards, she holsters her sidearm, reaches into her car, and grabs her long rifle instead. Loading the magazine into the rifle, she pulls the bolt back to load a round. *These assholes better drop their weapons and hit the deck before I find them.* Sara shoots a plate-sized target out to sixty yards with her pistol. With this rifle, Sara easily hits targets out to 250 yards while standing, and out to 400 yards once she lays prone.

Sara looks over at the other officer; he has his rifle up to his shoulder and looks ready. They both nod, and she takes off to the right side of the house. Walking tactically, S.W.A.T. style: rifle shouldered, knees bent, looking through the scope with one eye and looking far with the other.

As Sara gets far enough to the right, she sees the tall fence that surrounds the backyard, with the gate closed and grass untouched. Sara's hunting trips with her dad and uncles in Northern B.C. have given her skills that complement hunting suspects every week. She recognizes the familiar sound of tires screeching as two other cruisers converge on the street. She grasps her radio and tells them, "The two cars already here can secure the scene. Go search the area for the Walker or any other suspicious activity."

Wup wup wup. She hears the familiar sound of the turbine engine of an Air 1 helicopter as it swings in from behind the grey house. The chopper has a white fuselage and thick blue and yellow and red stripes . The helicopter is an EC 120, one of the RCMP aircraft that is always in the air. The radio lights up again. "Air 1 here. The backyard is empty, and there's no human movement in any of the yards or on the street that we can see."

Sara grabs her radio and suggests Air 1, "Get a little altitude and look for the light-suited Walker and any other suspicious activity." Air 1 agrees, and she hears the power added to the engine. The pilot pulls up on the collective controls and starts a fast and smooth ascent up another couple of hundred feet before patrolling around like a giant insect. Sara carefully walks over to the victim. Her right hand holding her rifle to her shoulder, she speaks into her radio in a calm voice. "Stay vigilant. I'm going to check the victim for life signs." The officer nods yes when she looks to him for a confirmation.

The blood from the head is a small pool about three feet long and one foot wide; the victim's eyes are staring out at the cruiser in the street. The cheek on the ground is stretched down to the chin, pulling his eyelid away from the eye, and his neck is cranked past normal range for comfort, from all the weight of the body pushing towards the top of his head. His right shoulder is under the weight of his pressing body, and his arm is protruding out from under the torso with the palm flat. Sara determines, *Nobody conscious can lay like this.*

She's able to get to his neck to check for a pulse. As soon as her hand touches his skin, she's almost certain there will be no life signs. After trying for twenty seconds, she finds no pulse. When hunting moose Sara is always amazed at how, from the moment of the kill shot on large game until the moment the hunting party arrives, the skin cools so quickly. The feeling of being alone arrives, even though there is another 'living' being right there. Dead feels dead, always the same. This guy is dead.

She looks around the scene and sees a .22 calibre cartridge closer to the garage, about ten feet away. When she evaluates the downed man, there's no blood on his back. With blood slowly trickling from his head and the shell right there, this is probably the work of someone he knows. *Is the shooter an associate, and this is a conversation that went bad?*

Screech, roar. Sara knows right away this isn't a cruiser approaching; this engine sounds like a drag car. She stands up quickly, but not in a panic; she is the one holding an assault rifle.

A slime-green Lamborghini skids across the neighbour's lawn, all four tires spinning at warp speed, spitting dirt in the air to get around the police cruisers. It stops in the driveway of the grey stone house at breakneck speed.

Sara lowers her weapon, because the look of horror on the driver's face says it all. 'I know that guy on the ground; I'm coming over to help.'

The other officer keeps his position at his cruiser, knowing Sara can handle the single crying woman who has emerged from the green race-car. Lambo lady wails, "Noooo no no!"

Sara jumps around the body on the ground so as not to interfere with evidence, and she meets the hysterical lady as the other woman clears the open car door. The screaming lady isn't planning on a fight; when Sara grabs her with her left arm around her waist and steps behind the lady's left heel, it's effortless to take her balance while turning her away from the sight of the dead man. As gently as turning a toddler, Sara puts the woman face-down on the back of the green car, kicks her feet apart, and holds her with a forearm across the woman's upper back.

There's no resistance, only bawling tears. "Ahhh no, please nohohoo…"

3

Damon turns left onto Highway 15, heading northbound out of the upscale neighbourhood. *For the last time*, he thinks happily. Damon keeps the car in the right lane as he gets up to traffic speed on the four-lane highway. The slow lane, as everyone calls it, but really it's the speed-limit lane. Everyone who has a fun sports car, or a company vehicle where fuel costs don't matter, drives in the left lane. And all the people who have to be somewhere in a hurry also race in the left lane.

Damon's blue Corolla is behind a newer green Subaru Forester. The car that Damon has pulled in front of is a ten-year-old grey Civic, and it speeds up and merges into the left lane, the driver wanting to prove that he has enough juice to keep a position in front of the Corolla. The hood of the grey Civic is past the back-end of the Subaru when Damon looks forward; the Civic has blocked him behind the Subaru. Then a wave of cars come up from behind. Damon knows that unmarked cars are normal. *This could be it, the cops are boxing me in.*

His chest feels as if an invisible hand is pulling on his lungs. *Head forward, breathe in for ten seconds, breathe out for ten, eyes forward hands at ten and two on the wheel,* his internal Coach reminds him, in the calm voice of an instructor who helps you train for a test and knows you can do it. *The only defence is not to exist. You are not who they are searching for, you are a regular civilian driving to work slowly.* The car that pulls up behind him is right on his tail; a black Ford Explorer with a broken headlight and a slightly crumpled hood to match.

This is not a duty car, his Coach assures him. *The police have plenty of cars that don't have broken parts.* The grey Civic has the older black Range Rover riding its ass. He assumes the cars have been racing, and are held up by Damon's boring group of cars. The little grey Civic picks up its pace to get ready to pull in front of the green Subaru in the right lane.

The black Ford Explorer, seeing the opening starting in the left lane, quickly pulls in about three feet off the tail of the Range Rover; the two vehicles are definitely in a street race. With his eyes forward but seeing the action beside him, Damon suddenly notices the red and blue flashes reflecting off the side of the Civic and blasting over the Subaru.

His inner Coach's voice says, in a level and reassuring tone that doctors use to tell people they have thirty days to live, *If they spotted your car at the scene, then the cruiser that's flying towards you will do a U-turn and pull up behind you, and that will be it. Air 1 will call for air support, and the rest of the police cruisers will head to you as well.* This time Damon answers his Coach. *Shut the fuck up, Captain Obvious.*

As the cruiser speeds by going at least 140 kilometres an hour, Damon doesn't even glance at it. The little race that the Civic, Range Rover, and Explorer on his right have been enjoying blocks all sight of the officer driving the car. All Damon hears is his heart pounding as the sirens get quieter and quieter.

A couple of minutes later, still heading north as he passes through Cloverdale on Highway 15, Damon checks his rear view mirror as two more police cruisers take a left back to the scene. Their lights are on, sirens blaring. This time his heart stays level; the police have no reason to pretend to head in the opposite direction. Damon knows the drive will be calm.

As Damon turns onto Highway 1 east, he reflects on how long it has taken to get this far in this job, and how long a day he still has to wrap it up. *Take all the little steps that were laid out months ago,* his Coach pipes up in a helpful and positive tone.

This time Damon nods slightly, with a feeling of weight lifting off his chest. The hit is done, and the debt will be removed. *I'll have time for normal things again*, he envisions in disbelief.

This 'easy job,' as he first presumed, has taken five months and twenty-two days, including today. And that doesn't include the upcoming two days it will take to legally remove the debt that Damon owes to the men who hired him.

He drives along the highway for about an hour, then takes an exit outside of a town called Hope. At the edge of the Cascade Mountains, Damon takes the car onto a gravel service road that gives access to logging activity. He drives for about twenty minutes at the best speed to not damage the car on the potholes and loose gravel.

Should be around here somewhere...there it is. A sharp turn to the right into the bush leads to a thin road, probably manicured by a four wheel drive club. About 100 yards down the road there's a campsite that has enough room for two vehicles to pass. Damon gets out as soon as he turns the engine off, locks the door, and heads into the trees on the right hand side of the car. Once he's about twenty yards into the bush he stands still, breathing very quietly. Checking his watch, he sees that it's 10:35 a.m. Damon remains motionless for ten minutes, listening to the forest. He read this is what special forces do when they're dropped behind enemy lines, the logic being that anyone who's already there will make a sound and you'll know you're not alone. There's silence, intermittent leaves falling, and after a few minutes birds starting to sing.

The slight trickle of a creek that Damon didn't notice before, most likely runoff from one of the mountains that surround the area. The sun is bright today, but the forest drips with water from the heavy rain that constantly saturates these hills. In the mountains around Hope the only direct sunlight is around noon, so the light is even, and with the ground being perpetually wet in this area, everything has a shine to it. The green foliage of ferns glows brightly.

Damon steps carefully so as not to make any unnecessary sounds. After twenty minutes of ducking under logs and climbing cautiously over a couple more, he finds the spot that he prepped five months and twenty-one days ago.

The earth is untouched by humans, so he walks around a pile of boulders that is about four-feet high and ten-feet around. Damon puts on a pair of white rubber gloves; then he reaches under the rock and pulls out a heavy black garbage bag, about half-full of supplies. Untying the knot, he pulls out a plastic freezer bag and a small white jug of bleach. He pours roughly three cups of bleach into the bag; holding the bag in his left hand, he reaches into his right-hand pocket and grabs the .22 caliber auto-loader. Damon places the bag on the ground and drops the magazine straight out of the gun and into the bleach bag. He rolls the pistol and pulls the slide back, the round from the chamber falls directly into the same bleach bag. Then, with the slide still open, he drops the gun in and presses the bag flat on the ground. Keeping the opening from spilling any bleach, he rolls the bag, removing the excess air as he seals it. He gives it a good shake, then tosses the gun and bag away from the rock pile about ten feet.

Damon pulls his shirt and pants off; the fresh air feels good as he pulls off his underwear and becomes completely naked. The forest is so quiet and calm. *I wish I always felt this relaxed.*

Damon stands naked, breathing in the fresh air. He feels a light wind blowing the hairs on his legs, which are never normally touched by a breeze. Damon is 6'1" and 190 pounds, with brown hair kept an inch on top and buzzed on the sides. He studies his legs and sees the hair moving in the breeze. The short fine hair is all blowing slightly to the right. He tenses the quad muscle on his left leg; it reacts by the top going flat and a split forming down the middle; at the bottom of his quad where the muscle connects to the knee, two round edges appear. Damon relaxes the quad and lifts his left heel off the ground, keeping the heel in the air he flexes his calf, which goes from round and smooth to corded muscle. *Man I have skinny legs.*

Although the truth is that Damon knows he is above average in fitness. He keeps his legs and cardio in better shape than his arm muscles, consistently going out to the trails that dot the North Shore Mountains next to Vancouver and Maple Ridge. He hikes with the goal to get better results every time he's out. Damon's stomach is flat but not a six pack; he loves chips too much to care about a beach body. 350 mixed crunches three times a week keeps his core stable. Damon has been doing this crunch regimen for so long he often forgets how hard it was to get up to 350 crunches in fifteen minutes. These days he doesn't even break a sweat; he's usually thinking about chores while going through the crunch drill.

Damon stands and examines his arms for any sign of evidence; there's nothing the naked eye can see, anyway. Damon has no tattoos on his arms or back; his upper chest has ink on it, though it's out of sight while clothed: a great bald eagle in the classic talons-out-front-grabbing-dinner pose.

Reaching into the garbage bag, he pulls out a new set of clothes; not brand new. Old clothes he packed here five months and twenty-one days ago, specifically for today. Blue boxers, white sport socks, blue jeans, white shirt, some brown slip-on ankle-high boots, a black jean jacket, and, last but not least, his black cap. Damon places all the other clothes he had been wearing earlier this morning, about $1,000 worth, into the black garbage bag. He takes the bleach bottle cap off and, keeping the bottle in the bag so as to not splash his new clothes, dumps the whole bottle in the bag. *What a shame to waste that nice coat, and I can't even buy one like it to replace it. I'll never own a beige waterproof sports coat, what a shame.*

He laughs out loud, at the thought of this being a problem.

Walking the open garbage bag over to where he threw the gun in the freezer bag, he picks the freezer bag up and puts it in the garbage bag, ties off the garbage bag, and gives it all a good shake and turn to mix the potent bleach into all the material.

Damon scans to his right and spots the little mound, about three feet high. It could be an ant hill, but if it is then he's the ant that built it. The pile is loose dirt from the hole at his feet. Damon gets on his knees and reaches into the old hole, pulling out the leaves and sticks that have fallen in. These he places to his left, and then he tosses the garbage bag into the hole. The top of the bag is only about two feet from the top of the hole, not really deep enough but far enough for this situation. The worst case is that the bag is found in ten to twenty years, and then what?

They do forensics on a bleach-rusted old gun that anyone, anytime, could have put here?

Damon always goes too far for evidence destruction. *Guys are throwing guns on the body and not getting caught, this hole is overkill.* Another voice in his head speaks; this voice is one that Damon never likes to listen to, the Simple voice that always advises plans. *Don't worry, shoot them in front of a crowd and run, it's fine, a guy in Toronto did it.*

Follow trusted methods, his Coaching voice counsels with confidence. Damon nods in agreement as he cleans the last of the leaves and fallen sticks off of his ant hill.

Taking off his black jean-jacket, he pulls the dirt into the hole by hand, then two hands at once, pulling like a kid in a sandbox. Once the loose soil is a pile about twelve inches above level ground, he pats the dirt. Rain will flatten it at least ten inches over the winter. Damon carefully places the leaves and sticks all over the freshly packed dirt, so it nearly matches the ground cover.

He rises and dusts his knees, then reaches to where his knees have made two little indents in the dirt, and gently rubs the dirt flat. He picks up his jean jacket and walks to the small creek, twenty feet towards the direction of his car. Peeling his rubber gloves off and putting them in his jacket pocket, he rinses his hands and arms in the creek. The ice-cold water feels so invigorating as it numbs the skin of his arms that he splashes it on his face, too; he allows some to go into his mouth, which is dry from all the activity with no water. Damon only drinks a few sips of this mountain run-off, knowing that any logging upstream or a dead animal in the creek could cause him a sickness he can't afford.

Anyhow, he'll be back to civilization within two hours. As he turns to leave the area, Damon scrutinizes the spot where the hole had been; it's gone. From twenty feet away, if you didn't know where to look, you'd never see it. After a winter of snow and rain, the ground will be hard and flat; and those boulders next to the hole assure that anybody who brings equipment through will pick another route.

The evidence is gone.

As the short twenty-minute walk back to the car is nearing its end, Damon stops at the twenty-yard listening post. He hears the roar of a semi-truck passing the little road he's on; the guy must be doing fifty kilometres an hour. These trucks work with local radio communication, so other big rigs know when they have the right of way. Little cars, like the Corolla, pay attention and pull out of the way; that's the system out here.

Damon stands listening for new human activity on his small camp road. He smiles because even if some guys do show up, all he has to do is come out of the bush and be friendly. "Hi guys, I pulled over for a piss, is that a four-inch lift? Cool, a winch on the front and the back! Well, gotta go, bye for now." Nobody will walk in here and start digging a hole; it really is over.

This is precaution and protocol for wrap up. After fifteen minutes nobody is around, so he ducks out of the tree line, gets in the car, and pulls out.

4

Detective Wolvsmere is known as the Wolf, mostly because of his name but also thanks to his job. Tracking criminals and eating them—well, arresting them anyway. The Wolf is fifty-nine-years-old and 6'3", and has the frame of an ex-linebacker. His hair is a grey buzzcut, his skin has a tan that tells of long golf days or a recent holiday, and he wears thin silver aviator sunglasses all day.

He sits in his unmarked service car, a black Ford Taurus with black tires and blacked-out windows. The Taurus isn't an undercover car, simply unmarked; his vehicle has an information-centre on the dash and all the other police goodies.

The Wolf sits watching the forensic team measure evidence locations and photograph the body of Mr. Fukadero, which still lies in front of his stone castle, hit by the full light of the sun from its high-noon position. Little yellow number cards stand by two .22 caliber shells. The body of Mr. Fukadero is being prepped to load away; he's still in his white housecoat, laid out flat in a body bag on a gurney. As they zip up the thick black bag, the Wolf lifts his chin, *This forensic team sure is efficient.* A moment later he lowers his head, accepting that the forensic and homicide departments work so well together because of all the grim work in Surrey.

When he was a young man, the Wolf imagined himself as a detective. With only a handful of murders a year, he had believed he could hound all of the suspects until everyone knew to not even bother killing each other. Now, with all the gang killings that have flared up, different communities fight for resources with the same desperation that they did back in their ancestors' home countries. It's more or less weekly that he's called out to a murder, and he definitely never gets out of a month without standing over a new body on the ground. The Wolf reviews the full circle this situations gone around, and how there is one more traditional path this will take.

The Wolf remembers a story one of his fellow officers told him the year before. This land developer who had a bunch of issues paying the trades was being threatened. "It's the police's job to help legitimate business men," Mr. Fukadero had pleaded with the officer. So the police arranged a sting to catch the violent Polish gang that was trying to extort Mr. Fukadero. The only reason they qualified as a gang was because they acted as a group of three, and used threats of violence to get paid.

"We have the courts to deal with arguments, not baseball bats," Mr. Fukadero stated affirmatively. He joked with officers about how, "out of touch these guys are with fair business practices. Signing legal agreements is what makes the world work smoothly, right?"

At the time, Mr. Fukadero was sitting in the police station signing the documents to have his place of business wired for video and sound. He wanted to catch these guys in the act of extorting him personally for the money an incorporated company owed them. The young officer was so happy to have a cooperating witness who would help him get a gang on extortion, he barely stopped smiling. He sat with the happy land developer to go over the wiretap legalities, confirming that Mr. Fukadero would participate in court as a witness.

"Yes, of course, if I need to go to court I'll be happy to. That's where business is supposed to be discussed," Mr. Fukadero had proclaimed when that document was brought to the table.

What the Wolf didn't know until he pulled the file up, here in front of the active murder investigation of Mr. Anthony Fukadero, is that this victim had a long history of 'helping' police.

When Mr. Fukadero was eighteen, he was pulled over for speeding. The officer smelled booze, and ordered him out of the red Mustang 5.0 with the five-star mags that his dad had bought him when he acquired his driver's license two years before. There was a fifteen-year-old girl with him at the time, and when officers asked her to step out of the car she started to cry and said, "The drugs in the trunk aren't mine, he told me we're dropping them off on the way to the movies." This statement gave the officer the right to search the car. Probably expecting to find some marijuana or a bit of mushrooms, the officer was more than a little shocked to see two kilograms of cocaine in a backpack. Mr. Fukadero, being ever so helpful, immediately offered to take the officer to the buyer if they would make it look like a random bust.

The officer did precisely that, and arrested both the buyer and the young Mr. Fukadero at the scene. The difference between the buyer and the seller was that Mr. Fukadero came from a wealthy family, and immediately synced up with the police investigation. The high-end attorney Mr. Fukadero's father paid for, Mr Livion, argued that the young Mr. Fukadero had been through enough; there was no way to have him as a witness against the person who supplied the two kilos of cocaine without endangering his life, and turning over the buyer was more than sufficient to show his cooperation. The courts agreed.

The buyer, Dean Schmitt, a twenty-two-year-old who lived in a rented apartment on his own, got a six year sentence, for which he served the full term due to violent tendencies in prison.

During that six years, it appeared Mr. Fukadero was an upstanding citizen. He began working for his dad managing rental properties, and when he was twenty-two years old he was even able to help the police in a major marijuana bust at one of the properties his family held as a rental, an acreage out in Mission B.C.

Mr. Fukadero had crashed the red Cadillac four-door that he had been given by his mom. The Wolf reads in the record that Fukadero had been drinking, and had driven straight into the back of a dump truck while speeding to pass. The dump truck wasn't severely damaged, but he felt so bad—and also didn't want to be charged for drunk driving—that he mentioned that he might have seen 130 pounds of dried marijuana in one of his rental properties. The officers liked the sound of a major bust over a drinking and driving charge, so they moved forward.

Sure enough, in the locked garage of the address they had been given by young Mr. Fukadero, was 130 pounds of dried and cured marijuana in 260 half-pound freezer bags. The tenants who were working in the grow-room at the time tried to make a deal, saying they worked for a kid who ran the business for his dad. "Hey this rich kid comes here, and he pays us to grow weed here. So like he is our boss, right? His name is Tony."

The officers took note of the accusations, and when it went to court the high-priced attorney who the Fukaderos' had kept on retainer for years tore the growers' accusations to pieces on the stand. They got five years for cultivation with the intent of trafficking, and were labeled as informants because they were on the stand pointing the finger. They did eight months on good behaviour in protective custody. When they got out they all put in a request with their parole officer to move to Toronto, and it was granted.

The Wolf effortlessly climbs out of his Taurus and advances across the street; the cameras are being put away, and the studio lights as well. He saunters around the area where the body had been and around behind the slime-green Lamborghini that sits with its driver door still open. As he passes each officer they silently nod a 'hello' and he returns it. The Wolf isn't one for small talk; everyone knows that. He's gotten quieter since the murder rate has soared so high in his area.

He takes note of the security cameras that are on every corner of the house as he heads through the tall red doors. There's an officer standing a loose guard on the door. He's proudly wearing blue pants with a yellow stripe down the leg, the sign of all uniformed RCMP. He also has on a brown shirt, with all the regular police utilities on his belt. The Wolf gives a quick nod to the sentry but doesn't look at him; he's keeping his eyes out for the widow he has been briefed about over the radio.

There she is, to the right of the large sitting room, finished in designer white; white wallpaper with gold 3D spiral loops stretches from the white carpeted floor all the way to the fifteen-foot ceiling. The curtains are a heavy white material covered with a gentle pattern in gold stitching. Someone has closed the front curtains, he assumes to give the widow some privacy from the scene out front. The Wolf can only imagine how many meetings it took to find, cost, deliver, and install such beautiful curtains; maybe they cost as much as his house's assessed value? His home is in a residential area in Maple Ridge, and was built in 1965; the building was assessed by the city at about $80 grand due to its age. He's kept up on the maintenance over the years, but knows he needs blinds or curtains. He'll talk about it with his wife later. *My mind is drifting again, focus on these people.*

The problem here is that the Wolf knows that the woman isn't going to say anything. Her platinum blonde hair, is hanging loose behind her shoulders, and she's wearing a white Chanel pantsuit with black trim. With both hands she clutches a little white Bichon with a fancy haircut cut on her lap, as if she's never going to let it get away again. Also the 60-year-old white male attorney, with pock marked cheeks, in a custom cut dark suit. This seasoned lawyer stands vigil and repeats, "My client is going to submit her official statement later." He'll block this investigation with all his legal right.

The Wolf enters the room and introduces himself officially to everyone. Only two people in this room of three don't know him; the other is Sara. The star officer who everyone wants on their shift; he has to stifle a smile when he sees her. Sara is thirty-three years old, 5'9", with champagne blonde hair that she keeps in a tight bun while on duty. She has keen dark blue eyes. Sara lifts weight in the gym since her life depends on it, and uses a spotter for bench and squat. Her thick thighs are solid, and her back and neck are thick from overtraining. The Wolf has trained with her on the mats as well. Without him using his size and weight advantages, they are equal, and he's sure that if they went toe to toe it would be anyone's fight. Sara has a lot of Judo moves that combat his forty years of mixed fight training.

Sara sits with a compassionate look, facing the lawyer and the widow. She hasn't let the woman out of her sight since the moment the widow jumped from her sports car; possibly she's suicidal or vengeful, and could run straight to a gun. Or the widow might plain old mess with evidence. And of course Sara is there for compassion; it's her job, and she does it all correctly.

The widow Fukadero gloomily sits, staring at a spot on the floor halfway from herself to where the Wolf stands. When he introduces himself he's surprised to see her lift her gaze and smile politely. Her bright red lips open, and he catches a glimpse of her perfect white teeth. Her attorney speaks up quickly and affirmatively. "Ms. Fukadero has been through a lot, and will fill out the proper forms a little later."

The widow closes her mouth slowly, and with elegant control, gazes to the centre of the floor.

The Wolf knows Sara has the lawyer's card, so he doesn't ask for it. "Sir, this is a murder investigation, and I'll need to see your ID, now." He informs, with enough steel in his voice that everyone in the room turns to the attorney to see how he will answer. Knowing the Wolf is trying to rattle his position, Mr. Livion reaches into his pocket and pulls out his wallet.

Mr. Livion stands staring at the Wolf for two seconds with the wallet in his hand, his body language is flippant. Then he quickly changes his mind and walks the wallet over to the Wolf, who never takes his eyes off the attorney. At the same time, he watches the widow's body language for any changes when the attorney moves away from her. She's a rock. Her face has been cleansed, and her makeup subtly refreshed.

The Wolf takes the wallet without inspecting it and voices over his right shoulder, " Officer," in a regular tone. Three seconds later the guard from the front door steps beside the Wolf, but not past him. "Take this wallet and photograph its contents for evidence." The officer takes the wallet and walks away quietly.

The Wolf stands surveying the beautifully furnished room, letting the air clear a bit. In a calm and kind tone, "Mrs. Fukadero…or may I call you Chloe?"

The attorney goes to open his mouth but seems to have a feeling that if he does, the Wolf might eat him. And since this is merely a friendly 'let me get your name' situation, he lets it pass.

"Chloe is fine, sir."

"Okay Chloe, please call me Bill. This is a terrible tragedy that has happened to you, so you have the right to call me by the name my mother gave me. To you I'm Bill, okay?"

Chloe directs her gaze solidly at the Wolf, and he sees in her eyes the confidence she has from years of making good choices and picking the right side. "Okay Bill, thank you." The attorney believes that the intrusion with his client is over, but as Chloe is lowering her eyes again she asks in a whisper that hangs in the air, "May I have your card, Bill?"

Bill smiles as he sees the attorney's many hours of work keeping Sara and all the other officers from Chloe go out the window; the other man's shoulders drop. *So he really doesn't want me talking to her,* the Wolf notes as he moves across the room. He makes it seem as if he's going to hug Chloe, but he stops in front of the attorney instead, over an arm's length away from the girl. He has to bend at the waist to hand his card over. "Chloe, I'm here for you. Nobody will stop you and me from having a relationship. I've trained my whole life to protect my citizens, and you're my main one right now." He pauses then; as he straightens up he fixes his eyes on the attorney, "We're all here to support you, Chloe. Please take comfort knowing that I'm *only* here to support you." Everyone in the room sees the attorney is taken aback by this large officer being attentive and talking so directly to his client.

Chloe lifts her head and glances toward the Wolf, and with a closed-mouth smile she lifts her right hand up so his card can be seen held between her pointer and middle finger. Her flawlessly manicured red nails match her lips so perfectly that getting them both in a person's view is this lady's game all day. *This one is a real player,* the Wolf senses.

Without taking her bloodshot eyes off Bill, Chloe places his card in her front chest pocket that's barely large enough to hold the single card. Then she returns her gaze back to the floor.

The Wolf drops the whole bother-the-attorney-and-connect-with-the-suspect act, and politely makes his way back to the door of the room. He stands there for a moment, and again in conversational voice over his shoulder, "Officer." The same man appears. In a courteous tone, the Wolf states, " I need you to stay here with Mrs. Fukadero and her attorney Mr. Livion. If Mrs. Fukadero needs anything you are to go with her and help. If she needs to go to the washroom, radio and Sara will come back to assist; if Mrs. Fukadero can't wait, then you are to wait at the door with it open and your back turned."

The Wolf turns to Chloe. "Ma'am, this is all normal operating procedure. We're here for you, and a counsellor is on the way."

Chloe, raises her eyes and nods a 'yes' with a quivering bottom lip. *She's probably sad we're not leaving,* the Wolf imagines; then his training comes back. *Don't put feelings on suspects without evidence.* "Sara, I need you for a few moments."

Sara makes eye contact with Chloe. "I am close. I'll be back in about fifteen minutes, and I'll wait for the counsellor with you."

It takes all of the Wolf's might not to stare at the widow to see what connection Sara has made with her; instead he allows his peripheral vision to inform him. Chloe locks eyes with Sara in a way that says, *You're my only friend here, and I never thought you'd leave, but I'm a big girl and I'll be strong, come back quick please.* Chloe whispers, "Thank you." This time Chloe stares into a far corner, away from everyone, as the tears start to flow. Her mouth loses all composure and begins to tremble through all the positions of anguish.

The attorney rests his hand on her shoulder in the most comforting way he legally can. The Wolf observes the attorney has a single tear dripping, and his other eye is welling up. The Wolf relaxes his stare before he turns to leave.

5

Damon has been driving west on Highway 1 for about twenty minutes. *I'm starving.*

Sometimes he packs a lunch, and if surveillance doesn't work out he eats on his way to the next appointment. But today he's been so excited about the uninterrupted time to meet the Fuk that he rushed his day. His plan had been that after all the driving and hiding the evidence, he would go and sit alone and have a proper lunch in his favourite Vietnamese pho restaurant; around 2 p.m. if all went as planned. Today he will be early for lunch.

As he comes into Chilliwack, though, he's hungrier than he had expected, and considers stopping at another place near a highway exit.

Yeah, that's what a boss does, when you're hungry you eat, offers his Simple inner voice. Damon hears its tone, a kid asking for candy when they know they're not gonna get it. His Coach voice pipes up. *The man in the field follows the plan that is given to him, that's how every military team that wins does it. Are you better than them?* Damon

43

avows in his head; his lips still move slightly. *No sir.* The Simpler voice is as quiet as an embarrassed underling.

Damon settles into the drive, happy to know he'll be making his lunch plan on time today. *I'm going to order spring rolls with my soup.* He envisions it as his lips curl up in the hint of a smile.

SURREY, 12:30 P.M.

As Sara and the Wolf leave the great white-adorned sitting room with him in the lead, he notices the officer upstairs, has some evidence bags lined near the top of the stairs. Other officers' voices come up from the basement. The Wolf doesn't have to walk around and check on any of his team. He has complete faith in their ability to find and log evidence. The evidence bags at the top of the stairs are most likely drugs or an improperly stored gun, maybe unregistered; that's why they've put them in a central location for pick-up. The Wolf knows everything these officers do today will be in a neat file on his desk by morning; he won't work this new case until the morning.

This house is huge; the spiral staircase is remarkable, the redwood railings and the dark wood stairs, topped off with all the custom white ironwork, it's a masterpiece for all visitors to admire. The Wolf keeps Sara walking out the front door. He knows the way Sara will handle this situation, and is glad to have her to confide in. "I know this has been a long morning, but can you skip the minor details and tell me anything important?" he encourages while they descend the three long steps and pass around the Lamborghini.

Sara starts as soon as he finishes his last word. She has a psychology background from university, and has been evaluating Chloe and Mr. Livion for hours. "Chloe arrived after the neighbour, Nancy, the lady who called 911, texted her about a possible shooting at her house. Officers are at Nancy's house getting a statement, as well as camera footage and evidence." The Wolf nods as they get to the back of his blacked-out Taurus. They both stop and turn to keep eyes on the grey stone house. Sara rests her hands on her hips. "Chloe did everything in her power to try and get me to let her go upstairs alone; man, she can talk. Crying mixed with reasoning. I gave her an out after ten minutes and asked if she wanted to clean up her face in her powder room, saying I had to come along. She dropped her shoulders and accepted that as 'her reason' for wanting to go up there alone. I directed four officers to dissect the upstairs." The Wolf nods to show he agrees.

"I don't know who called Mr. Livion, but he was here within forty minutes. Right away he started asking what Chloe had said, and that I 'was to leave them alone.' I didn't, obviously. I asked her 'the question' already, and her first answer was, 'The Polish guys killed Tony.' She never said anything else of importance. Her body language was angry, not sad. Anger was her mood; she tore a picture of Mr. Fukadero, Tony and her, off the wall in their room. The sorrow came about an hour after her arrival, a few minutes after the attorney."

All of this is old hat to the Wolf, he's waiting for Sara to confirm a couple points before he sets one of his plans into play. "I'll go over the file with you tomorrow when we start our next shift, but I can tell you these people are going to try and use us. How they will try to use us, I'm not sure. Can I ask you for some overtime hours on this job?"

Sara cannot believe he asked her permission for extra help; she's a bit insulted. When she looks at his face, the Wolf has a slight smile. Sara leans forward. "You have a funny side, sir. Of course, what can I do?"

SURREY, WHALLEY, 1:20 P.M.

Damon pulls into the generic one-level strip mall, a popular style from the 70s and 80s that usually contains mom-and-pop businesses: a barber shop, a tax office, a laundromat or whatever business doesn't need a building from this millennium. This particular strip mall is a six unit, with parking in the front and back. Damon pulls into the parking spot he has been using for this blue Corolla for the past five months. He has wiped his fingerprints off the surfaces and driven with rubber gloves on since he left the bush. *This is all you can do to hide your involvement with this vehicle. Somebody knows you have it,* his Coach explains in a voice that we all know as, 'It is what it is.' Damon doesn't bat an eye; this business is ripe with concerns, and this isn't a major one of them. He gets out of the car and puts the key under the driver-side mat, locks the door manually, closes the door, and turns and walks off through a thin hole in the cedar hedge that directly faces the back of the building.

After walking for eight minutes, Damon gets to his personal vehicle, a white Caravan that's three years old. Reaching into his jacket pocket, he pulls out a plastic bag with his keys and his wallet, unlocks the van, and gets into the driver's seat. His mouth is dry, and he grabs the litre of water from the cup holder that he brought with him in the morning.

Rookie mistake leaving your water, Damon. His inner Coach chimes in positively. *Hey, you won't do it again. It was an early morning operation with low intensity and medium temperature, you were never in a condition to dehydrate, only to suffer a little discomfort. Which of course leads to slower reaction times...* Damon shamefully cuts in, "Okay okay, better next time." Damon is alone; to make even the small mistake of not having water for five hours is one too many mistakes. He starts the white van, putting on his turn signal as he pulls away from the curb.

12:45 P.M.

"Sara, I'm putting your name on the file so you can access all the info I get. Will you review it before you see me at 10 a.m. tomorrow?"

Sara nods, the Wolf is about to lean on her; she's proud, but at the same time a little pissed at the time crunch. However, she knows the Wolf is a serious officer and has a vision that will succeed, so she cheers up right away. "Any direction for my dealings with Chloe?"

The Wolf smiles from ear to ear. "Get back in there and make sure your new best friend is all right."

Sara immediately walks back to the house as the Wolf turns to his car. They've spoken enough throughout the few years since Sara transferred to the Wolf's precinct that they know they're of one mind.

Everyone is a suspect.

LANGLEY, 2:15 P.M.

Damon is halfway through his large rare-beef noodle soup, and has half of a spring roll left. He has put a spoonful of chilli oil into the soup, and all his sprouts. On the spring roll plate he makes two even lines about three inches long, one of hot sauce and one of barbecue sauce, to dip the spring roll into. He has the newspaper open on the table above his food. The paper is already covered in drips from the lunch crowd, so he eats liberally and doesn't worry about the splashes that dot the newspaper. With his teapot and water glass empty, Damon raises a finger to the waitress, who knows him well. She dismissively waves and heads to her till. Grabbing a piece of paper with exaggerated roughness, she comes charging toward him.

"You wan beel?" she pipes in her broken English, with a huge smile and confidant eyes.

They both laugh as he pulls out his wallet.

"Ware jor famly?" she pries with mock disappointment in her voice and body language.

"My wife is getting ready for a family visit and my boy is at school."

"You bring dem here soon. I miss yer boy, he so cute, like da mom, not you!"

They both have a good laugh.

"Of course, they love you too, and your pho is the best in the area. Thank you, keep the change."

The Vietnamese lady walks off smiling. Damon wonders if she can tell he's a person under a lot of pressure. She always works to cheer him up, and it always works; she has a light heart and easily shares her joy. *Is it the soup or her that makes this place so great?* he wonders as she walks away. He picks up the bowl and drinks the rest of the broth, then uses the chopsticks to grab the last bites of meat and noodle. Standing with a high wave to the waitress, he walks out the door to his Caravan.

6

Damon pulls into his driveway in Langley. A quiet cul-de-sac in Walnut Grove, the entire yard is loose dirt all the way to the edge of the new house. The 2400-square-foot house was completed two months ago, and he has no time or money to finish the yard. There's a concrete driveway that holds four parked cars, but the front and back yards are still dirt pits. He's apologized to his neighbours so many times, because on windy days it paints their yards, cars, and houses with dust. Everyone is really understanding, and are all genuinely happy that a new home is on their street. Most of the houses have been built around 1980; this is the first newly built house, and it has been by luck how it has come together for him and his family.

His wife is picking their son from school, so Damon throws in a load of laundry, including the clothes he's wearing, and steps into the master bedroom's ensuite shower. Damon is happy with the tile-work and the heated floor. They have a soaker tub that fits only one person, but it is a comfortable three-feet deep. The double sinks are set in good quality quartz, and the satin-chrome fixtures all match nicely.

He gets out of the shower and brushes his teeth, drops his towel on the ground, and then jumps under the covers of the queen-size bed for a nap. His head is spinning from eating the large soup and concentrating all day.

"Hun? Damon? Are you up there?" His wife is in the kitchen downstairs. He hears his son throw his school bag in the middle of the floor. "Pick that up," she yells down as she comes up to find her husband. He wonders for a moment how she knows he's here.

She comes into the room and sees Damon in the bed, blanket up to his nose in a barefaced hide, he smells that she has recently cleaned the sheets. They lock eyes for a moment; smiling as she turns to the bathroom door. "Seriously Damon!" She becomes mad instantly, all her cheer gone. He knows right away what she sees. "You throw wet towels on the ground? If I don't find them they'll stink."

Damon defends himself weakly. "It's in the middle of the floor, not hidden. I was going to use it as a foot mat later."

She reaches down and grabs it. "Yeah right, how will we teach our kid anything if you can't even put a towel in the hamper?" She's going through the motions of getting a little dig in for fun.

"So are you in bed for the night, or are you going to get my parents from the airport tonight?" she asks, with the desperation in her eyes of a tired parent and wife.

Damon knows the pick-up is at 9 p.m., but plays a bit in his answer. "What time are they at the gate?"

"Nine tonight."

"Oh, I planned on sleeping until nine, then watching a couple episodes of whatever on Netflix. When you get back with them will you all be quiet?"

Her smile comes back; she knows that is a yes. Damon rolls over and closes his eyelids, which seal instantly. "Would you wake me up at dinner please?"

She's already gently shutting the door.

A second later, the sound of a siren makes his heart jump. His eyes blink. *Ree ooo ree ooo.*

Damon takes a long deep breath and makes a note to toss out his kid's damn toy police car. He chuckles about being a chicken shit. Scared by a toy. He drifts off to sleep.

LANGLEY, 6:30 P.M.

Damon is woken by his wife talking to him as though he's already awake, speaking lightly resembling waking a baby. She's talking about the next few hours as if to get the baby ready for the day. "Hun, hun, it's six-thirty, dinner is on a plate downstairs. I'm going to get our Benji from his gym, he's done at seven. If you leave for the airport right after you eat then you could stop and grab some groceries on the way."

Damon opens his eyes and feels fully awake. He hears Naomi in the dimly lit room and sees her by the closet at the end of the bed. She's pulling her pants down and he notices she's wearing a little purple thong. *Why would anyone wear a string up their butt?* He pushes the blanket off. The skimpy underwear are for his viewing pleasure, so he climbs out of bed with a quick purposeful motion that his wife knows well after ten years of marriage. He has a nap boner, their son is out, and with in-laws on the way, this is a golden opportunity that he's not going to miss.

Naomi hears him coming and before he gets a hand on her, she smiles and insists, "You be fast, I gotta go pick up Benjamin."

Damon answers as he grabs her on her right hip with his right hand and pulls the tiny underwear down with his left hand. "Then you stop talking about chores and I'll be quick," he replies with a hint of a playful order. She helps him take down the panties; when she bends over to pull them off her ankle he uses his left hand to grab the back of her neck and keep her bent over. He turns her towards the bed, and she's happy to have the bed to lay her torso on.

Damon moves his left hand off the back of her neck and moves it to the centre of her back, keeping a bit of downward pressure. Using his right foot he gently pushes on the instep of each of her feet, until she is standing with her legs apart. He then grabs his hard member and gently rubs the head on her lips; as soon as she is a little wet he pushes in halfway. She gasps, he pulls in and out a few times, then sinks all the way in.

He is done fast enough.

LANGLEY, 7:00 P.M.

At the grocery store that's five minutes from their home, Damon walks with an after-sex glow, wondering if it would be weird to wear sunglasses in a store. *The lights are so bright.*

After going through the grocery list Naomi has texted him, he grabs a few extras. He pays and leaves the store.

Outside, four young guys stand off to the side with their purchases in four bags; their shopping bag contents are age-appropriate: red drink cups, Cola, and chips. The guys are about twenty-five years old, and have the air of being well cared-for by adults. One is in a golf shirt, another has proper gym clothes with melon sized biceps. Damon surveys the guys standing there, one of them is staring right at him with squinted eyes. *'What the fuck are you staring at?'* Upon a closer examination, Damon determines these guys are already drinking. The right age to be university grads; nice clothes and good fitness, but young enough to stand around smoking and picking fights with strangers who are buying jugs of milk.

"You wanna say something?" The young guy snaps in a tone that foretells a fight. Damon is happy with the language he used, because it's a genuine opportunity to walk over and say something. Damon doesn't fight strangers in parking lots anymore, but if he did this guy wouldn't be a problem; so he changes direction and walks over. The other three guys are all taken aback by their pal's comment, and the fact that a man is coming over who they might all have to fight.

Checking each other like a hockey game is starting, they all need to see if the team is ready. The Bad Attitude kid keeps his eyes locked on Damon as he comes closer. This kid has probably won a few fights around parties and has never had his ass handed to him, or he'd know not to call out strangers.

Damon smirks as he closes on the group. They're all at least as big as him, and Bad Attitude kid is about 215 pounds. Damon stops about one-and-a-half arm-lengths away, with unblinking eye contact with the big kid. "How about, 'nice evening eh?' Or, 'glad it's not raining, I'm drinking and driving tonight.'" The three back-up guys start to relax at the nice evening part, and Bad Attitude is confused by it. All four look guilty once the drinking and driving comment is out.

These kids are so delicate. He watches them go through their emotions. *Someone has gotta tell them the truth,* Damon decides. "When I was in my early twenties I wondered how the police always knew to focus on my friends and I when we were out drinking, but when I see four guys with pop for mix, red drink cups, and bags of chips smoking in front of a grocery store picking fights. It's clear this is how the police picked us to check on." All this is said without taking his eyes off of Bad Attitude; the other three are blinking and looking over their shoulders. "Are you a black belt?" Damon asks the Bad Attitude Kid, politely enough.

In a cocky smart-ass way the kid answers, "Don't need one, I always win."

Damon doesn't miss a beat. "I know you're not a black belt, you know how I know? No, never mind, I'll tell you. People who train to fight at a top level never ever choose a random person to fight. It's basic survival. Is that guy a ninja? Is that guy a cop? You see, your actions tell me everything. You're a young man who's out having a few drinks, making a few bad decisions." Bad Attitude is frozen in confusion; he knows he's not going to attack this man who just walked up, but he's stuck in this weird spot. Damon helps him out. "I want you guys to have fun, I don't want you to get in trouble. I live around here, do you?"

One of them answers, "Yeah we all do, and I'm not drinking. I'm the DD."

Damon smiles to let them know this is all for fun, and they all do the same, even Bad Attitude. "Listen, we have every day to make good things happen, it only takes one bad choice to ruin it. I'm gonna introduce myself before I go, the next time we meet be cool and tell me something good okay? I have enough problems, I'd rather have a few more pals." At that Damon walks towards them with his hand extended. They all shake it and introduce themselves.

Damon is about twenty feet away, he turns and yells back to them. "Next time, a nice big smile, and a handshake eh?"

The big kids wave goodbye, with smiles.

7

HIGHWAY 1, 7:15 P.M.

Damon gets on Highway 1 via the 200 Westbound exit from Langley; his white Caravan synchronizes with the 100 kilometre an hour traffic easily. He heads for the 176 exit that will take him onto the 17 Connector to Delta. The connector is mostly used by trucks pulling container trailers to and from the ports and train depots. Most commuters drive at the speed limit because of the gauntlet of speed traps the police set up. Damon is no different; he falls in behind a container truck and hits cruise control at 80 kilometres an hour. The drive to the Vancouver airport is less than an hour at this time of day doing the speed limit.

The sun is on the horizon, the sky has a glow that indicates it's either sunrise or sunset. Damon ponders how many sunsets he has left, and how so many people seem to want to shorten their sunset count. They're daring someone to send them to the afterlife. History is full of these stories. Damon is sure every single guy who steals and bullies believes for some reason that he won't meet the reaper. There are the few who seem to really not care, and they talk in a way which tends to freak people out. *I don't care if I get killed, I'll be dead,* is the common trumpet these guys sound off when someone warns them of impending doom. But for sure not being afraid of death is no defence against death.

Crack! The sound is loud. The visual of an incoming rock hits the window right above the steering wheel, and suddenly a spider-crack appears, two inches round. Damon's heart pounds; he laughs nervously, because he knows that if that had been a shot from a passing car he would be on his way to the afterlife. *It's that fast.* He takes in a big breath and lets it out with sound to relieve the sudden tension.

He never wants his targets to see it coming for one reason: they might be the best at dodging bullets. And then it's eight shots instead of two. *Bang, bang, bang, bang, bang, bang, bang, bang.* Or *bang, bang.* It's no question it should only be two shots. If everyone froze, as one target had once, then it would not matter. But usually, these guys are already peeking over their shoulder. If they have half a mind for self-preservation, they'll have some kind of dodging and drawing a gun plan. Surprise is the number one option. And it had taken five months and twenty-two days to surprise the Fuk.

Damon reminisces about a few of the close calls the Fuk had pulled off without even knowing it. The Fuk's office was the show-home trailer for the development that he had been running for two years. At first Damon had gone to his office in disguise, and found that the

Fuk never sat in his actual office; and it was wired with cameras everywhere.

The place was filled with Barbie Doll realtor girls; none were over thirty, all in high heels and skirts with polished hair and makeup. Even if these girls weren't in makeup Damon figured they would be gorgeous. This was a spot to get a lead, but not the spot to do the task, Damon determined, though it took four weeks of close watching with a mixed pattern of walking by, riding a bicycle by, driving by, and jogging by at two-and-half hour intervals. And always in different clothes. The disguise to fool the cameras was so elaborate that Damon got tired of getting ready and taking it all off for a 'maybe' shot at the Fuk. Long days alone, with only his thoughts to keep him company.

"When behind enemy lines with no communication, it's important to keep morale high by remembering you're serving your country's highest needs," he read once. Damon edits that to read, "serving your *family's* highest needs."

His strategy, of course, was a lot of work, and someone had to pay for it. He's worked out a sweet deal this time, but in every deal there's a consequence for not succeeding. Failing is not an option; there is no retreat, the target must be eliminated. He chuckles to himself at his last thought. What is he, a Terminator robot?

If he were, the job would have been done three and half months ago. That's when the Fuk went to his gym on a half-ass regular basis. Damon had caught a glimpse of his car and then picked up his schedule by seeing his Cadillac there twice. The second time, Damon had sat at the farthest distance, in a neighbouring commercial warehouse across the highway, and watched the Fuk's car with binoculars. The target walked to his car alone at exactly 2:10 p.m. Damon checked the gym's schedule and saw there was a bootcamp-type class that ended at 2:00 p.m. Regular schedule + a fresh sighting = actionable intel, by the methods that Damon adopted.

Damon picked up the blue Corolla the next day from the regular spot. He drove to a safe spot and dressed in ninety percent of his disguise. Of course since it was a gym, it was one of the only places someone should wear a sweat suit with the hood up. The cherry on-top was his gym bag.

Damon remembered how he came back that night and walked the area to take note of camera locations and angles, not *if* there were cameras. He found the spots and determined his path in and out, and what direction doors opened on the other units so he only had to watch a few, not all of them.

The next morning, Damon walked from the Corolla around the building, schooling his head and keeping his ears open. *Lots of human traffic here, gonna need fast hands today.* He got to his spot by the garbage can at 1:59 p.m. After about thirty-seconds he reached into his left pant pocket and pulled out a cell phone, pretending to answer it and talk. The phone had no battery or SIM card, of course; another part of his disguise. With the rain a downpour, it was okay to have the blue sweater's hood over his head

At 2:10 p.m. he saw the Fuk, grabbing the door and walking out; quickly he turned, stopped, and started yelling a joke back into the building.

Damon kept the fake phone to his left ear and reached into his big kangaroo pocket on the front of the hoodie. He pulled the small pistol out of its holster with his pointer finger while lightly pulling on the pistol's grip with his thumb and middle finger. As he cleared the trigger guard of the holster he put his finger in the trigger guard and nudged the holster off the end of the gun. The gun was in his grip and free of the holster in less than two-seconds, with little or no tells to the outside world.

As far as Damon was concerned, drawing the gun should be invisible. The lifting of the arm to target is only one-second, and two shots are only two-seconds or less. With the arm going down and into its hiding spot in another two-seconds or less, it's only four-seconds with gun out. That felt like an hour, but no matter how much he drilled this move with a concealed pistol it always took the four-seconds.

Damon had modified his holster for the big kangaroo pocket, since the jogging pants wouldn't support the gun's weight well. *Oh my god so much time wasted in my life, cutting fabric and sewing. So strange,* he thinks in a disappointed way. Then his Coach's voice comes back in with a confident and forceful tone. *We assessed the situation and the situation determined that you had to sew a holster, are you above getting ready for a mission?* Damon is a little surprised by the sudden company he has in his mind. *No, and I'm glad we put that all together.*

Damon is always a little concerned that if he doesn't respect the Coach in his head, it might leave. Then what? Damon and the Simple voice would get himself killed or jailed. So he always answers politely and follows any plans that come from the Coach.

The Fuk went back into the gym, laughing, and Damon talked to no one on the phone, knowing that people in the parking lot would only see him for a minute or two while they transitioned from car to gym and vice versa.

The Fuk came out slow. "Come on man, we'll go right now, I'll drive, it's nothing."

A big brown guy came walking out, talking on his own phone. "Yeah yeah, don't bother, Tony is driving me. I don't care what happens to the Charger, a tow truck is on the way." The brown guy was ten steps behind Fukadero and on the phone. This presented the age-old question, 'How important is this hit?'

Are we averting a war between two nations? Nope. The brown guy being on the phone made it far riskier. 'Oh my God, man, a guy shot Tony, no no not me bro please,' all this with the phone on. Plus the big brown guy had the build of a linebacker; if he instantly charged after the first shot, Damon didn't know if he'd be able to turn and shoot in time. Either way it would be twice as much shooting, even if it went smoothly. Two guys = four bullets, unless the second guy is the best at dodging bullets. Then it would be the other eight to get him, which means a magazine change, and that's another three-seconds.

So Damon watched the back of Tony's head for the thirteen-seconds it took him to walk to his beautiful

Cadillac four-door, all black with black mags. *Vroom*! The engine roared as he turned the V8 over. This Cadillac was souped-up with over 700 horsepower. Damon bent and unzipped his bag as the car drove past and raced outta the parking lot.

At the moment the car passed by him the Simple voice in Damon's head piped up. *You had him, who cares about that other guy. You just sentenced us to this stupid job that will never end, are you even going to do it? You would be embarrassed if your family knew...*

Damon holstered the gun and pretended to turn the fake phone off. During that time he listened to the voice. Once the Cadillac was well gone and the gun holstered, Damon answered back sharply. *I can't think of a single thing that you've done for us in our adult life. Your stupid ideas are why we're here at forty years old. Have another drink, Damon, you're a boss, quit that job, Damon, they're assholes.* Damon was walking away, toward his borrowed Corolla, so he kept on telling the Simple voice off. *I don't need you, you sound stupid. Die already, never speak again and maybe I'll get smarter advice.*

In that instant his Coach spoke up. *Damon, this is an active mission, ignore anything that is taking away from the task at hand, which is getting away smooth and by the clock. This is now a full dress rehearsal training session, get into it and see if we can improve anything.* Damon nodded affirmative. It was a long ride back, including getting out of disguise and transferring cars and hiding the gun.

HIGHWAY 99, 7:50 P.M.

Long fruitless day, he reminisces as he reaches the exit onto the Highway 99 Northbound, en-route to YVR.

The thought of his son going from his gym straight into the shower, and off to bed again without seeing his dad, suddenly hits Damon. His heart aches knowing that he's stuck in the same cycle so many parents end up in: work for your kids but then don't see your kids. *Naomi tries to sync up the family all the time,* he recalls with a huge feeling of debt to her. Naomi constantly tells Damon about plays and play-dates, and always informs "If you could make it, we'll be there from four until five-thirty," in the kind way a nurse talks to patients who are trying to live, and have a chance of recovery. It's ten-to-eight, and Damon's white Caravan is approaching the George Massey Tunnel, which goes under the Fraser River on the way to the airport.

The tunnel is bright, on the ceiling the big orange lights line up in a row end-to-end, with a small amount of burned out lights missing from the chain.

There are only a few kinds of living dead men. *What kind was the Fuk?* Damon narrows it down to two kinds the Fuk seemed to fit into the most accurately. He was the kind who had recently come into financial trouble, so he resorted to stealing and bullying and ratting; or he had always been that way, and had a long history of destroying people to get ahead.

Damon has no evidence to know which, other than Fuk's lifestyle and the events that led to the hit, which was stealing and then getting the guys he stole from arrested. Damon knows his clients' type well, and feels safe with them. But knowing the Fuk's type will help him in the future.

It's not over, he growls to himself. He focuses his mind's eye to see the next target, but it's blank. A crowd of associates and a young gorgeous wife, no defined target yet. And it doesn't matter. *I'll be paid out soon, and not thinking about these people's problems in the next few days. 'Don't trust scumbags' will be my advice to my clients.*

It's good to know who supports the Fuk, to get more work for us, The Simple voice adds, in a supportive way, so as not to offend Damon. The truth makes Damon stop breathing; his clients' big play isn't over. And they'll need him to carry on removing any blockers to their millions of court-held dollars. *I could make another huge payout off these clients. This is amazing how good a spot I'm in.*

Then he feels guilt and happiness at the same time. *How much can they afford this time?* He knows his own future more clearly. Clearly he's ready to accept an offer to carry on for the right amount of money.

What is this revolving door that I keep going around in? How does this keep continuing? When the message is delivered from a voice from God or some higher being. The message comes from a voice that speaks up occasionally with calming facts. It's not the Simple voice and it's not the Coach, but whatever it advises always seems so accurate. Damon isn't religious, but he has always been delivered from hopeless situations by a solid piece of advice delivered to him; the thought rings, and light becomes brighter, and sound crisper at the moment of the message. As long as he's true to his missions and never quits, he knows a message will arrive; then he will act on it, and succeed.

Damon takes the last exit for the Vancouver airport. He arrives early, so he turns into the Tim Hortons at the exit. The place has two marked police cars running, with their officers at the wheel. The cars are parked opposite each other so the police can talk to each other through their open windows. Damon is glad they're here; he hates worrying about car thieves, and with marked cars here he knows crackhead car thieves will steer clear.

VANCOUVER INTERNATIONAL AIRPORT, 9:10 P.M.

Damon drives up to the domestic arrivals and sees his in-laws right away. He pulls into a spot on the curb, puts the van in park, and jumps out. His father-in-law is dressed similar, in blue jeans and a white shirt, and they both have black shoes on. Damon pinches Sammy's sleeve with his thumb and index.

Sammy jokes, " We could start a band." The three warmly hug each-other. His mother-in-law, Vicky, still has her looks and her smile lights up as she embraces Damon. Damon has to break the eye contact that the wise woman is locking on him in attempt to gauge his general mood. Damon holds a big smile and grabs their bags; he's happy she cares about his well-being, but with her years of taking care of her husband she could sniff out any problems Damon might have pretty easily.

Once they're all seated in the van Damon pulls out a CD. "You two mind if I put in Led Zeppelin live?"

The in-laws smile and nod happily. They went to the 1978 live concert in Seattle. Sammy points at the crack in the windshield. "How long have you been driving around with that?"

"It happened on the way here, scared the crap outta me," Damon exclaims. They turn up the music and head home in the dark.

The three talk easily about how Sammy and Vicky managed the day's travel. The two hour flight was almost not worth it compared to the five-hour drive, because it included this one hour drive and the one hour for Damon to get there, which is four hours. They banter about how many options are available for travellers these days.

"In the 1800s that trip was only done in the spring, and would take over two months with horses; and we whine about five hours in a car or a plane," Vicky points out in jest. The Okanogan is a retirement paradise, with lakes and flat trails everywhere, and Damon's in-laws moved there at the right time in their lives.

They turn back onto the dark highway heading home, and Damon unintentionally tunes out the casual conversation. He's answering with, "Mm-hm," and "Oh yeah," while his mind asks a clear question. *Who will hold the violent demon next?* This is a serious question, and his mind's eye sees only darkness, but he knows someone will raise their hand at the chance to feed the greedy demon inside them with the promise of riches and glory.

The older Damon gets, the less surprised he is each time good people change and start risking their lives for money and power, as if suddenly guided by a demonic entity. He knows it's demonic because they daringly announce, "Nobody can kill me, I'll have them killed first," or "Everyone better fall in line, or else." These are daring statements for a delicate human to make. What makes them believe these things all of a sudden?

Of course, this has always been the case. The minute that one possessed human is stamped out, another one or two will immediately jump to fill the spot. This repetition is repeated throughout history. One king goes to another kingdom to kill the monarch there and gain the crown. Once that war is over, one of his people kill him, and on and on.

The church speaks about being filled with the holy ghost; it's safe to assume folks could be filled with an unholy ghost just as easily. Damon believes it really is a fight between good and evil. *What does that make me?* Damon asks in his mind.

As he sits in the silence of his mind, waiting for an answer, he hears, "Damon, Damon, Earth to Damon." Sammy is waving his hand off to the side of Damon's vision, trying to wake him.

Damon pokes fun as he turns towards Sammy. "Whoa sorry, it's been a long drive. I'm so tired, maybe we should get a hotel."

Sammy and Vicky are nervously smiling, and Sammy offers to drive, "Holy Damon, I said your name five times. Are you on drugs?" Sammy knows Damon never drinks, and only has a few puffs of a joint on occasion to help him sleep.

Damon answers back in a level, serious tone. "Yeah, a guy I know gave me some horse tranquilizer to take the edge off, he told me it's safe for humans." They all laugh, and Damon quietly vows to have his personal thoughts when no one is around. He always gets so lost in his head, he really wonders sometimes if ancestors talk to him or an angel. Or maybe he's lightly insane. *If I'm insane, how many others are? Does the most insane person win?*

10:15 P.M.

When they get back to the house, Sammy digs into Damon's plans. "What do you plan on doing out here? This is a huge job." Sammy has owned three houses and improved them all, but this one has no yard to improve; it's not even level enough to spread seed.

Damon knows the answer. "When I get a few more bucks I'm going to landscape and build a fence. I want to run power to each corner of the property for future use, and some stone-work for gardens. Finishing the yard is actually more important than finer finishing inside."

In a sober voice with a touch of a smile, Sammy asks, " How much do you figure for it all?"

Damon knows the answer almost to the dollar. "About fifty G. The levelling and stonework, plus the good planting dirt, will be about ten G. The electrical and the fixtures we want will be another ten. The fence alone is almost fifteen G, and at the same time I want to build a deck out back that's going to be wired for power, and have a lighting package along with a piped-in barbecue. That'll eat the rest of the estimate."

Sammy rubs his chin, and Damon notices his sleeve tattoo poking out from under his long-sleeved shirt. Sammy had sleeve tattoos thirty years before they were cool, back when it labelled you as trouble, not trendy. "Don't you still owe for the land and the house being built? Are you seriously thinking of taking on another fifty thousand in debt?" Sammy delivers his comment with respect, examining Damon to decide if he's thinking about these details.

Damon feels so tired, and a little ashamed at having so much debt, but answers as cheerfully as he can. "I've been working on some things, I think it will work out real soon. Let's go in. I've gotta go to bed, I'm getting up early."

Sammy smiles as he remembers being young and trying to get over this same hump, and so he adds, "We're here for you and Naomi in any way."

Damon knows how far his father-in-law will go to help him and what he is capable of, but he has too much respect to drag him into some little spat about money. They head into the house, talking and joking all the way.

Damon announces goodnight to all and heads to the master bedroom. On the way he pops into Benji's room, which is next to theirs on the back of the house. The young boy is out cold, laying diagonally across the bed, on his back, in the starfish position. Damon smiles and shuts the door.

As soon as he's in the bathroom, Damon pulls his cell-phone out and checks the news. Nothing on this morning's hit. He checks a few news outlets, but there's still nothing. His heart beats a little faster. *What are the RCMP doing with the investigation that they don't want it in the news? Maybe they have a witness and an informant, and twenty men in black suits with masks and rifles with flash-lights are on route to smash down my door tonight once everyone is asleep.*

His heart speeds a bit; he has no way of knowing what's going on with the police investigation, or if one of his clients' wives or brothers has dropped the dime to secure citizenship. *Fuck, this is gonna be a long night.* His Coach chimes in. *This is still a live mission, you need rest, so wash up and be in bed in ten minutes.*

With no better plan, Damon listens. He uses a technique adopted from a government agency manual. "When behind enemy lines and in a constant state of battle, rest is important. Count backwards from 100 and repeat until you fall asleep. Keep your eyes closed and breath long controlled breaths."

He drifts off in the fourth round of the countdown.

8

Damon sets his alarm for 5:30 a.m., but turns it off at 5:28 a.m. He's been wide awake since 4:40 a.m. *I'll sleep well tonight.*

Damon sits up and puts his feet on the carpet. He reaches for his cup of water on the bed-stand. As the cup touches his lip and the room temperature water pours into his mouth, the faint voice of Naomi breaks the silence. "You going hiking?"

Damon stops drinking at half a glass to answer his sweet wife, who he knows wants him here while her parents visit. "I'll come back at eleven and we will all do something together."

With her head still on her pillow, she yawns, "Kiss me." He obeys and she closes her eyes.

Damon loads his van with the things he'll need, then calls the dog, Patch, over. He jumps in, too, and they drive out in the morning dawn.

He drives north over the Golden Ears bridge, and ends up in Pitt Meadows. The little municipality has a dyke system that holds back one of the largest tidal lakes in the world, Pitt Lake. After he parks his van, Damon gets himself and the excited white Boxer out and heads along the Fraser River. The dyke has a ten-kilometre loop trail back to his van, and the sun will rise at 6:30 a.m. He'll have a perfect view.

Damon brings his backpack, with a few things in it, and takes to the trail at a fast walking pace. His dog is off-leash in this casual country setting, which is the norm. At 7:00 a.m. he turns back, knowing that he walks at five kilometres an hour with the dog, so a half hour in and a half hour out, makes a healthy start to the day.

He's resisted the urge to open his cell phone since he woke, and he decides not to check the news until he's on his way back to his house; then he'll have a better overview on the week. He marvels at the other close call the Fuk had lucked into. He was at a coffee shop that Damon had, again by chance, spotted him at. This time it had been a small miracle that had saved Damon from disaster; not a disaster for his clients, solely himself and his family.

———————————

Damon had the Corolla and was doing a circuit of the known spots the Fuk frequented. This was standard procedure when he was on the hunt, with no hot leads. This type of hunt was unrewarding and mentally draining. He had gone through the car trading routine, dressed in a casual disguise that would work in any situation. A cheap suit and, if he saw his chance, a large fedora and sunglasses. It was casual enough to walk into an office or a construction site and not be bothered. This costume took time to get into, and also to don the tie and belt. One good part was a regular conceal holster clipped on the inside of the belt, so the gun was in a solid spot all day. If he saw his target at any point he simply had to park discretely and walk straight over. After four seconds of gunplay it would be over.

Then back to a quiet and nerve-racking drive.

That day, Damon was heading between the gym, the construction site, and the show-home. He spotted the Fuk driving in front of him, three cars ahead. Immediately Damon checked his rear view mirror; it was a mom, with car seats, in a van; that was good, no tail. He shadowed the Fuk, who was in his limited-edition black Cadillac. The last car separating them pulled over to the left lane and they got stopped at a light, with Damon in the blue Corolla right behind the Fuk. Damon checked the licence plate to confirm it was him; Damon had memorized the plate a long time ago. *Quickly, get out and run over and take the shot.* The Simple voice urged to him. Damon snapped back. *Not now, be quiet, this hit is live.*

The Fuk pulled into a coffee shop and Damon continued driving straight, carrying on in the same direction. Damon marked the time as 10:07 a.m. *A coffee stop takes four minutes if there's no lineup,* he noted. He took a right turn at the corner and another right into the commercial alley behind the upscale strip mall. He put his hat on as he turned into the alley and then parked beside a dumpster that was empty. *No pick up, most likely.*

He put his big sunglasses on and stepped out of the car. It was 10:09 a.m. He knew the little mall was usually a busy, trendy place, but being 10 a.m. on a weekday, it was a ghost town. He was walking at a fast pace, but slow enough not to project that he was a cat in the final stage of the stalk. *Chill, relaxed arms and body*, he told himself. *There he is coming out already, dammit I'm too far away.* The Fuk was parked right out front, and the parking lot was empty except for the Cadillac and the Explorer right next to him. *Should I run?* Damon thought in a panic. At that moment, the Fuk dropped the muffin bag that he had been balancing on top of his coffee. Another gift from God, he bent over and put the coffee down to rebalance the muffin on it.

Damon could tell that he had him. It was the perfect place for the Fuk to be shot, bent over. Anyone who heard the shots wouldn't see the body fall, or see Damon's arm aiming and swinging down. It might be five minutes before another patron noticed the downed man. With his left hand Damon started pulling his button-up shirt out of his pants, his right hand was reaching to meet the pistol grip that his left hand was presenting, both hands suddenly froze. His left hand let go of the shirt and his right hand casually dropped back to the walking swing. To a bystander it would have looked as though he had an itch, and scratched it. Damon was right on top of the Fuk, but doesn't stop or glance at him. He heard the Fuk complaining to himself.

"This damn muffin is a joke. Why the fuck does she not just get her own food?"

As Damon walked off knowing this day was a bust, he couldn't believe that an unmarked police car with an officer sitting in it, was five feet from the head shots that were literally under five seconds away. Would that officer have jumped out and started firing, or turned his lights on and called for backup, then jumped out and started firing? Either way, Damon was sure he would have shit his pants at the shock of everything in his life being ruined from not being alert.

7:10 A.M.

During this bright sunrise, Damon asks the same weird question that has no answer. *Was that my good luck or his?*

Because the Fuk is still dead, and I'm enjoying this morning. Is there some cosmic or heavenly measuring system that offers a chance to make things right? And he clearly keeps telling them, 'Nope, ain't nobody gonna stop me.' And so they finally send me the message, and I get my clear shot.

Who is helping me? Damon asks politely to the morning sun. "Patch get over here, get outta that mud. Damn it!"

The dog has run through the low-tide mud of the Fraser River, and is covered from shoulder down. The ninety-pound boxer is smiling from ear to ear, and comes running right at Damon with the intent of bumping his owner with his muddy body.

"No no, Patch, don't you dare, get, get outta here." The dog stops about fifteen feet away and freezes, with his ears perked and his docked tail pointing straight up. Patch has a look that Damon's sure is a dog joke. 'Ahh you just called me and now you want me to go?'

Damon affectionately laughs at his dog being such a dog.

MISSION, 9:30 A.M.

Damon loads the magazine with four rounds and quickly holds the rifle to his shoulder. Through the scope he can see the plate-size target moving around the crosshairs of the scope. As the crosshairs pass the bullseye he squeezes a round off; lowering the rifle, he operates the bolt and loads another round. He shoulders the rifle again, and this time is able to time the movement of the scope over the bullseye and squeeze the trigger a little quicker. He repeats this two more times.

After dropping the hunting rifle's magazine and pulling the bolt out, he blows a quick breath down the barrel for fun, to see the smoke come out of the end.

No reason to let that burned powder settle in the barrel.

"Which target you shooting at?" an old man's voice asks him. Damon answers through a smile. "The two hundred yard I hope, you want to walk out with me and see if I hit it?"

The old man smiles and nods. It's normal for a few guys who don't know each other to be out at the range, and to group up and B.S. about the type of rounds they hunt with. Today it's Damon and this old grey-hair, who is well into retirement and has had a full life, judging by the guns on the bench and the newer one-ton truck parked outside.

The old man asks a question to see if Damon is a hunter or a sport shooter. "How far would you take a standing shot at an animal?"

Damon is happy he asked. "Well, my gun is a thirty-aught-six, and at two-hundred yards there's a two inch bullet drop, but at three-hundred yards it's eighteen inches. So this gun is accurate at two-hundred yards and under from standing, after that I'd really think about my shot."

The old man nods in agreement. "We'll see in a minute if you're right, won't we."

They both smile and start the walk out to the targets, "What are you shooting?"

The old man is full of enthusiasm, "Anything that I can put ammo in. I've been shooting longer than you've been alive. All my shooting is from the bench rest nowadays, but you'll see, it happens to everyone. Today I'm making sure one of the guns I own is still sighted at three-hundred yards, a Mauser 8mm."

Damon's eyes light up. "How long have you been shooting that rifle?"

"How old are you?" The old man solemnly makes eye contact. "I've been shooting this rifle for sixty-five years, it's an old Polish service rifle; it was my father's, he gave the rifle to me." Then he adds, "It's actually an 7.92 by 57mm."

Damon acknowledges with a nod. "I didn't know that." Damon is old enough to know that a man this old, from Poland, knows hardship; from German bombings and invasion, to Russia 'liberating' them. This is a touchy conversation that Damon isn't qualified to be in.

The old man shakes his head slowly with a finger wagging around, looking for missing holes. "You're lucky animals are bigger than this plate, I thought you took four shots?"

Damon surveys the target. He crouches and does a serious, albeit mock, inspection. Damon is embarrassed but still happy to point to the half-moon of a bullet with the telltale black grease on the edge of the target. "Half a bullet on the edge of the paper is four hits." Damon knows it's not great shooting, but he had rushed the shots for fun.

The old man clasps his hands behind his back. "Do you want to walk out to the three hundred and see if my Mauser is still sighted?"

"My pleasure, you lead," Damon answers. The two walk along, and Damon has to wonder how people from war-torn places can be so happy. All the death and cruelty doesn't seem to affect them.

As they arrive at the only target at three hundred yards, Damon's eyes widen at what he thinks is an illusion.

It's amazing to see it, this shooting is a miracle—the way the bullets always leave a little black ring around the first piece of paper they pass through. A shooter never has to wonder if a random hole is from a bullet. And here are four bullet holes with the grease from the round, in a neat row that drifts low on the right, all touching and all over-lapping, by exactly a quarter of the diameter of the shot, with the next round.

The old man speaks softly. "Son, if you have some time I've got a few more rounds. I can show you a couple tricks my dad taught me."

Damon readily accepts, and again feels his guardian helping him become a better hunter.

SURREY, 10:00 A.M.

Yakub is an hour into organizing the tile storage for an upcoming apartment building contract. He bought the tile originally to do 250 apartment bathrooms, but the job had been cancelled after all the bad publicity surrounding the Fukadero job.

Today will be a long day of moving the large format tiles, by hand, off the racks and to the truck out front. From there it goes to the site and up into the building they've won the bid for. He brought in two general labour guys for the job, fresh off the boat from Poland and wanting to show they can work. Yakub will give them breakfast and lunch, and, depending on how they work, a bit of pocket money.

Yakub ponders while going about the day's work. *We're almost working at the cost of the tiles and the labour to install. How am I gonna pay my warehouse's mortgage this month? Damn it, this is a cursed situation.*

We never did anything but work hard, and now I have these good guys working for food! I hope my wife is able transfer two hundred dollars by the end of the day so I can give these guys something. The one guy has a baby, and the other is taking care of his parents. Yakub has been up in the racks passing the tiles down, his focus on the tiles and at the guy he's passing them to since he climbed into the racks. So when he hears a deep voice call for his attention, he's a little embarrassed. He lifts his head bashfully, as if to apologize for working in his own building.

"Hey guys, I'm looking for your boss, Yakub," the man yells in a polite but loud and deep voice.

"I am he," Yakub answers with a wave of his big thick bear paw, earned over a lifetime of heavy work. Mainly hauling tiles and carrying bricks. Yakub climbs down the ladder, and he gets his head in the game. *I've never seen this man, he's massive like a football player from the NFL, and so well dressed. So this wealthy guy wants a good deal on something, that's why a South Asian guy would come to a Polish guy for work. Or maybe he has such a vast job he needs a huge crew, jeez I don't know if I could carry a big crew through one draw. Oh well, it's work anyway.*

"I'm Yakub," he booms. He turns from the ladder and makes eye contact from twenty feet away. The man is fixedly staring, and appears prepped to run over and try and kill him with his bare hands. "What's up my friend?" Yakub inquires in a level tone that is still polite. Both of Yakub's day-labour hires take a step to get in front of Yakub, but Yakub touches both their arms, "Can you two keep working on the tile transfer?" in the mannerly tone a boss perfects after twenty years. The two Polish day labourers glance at each other and nod; they get back to it. But, they keep an eye on the meeting.

The 6'6" Indo-Canadian stands watching Yakub, and only Yakub. His shoulders and body are relaxed. His pants are the new style of expensive black jogging pants that are tapered at the bottom, and he wears a heavy black sweater with some crest on the chest that makes it clear it's a fancy brand. His shoes just came out of a Nike box. His fists ball up, then release.

Yakub is forty-five years old. He stands 6'1", and his 250 pounds is all back and neck muscle, resting on two thick legs. His neck and chin are one mass of flesh. Yakub's blue work jeans are covered in tile dust, and his white shirt, yellow from wear, rests under an old jean jacket that might be twenty years old or maybe only two years of heavy wear. Back in his native city of Warsaw, he was part of a dedicated Judo team from the age of ten until he left the county when he was twenty-five to work in Canada. Yakub judges the huge man. *This is a juice monkey. This young man is maybe thirty-five years old, and he has overdone the weights and the testosterone. He's about to have his body very hurt if he comes near me.*

"I'm Suhki, a good friend of Tony Fukadero. He was killed yesterday on his lawn by some chicken-shit fuck."

This is news to Yakub, and maintains eye contact with Suhki. Taking note of his thick arms hanging at his sides. "So why you come here so mad and tell me this?"

Suhki caught Yakub in a trap. "Who said I'm mad?" Suhki tests, his eyes flash for a moment.

Yakub's lips press into a frown. *What does this huge kid think is going to happen here?* Yakub notices the two heavy brown guys, about 220 pounds of solid muscle each. Standing guard, rubber necking from the bay door.

"Listen Suhki, I run a legitimate business. If you think I'll say something dumb on a camera, the way your friend Mr. Fukadero did to my brother and cousin, and get me thrown in jail, then you've got me all wrong.

I'm a simple, hard-working family man who has a damaged and struggling business to run. If you have no business here, can you please leave?"

Suhki answers in a quick, low voice. "Of course I'll leave. Nobody stays anywhere forever. But I have to make sure you know something, fat man. So listen." At this Suhki takes one step closer to Yakub. Then Yakub takes a step, both with their eyes locked on each other like two alpha dogs.

Suhki relaxes his eyes, and in a conversational tone, "You bunch of low bottom-feeder general labourers think that if Tony is gone, his company will drop the case; and the one-point-nine million that's held by the courts will be released to your company, right? Come on, just say it, I'm listening. Relax, I can see you don't want to admit what you want. How will you get it if you don't say it out loud?" Suhki's tone stays casual, similar to discussing a used car sale, all smiles and relaxed.

Yakub gets right into this game by answering in a gentlemanly tone. "My company's lawsuit has nothing to do with anyone named Suhki. I'm simple, but I've read the papers our lawyer gave me." Yakub peers to the ceiling, trying to recollect if the name Suhki is in any papers. "No, hmm, no. I think you and I should start fresh, because you never stole two million dollars from my company. That sounds better, right? New friends, ones that don't steal and rat?" At that last word Suhki cringes; the micro reaction makes Yakub smile.

Suhki scans the warehouse and chuckles as he points to the corner of the room. "Hey it's you who has the cameras, they're out front as well, I see." Suhki lowers his voice. "So I guess I'll have to come back when the power's off, or maybe a relative will come by when you're loading a truck."

Yakub decides as soon as the big kid starts to threaten that he can't contain himself. Yakub walks closer, a peace-maker, with his hand low and palms open and facing forward.

Yakub gently approaches. "Look my new friend, there's plenty of room in this province for all of us."

Yakub is about ten feet away from him at this point, and Suhki hasn't moved again; he even appears a little concerned with the confidence of the big Polak. Yakub recalls that it has been twenty years since he trained Judo, but he had taken it absolutely serious, training six days a week at a minimum of an hour-and-a-half, with conditioning. *When I get close enough the big guy will charge, and I'll get a toss on him. Or I'll reach up for a chest grip on that great big sweater and I'll grab his elbow with my other hand. When he charges I'll get my toss, and worst case if he pulls away I'll trip him backwards with a leg hook.*

Suhki glances over his shoulder at the exit.

"Yes, I agree there's a lot of room here for all of us." He wipes his palms on his sweater and licks his lips as the big confident bricklayer moves closer.

"Just that you pieces of shit will be in the gutter where you belong and my people will be living good."

By the time Suhki has finished that line, Yakub is gently reaching for the two main grips he needs to throw Suhki onto a pile of hard sharp tiles.

In less than a blink of an eye Suhki snatches both of Yakub's arms by the tops of his elbows and pins them so hard against Yakub's ribs that air shoots out in a quick burst. Yakub saw it coming once he felt Suhki's hands get the grips on the tops of his elbows. He starts a turn to the left, knowing the big man is pushing forward and will fall right into a sacrifice technique that will land them both on the ground, with Suhki taking the hard fall.

Suhki immediately releases his two elbow grips and steps his left foot to the outside and a bit behind Yakub's right leg. At a speed that Yakub had not expected, Suhki lowers his torso level, low enough to bear-hug Yakub's arms below the elbow. He squeezes so hard it stuns the 250 pound bricklayer as he is lifted into the classic wrestling back-body drop. Yakub knows, right when the squeeze locks his arms, which way this huge man is going to throw him, and his only thought is about trying to absorb the concrete with no arms and while landing on his face.

SURREY, 10:05 A.M.

Suhki is acting a little nervous as he gets Yakub to head over. Due to his large size, he's been training with his older cousins since he was twelve years old. When he was in grade eight and formal training started in his local MMA gym, he was already 6' and 185 pounds. He joined the school wrestling team and stayed on it until graduation; Suhki even made the university team. The problem had always been Suhki's size.

"Dad, I beat everyone already," he had complained to his father in grade ten when he wanted to stop training.

Suhki's dad would answer back, "It's not about beating everyone, it's about getting to know people and not getting beat. You are the eldest son of this family, I need you strong."

So Suhki trained, and learnt that to have a solid fighter even try against him, he had to put on this 'scared' face. They all fell for it.

Today, this big Polak is walking right into it. Suhki knows immediately that Yakub is trained, because everyone is either afraid of a 6'6" and 265 pound jacked dude, or crazy tough.

As Yakub reaches for his grips Suhki withholds a smile. *Judo.* He stands still and lets Yakub get halfway to good throwing grips. When he snatches Yakub's arms out of the air and the Polak goes for a sacrifice throw, he lets him turn a bit while he goes in fast for his grip, a bear hug. He feels the big Polak go limp as soon as he gets the bear hug.

Best chance to land half decent.

Suhki respects Yakub for trying, as he lifts the heavy man up and over his shoulder. For good measure Suhki jumps up and back so that the full weight of both of their bodies will land on the man's upper shoulder and chest. Suhki directs the throw so that this guy's head doesn't smash on the concrete, avoiding a death. He wants broken bones left here, not bodies.

"Don't hurt anyone while you train, it will give you and the family a bad name. You don't always have to win." His dad's voice sings in his head as he rolls off the unconscious man. With one big push up and a hop he is back on his feet, squinting with his chin tucked. Suhki's hands outstretched, waiting for challengers. The two workers who are at the racks stand motionless, their mouths open.

The one worker on the ground yells, "Aleksander, call the police," to the guy in the racks. He looks to Suhki, and gestures with his hand politely to say, 'go please.'

Suhki mocks, "Whoa, did you see him come at me? It's on those cameras. I was so afraid, I can't believe what happened."

At that Suhki turns to leave. Smiling, he shakes his head in disappointment. "I just came to talk, these people are crazy."

9

The Wolf arrives at his office, on an upper floor of the purpose-built one billion dollar RCMP station that houses the E Division. Sara lifts her focus off her phone, where she's been reviewing the Fukadero case facts that she intends to touch on with the Wolf. She stands from her seat on the couch that everyone knows is for waiting when you show up early to meet the Wolf.

The Wolf walks into his office, expecting Sara to be there and ready to go over her views on the case they had worked yesterday. He slept for his regular five-and-a-half hours last night, and kept to his routine of a morning two-kilometre jog. He's been working since 6:30 am.

Sara had less than her regular sleep of six-and-a-half hours, and only got five. The Wolf asked for her help, so she's already put in an extra eight hours of overtime on this case. *What is the Wolf trying to achieve in this investigation? To protect an informant? To follow the drug trade? Or simply to solve a murder with no care about any other agenda?* She contemplates while she takes her seat at the Wolf's desk. He's hanging his blue RCMP rain-coat and duty-hat on a hanger. *He's wearing full uniform, grey shirt and dark blue pants with gold strapping held up by a utility belt kit, and a gun with three magazines,* Sara notes with more than a little admiration. This man never misses a beat in his personal life, his health, or at work, as far as she's ever heard.

"How's your husband, Sara?"

"Fine Bill, thanks for asking," Sara answers, but never asks a question back; waiting for her boss to begin the meeting. Bill is the Superintendent of I.H.I.T, the Integrated Homicide Investigation Team; for years, he's proven a leader in teamwork management. Sara eagerly wants to follow the plan she knows he has ready.

"Sara, how long have you worked in Surrey at your current position?"

Sara is taken aback by the inquiry.

"Five years."

The Wolf already knows this, she flashes a smile and asks, "Can we focus on the case and talk about work and family at lunch?"

The Wolf reciprocates a huge grin, "Absolutely."

On his desk, there's one file folder holding two identical, thin, bound notebooks. The Wolf hands her one and she opens it to the first page; there's a summary of the relationships Mr. Fukadero had enjoyed with the RCMP. The next page is an index; in each chapter there's an organized timeline and dated history recounting what the RCMP know about Mr. Fukadero and his family, both from their own accounts and the soft sources that surround them.

The Wolf begins his narrative. "Dean Schmitt is the first person that Mr. Fukadero turned into the system to keep himself out of it. It was for the cocaine that Mr. Fukadero was delivering to Schmitt. Schmitt did six years and has lead a criminal life ever since being released from prison. In all future dealings and by all evidence; Dean is unaware that Mr. Fukadero was the main witness who sent him into the system for six years."

Sara nods in agreement, which makes the Wolf happy because he sees that Sara only got this file last night at 9 p.m., but has read it already.

The Wolf carries on, "The Polish contractor group that we've codenamed Trowel has three people in the system, because Mr. Fukadero testified, under oath, that they're a criminal gang that uses extortion. Those are legal facts.

"In high-level hearsay we also have Mr. Fukadero being brought up in the black market business of smuggling cannabis, working actively from 1998-2005. Allegedly he was also bringing in small amounts of cocaine from the U.S. He had been fingered unofficially as a street-level supplier of single kilograms of cocaine, and rumours are that he had completed bigger deals.

"Mr. Fukadero was always found in the company of high-level street dealers, most notably Dean Schmitt." After the Wolf utters that name, he and Sara lock eyes for two-seconds. Trying to read what the other's take on that ugly fact is. Both are unmoved. The Wolf carries on as the rain outside his office window pours; there's no sound from the downpour, as the building is overbuilt. "Dean has made a lot of friends in many crowds due to his constant supply of cocaine, and people on the street say the supply comes from his close relationship with Mr. Fukadero."

The Wolf goes on from memory, but continues to flip the pages to keep Sara company while she follows each story with her finger in the notebook. "Dean Schmitt did the time behind bars for Mr. Fukadero, and has not found out that Mr. Fukadero put him there. The Fukaderos kept Dean's lawyer paid and his canteen full, and bought a few gifts on special occasions for Dean's close family. As soon as Dean got out of jail, at twenty-seven years of age, the Fukaderos had him working for the family real estate business, which included but was not limited to buying bare land and developing it for residential use. Also lending money for mortgages with a history of fast foreclosure. Some of this is from Dean's written account on his release papers after his six-year sentence explaining his work intentions; he followed up a few times with the counsellor that he talked with in prison."

Sara already read the full report on her computer last night, and thought about how she would handle this package of information. With so many moving parts she only sees an 'okay' way to investigate, and is curious to hear how the Wolf has interpreted the case history.

"The Polish group that owns the construction company is currently in an ongoing lawsuit with the Fukaderos over unpaid material and wages. We know for sure that the Polish group, Trowel from now on—" the Wolf speaks loud and clear, like he is speaking to a court reporter. Sara is waiting for this man to have a flaw, but he's a machine. "Trowel has had dozens of men at all levels of construction on the Fukadero sites for at least two years, plenty of evidence that Trowel is a company that has built high-end residential. I say Trowel is a company, but it's more of a commune. They trust each other to do the job right for fair pay. They're all fresh Polish immigrants, with the core being relatives who started a tile company together when they first arrived in Canada twenty years ago. That tile company is primarily a general contractor that sublets out all their quotes. The company is run by two men, Yakub and Kuda Kalowski. Kuda is currently in prison doing five years, probably out in two plus. These two men are the centre of Trowel."

At the end of that sentence, the Wolf indicates with his eyes toward the window. Sara is hopeful that some fantastic evidence will be sitting there. Sara breathes out with a light laugh when what she sees instead are curtains dropping from the ceiling over the glass window-walls.

When Sara looks back at the Wolf, he's leaning back in his chair. He holds a small silver remote. The Wolf breaks his stare after giving her an agreeing nod. He focuses over her shoulder, and loses all animation from his face. Sara turns her chair on its swivel and sees a ten-by-eight screen coming down the far wall. It stops six inches above the backless couch she had been sitting on. She leans back in the theatre quality seat.

The picture is perfect, the set-up using a crystal-clear speaker system Sara hadn't noticed in the ceiling. She knows the scene from the report. Sara grabs the chair's arms and draws a long breath. Ready to glean any clues about the Fukadero and Trowel relationship from this evidence video that was used in the arrest and sentencing of three Trowel members.

There Tony Fukadero is, alive. Sara is glad she's sitting back in her chair, because this is a blow to the centre of her calm. *I pronounced him dead over thirteen hours ago.*

At this moment the Wolf asks, with a fatherly leadership voice, "This is powerful stuff, should we stop this video and work on something else? Or you may want to see this video later, you can pull the file."

Sara turns around to meet his eyes. "Sir, I can work through the discomfort. Please keep the evidence rolling."

The Wolf makes extended eye contact, "Thank you for doing this extra work with me, I need your help."

Sara turns back around as Bill clicks the remote to start the video evidence again.

It's a split screen with four boxes. One screen has Mr. Fukadero sitting at a desk, in a large office that's similar to his house, with all-white walls, furniture, and desk. *The place looks like a sci-fi movie where an android lives.* Sara muses.

There he is talking and drinking a coffee from a tall glass mug the size of a large from Timmies. Time on the clock reads 9:00 a.m. Tony Fukadero is wearing a white blazer that's cut perfectly for him. His upper body is solid, hair is perfectly styled with gel. On his desk appears to be an office phone and two cell phones: one Blackberry and one iPhone. He's mostly sitting there texting. Mr. Fukadero eyes dart around at every sound.

On the other screen, a van pulls into a parking spot. The van is tall enough to stand in, a Mercedes Sprinter. Three guys get out, and she spots each Trowel member right away.

Kuda getting out of the passenger side. He's about forty years old, He eats healthy, not too much alcohol, good even skin colour with brown hair. The driver and the guy who get out the side door are two cousins by marriage of Kuda, their names are Jan and Nikki Nowalk. They are relaxed and at ease, no weapons. Walking casually, three guys going to work; no one is searching for witnesses, and they're not leaving a guard. As they go in the front door, the video turns to two screens. Tony Fukadero noticing them entering on his forty inch office wall TV. Sara's eyes are going back and forth between screens, as the assault she has read about unfolds. Sara read that Judo is Trowel's central martial art. Thirty percent of Trowel have trained for more than ten years in Judo, both back in Poland or here in Canada.

She watches the living Mr. Fukadero in his chair, obviously waiting for a heated conversation. And she can't help but wonder where he hit the wall with this group. The houses were built correctly, and they were all selling fine. Tony had plenty of tough street guys around to help with tough conversations. Why did he cop out of his circumstances?

Tony watches the security feed on his big screen as the Trowel members get out of their cars and head up the stairs. As they enter the building, he uses a remote to change the security cameras to a business news feed.

Tony has his thick Italian hair greased back. *His skin has a warm glow compared to when I last saw him on the ground, going cold.* Sara has only professional feelings now; the overwhelming waves have passed. Tony's skin has that tanned shade from recent long trips to hot places. His skin is well cared for. *Typical rich Italian playboy.* She observes him watching the door of his office as the three approach.

The video's two screens turn into one, since all the people in the case are in the white office. *This video is edited for the court,* Sara notes as she hears the men's footsteps and the chairs being moved around for the three to sit. *Tony doesn't offer his hand to them, he's focusing on the Blackberry.*

"One moment, guys, I have to send this email," without even looking at the three Trowel members. The three Polish men don't take their eyes off of Tony, and are not talking to each other.

When Tony lifts his head, he's smirking. Trying to be friendly? He sounds confused. "So guys, what can I do for you today?"

Kuda is sitting on the end to the left of the desk, he quickly glances to his cousins wide-eyed.

Then he vents. "We've been at this for so long, will you pull out a chequebook and catch us up?" His voice is a pitch or two higher and faster.

Tony stares at them for ten-seconds, his face losing its smile. Cousin Nikki, who runs the flooring branch of Trowel, speaks in Polish in a quick quiet voice that is translated on the screen. "I told you he's never going to make good on this."

Kuda dismisses the comment with a wave. "Tony, we came to your job site in full force and pushed the job through; we beat all the timelines you set out. And even though *your* contractor took off with your company's money, you told us to not worry and keep going. You'd take care of us, right? When the properties started to sell, right?"

While Kuda is talking Tony picks up his iPhone and types. He glances up. "Sorry guys, it's work related, I have to answer," Tony explains as compensation for the interruption.

Jan hits his fist on the desk. "This meeting *is* work, you fucker."

Tony sits back with a Cheshire cat grin. "I'm always working, sometimes it overlaps. Jan, I saw you at work texting. Is it okay for you to do but not me?"

Kuda puts his hand across Jan's chest as Jan immediately defends himself. "When I was on your site paying my crew with my credit line I made many calls about your job. Get out your chequebook now, you low-life. You said the whole time not to worry about the guy *you* hired that ran off with *our* draw. Pay us, right now!"

While Jan is angrily telling his side, Tony moves his eye-line to the big TV, still playing business news. Sara concludes. *Tony Fukadero was using the court to rob these guys. He used this police sting to seal their fate.*

Kuda speaks up, as Jan finishes. "Look Tony, we're maxed out here, out of money. We can't do another job. You've sold some houses, why aren't you paying us? Could you give it to us in pieces as each house sells?"

Tony stands and looks over the three of them. "You guys filed a court case against my company for your lost draw. This situation will be handled in court. Good luck, and no hard feelings."

Kuda pops up into a wide stance. "Tony, our tax lawyer told us the case had to be filed, for our protection. This won't be going to court. You're going to pay us like you've been saying the whole time. Even last week when I saw you, you repeated it. Right here and now, you get out your chequebook and pay."

At that last comment Tony makes his move. "I'm not standing here, in my office, and being threatened by you and your crew," disdain wrinkling his face.

Nikki speaks firmly. "We haven't threatened you, and we're not going to. I'm going to smash your face in a minute. That is not a threat, it's a fact. Fifty-six seconds left, you leech." At the end of his sentence, Nikki jumps up with veins throbbing on his neck. Jan slowly stands, his chin jutting at Tony.

All four men are standing, and Tony puts the icing on the cake for the cameras. "I'm not violent, never have been. If you came here for a fight, I'm sorry, but that's not going to happen. I'm leaving my office so that I will be safe from your crew, Kuda. I never want to see you again, until we're in court." At that Tony tries to walk by Kuda for the door.

In Polish Jan softly asks. "What the fuck is this guy trying to do?"

Kuda reaches with his closest hand automatically, and with no expression he stops Tony by grabbing his bicep. "You don't walk out on this meeting without paying us something. This is not the end of us, but this could be the end of you."

Tony pulls his arm back to release the grip Kuda has taken, and Sara sees it coming a moment before it happens. Kuda steps forward and places the heel of his left foot against the back of Tony's left heel. In one big sweeping motion he pushes the arm holding the bicep and pulls his own heel back. Tony stares forward as the single leg-throw makes him swing so fast his two phones fly out of his free hand. As he's about to hit the ground Kuda keeps control of the arm, lifting Tony's head so as to not let him hit it on the ground.

That's Judo, full control and not hurting the person who's getting thrown.

Sara recognizes the intent right away; it was only to throw Tony down, not hurt him.

Nikki, who is standing beside Kuda, delivers a quick punch to Tony's face as Kuda holds the recovering Fukadero on the ground. Kuda shakes his head at Nikki with pursed lips.

Tony weakly stands, Kuda keeps his balance by his arm. Tony aims his yell at the door. "Help me, these guys are crazy, help, help!" Tony pushes wildly at Kuda, who lets the little outburst happen.

Then Nikki explodes, yelling in Polish. "You want to see crazy?"

Kuda turns to hold Nikki back as Tony pushes wildly against him. Jan hops around Kuda; he has Tony open from the other side. Grabbing Tony across the chest with his right arm and fully stepping behind both of Tony's legs, with everything he can muster he does an ugly hip toss, throwing Tony onto his desk; the full coffee cup explodes all over the white desk. *That was with the intent to hurt for sure,* Sara notes.

Jan lets Tony have a moment of shock and pain as the air in his lungs shoots out with a loud yell. Tony rolls over, so he's belly down on his desk with his feet on the ground again; his entire white blazer is covered in coffee. Tony does a push-up off the desk with shaky arms, and speaks quietly. "I'll never pay you for company debt, let the courts decide."

Kuda lets go of his cousin as Nikki, who jumps on Tony's back with his full weight and yells in a rage. "How about we handle this right now? You low-life thief." Holding the middle of Tony's coffee-stained white blazer, he fires three half-strength punches to the side of Tony's ear. "Can you hear me now? Do you need a judge to tell you to pay or can you hear me?"

Kuda stares with wide eyes and raised eyebrows, "Tony, we're only three of a large group of furious contractors. You said you'd pay us. Everyone heard you. Pay and we'll stop coming here."

Tony, knowing all of this is for a video, asks. "If I don't pay you, will you keep hurting me?"

Nikki speaks to Tony while still holding the back of his coffee-stained white blazer. "I'll come to your house with a group of friends and we'll make ourselves really comfortable. I'll beat the shit out of you in your bathroom so you can clean up easily. That's a fair deal. No?"

Tony keeps it going. "If I don't pay you, you're going to come in my house and beat me?" His pleading eyes streaming tears.

Kuda warns. "It's not just us, Tony, we have lots of guys who wanted to come here to see you. We told them we would come and talk first, and now this has happened. Will you pay us today?" He wipes sweat off his nose with the back of his hand.

Tony makes a run for the door, but Jan catches him in a real clean hip-toss. Sara cringes as she watches Tony leave the ground; his head is down, his feet pointing to the ceiling.

Jan hates this guy. I've never thrown anyone that hard.

Jan lets him go, so that gravity and the wall combine; but a small shelf that Tony hits, upside down, does all the real work. Kuda rolls his eyes before Tony hits the ground. Nikki jumps forward and squats, yelling in the unconscious Tony's face. "You pay us or we will kill you. You rotten piece of shit."

Kuda grabs Jan before he hits Tony again, speaking in Polish. "Let's go, guys. We've done enough for today."

SURREY, 11:50 A.M.

The Wolf stops the video, and the lights come up slowly as Sara turns her chair back around. The Wolf begins his monotone dictation. "So we have a large group of violent contractors who threaten death over a debt. The three we would blame, for the Fukadero murder, are in jail for the threats and violence we just watched. We've already subpoenaed the prison communication recordings that the three Trowel members have had since they've been incarcerated. It all needs to be run through a Polish translator, because that's the language they speak on the phone to family and friends."

Sara and Bill keep unblinking eye contact during this last narration.

"Sara, there's more going on here than a one dimensional murder investigation. I'm sure you've surmised that."

"Yes Bill. I'm here to help, and I'm not putting my own judgment into this situation. What can I do to assist you?"

The Wolf warmly studies her. *Sara should be able to stay above it all and get some serious police work done.* "Grab your file, we'll go down the hall and meet a group that you'll have at your disposal for this case. Then you and I will go to lunch, and we will catch up." Bill jumps up, leaving his coat, and gets to the door before Sara, holding it for her. "This way, Officer,"

10

The phone rings on Bluetooth in the white Caravan as Damon drives along the two-lane country road, leaving the gun range. "Hello!" Naomi's voice sings in a happy note that's meant for him.

Damon answers back with a little less enthusiasm but in the same spirit. "Hello my angel. I'm a little late. I'm in the van about forty minutes away from the house. Are you and your parents still home?"

Naomi's accustomed to her husband's schedule. She knows he would spend every moment at home having sex and sleeping, if work permitted. She always takes it easy on him when he's a little late or doesn't come back at all for something they have planned. "Oh yeah hun, we had a late breakfast and we're talking about what to do when Benji gets out of school. Will you be around later?" The moment the words leave her mouth Naomi bites her lip, aware that Damon really dislikes talking about timelines on the phone. Naomi accepted this little personality trait soon after they started dating. The few times the police or close friends started asking about where Damon was at such and such a time, she comfortably answered, "I don't keep track of his schedule, I'm busy and he's busy." It felt good not to lie.

Damon answers her right away, and sounds genuinely happy to respond. "I'll be home soon, and I'll stay home for the night."

Naomi smiles as she imagines everyone eating a meal together, rather than alone with her parents, who would no doubt ask, in the politest way, "So what's Damon working on at dinner time?" while they stare at their plates, not wanting to add to Naomi's marital pressures.

"Oh, okay. What should we do for dinner then? If you're going to be here why don't you choose?"

Damon delivers, "Barbecue steak and baked potatoes with all the fixings, you choose the other side dish. I'll stop at the grocery store, text me whatever we need, please." They say their goodbyes with both of their hearts glowing a bit at the beautiful day and the evening they have waiting for them.

Damon sees the fuel in the Caravan is at half, so he pulls off the highway to fill the tank. He pulls into a big chain gas station that has a burger joint attached to it. He's gotten hungry since training with the old man on that Mauser rifle. *Man, that guy drilled me on his technical system of shooting, I must have shot twenty-five of his rounds. Gabriel wouldn't accept a dime, either. He didn't seem to need the money. He just wants an apt pupil. I feel that I'm a little sharper on the long gun, he succeeded in drilling me.*

Damon parks, gets out, and uses his credit card to pay at the pump. As he pumps he keeps thinking. *I'll write down what Gabriel was giving me, that knowledge is valuable. I'll practice more rifle in the next six months so I will get those drills into my muscle memory; yes, at least forty rounds once a week for two months, then every second week for the other four months.* This is the method Damon has come to adopt over the last twenty years of adulthood; when a helpful stranger gives valuable information that's directly related to Damon's life, he studies it extensively. He's even taken courses when he maxes out on self-teaching.

Damon gets back in the van, and parks it in sight of the empty table he plans on sitting at in the gas station. He walks in and orders a fully-loaded burger with onion rings on the side. *Not even trying for a six pack, eh?* his mind jokes with him. *Nope,* he answers back while smirking. He goes over to the window so he can watch his vehicle while he eats.

Look at them all. Almost every one of the public is half asleep while walking and driving around. They have no life-or-death challenges. They think when they're hiking that slipping and getting hurt is a major concern. Maybe because they'd have to crawl out on their belly with a shin bone sticking out through the skin? Driving at night on a distant highway puts fear in normal people, I've heard. Why, because your car might flip into the ditch and you'd have to stand on the side of the road for a few hours with no food? They're so lucky to think that those are even problems.

Man, this burger is so good. I wish it was twice as big. Damon has always seriously believed that any problem that doesn't involve having a group of guys who want to kill you slowly in a remote underground windowless room, with saws, is not a problem. *Whoa whoa Damon, nice little pity party.* Damon's personal thoughts have joined back in; this is his conscious mind that helps him make normal decisions. *Have you forgotten about sick kids? Or widows of good men? Children with abusive adults in charge of them? You should be ashamed of yourself for thinking that you have it rough in any way.* Damon listens to the speech from his mind, wearing an embarrassed grin while he eats. He doesn't need to answer. They both know his pity party is over.

The burger is gone and he's dipping the onion rings in some ketchup as he notices that everyone around the gas bar, and in the store, has a glint of joy in their eyes. Dim in some, brighter in others.

The general population is so safe, if you don't go around stealing and causing mayhem generally nobody is going to kill you. How would that safety feel?

Damon's mind is blank. He acts like them, but they have nothing in common.

Everyone here had been safe in their beds as kids, listening to soothing stories from their mom and dad. Meanwhile, Damon had watched his mom's boyfriend leave the house one night, promising eight-year-old Damon that he would be back before he was awake the next morning. Chuck assured Damon's crying mom that it was an easy debt collection. Instead, he got himself shot in the stomach while knocking on the door of a speed-freak thief who had been ripping off kilos of coke, and using most of it himself. The murderer had already killed two other collectors; Chuck had been number three to go in the trunk with his head and hands cut off. The killer got a life sentence. He had done his twenty years, and was out on parole for life.

Come on Damon, everyone was not safe in bed, his mind soothes. Damon chuckles this time. As he walks back to the van, he has the old passing thought, *So all the people who I relate to have dealt with harsh things in their lives…Akin to someone from a war-torn nation… No. In Iraq, dead civilians are rotting under rubble with kids walking past to get to a makeshift school. I'm so weak when compared to them.* He unlocks the Caravan as he approaches, gets in, and starts the engine.

As the van gets on the highway, Damon really ponders his place in the world. *I know better than most about the destruction of revenge-murder, greed-murder, and the other murders that lurk. The classic, good old rage-murder and drunken-murder and on and on. So I choose to be up to my ears in these dark, heavy, murderous situations that people get into on purpose. I don't feel evil. I don't even enjoy killing anything, or anyone.*

I eat meat, so I shoot moose. I need money, so I shoot people? No, no, it's more than that, just say it to yourself. Damon asks the deepest part of his mind. The part that's always so sure when the message comes in. The deep place that makes him believe there's some kind of protection that Damon and all his ancestors have been blessed with. Damon asks again, soberly.

Why am I stuck in this murder cycle?

Silence.

Damon feels the question linger. *No, no, it's more than that, Say it to yourself.* Damon's mind is still and quiet, so he asks again. *What do you think it is?*

Silence rings in the air. He turns on the music in the Caravan.

'I'm on the highway to...'

SURREY, 12:00 P.M.

Sara finds it hard to be informal with the Wolf as they walk along the lengthy hall. She notices everyone they pass taking a look at them. Sara is reminded that the man next to her is in charge of over 120 employees, and today she is one more. "Bill, maybe we should skip casual lunch today? I will grab something on the go after this next meeting." Bill is leading the two of them, because Sara has never been to the meeting room for I.H.I.T.

He ignores her comment with no emotion. "This meeting will have eleven different department representatives, each of whom has a full staff. Everyone will meet you in person, with me present. You're going to lead this investigation, with me overseeing you."

Sara slowly presses her lips and furrows her brow.

He follows up, but a smile creeps onto his face. "If you don't want to participate in this investigation at this level, now is the time to tell me, and I'll assign one of the officers in the meeting to lead the investigation."

Sara recovers her composure and answers with steel in her voice. "Sir, I believe in myself, and I believe in you and your department. I'm ready to work with you and your team."

The Wolf stops and turns toward her; she turns to face him, and they make eye contact. Bill slowly reaches around behind her,

"The door to the meeting is behind you."

They enter the room laughing.

Sara is hit with the layout and attendees of the room all at once. Two empty places to sit have cups of water on napkins and folders in front of them. The eleven attendees quiet as Bill and Sara enter. The table is long and, judging by the thirteen spots that are set for the meeting, there are at least another eleven seats that could be filled. One young male officer is standing approximately behind the position that is clearly the Wolf's at the far end of the room; Sara's spot is to his left. As she walks along, she notes an even number of men and women. The group has the same file she and Bill had acquired in his office; all the books are open to different spots. She's happy that she studied the email of the case last night. Sara has a sobering thought. *Everyone here is a top-level career-orientated officer and civilian. This could go well, or they could eat me alive.*

Bill shows Sara to her seat via a polite wave in the direction of her chair. She sits, while Bill stays standing and begins his monologue before her butt hits the seat. "Good afternoon everyone. To my left is Officer Sara McDonald. She is my choice to lead the Fukadero investigation. I chose her because of her background in psychology, and because her career record with the RCMP has been exceptional. As I call out your department, raise your hand so Sara can see you: Investigation Support Unit, Public and Media Relations, Family Victim Support, Legal Application, Evidence Secretary, Communications, Emergency Response Team, Street Patrol Car Dispatch, Air Support." Each person raises their hand and introduces themselves by first name. Sara nods, acknowledging each person; she gets the feeling that they've been through this a few times before.

The Wolf reveals a promotion, "Sara, you will be acting in the position of Major Case Management." The room breaks into a supportive applause, all eyes on her to gauge her reaction. Sara smiles and reaches for the notebook and taps a finger on the cover. She looks at Bill to carry on, he nods, "Of course," He sits and dims the light as the screen comes on at the other end of the room.

As the screen comes on, the mid-thirties man who raised his hand for Evidence Secretary speaks. "We have some video footage from the victim's street." After that statement, he hits a button on his remote and the video plays. Sara's heart accelerates, *Oh my god that's Tony's front yard. This is the big stone house's security camera. This is going to show us the killer at the moment of the murder, is this a joke? They don't need me to do anything.* After her last thought, Sara reminds herself, *This is not a popularity contest, I've been asked to do a job and I better focus.*

The big screen has a singular camera feed, the front door camera. *Tony comes walking out the front door in that white housecoat. He has a strong build and swings his upper body while he walks.* Sara observes Tony look to his right as he walks. At that moment the screen splits in two, vertically, with the Tony screen on the left and a street view that seems to point north on the right. *An old man is tying his shoe, he's standing and walking along casually. Tony is engaging him, the old man waves, Tony waves back. Is another vehicle going to turn up? What is Tony yelling at?* At that moment the screen splits into three vertical lines to show the angle from the corner of the house, and Sara sees the little dog going into the garden.

It's him, the old man. Sara retracts her notion that the shooter is an old man because she has no idea of his age. It's the way he walks along, maybe a bad back or bad knees? *Do they know each other? The old man is acknowledging the dog and laughing with Tony. But Tony's not laughing, he's mad. The old man is leaving?* As Tony turns, Sara's mouth drops open. *That gun was drawn fast, the first shot is within the first second of the draw, that little two-step to get the follow-up shot is a practiced move. Shooting on the move,* she notes. *And with the draw and re-holster. Is this guy a government agency staff member?* Sara shudders. *What the fuck did this Fukadero guy get into? I'm going to need some direction from Bill on this.*

The Evidence Secretary, freeze-frames a close-up of the assassin. His hat is pulled over the tops of his ears. His glasses are huge, covering everything from the cap down to the middle of the cheek. He's wearing his coat completely zipped, and snaps cover his neck; his chin is tucked into the collar of the coat. Sara's best guess is he's white or light brown.

He even keeps his mouth shut, no teeth in the frame.

The Evidence Secretary flips the screen to a four split; it's all different cars. "All four of these cars were seen leaving the neighbourhood at the time of the crime; we've only been able to pull the plates off two of them, and they check out as local. The other two we follow by traffic camera for a while, but they get lost in traffic after ten kilometers." At that, he switches to one screen, the one from Sara's car. It's a shot of a group of cars; he has the video stopped and a red arrow edited into the video to point behind the group of cars, specifically at the roof of a blue car. The Evidence Secretary continues. "We follow this car to the highway, and then we can't be sure which exit it gets off at; we had to back off when it got to following fifteen of these cars off exits ramps, and we don't even know if the vehicle was at the shooting."

Sara's blood boils at the thought of possibly being one lane of traffic away from the shooter. Bill turns the lights on and speaks, his voice loud enough to wake anyone. "Media, get the shooter's picture on the six o'clock news and in the paper in the morning. Also, this morning a well-known up-and-coming South Asian street thug, close friend of Tony Fukadero, was involved in a major physical assault at Trowel's contracting headquarters. An ambulance was called; a witness told us Suhki Trivedi picked up Yakub Kalowski and tossed him over his shoulder, smashed him into the concrete at his place of business. Yakub wouldn't tell us anything other than to say, 'I don't know who did this.' It was one of his day labourer's who gave the ambulance a description of the big Indo-Canadian who drove off in a purple Charger with black mags and loud exhaust pipes. Suhki drives a purple Hellcat Charger. So for now let's assume Trowel and the Indo-Canadian group that we have on file as Basmati is going to war over the debt that Mr. Fukadero was fighting in court, and the assault that Suhki just committed is retaliation."

Bill stands to talk. "Sara, you'll have access to every department. Here's the schedule, direct email, and telephone contacts of each officer who will be on duty twenty-four hours a day. All of your requests for assets are to be thought about before asking. An example, when you want undercover officers, check how many are on duty. You will see if they're busy before you ask. Study the schedule for them and plan your operation for the next opening. This group is fluid in nature; the schedule is always up-to-date. Review each department's schedule and make a game plan, you're the Major Case Management officer on this, so manage everyone to work smoothly and nobody will tell you no. They will only advise you on coordination.

"All your requests for asset direction should be placed through the laptop in front of you. All schedules and movements of this department are top secret. You are not to have a single casual conversation with anyone outside this room about asset movement or how we are operating. Do you understand?"

Sara scans everyone in the room, then answers in a firm tone, "Yes sir. I will take the utmost care with my duties."

The Wolf wraps up the meeting, "We have a lot to do, I expect everyone to play nice and show the new kid around a bit. Call me directly if you see anything Sara does that you think is inappropriate. Now, I promised Sara a lunch after we have this meeting, but she has since told me she would rather get to work. So, Sara, do you have anything to say to everyone before we break?"

Sara stands and speaks clearly to the room. "Thank you for welcoming me onto your team. During this job, if anyone has any suggestions, I'll expect emails on this computer. Also, when I call you, if my request is nonconforming or you have a better idea please tell me, so we are as efficient as possible. Be direct with me. I'm here to serve all of you, I expect you to serve me." The crowd nods and smiles.

Bill starts to leave the room without Sara, then turns grinning, "Sara, the lunch we were going to is with the Deputy Commissioner of E Division. I think you should come and tell her yourself that you're too busy to eat with her." Every head in the room turns at the same time to see Sara's reaction. Sara grabs her notebook and follows Bill. She is not smiling; the deputy commissioner is the absolute top cop in the E Division, a high-ranking officer that Sara only could have dreamt of eating with five years ago. Today during a murder investigation, she's waiting to eat with Sara. *What is going on? What do they really want me to do?*

11

Chloe is at home, upstairs, in her walk-in closet in the master bedroom. She hears the crowd of people murmuring down in the great white sitting area. That's where Chloe told her sister and mom to send all the well-wishers and associates. The kitchen is where she will sit with family and close friends. *Who will claim his death? Why was Tony such an asshole? I loved him. Did he love me, or was I nothing but a trophy wife? It doesn't matter anymore, he was my husband and we are a family. I'm in his family, I run this part of the family now. Who will help me? My sister only looks hot and screws. My mom has no business or family sense, and my dad never even came over for holidays. I can do it, I have it all now. Everyone will help me; this is all okay. Yes, all is as good as it could be in my life.*

Chloe is covered from her ankles to the bottom of her neck, in the loose-fitting black silk pantsuit she bought while in Italy last year with Tony. On her feet are polished nude flats styled after the ballerina slippers she had grown attached to in her younger years.

The walk-in closet is a duplicate of Chanel, in France. With dark cabinets, a white ceiling, and a plush carpet with large black-and-white squares that stretches from wall to wall; a Chanel symbol sits in the centre of the elegant room. Chloe loves that the lighting adjusts to match the venue that she's dressing for, from dim light for a nightclub to the fully lit stage.

Chloe freezes facing the mirror. *What do others see when they look at me?* She stares into her eyes. *Under thirty, high cheekbones, slender neck, long toned arms, and svelte firm legs. Smooth white skin, no blemishes even on my chest and back, perfect nails, no roots in my blonde hair. Yes, this is a perfect presentation.* Then Chloe goes through another list. *What* don't *they see? That I have trained and preened myself to be a trophy wife, and I had no plan to run a multi-million dollar real estate company. Will good looks and charm help me run the black-market business that Tony had been up to his ears with, since before I met him? Is that business somehow mine now?*

Chloe feels a sprinkle of joy hit her, the same tingle she has received her whole life when she has a useful idea. *They can't see that I have no one, everyone will think I have everyone.* Chloe takes in a long controlled breath, and releases it quickly with no sound. Then another deep breath. *How about a run through some basic footwork drills, I have all these mirrors in my dream Chanel walk-in. I'm going to use the mirrors each day for twenty minutes, minimum,* Chloe vows.

She's standing about three feet back from a bank of mirrors, with her feet shoulder-width apart. Evenly, and with straight legs as if possessed by a beautiful ghost, Chloe drags her heels together so that her toes point straight out. As her heels move, her relaxed hands, which hang in the front and centre of her body, begin to lift. While making round elbows and wrists, her fingers hold a soft feeling at their tips resting below her solar plexus. "That's one," Chloe whispers. She stands and stares at her form. *The most basic move performed with a skill that people used to pay me to see. Yes, this is okay.*

Chloe's eyes come alive before her body moves again. Her left arm lifts in a delicate movement. At the same time her perfectly straight right leg carries the heel to the centre of the other foot, Chloe's right arm comes to life. It comes to rest straight out, at her belly-button height. *I am at my peak. I was born to be on a stage. I'm the perfect age to run all this.*

Chloe holds the basic third position while prolonging her own gaze in the mirror. *This is what they see, a mix of perfect form and drama. I'm going down to my white sitting room to see who's going to help push this development across the line. I need eight to twelve months of backstopping from everyone. They will all help me, with smiles.* Chloe relaxes out of her last position and takes three deep breaths with her eyes closed. Turning, she heads for the dark heavy door, relaxed in the personal Chanel boutique she built. She hits the crystal light switch and shuts the door.

Chloe pauses at the spiral stairs, listening to everyone chat. "How'd this happen?" "Was it the cartel?" "Those Polaks did it, I bet." Everyone is making guesses.

Maybe the killer is here? She slinks down the stairs with her face made-up at a tasteful level and her hair pulled into a tight bun. Chloe pauses on the last step unnoticed, staring into the great white room, and evaluates everyone. *Deans devastated, he's weeping into my sisters shoulder. His crew is here. Four of them, they are ready for anything. Two of them are wasted on booze and pills, of coarse. Tony's childhood best friend, Danny, is very uncomfortable around Dean's crew. Where is my mom? Probably outside smoking. Better be outside smoking.*

Danny notices Chloe standing on the stairs and heads over with his arms lifted, palms open. "Ah Chloe, you poor girl."

She walks toward him and lets him hug her; she hugs him back. This is Tony's only childhood friend, other than Dean. *Nice of Danny to come here, but I bet he'll leave soon. Danny never approved that Tony led a thug life. He has a pleasant wife and kids who are so lucky to have him; he's never tried anything creepy with me. Always so polite.* "Thanks for coming, Danny," Chloe sniffles. Giving more support to Danny, than she expects to receive from him. She's right, he's terrified. Danny has no idea who half the people Tony knew are. "Danny, how are you doing?"

With straight arms Danny holds her shoulders. "How did this happen, Chloe?"

Her eyes well up fast as her mouth trembles open and closed. She never breaks the eye contact Danny wants. "I don't know," she quietly whimpers as she falls to his chest. She knows everyone is blaming everyone, and that's what makes this so terrible for her. Nobody can even take a solid guess other than to think of the most recent wrongs Tony had pulled off. "The Polish guys said they would kill him, right? Right?" She pleads to Danny, for a solid answer.

He stares back as the tears begin to flow. "I can't even begin to point the finger," he whispers. She tunes in that Danny's ready to leave.

He only wanted to ask me who did this, he's not going to be here to take on my problems.

There's a faint knock on the front door, *tap tap tap*. Light enough that if Chloe wasn't standing in the foyer, she would have missed the knocking under the drone of chatter in the sitting room. Danny peeks over to the door at the same time Chloe does. He heads towards the door while holding his trailing arm up with his hand in the stay position. "I'll get it, Chloe."

Danny pulls the heavy red door open with his left hand and stands to block the entrance with his body; his free hand is palm up. "Who are you here for?" As the door opens, Chloe catches a glance of the thick brown hand that she has seen in her kitchen holding her Boch French garden teacups while meeting Tony many times over the last year and a half.

Suhki towering in the door frame gives Chloe a level of calm that she has not felt since Tony died.

"Suhki, thank you for coming."

Danny looks Suhki up and down as he reaches for a handshake. "Hi, I'm Danny, Tony's best friend." Then

Danny walks back over to Chloe, grabs her in a hug, "I've got to go. I'll be in touch soon. If you need anything, please call right away." At that, he turns and walks past Suhki, who is standing with his head and shoulders low .

Chloe walks over to the door and takes Suhki's hand to draw him in; he walks in gently, with his eyes down. When he peers into the sitting area, he spots Dean in a chair, weeping.

"Chloe, I'm going to say hi to Dean, then could I talk to you for a minute in the kitchen?" Suhki asks with a confidence he has grown accustomed to as Tony's friend.

"Of course Suhki, I'll go put on the tea."

He nods politely. They both turn and go in different directions. As Suhki walks into the room, the two sober guys in Dean's crew become instantly alert. They've all heard about his temper and the beatings he lays on guys who are in his way. *They say he's always laughing during a fight because he has never lost,* and *He killed all these guys in India with his bare hands over his family's territory,* are a couple of the legends guys think about when they spot him. One of the thugs tap Dean's shoulder to get his attention.

Dean takes his hands off his face and lifts his head. "What the fuck bro?" Then he spots Suhki. Dean stands quickly, does a step change and walks over with his arms open. "Holy shit bro, thanks so much for coming over for this," Dean's honest reaction helps everyone relax.

At the end of the big hug, Suhki grabs Dean by the shoulders, holds him, "I'm here for you and your family, you call me as soon as you are able, and we'll go over some stuff."

Dean nods, tears welling up again, and speaks through a new wave of tears. "Thanks bro, we need you right now." Dean turns, his tears flowing, and staggers back to the chair, where Chloe's younger sister resumes manning his side with compassionate back-rubbing. Suhki turns and strides out of the room; nobody asks him where he's going.

SURREY, 12:45 P.M.

Suhki enters the blue designer kitchen, with its white trim, and sees Chloe pouring hot water in a teapot for them. "Let me do that," Suhki offers in a quiet voice as he walks over. He takes the kettle from her hand gently, she releases the teapot with delicate fingers. Chloe drifts over to the grand island in the middle of the kitchen, where she has teacups waiting.

Suhki glances at Chloe, standing with her back to him with her hands in front of her on the counter. Her head tilts so gently to the left, and her left knee is bent as well, giving the impression she might fall over any second. He walks over and moves around her widely, not crowding her. She doesn't react as he pours the tea in the cups in front of her.

The moment he places the tea kettle onto the counter by the teacups, she falls into his arms and rests her head on his chest. Chloe isn't wailing or bawling. She completely leans on Suhki with all her weight. He holds her around the back like a giant bear, rubbing and patting her back gently. She stretches her arms around his massive torso, with her hands resting lightly on the small of his back.

Chloe asks a generic question that usually no one can answer. "What should I do first Suhki?"

Suhki has one thing to say. "I went and threw that fat Polak on his head an hour-and-a-half ago."

Chloe is startled to the present by this comment, and grips Suhki with her arms. In a sober voice, she asks, "You already did that, or you thought about it?"

Suhki tells her about lifting the big bricklayer and doing an over-the-shoulder throw, leaving while the guy was still out cold. Chloe cries with joy and salvation into Suhki's chest, and he pats and rubs her back.

"Suhki, will you help me with the business that Tony started?" Chloe wimpers as she pulls her head off his chest, looking for eye contact. Their eyes meet, she draws the tips of her fingers ever-so-gently down the centre of his back. Suhki is shocked by the attention Chloe is giving him so soberly and sincerely; he feels a connection with her right away that he never noticed before. *This woman is full of intelligence.* The hairs on his neck stand up. "Yes, Chloe. I'm a businessman, and your family has helped my family. I'm here for you."

Chloe reaches up the centre of his back and hooks her hands over his thick shoulders. Letting her body hang, she buries her face back in his chest and weeps; he holds her weight with his big hands. After thirty-seconds of gentle crying into his massive chest, Chloe takes her weight onto her own feet. A moment later she lets go of his shoulders and drags her arms through his. Suhki is a little embarrassed that he feels so intimate while they are slowly separating.

Back on her feet, she reaches for her tea. Feebly she pushes a cup towards Suhki. "Please drink this, it's an herbal tea that supports your immune system."

Suhki dutifully obeys. Chloe mimics him in silence.

Chloe breaks the silence. "Will you meet me at the office tomorrow twenty minutes after closing? I'll prep some documents for us."

Suhki plays it cool, but during the silence he has noticed how Chloe holds her teacup with her pinky outstretched, and the way the gold trim sinks deeply into her plush lips.

"Yeah of course. Are you sure tomorrow?"

Chloe blankly stares across the kitchen. "I'm going to ask everyone to leave soon. I'm going to make a fresh juice and a small piece of fish on rice. I'll be in bed early. In the morning I'll work out lightly here at the house. Then I'll go into work and keep all the girls selling the properties. Be ready for our meeting around dinner. Okay?"

Suhki straightens his spine. *This woman is an angel. She seems sad and efficient at the same time. Perfect, we're going to get a grip on any loose ends.* "I'll be there for sure."

A knock on the back door. In comes an older Italian couple, and close behind them is another Italian couple and two Italian guys who are under sixty.

Suhki greets them, "Hello Mr. Fukadero, Mrs. Fukadero. I'm here to show my support for your family."

The senior Mr. Fukadero smiles and speaks in a thick Italian accent. "Thank-a you son, you have-a been a good friend. Come give me a hug, then excuse the family so we can talk."

Suhki smiles ear to ear, and almost runs over to the older man for the hug. "Sir, you have my number and can call me anytime, my family sends their condolences." And at that Suhki turns and heads towards the foyer to exit.

The old Italian woman walks over to Chloe. "Coma sit, you gotta eat. Wadda you want?" Chloe asks for the fresh juice and fish, the ladies smile. "Okay dear. Anything fora you. Go sit-a down and talk to your father and uncles about this-a miserable curse."

12

Damon emptied his van and locked his hunting rifle up right when he returned home. He also put the steaks in a freezer bag, adding his favourite sauces to marinate them for the barbecue. Damon hung out for the day hearing about life in the Okanogan from his in-laws. Naomi made their son Benji work on some after-school math. The boy kept fooling around, so Damon banned his video games for the weekend. The child whimpered while doing his homework; but when Benji was done he had forgotten about the loss of the video games, and was jumping on everyone and talking about the latest games the kids play at recess.

The news comes on in the family room; Damon goes and sits to watch. The music and newscaster's voice blast from the TV. "Another murder in Surrey yesterday has started a province-wide manhunt. We will show you a picture of the gunman right when we come back from commercial."

Damon's whole body has waves pulsing up and down. His son runs in the room and belly-flops onto his lap.

"Boom!" the boy yells as he lands heavy. Damon laughs and plays like he has been bombed; he rolls his eyes and his body goes limp. His father-in-law comes into the room and grabs the remote. Damon has to intervene. "Sammy, leave it on, I want to see one of the news stories."

Sammy still has the remote, "Google it." He examines the remote like he's trying to decode a bomb.

"You go Google your hockey, I came in here to watch the news. It's not that I happen to be in here and the news came on. I came here to watch it." As Damon explains this Benji is sitting on his lap, looking back and forth between the two.

Sammy laughs. "You trying to watch the weather girl or something?"

Damon deadpans. "Nah, I hear there's a new story about men going to other men's houses and randomly flipping through the channels, I want to see how to get them help. You should watch."

At that Sammy rolls his eyes, "Let's go Benji, your room will be more fun than the news. After the news are you going to throw the steaks on?"

Damon gives a big nod. "For sure, I will."

The news comes back on, and there's a close up of Damon's face right there in his living room. The hat and glasses are blurred into one, and his coat and skin are seamless. Naomi comes into the room, glances at the TV.

"Can you start dinner? Everyone is hungry."

Damon studies her for any sign that she just saw him on TV. Nothing registers on her face.

"So will you start the barbecue, or are you going to sit here and try and solve a murder from a blurry picture?"

She puts her hands in her joggers and steps in front of the T.V .

"Why do they even have cameras, the picture is always a blur eh? This guy isn't even in a mask and we can't see his face. Barbecue now?" The last part is said with a mock pouty-face.

"Yeah, I'm starved too, my angel, I'll fire it up."

Naomi feels a brief shock when she sees the face on TV.

It's just a blurry face.

She always feels that her husband is a bit naughty, but he's not out shooting every gangster in B.C.

He doesn't have the time.

As Damon fires the barbecue he yells in to the house. "Let's all go to Science World tomorrow, I've been trying to have a meeting with a notary for a while. It will be less than an hour." After the barbecue is lit, he walks over to his wife in the kitchen and gives her a hug. "Hey hun, tomorrow we sign off the debt that's on the title for the house build." Naomi knows this is huge news; they've been barely able to make the interest-only payments to the contractor. This is a miracle. Naomi closes her eyes. *We need some work so we have some cash.*

LANGLEY, APRIL 8, 6:15 A.M.

Damon pushes against the ground with both hands; his back is straight and he's on his toes. "...nineteen, twenty." He pushes out the last twelve push-ups with gritted teeth and blurred eyes. The routine is five sets of twenty, each set of twenty being a different style of push-up. He's already hung from the ceiling on his custom built pull-up bar for five sets of twenty pull-ups. This is the lazy workout that he puts in on off days. Now the crunches begin, fourteen different crunch techniques in sets of twenty-five. After all the years of conditioning he doesn't break a sweat. This little workout takes about thirty-five minutes.

When Damon goes into his garage to work out he only turns on one small light, no music. Being awake this early gives him the feeling of being ready for the monsters of the world. The main benefit to no music and low lighting is that if the beasts get the bright idea to come by this monster's house, they'll find it nice and quiet. The last thing they might see is the barrel of his 12-gauge shotgun. *But you can't see when the shotgun's flashlight is in your eyes, so the last thing they'll see is a bright light. Wait, wait, if you shoot from here to the street, most likely it won't be a kill shot, so they'll be crawling and bleeding before you get there to finish them off.*

These are the casual workout thoughts that run through Damon's head while he listens for light footsteps around his house or on the street. He doesn't want a shootout at his home, but Damon's not going to miss a great chance to take out a dedicated killer either.

You know a guy might only be coming here to scare you? Maybe a friend dared him or he's trying to show off. Damon's one sensible voice gets to ask a lot of questions that all get shot down like paper airplanes in a rainstorm. Damon counters with the same answer he's been giving since he was a kid. *If someone is hounding me so hard they're at my house, I'm not going to wait and see how they want to play my family and me out. They are done. I get their ID out, and I go after their people as well, at their houses. Once someone comes to my house, if they're not killed here, I'll be after 'em like the Grudge. I don't make that choice, they do when they come here.*

Going through the crunches, he wonders if there's another ab workout that would be hard again. 350 in thirteen minutes and not even a light sweat. *I can't believe that I used to have a hard time with 100 crunches. Should I be trying harder? Is 350 even a workout?* Working out alone, he doesn't have anyone to challenge; anyway, he doesn't want to challenge anyone. His workout is done for work. *The police and military have minimums for fitness depending on your duty. I'm a field operative, I have to keep a higher fitness level.*

So Damon made this fitness regimen from different government fitness minimums and maximums. It includes running times, and hiking times with a weighted pack on. On top of that, there's shooting practice and familiarity drills, costume design, and transportation competency. *How come I never joined a government agency when I was young? They get paid to learn all this, and a pension.*

Damon knows the answer. He was raised with little education and no participation in team sports. The adults around him would mock authority. "Those guys are sitting around eating doughnuts and robbing pimps for money." Damon shakes his head at the memory.

Why should a pimp not be robbed? He's robbing the women of their dignity, any adult must know that. This last thought makes him smile, because in this view of right and wrong herein lies the essence of care that the world has for murdered criminals. They don't care about someone who benefits by cheating while they work so hard. Everybody wants a criminal to be served justice one way or another. Damon has an afterthought. *When they're dead they don't cost taxpayers any money, either.*

It all looks so different as an informed adult, he often reflects.

Damon stands and stretches his lats and hip with a standing side stretch. He holds each side for four breaths and alternates three times between sides. This is a relaxing workout day for sure. He stands in his low-lit garage staring out a small window towards the street, morning light bathing everything in a blue glow. *Neighbour with the f150 next door pulls out at six on the dot. The next one with the blue VW Wagon leaves at six-forty-five. All is as it should be.*

Damon dreams of quietly watching a would-be hitman walking casually along, not sneaking or acting suspicious; nevertheless Damon would notice because he knows the neighbourhood pattern entirely. As though everyone on the cul-de-sac is in his family, he knows all of their patterns. So this dream hitman would be trying to blend into 'nothing' because he isn't from here. Damon would let him get right close before squeezing off a single round. *Depending on timing, maybe the head or maybe the chest. If the chest, then I'd close the distance and get his weapon under control before cutting deep into his neck with my eight-inch Cold Steel Tanto blade. Possibly covering his mouth to keep the last yell muffled; with only one shot and it being on my property, I would probably have all day to hide the body. Would neighbours come after one single shot? Not likely.*

However, this has never happened yet, and it did not happen this morning either.

"Morning hun," Naomi is optimistic when she pops her head into the garage and sees Damon is home. "I don't want to bother you, but I'm making breakfast for my parents; are you still going to be here today?"

Damon is happy and disappointed at the question; happy that he can answer, 'yes we are going to the notary and Science World today.' Disappointed because his wife never really knows when he's coming or going. *How would it feel to have a normal schedule, to have no violent repercussions?* Damon's Coach answers loudly. *Don't sit around wishing you had a soft life, you don't and you never will. Train, be alert, and plan. Go eat a good meal with your family, you deserve it. Your last mission was a success on every level. Good work.*

HIGHWAY 1, 10:00 A.M.

Damon's white Caravan is on Highway 1, doing ninety kilometres an hour and heading west on the Port Mann suspension bridge over the Fraser River. "So Damon, what type of notary is open on a Sunday?" Sammy asks for the second time this morning. Naomi smiles while her dad grills Damon; her mom enjoys the view of the river, while little Benji reads a graphic novel.

Damon answers politely and informatively, "Well the city is so competitive nowadays that most often you can get any service industry, even a notary, to accommodate your schedule and they're happy you asked."

Sammy has his references ready this time. "Well I've bought and sold three houses, so that's three property transactions. I've always had to wait until Monday for legal services. What's this guy making on your deal?"

Damon answers confidently. "You nailed it. For him to discharge the debt off our title and gather the lender and borrower signatures, he'll get twelve hundred dollars. So when I asked him to accommodate my schedule, he was more than happy. This way I sign it all today and grab the promissory note I signed, and tomorrow he'll go to the Land Title Office and remove the lien from our house's title."

Sammy is smiling; he has more questions. "So sometime last week you called him and requested this Sunday, when we're visiting, to go and do this transaction?"

"I've been super busy and I don't consider this work, so we can blend a bit of family time in with a quick filing appointment. You guys can go get an early lunch close by while I take care of it. Then we will go to Science World." Everyone is bored with the topic, and Naomi changes the subject.

Damon's Simple voice blurts out. *Don't you think you should have come to meet the notary armed, and arrived tactically, with surveillance and proper approach?* The Coach chimes in. *You did not profile the notary? The amount of time he's been at the same location: thirty-five years; his age: about sixty-eight; his wife works the desk and his son's law firm has cards on the front counter. You ask a good question, but show you're not paying attention.*

The Simple voice comes back level and firm. *Yeah, I've thought about all that, they have the best cover. This guy could be the best assassin ever, wooing you with his old reliable act and then poisoning your tea.*

Damon is listening to the banter in his head and agrees with both of them, so he adds in, *Fine, if this guy is the ultimate killer, I'll go out in a quiet office.*

As his argument ends, he remembers a fun question for everyone and asks everyone in the van. "Suppose vampires are real, but the only person to see them in full fangs is the person they're about to eat. Would anyone in this van want to meet a vampire?"

Naomi rolls her eyes and laughs. "This one is for you, Dad. He's always going on about old monsters from the movies."

Sammy smiles. "Well, you might be the one they're going to turn into a vampire…"

Damon laughs and checks for eye contact in the rearview mirror. "That's the burn, vampires put that rumour out. 'If we bite you a certain way, you live forever.' The rumour is so that when we see one for the first time in full fang, we react, 'Oh this might be my chance to live forever.' Vampires are geniuses, they have a marketing campaign so their food doesn't resist."

Everybody in the van groans. Benji pipes up, "Daddy, are vampires real or what?"

"I can't say yes or no because they eat every witness, but if you see fangs coming at you, *fight*."

The boy nods affirmatively, with conviction in his eyes. They all enjoy the fit of laughter that breaks out in the van.

13

Damon parks on Commercial and 12th and walks the family into a little mom-and-pop diner. He gives them an ETA of roughly forty-five minutes and leaves for the notary on foot; it's across the road. Going to the corner of 12th and Commercial, he waits for the light, even though there are few cars. Damon is observing the street. Do the closed stores have too many cars? Is anyone watching for his approach? No, this street appears as it should. It has not changed since he was a kid growing up three blocks away. Pedaling his biycle through Clark park.

This is a typical Sunday; the notary's car is the only one in front of the office. That makes sense, since Damon is his only customer today.

He reaches for the glass door; it bears an old sticker that's gold with black trim and reads Notary Public. The door's classic aluminum frame must be as old as Damon. Through the open blinds, he sees the secretary sitting in her seat. The lady has grey hair tied in a bun and wears a blue business jacket; Damon knows she will have a dress that matches the coat. This is the notary's wife, Olga. Damon always gets the impression that the secretary does all the work in a notary office, and then accepts he has no idea of what a notary really does. Not that it matters; they're always involved at the beginning and the end of every mortgage deal.

He walks inside, and is quickly greeted. "Good morning Damon. Alexi will be right out. Have a seat please."

"Good morning Olga, thank you." *If this lady, with her grandma-weight rear-end is going to kill me, it will be the sweetest death. She has nothing but kindness in her eyes. They're not trying to kill me. She considers me a troubled boy who is lost. Olga is afraid I'll misunderstand and act poorly. She and her husband are straightforward folks, that's my only feeling here. They raised a good family and probably don't aim to be around any killers if they can help it. Being of a certain age and seeing men steal and lie, they will work any angle to keep their family safe. This notary is Yakub's great-uncle by marriage to his wife, so this notary has a family connection to Kuda, who is locked in the pen. I know this type of client well, they have been hurt and need band-aids. This is not their way, it's a way.*

"Damon! Good morning, thank you for coming to our office on this busy Sunday. May I offer you tea?"

Damon smiles at the question and knows this meeting is going to take at least twenty minutes, so he accepts graciously. "Yes please, I'll have whatever you're having."

"Come into my office and have a seat. Olga will bring in the tea when it's ready."

Damon follows and takes the first seat. The desk is completely clear, ready for fresh business. He sits, eyes locked on the older gentleman, leans forward and lays his hands flat on the desk. Alexi smiles knowingly, reaches into a file, and pulls some papers. Damon relaxes and leans back. This is not an act. Damon has a jaded outlook on everyone's intentions, and has hardened from far too many renegotiations after a job. Damon is sure there will be no mention of the hit during this document signing.

Alexi is old enough to know that you never speak of a past murder again. Anyone who does mention old murder is suspected immediately of being an informant.

The hit is done, the deal is complete. The day after it's on the news, meet here and sign off the debt for the building of Damon's house, they had arranged. That's it. No reminiscing, no renegotiating.

Alexi relays the news offhandedly. "Your clients want to meet to offer you more work."

Damon holds his mouth shut and watches the aged notary's face, then politely states, "I've come here to sign off a debt I've paid. More work can be discussed after the debt is removed." *Ah fuck, everyone is the same. This nice old man is a fucking liar and a scammer. They think I'll keep going until I'm dead or in jail, then they don't have to pay me. This is not my first rodeo, fuckers.* "Listen to me clearly, Alexi. I don't care to even hear any other conversation that you have prepped until the debt is signed off and you have been over to the Land Title Office and cleared the lien." Damon looks to his left; Olga is standing in the door with her eyes wide, holding two teacups. She's trying to judge how badly Damon is reacting to the conversation. Damon relaxes his face and is a little ashamed, she proceeds to slowly bring the tea in for them.

Alexi addresses her while nodding quickly and confidently. "Thank you for the tea, we are fine. Just chatting, sweetie."

Damon asks, "What kind of tea is this?"

Olga carries the habits of a professional lady. "We have imported English breakfast tea, to us its better than coffee."

To be polite Damon adds. "Yes, a black tea has enough caffeine for me, thank you."

Olga nods and smiles as she leaves.

"Damon, your papers are right here. You can sign them and not listen to another word from me. However, I have to say, you made a good deal with your clients before, and they want to pay you a lot more. Will you please listen?"

Damon stares while saying, "Pass the documents over and I'll review them." Alexi turns the file with a professional smile, then he starts on page one and walks Damon through, adding his signature in the appropriate places. After the signing, Damon stands to leave. "Thank you for the tea. You will be filing this tomorrow morning?"

Alexi nods. "It is the first thing I'll do."

Damon turns to leave, knowing he will be followed out of the office for a last-chance proposition from the old notary. At the front desk he turns, and sure enough, Alexi is right behind him. "Damon, may I walk with you to your car?" *This guy is so polite, I want to believe he's nice.*

"It would be my pleasure Alexi. Good day Olga. Thank you for your work this Sunday. Did you miss your service this morning?"

Her eyes light up; young folks never talk about Sunday service anymore. "Why yes, but we will go to the afternoon service, after work."

"Thanks again, Olga."

Damon holds the door for Alexi, who follows with slumped shoulders and head low. He's at a loss for words but desperately needs some in the next ten seconds. "Damon, you know my family is close to this work, so I'm not only working here, this is family protection. Yakub was attacked yesterday."

Damon has to steel his body to not glance at Alexi. "Go on." Damon keeps his eyes forward while they walk.

Alexi rushes through his case, "The police are everywhere, watching our entire family and even our friends. We can't make a move to help ourselves. You understand how important it is to keep momentum or all will be lost."

This old guy is doing a good job. He's not mentioning the last hit. He's not mentioning any new targets. He has not asked me to do anything. I trust him.

Damon stops and steps into a restaurant's door-stoop, Alexi follows him.

"What are you thinking?" Damon stares at Alexi, reading anything he can from micro-reactions on the old man's face.

Alexi looks like he has taken a breath of air after being under water. "Go over to Trout Lake and meet Yakub, he will talk to you. I'll wait here to draw up a new agreement."

There it is, so the papers I just signed are garbage I guess, damn it. I'm stupid for even listening. Let's wrap this up and go to Science World.

Damon leans in a little and lowers his voice. "Once you file that document I signed I'll have a meeting, not before."

Alexi smiles; he knows the young man has misunderstood the proposition. "Let me explain more clearly. The first debt on your build is over, I'll file it tomorrow. You go meet Yakub at the lake, and if you make another deal I'll write it up today."

"Look at my face old man, do you think for a second that I'm confident in my papers being filed? The papers sitting in your office on a Sunday. What if I was to die today?"

Alexi recoils and squints. Damon widens his stance. *Good acting, pal.*

"Damon, Yakub has brought his whole family to the lake for a picnic. There are twenty-five woman and children, with their husbands. I'm to ask you to join their picnic for your talk. We are not the kind of people you are thinking." Alexi is doing the staring at Damon, but with compassion for Damon's ugly ideas.

"Okay, I'll go over to the lake, I have my wife, son, and in-laws as well."

Alexi relaxes, "Good, good, thank you for listening to me. I'll wait at the office until five p.m."

"What about afternoon service for you and Olga?" Damon asks inquisitively.

"We are all sacrificing for greater good, I'll read the Book with her tonight."

EAST VANCOUVER, 11:30 A.M.

Naomi notices Damon before he grabs the door; she sees the familiar look of an unexpected change of plans. Damon cheers up as he approaches the table. "Hey everybody, good news, the contractor who built our house is down the road at Trout Lake, having a barbecue with thirty family and friends, and we've been invited."

Everyone looks at each other; it's Benji who asks the first question. "How big is the lake?"

"Oh, it's not too big, but it's the only one I know of in the city. You should have seen it by now. I used to pedal my bike there all the time as a kid."

Benji is into it right away, so Sammy chimes in, "We'll save a fortune not going to Science World, let's go. I used to run my pit bull up trees there when you were a baby Naomi. Let's see if those trees are still there."

Damon asks if anyone has anything in the van they need, because they'll be walking four blocks to get to the picnic, the family is ready to go.

The happy family walks along 12th until they get to the next light; turning right, they keep up the pace to get off the busy side street. "Daddy, was there this many cars here when you were a kid?"

Damon reminisces. "Yes, it was about the same. These are old roads made for fewer cars. See how bumpy the street is compared to our neighbourhood in Langley?" Benji looks around, but it's clear he doesn't recognize the difference. "Don't worry Son, now that you've seen old bumpy roads, you'll notice the new roads around our house next time you look."

The boy looks around as they walk. Soon he has another question. "Why are all the houses so old and big?"

"That's a good question. These are Vancouver specials. This was a suburb a long time ago, they built them as big as the land could hold."

They soon arrive at Trout Lake. Strolling in the alley that surrounds the park. Over at the south east end of the small lake, they all agree the big group with the barbecue smoke and all the kids running around must be the contractor's family picnic. Sammy investigates, "How did you meet these guys? They seem like a hell of a group. Building houses and carrying mortgages for young couples is amazing."

Damon was ready for this question six months ago. "I went to school with one of the guys here in Vancouver. Peter is his name; we lost touch for fifteen years. We saw each other on a construction site where I was installing an HVAC system at a mansion. His family were the builders, so they started giving me more work over the years. Then last year they started talking to me about how I could have a house, and the costs. Eventually, a situation came up where we put it all in motion. Very easy to deal with this group, hard-working, honest, old school. Sammy, you will have fun at the barbecue, they tip a few beers on days off." Sammy contented, lifts his head a bit and looks closer at the crowd.

As they stroll over, Yakub lifts his chin at Damon with a subtle smile. Damon gently nods and feels at ease, even happy; seeing all these people having a good day is a treat. After the introduction of the in-laws to a few folks, Damon brings little Benji over to a soccer game that twelve kids have going on. Yakub asks if Sammy is okay to hang out with his cousins while he and Damon walk around to say hi to a few guys. Sammy nods a yes while taking a beer that's being handed to him. The girls are taken in by a big group of ladies of mixed ages; Naomi has met a few of the wives over the last couple years, and has grown close to the moms who have children the same age as hers.

As soon as they're out of earshot, Damon mutters, "I don't want to go around shaking any hands today, this isn't my celebration. I'm only a guest."

Yakub speaks through his smile. "The guys who built your house will want to say hi and hear about the house; it would be odd not to say hi. Relax, everyone will be normal." Damon takes a breath and prepares for knowing smiles, extra-long handshakes, and unnecessary thank yous. *This is a terrible idea,* his Coach utters quickly. *No, this is great. Everyone should be thanking us,* his Simple voice chimes in. *Don't worry, you'll be surprised by these people, just breathe,* the all-knowing voice soothes, and everyone shuts up.

The first family Yakub and Damon approach is the concrete guy's. The man introduces his wife and points out his kid on the soccer field. Concrete guy lets his wife know that this is the owner of the Walnut Grove build in Langley. His wife doesn't bat an eye, and firmly shakes Damon's hand, glad to meet another client who's happy with her husband's work. Damon and Yakub go around to all the families; some of the guys Damon knows well from different jobs. They've worked on his house as well. It feels good to talk about harmless stuff; Damon feels healthy for the first moment in a long time. The job is over, and he doesn't have to keep ten strangers' schedules in his head so that he blends into the background of their lives, all so that he can take a life. *It's so much harder to take a human down than any other animal. Damn it, this is not the time for comparison games.*

Damon snaps back to the present. Yakub waits for eye contact and asks, "You get any rest lately, my friend?" Yakub has a brother and many close cousins; he has no problem talking to men about taking care of themselves.

The two walk over to some chairs under a pop-up gazebo that blocks the sun from the food table. Yakub has his left arm in a blue canvas sling hung around his neck, and Damon gestures to it with his eyes.

"It's nothing, just a thin fracture on my collar bone. I'm supposed to hang the arm in the sling to remind myself to let it rest and heal. When I was younger I wouldn't have used this. But I have to help myself heal, I have enough problems."

"What happened?"

Yakub tells the short version of the big kid tricking him and getting a solid over-the-shoulder toss. Yakub is a good sport about the beating. "Suhki had enough control not to hit my head on the ground, otherwise I would be dead for sure. He had my feet five feet off the ground in a split second. I never trained with anyone that big back home.

I was the biggest. Very few times was I lifted so high, in fifteen years of training back in Poland."

Damon's stomach turns to butterflies when he hears the name Suhki. He's only heard the street stories about Suhki; with this first-hand account that Yakub gives him, he belives they're all true. Yakub has a large belly, but it goes well with his substantial back muscles and thick legs. Since Yakub was young he's been known as unbeatable because of his size and his style of Judo. *Suhki is a real monster,* Damon envisions. Then in the time it takes for Yakub to take a breath Damon's mind has three distinct thoughts. *You saw Suhki with Fukadero at the gym. This man is possessed by the demon now. Suhki is the next target.*

Yakub is waiting for eye contact as Damon comes out of thought.

"Yes, I see you already know what we need," .

Damon gives an order. "We should stand and talk."

"Sure if you want to walk and talk, it's okay with me."

"No, we need to stand under the gazebo."

LANGLEY 12:00 P.M.

"Hi, I just got an email from communications, my ID number is 4576." Sara is calling the number for RCMP surveillance communications for the first time.

"Yes, hi Sara. We met in the office yesterday. What can I do for you?"

"Is the information in this email real-time?"

"Let me open the file, I'll tell you. Oh yeah, this was two minutes ago," the communications specialist answers back.

"We have fifteen Trowel members at Trout Lake, right now?"

Her contact answers back. "Yes, a gathering of twenty wives and associates. You'll get a full list of all the phones that are in the area of that barbecue for more than ten minutes, and you'll get who's standing next to who in a flowchart. It will show who's the most popular because the chart will show by time who stands next to who and for how long."

Sara already knows this and needs to end this call. "Thank you, sir, I've got to go." She hangs up without waiting for a goodbye and makes another call. "Hello, my ID number is 4576, I'm Sara McDonald." Sara has the swing of this already.

"Yes Sara I met you yesterday, what can I do for you?" The air traffic controller for Air 1 is all business.

"I'm sending you a request for surveillance at Trout Lake in Vancouver. I'll need a log of all the people and the cars in the parking lots. Would Air 1 get over there in the next half hour? I sent an email request to you, just now."

The air traffic controller answers immediately. "Air 1 is over Surrey Central. Searching for a stolen car that fled a store robbery, and has forty-five useful minutes of fuel left. Do you feel there's fruit to be had at Trout Lake, or is this nothing more than a look?"

Sara challenges. "If I have the authority to direct Air 1 then I want that EC 120 over Trout Lake filming and logging Trowel's most current get-together. If I don't have the authority then don't do it."

The air traffic controller answers as the last word comes from Sara's mouth. "We have diverted Air 1 to your location, facial recognition should help identify Trowel members. Their cars and their friends' cars will all be filmed and logged as well. Your video file will be uploaded as soon as they leave." At that the air traffic controller and Sara hang up with no good-bye; both are busy and need to focus elsewhere.

14

"Do you hear it yet?" Damon stands with his mouth open so he hears slightly better.

Yakub turns his head and keeps an eye on Damon.

"No Damon, I don't hear any spy helicopters." Yakub peers under the gazebo-edge toward the sky. Damon doesn't care if Yakub is caught at his own barbecue, but he himself doesn't want to be visualized here. Especially if they're making a film log of who's here.

"Yakub, you know I'm a pilot, right?" Yakub nods politely, like he is talking to an upset little brother. Damon goes on. "The RCMP helicopter is an EC 120, its rotor blades direct sound straight down. So you won't hear the helicopter the way you're imagining, you'll only hear the whine of the turbine engine. And only when the wind is coming from behind the helicopter and straight at you. So if you want to check out the big white bird, turn your focus fifteen hundred feet up and about a kilometre away; with the wind coming from the south that's where she is.

The aircraft will be coming out of cruise flight, transitioning into a slow-moving hover."

Yakub steps out of the gazebo to prove to his little brother that there is no ghost out there, but as soon as he looks up to the South.

"Holy shit man, it's right where you said it would be. I can't hear it. Oh oh, I hear the whining sound. Yes, so strange how it's so quiet."

Yakub ducks back under the gazebo to see Damon smirking,

"Hey I have no idea if that bird is here for you guys. Supposing it is then why would I want my pretty face sitting here? It will only stay for a half an hour or so if it's logging everyone."

Yakub's face sours. "What do you mean, logging us?"

Damon explains, how the cops don't watch and make notes; the tactic seems to be a video log of everyone. To have file footage for long-term information helps them make better choices when after different groups. "Think about it, Yakub, they have a solid case that your group is capable of anything. They will scan everyone here and decide how they will optimize officer time."

Yakub's mouth gapes and the colour in his cheeks drain. "You sound like them."

Damon smiles gently. "It's the oldest tactic in the world to study your opponent. Right now I'm not on a video. I'm not being followed by teams of athlete RCMP officers and their resources. Once you get heat, your hands are tied." Damon points an open hand at Yakub.

"You know about heat. They're all over you."

Damon has his head touching the top of the fold-out tent, so Yakub asks if he can sit while they talk.

Damon cheerily waves his hand towards the chair, "It's your barbecue." Damon examines Yakub; he decides the man is at his wit's end. A natural look when clients are talking about a murder. The other way clients talk is over excited. *Let's get this guy in the ground. Fuck him and his guys. We'll kill them all eh?* is the basic outline of the brave talk that is used. But Yakub is tired, and needs a miracle not to end up with nothing for him, and his work crews. Damon admires that Yakub is committed to do something about it. Some people, who Damon can't understand, will say *That's how they act, not me. I'll get flush somewhere else. Karma will get them.*

Almost every one of them has money to fall back on; it's the desperate who take desperate actions.

These people are done. Take the money and stop calling them, The Simple voice is laughing as it speaks, *They can't do shit. Join the big brown guy and reverse the job.* Damon gently rolls his eyes at the suggestion. "Yakub, how will you pay me? You're tapped. I need the payment up front. This is turning into an open war. And there's no guarantee of any outcome. I can't float a job on my dime until a court case gets thrown out because everyone is scared of getting killed. It's a huge risk you want me to take."

Yakub keeps eye contact during this negotiation. As he opens his mouth to talk, Damon cuts him off. "You're a good man and I'm going be straight with you. The payment for the last job was very generous of you and your people. The wholesale cost of material was at least two hundred and fifty-thousand. Everyone's labor was a minimum of another hundred and twenty. I'm not trying to grind anything else out of you, but I need you to understand my position. I had nine thousand saved before that last job, but it took months and I had a lot of costs that I won't begin to explain. That job was very time consuming. I spent over fifty-thousand on job costs during the last six months, and I'm forty-thousand in debt to my credit line, with four thousand left. I can't take another job for trade. I need work that pays me right away. I'm an air conditioning mechanic, you know, I'm qualified to find safe work."

Yakub's eyes have softened as Damon speaks, he hears the truth in the words. Damon explains his reality, "I don't have fun doing these jobs, it's not easy or quick. I'll need one hundred thousand dollars to take this work."

Yakub steeples his fingers. "Thank you for disclosing your finances to me. I respect your position. I already kind of knew that from clues; you would be happier if you were getting rich, I bet." At that Yakub chuckles. "You need your yard finished, right?"

Ah shit he's going to offer trading work again, this guy is at the end of his rope. After a little back-and-forth I'm going to wrap this up and get over to Science World. Damon answers sadly, "Yes, you know it's a dust pit at my house, but I don't have enough money to carry myself to make this happen. If I had some savings, the deal for trade in work would be great, but I don't."

Yakub smiles. "Okay, I don't want to waste your time, so I'll put all the cards on the table."

Damon smiles along, "Alright," in the way you listen to a kid's plea to not go to bed. "Wait, Yakub, Air 1 is dropping altitude. I've gotta turn around, I think they're trying to see who's under the gazebo."

Yakub asks. "Why would they go lower to the ground?"

Damon has already turned and keeps his head touching the top of the gazebo as he answers. "The camera hangs from the bottom of the fuselage. To get a snap of everyone's face, the whole chopper will have to lower. This is good, they can't go low enough to see my face, and they have to suspect that we're not aware of them. They'll swing around to try and get this last shot, then we'll know almost for certain that they're using full police coverage of your group. I want you to stand and look busy on this other side, as they swing around you move back and I'll follow; that way we are not hiding from the chopper. Then they will rack it up to not an ideal photo log situation."

Yakub obeys; he does not question this bizarre act Damon has asked him to perform. *Who trained this guy? He's not slightly worried that the police are flying around looking for him at a Sunday picnic.*

Sure enough, the white EC 120 with the RCMP red, blue, and yellow stripes swings around ever so slow and smooth. *If Damon hadn't noticed this helicopter there's no way I'd have heard the engine or noticed the bird circling around my family. He's worth the money. We need him to do this job for us.* Once the turbine helicopter gets to the other side, Damon and Yakub are turned so that Damon has his back to it while it circles.

Damon turns around to face the first direction, the bird swings back around. Damon and Yakub keep the dance going as well, with Yakub going back to the barbecue and Damon following. The multi-million dollar bird, with two officers in it, follows again. Damon hears power added to the engine to accommodate the sudden change of direction at each end of the giant circle.

"What do you think, Yakub? What else might that expensive bird be doing hover

circling? It costs around a thousand dollars an hour to keep that EC 120 flying with two officers, and that doesn't include the support crews they're talking to."

Yakub nods his head, his eyes closed. "Yes, we have to assume they're here to watch us."

"They'll leave soon; this is only info-gathering. They have the cars in the parking lot to sweep as well." Yakub knows the little blue car Damon had driven to kill the Fuk is parked in the lot. He stares at Damon with rising concern, Damon stays cool. "There are a lot of cars, Yakub, many different colours in many places. Even if they have a plate, your friend won't talk with them if they knock on the door asking about times and dates they've had their car, right?"

Damon holds his breath, until Yakub's reaction to this question is delivered. Yakub smiles confidently. "She barely speaks English and has been told to never speak to anyone, *ever*, about her transportation over the last six months. Her second cousin is in jail with my brother, Kuda, on the assault charge, and her husband is owed seventy-thousand dollars. Nobody here is helping the police. The RCMP definitely didn't help anyone here in the courts, or in that set-up the Fuk pulled on us."

Damon motions with his eyes for Yakub to listen; Air 1 is adding power as the helicopter goes into climbing cruise altitude. Yakub tips his ear up to hear better, and nods as he stands to pinpoint the bird's movement. "Yes, they are flying away fast towards Burnaby."

Yakub slaps his thighs. "Okay, here is what we have to offer." Damon lifts his brow and intertwines his fingers.

"We have raised twenty-five thousand dollars cash for the down payment. We are offering the yard job, which is about fifty thousand dollars, and another twenty-five thousand dollars when the courts release our draw."

The two men stare at each other. Damon counters. "The yard work is to begin the week after the job hits the news, regardless of the courts releasing your draw."

Yakub recoils his scrunched face. "If that's the deal you want, then that is the deal. The notary has the twenty-five thousand cash at his office, and some tricky words that you and he will fine-tune in the contract. I already signed the blank paper that you two can write this deal on."

They shake hands in one solid up-and-down.

Damon is looking at the ground while he scratches behind his ear. He gets an old thought out. "You're owed two million for the work you completed; with the last payment to me and this arrangement we just made, I've got to ask you, is there any profit in the court-held money with me getting four hundred and ten thousand dollars?"

Yakub is still sitting; his head drops low in his shoulders. "No, we lost money on the first payment to you, and the lawyer, who did not get any results, still cost us close to fifty-thousand. But with everyone here having the money they invested into those mansions back in their pockets, we will work again. Today we can't even build a rancher with all our resources. We'll all be working for someone else if this money doesn't come back. Forty years of our family's work, and we all become employees again like we just got off the boat, with nothing."

Damon has his hands in his pockets, "Yeah, I thought so. I'll give it my all. I won't stop until they do. I'll pull out all the stops, no mercy for anyone in the presence of that beast. I'll strike so hard that nobody else steps up. I'll try and take a group of them at one go. No more Mr. Nice Guy."

Yakub smiles as he stands, and hugs Damon while speaking quietly. "Thank you. I know you will. We all feel you're a godsend. All of us have your job in our prayers."

The hug feels genuine; Damon is hugging back when he sights someone he hadn't noticed. "What the fuck is going on here?" His body rigid as they pull apart, Yakub's eyes widen.

"What Damon, what is going on?"

"You tell me. Who's that old man and what kind of game do you think this is?"

Yakub turns expecting to see a ghost; he sees the old man in a chair casually watching the gazebo from afar. "That's one of my uncles, Gabriel. Do you know him?"

Damon is stunned by the sudden appearance of the old man he met at the shooting range yesterday; he was obviously following Damon. "Do you guys really think I give a shit if you know where I am? And how could you possibly have known that I was going the range if I didn't tell anyone?"

Yakub's hand hover a few inches off Damons shoulder. "Damon, nobody here follows you at all, we trust you. Only the notary, one other person, and I know what you do for us. That one other is your friend from when you were young, Peter."

Damon's heart pounds as his body gets ready for fight or flight. He demands Yakub to walk over to Gabriel with him.

Yakub heads over. "Let's go, my friend. We will see what this is all about."

Yakub and Damon walk side-by-side so Damon can watch both him and Gabriel; as they walk closer the old man gently claps once.

The old man stays seated.

"So you are the one, eh?"

Yakub asks the old man in English. "What is going on here! Uncle, what are you smiling about? 'The one' what?"

Gabriel stares at Damon. and questions, "Who did you tell that you were going to the range?"

Damon told no one; he keeps no schedule for his range practices. He regularly sweeps his vehicle for civilian-quality trackers, and none have been found on this van. Damon responds. "Why did you go to the range that morning?"

Yakub looks back-and-forth between the two with shock and confusion. Gabriel answers, "The same thing that made you go to the range. When I opened my eyes that morning I knew I'd go to the range after breakfast. I had no plan to go before that." Gabriel digs further, "When did *you* decide to go to the range?"

Damon relaxes his shoulders. "I woke up and decided while I took a piss, to head out to the range that morning."

Yakub speaks under his breath. "What the fuck are you two lunatics going on about?"

"Yakub, why don't you introduce me to your friend,"

Damon asks while keeping his eyes fixed on Gabriel. When Damon says, 'friend' Gabriel winces and gestures to Yakub.

Yakub says flatly. "This is my great-uncle on my dad's side, Gabriel."

Damon is sure this is one of the universe's little miracles, and is happy to get to the bottom of this opportunity.

"Is it okay if I keep your uncle company for a while?"

Yakub looks to his old uncle for direction. Gabriel smiles and nods. "Damon and I have lots to talk about. We are kindred spirits with matching old souls."

Yakub nods to Damon.

"Would you go over and see that my father-in-law is having fun? Sammy is a solid guy who has owned a few houses, and will pick your brain about a renovation he's been thinking about."

Yakub observes the two 'old friends.' Finally he walks away, shaking his head.

Gabriel is sitting in the only chair. Damon decides all the extra chairs are too far away; he feels too big standing over the old man, so he sits on the ground cross-legged, facing Gabriel. Damon talks first. "What are you thinking?

You've been at this whole life thing longer than me. What are your thoughts on you and I?"

Gabriel smiles and talks to Damon as he did at the range, when he was showing him better body-framing when holding the rifle while standing and shooting; as an old instructor to a good student who doesn't need to be coddled. "You came to the range the day after that thing, all by yourself. You don't celebrate success with some people?"

Damon relaxes further, once he hears the way Gabriel phrases it all. The old man makes no mention of the Fuk hit. If someone didn't know what they were talking about and overheard, they wouldn't have a clue. But they both know Gabriel is talking about the end of Fukadero being something worth a customary reaction, joy or fulfillment for the successful hunt.

Damon keeps eye contact. "I don't think anybody is delighted when things are going that way; maybe the guys who are the most impacted by the evil deeds he committed are sleeping better on their hard cots. But I'm not happy, nobody here is happy about violence looming over everyone." Damon knows that with Gabriel being the great-uncle of Yakub, then he is also the great-uncle of Kuda, who is sitting in jail because of the set-up the Fuk orchestrated. Damon carries on. "How can I celebrate this? I don't talk to anyone about anything to do with a job. No one knows when I start or finish one; anyone who makes it a team effort is going to jail one day, or dead when their partner wants to one-up them in a deal. No celebrations other than a good night's sleep and an early morning with no weight of a job hanging over my head."

Gabriel stares coolly at Damon while he speaks. "As soon as I started to watch you practice lifting the rifle so quickly to shoot, I thought, 'That's a drill for sharpening, reacquiring, and reloading that my dad had me doing when I was a boy in Poland.' I came over to test the water and see what kind of a guy you were. When we walked out and viewed your terrible accuracy, the way you joked reminded me of my dad when I was kid."

Damon laughs at the unexpected burn from the old man; Gabriel never cracks a smile, which makes it funnier. Damon accepts the recognition. "Thank you. What did your dad do back home?"

Gabriel proclaims. "Polish Underground State sniper for six-and-a-half years. From September 1939, when they got going, to the first half of 1945, when they dissolved to avert a civil war."

Damon is unschooled in Polish history. "I'm a little embarrassed to ask, but was the Polish Underground State part of the Polish Resistance to Germany?"

Gabriel is used to the younger generation not remembering the sacrifices the Poles had to endure during WW2. "The Polish Resistance was the largest underground resistance movement in occupied Europe, covering both German and Soviet zones of occupation. They had big success on the Eastern Front disrupting the German supply lines. They provided a lot of military intelligence for the British, as well. They saved many, many Jews. My Dad was a part of it from the beginning until the end."

Damon frowns. "I'm not anything like your dad; your dad was a hero who tried to save a nation. I'm working for pay. I try and stay on the right side of things, but I'm not your dad in any way; he's a national hero."

"My dad, Jan, always said. 'The heroes in that war all died. Katyn massacre is a good example of twenty-two thousand heroes. They stood tall and proclaimed their rank and died for it. All I did was camp and shoot people from afar.' This is how my dad truly felt, even though he killed more than one hundred Nazis and saved who knows how many lives. But he never celebrated his time as a resistance fighter."

Damon asks softly, "Did you say twenty-two thousand died at once?"

As Gabriel answers, on cue, a vast cloud blocks the sun. A shadow covers the entire park, the sun warmth is 500 yards away, and a cool breeze kicks up.

"Yes, twenty-two thousand. About eight thousand officers and six thousand police; the rest were a mix of landowners, factory owners, lawyers, and priests. It was the Soviets that did it, in 1940, April and May. My father had always bowed his head to all the dead and wished he had done more. But he couldn't have, he lived in the forest for six-and-a-half years and took all the missions that he was delivered. He never went to victory parties.

"My dad used to say. 'As long as I'm always in the mood for the hunt I'll be ahead of the Nazis,' and it worked. He was able to move around at will because he was always tuned into the area he was in. He would wait at a bend in the road and shoot the first driver in a column, then pick off Nazis until dark, and walk away comfortable in the knowledge that he would get in the woods before total darkness fell. I'd ask my dad, 'Did you ever think you would die?' When I was old enough, he told me his secret. Here it goes Damon: 'You see, Gabriel, we have a voice in us that tells us the truth no matter how at odds with common sense it seems. Once you know that voice, you are invincible. But you have to be quiet to hear it. No parties, no bragging. It's a personal relationship between the voice and you.'"

Damon nods wholeheartedly; another clear example of believing the voices in his head.

Gabriel continues. "One of the more eventful tales my dad told me was that he had planned on firing shots at a passing train full of Nazi soldiers. This was the beginning of the resistance actions; he hadn't seen a train stop before, so he thought a train took time to stop, one mile or so. After a shot or two, the wheels of the train locked up and it stopped fast. Nazis started pouring out and firing at the hillside; a few of them were on his position, so he was pinned down real bad and was only able to run occasionally. The Nazis surrounded his position.

"My dad said. 'They ran full-speed off that train like it was a track meet, and flanked me on both sides. I laid in this little divot in the ground, bullets raining around me. I heard voices yelling, 'This way, over here.' The circle was getting smaller around me. I was waiting to die in a last chance firefight, once I had a target or two. Suddenly, deafening rain pours. I can't hear any of them yelling anymore, it's too loud from the rain. The bullets start falling around me less and less. The train whistle goes off three times. The shooting falls off enough to let me know not to move.

"'Finally, I hear the train moving again, so carefully I get my eyes on them; the Nazis have loaded the train and are leaving. They left twenty guys to guard the tracks, thinking the lone sniper would leave with his tail between his legs. I didn't leave. I knew the men would do one of two things: have a fire and enjoy this little gravy post, or have no fire and be ready to hunt in the morning. They had a fire that night; I got to shoot six Nazi bastards before they got out of the fire's light. Then I left, walking along a nice moonlit trail that they had no way of knowing about. For sure they laid in the dark not wanting this local sniper to get them. You see son, as long as you give 100 percent and stay real quiet, you can do more than the noisy people. It was the celebration fire that killed those men. Celebrating a nice quiet post, when they should have prepped for war. You stay in the mood of hunting and war, let the others celebrate their participation.' Damon, that's what I mean when I said you remind me of him. Your way of being, not your actions."

Damon licks his lips and nods slowly. He can't think of anything to add, after being told such a personal story about such an unsung hero who gave it his all. "Gabriel, I have no idea what I would do if a massive evil army took over my city. But we know what your dad did, he participated in the centre of a brutal war, with no support. The only thing that happens to me if the occupying police force grabs me is a hard bed and gym for twenty years, with TV. Nothing I'm doing is like your dad. The numbers I've accumulated don't come close him either. I'm a regular guy who does a challenging job."

Gabriel leans forward, "Kid, you don't know who you are yet."

Damon is taken aback by this statement, and throws up his defence.

"I'm a hard-working family man,"

"How do you meet like minded folks? How does it happen? People who feel they know you. You feel close to them as well."

"By chance, almost every time."

Gabriel speaks calm and true. "Good people attract good people. The next level is, men who take care of the shit situations attract other men who take care of the shit situations. We stick together."

Damon agrees with the old man completely. The right person or idea comes to him consistently; he doesn't worry nearly as much as he did when he was younger. The sign happens one way or another.

Gabriel sits back. "Take out your pen and write my number. When you have some time, you call me. I have something you need."

Damon wiggles the pen between his thumb and trigger finger. "What is it?"

"You'll know before you call, I know that."

Damon cranes his head back. "Come on, Gabriel, neither of us is getting any younger.

Tell me, so I understand when I should make time for you."

"We can go back-and-forth all day, but I can't tell you today because I'm not exactly sure how to say it."

Damon is more than a little pissed at the riddle, but he smiles. "I'd be honoured to shoot with you again one day, so expect my call, but do not talk about me on your phone to anyone, please."

Gabriel beams. "They aren't the Nazis, but we still have a large force aiming to destroy us, eh?" At that, they both chuckle as a way to blow off the seriousness of the mess this family is in with the Fukaderos, Suhki, the law courts over money, and the police.

15

TROUT LAKE,

Gabriel's attention turns over Damon's right shoulder. Damon follows the gaze; he's relaxed because Gabriel's eyes show no urgency. All the Polish men are walking fast toward the soccer field the kids have made among the cement picnic tables, on the edge of the little lake. Damon focuses; Naomi looks for him with the concern that a mom has when there is an issue with her baby.

Damon turns back to Gabriel, who puts his hand out to help him off the ground. Damon takes the hand and pulls a bit of weight so the old man feels he helped him stand.

Gabriel offers encouragement. "Better get over there, Dad, seems to be a commotion on the soccer field. You call me one day, we'll go to the range and I will teach you how to shoot properly." This time Gabriel acknowledges his joke. Damon nods and takes off in a quick jog toward the commotion.

His heart beats quicker as worry sets in for his son, he doesn't see him standing with the crowd, and everyone is looking down at the ground. Damon breaks into a full run when he is 100 yards away; Naomi has gotten to the edge of the onlookers. Naomi turns with the group to see Damon coming in at full speed; she steps aside, nodding to confirm to Damon that it's their son Benji who's down.

Damon has level-three industrial first aid, and is ready for a bone sticking out of the skin. His main concern is that his boy is awake and coherent, and that it's not a head injury. *Please no head injury,* Damon pleads to any higher power that will listen. He pushes his way past the last onlookers, his mind is calmed by the wailing of his son's voice. Yakub is over the boy rubbing his back.

Yakub looks at Damon as soon as he breaks through the crowd and his eyes say it all. 'No serious injury, only tears and whimpers.' Damon composes himself, everyone's eyes are on him. He hears in his son's cries that have past the peak, and he needs to be inspected by a parent to feel safe again. Damon calmly asks, "Would everyone take a step back?" He kneels, and Yakub relieves his spot as the comforter. Damon looks around, wondering why everyone isn't dispersing; he sees a group of older boys corralling a heavy boy a year or two older than Benji. The husky boy has dried barbecue sauce on his cheek, his white shirt is stained with pop from drinking too fast. Yakub makes eye contact with Damon, making him aware that the husky boy has done something to Benji.

"Benji, I'm beside you. Can you hear me?" Benji is lying face down, his hands covering his face while he cries. Damon knows something must have happened for his son to be acting this way, he never cries when he has little falls.

Benji gets a hold of himself and takes his hands off his face.

"Of course I hear you, you're right beside me."

Damon sees that Benji has scrapes on his chin. And as the boy gets on all fours, Damon sees his right arm has a grass-and-dirt rash, with cuts spotting his forearm. Damon investigates, "Did you hit your head?"

Benji wimpers, "My face, when I hit the ground. He was on my back and had his hand on my head. He did it on purpose! I never even saw him coming." Benji points at the husky boy with one finger and an outstretched arm.

The crowd turns to the husky boy and asks in a mix of Polish and English, "Is this true, you attacked the little boy?"

The thick-set boy answers in rapid-fire Polish, as the older boys grab and push him. The biggest boy is about twelve, and he yells, "Speak in English, don't be rude!"

Yakub supports the boy. "Kuda, slow down and tell us your side." Damon knows right away this is Yakub's nephew, the son of the older Kuda, who's in prison.

Kuda Jr. starts up fast in English. "This kid comes here to our barbecue, and he keeps taking the ball from me, so I gave him something to think about."

The crowd is quiet with anger at the comment, everyone lightly shaking their heads.

The older boy grabs Kuda Jr. by the back of the neck. "You're bad at soccer and you're a bully! We're not going to let you play soccer with us anymore." The other kids are nodding with approval.

One of the adults yells into the crowd at Kuda Jr., "You're going to sit by us for the rest of the day, you can't go around beating little kids."

Kuda Jr. swivels his head with fury in his eyes,

"I'm not letting someone take my ball, my dad wouldn't let anyone take his stuff, that's why he's in the jail!"

The crowd of families erupts in anger and embarrassment.

"No, no, nobody ever taught you that, Kuda."

Damon helps his son to his feet, then speaks loudly enough for everyone to hear. "Benji, are you okay? Can you move all your limbs? Can you see straight?" As the boy answers yes to all the questions, the crowd is put at ease. Damon focuses on Kuda Jr. "Kuda, I know your dad from work, and he told me his son is good at reading. Do you have a brother?"

Kuda Jr. answers back fast. "No, a little sister."

Damon goes on. "So it's you, then, who reads so well?" Kuda Jr. nods and looks around to see if anyone else cares about his reading ability. "Kuda, I think I speak for everyone here, we've all tried pushing others to get what we want at some point in our life. It makes things harder usually, you understand?" The boy's lips are pursed, so Damon continues. "A game was on, Benji took the ball; if you hadn't pushed him we wouldn't be standing here talking to you and giving you trouble, would we?"

The crowd is nodding and agreeing. Kuda Jr. sees it, he answers back polity, "No."

"So all that would have happened is the ball being played by faster kids, the game would still be on, right?"

Again Kuda Jr. nods a yes. "How about on this barbecue day, you make it a day where you learned a lesson, and you try to use your words?"

Kuda Jr. is seeing the light at the end of this tunnel and smirks. "Okay."

Damon has a test for him, though. "You pushed Benji down in front of everyone, so let's hear you say sorry in front of everyone."

Kuda Jr. turns bright red and furrows his brow. Yakub gently coaxes. "Kuda, it takes a bigger man to make things right with words, go ahead and use your words. We are all family here, it's for the best."

Kuda takes a breath, shakes the older boys off his arms, and takes a step into the central opening where Damon and Benji are standing. And makes eye contact with Benji,

"When you took the ball from me so many times I was mad. I jumped you from behind because I wanted you to stop. I didn't think you'd fall so easy. I tripped, and I used you to break my fall. I'm sorry I hurt you, Benji."

The crowd is calmed by the boy's words. Damon asks, "Benji, do you accept his apology?"

Benji stands blinking at the husky boy, everyone sees he holds no animosity,

"Yes, but I get the ball when we start playing next round." The crowd disperses happily.

Damon smiles and pats Kuda Jr. on the back. "That's the smart boy your dad told me about, keep using your head and not your big muscles, okay?" Kuda Jr. smiles as the kids go back to their game. Kuda Jr. waits for Benji and they walk off together. Benji pointing at the cuts and rubbing his head.

Yakub walks over to Damon and his family, "Kuda Jr. has been in so much trouble since his dad went to the jail, his mom can't handle him. His dad used to take such good care of him."

Damon hints, "Any of your family going to Judo still?"

Yakub nods affirmative, "Of course, the family goes to a few different dojos around the lower mainland. Ah, I know what you're thinking Damon and yes, yes, we will get Kuda Jr. going to a dojo soon."

Damon agrees, "Give him the goal of getting his black belt. Junior and his dad will train when he gets back. He needs to learn his strength."

Naomi and her parents are talking to another group now that the kids' drama is over,

Damon strolls over to join them.

TROUT LAKE, 4:15 P.M.

With bellies full and lots of laughs, it's time to leave the Polish barbecue. Damon feels good about the job he has taken on for these people, which isn't always the feeling.

He wonders, *How would it feel not to care about killing?* Before he says his goodbye to Yakub, his Coach answers him in a quick whisper. *That's a sociopath, even the army doesn't want them. They are not natural.*

Yakub one arm hugs Damon; everyone is giving goodbye hugs. Damon's family walk off together. Benji is holding his dad's right hand, and Naomi is on his left. Sammy and Vicky have their arms linked as well. *Maybe for balance,* Damon reasons, Sammy was handed a lot of beers.

The sun is low on the horizon on the west of the lake, and the sky is bright blue; if they stay a little longer it will slowly change into a colourful sunset, but Damon knows it will take twenty-five minutes to walk back to the notary office where the van is parked, and another thirty-five to get home. Benji needs a bath, and everybody needs a shower.

The walk back is quiet, as everyone is tired from all the sun and eating. Benji has grass stains on the front and back of his shirt and dried blood mixed with dirt on his arm. *He'll sleep in the van for sure.* The cars on 12th are intermittent at best, a quiet Sunday night around his old East Vancouver neighbourhood.

They walk into the old notary office. Sammy is happy to get to see what kind of a notary is open on a Sunday. Naomi knows these people are helping with her family business in some way, so she puts on a good face even though she's tired from a day in the sun.

Olga glows when she sees little Benji all covered in the day's dirt. "Can he have a cookie?"

Damon replies, "It's up to his mom."

Naomi nods, "One more sweet can't hurt. The barbecue had so many homemade cakes I think that's all we ate today."

Benji is eating the cookie when Alexi comes in and gets the introductions out of the way. Alexi invites Damon to his office, "for a quick bit of business" before the family gets on the road.

Damon follows him. "It means a lot that you're helping us, I know these documents we're creating could never go to a court of law. They're a way of keeping everyone on the same page. You're a good man, and your family has been through a lot in the last hundred years."

The last sentence makes the old notary's eyes go wide, "Who have you been talking to? You do ask a lot of questions, don't you?" Alexi smiles as he pulls out the cash from a drawer, "We should count it together."

Damon confirms, "Did you count it already?"

"Of course I did; when they dropped the payment and again before I put it into this drawer. There's twenty-five thousand dollars."

Damon grins. "I'm sure you're more efficient than I am at counting, sir, please put it in an envelope." The money is in three stacks, all twenty dollar bills. Two $10,000 stacks, each with five mini-stacks of $2,000 strapped with matching blue rubber bands, and one stack with two mini-piles of $2,000 and one thin $1,000. Alexi has a big envelope. Alexi takes notes while Damon briefs him. Alexi states what they're both thinking, "You come back tomorrow and sign after I've drawn the agreement?"

Damon puts his hand out, "Thank you for your time, I'll be in after Tuesday. You'll clear the title of the first loan tomorrow?"

Alexi is smiling from ear to ear. "Yes, first job tomorrow morning."

When Damon comes out the family is sitting in the waiting room with water from Olga. Benji reads an old book. Damon warmly smiles at Olga, although he wants to hug her. "Okay, we can go home, Alexi has everything so well prepared that we're done already."

Benji's eyes flick up, "I'm halfway done the book though."

Olga chimes in, "That book has been here for about thirty years, when you come back you will read it while eating another treat." Everyone says their goodbyes and heads out onto Commercial Drive.

After loading the family into the white Caravan, Damon drives along 12th Street towards Highway 1. They pass Trout Lake on the right; all the adults look to the park and see the entire Polish barbecue still out there, kids running and the barbecue still smoking. *They don't take many days off, this is a celebration of the Fuk's death. Damn it. The cops came and took full advantage of the get-together. Gabriel was right. 'Don't go to celebrations in a war.'*

Damon's Coach comforts him. *Your vehicle was not video logged by Air 1, and your phone was in the van a kilometre away. You heard them and avoided the long lens of the law, most likely.* But that's it: *most likely* is all the security he has.

Damon hadn't planned on being at a celebration, and following the notary's advice, he had been put right in the line-of-sight of one of the most advanced police forces in the world. *Did they set me up? Is this the game to get their family out of jail?*

Damon's calm all-knowing voice takes over. *Don't think that way. You're their champion, it was an honest mistake. These people don't understand the methods of the police. They wanted you to be happy and feel safe. Don't waste energy on thinking about them double-crossing you. Okay?*

Damon takes in a long slow breath, and on the exhale speaks out loud, "Okay."

Naomi turns in her seat, "Okay what?"

Damon guts turn as he tells himself to keep his thought to himself, again.

He answers her cheerfully. "I was just thinking about the yard being such a dust pit, then I realized it's going to be okay."

" Allright…" Naomi looks at him sideways.

16

The legal agreements are in order on the desk in front of Chloe. The lights in the show home foyer have been dimmed to after-hours levels, with only a few LED lights over some pictures on the walls. From her office, formally Tony's, Chloe sees all the flowers her realtor girls have brought in throughout the foyer.

"No cards on the flowers, so they brighten the show-room." Chloe had put the request out on her office Facebook; at the same time, she asked that all realtors keep their shifts the same at the show house. "If anyone is too upset to work, please trade shifts. We need to be professional and sell the development. We have investors who deserve a professional show house up and running. I'll be in for the afternoon, and will be going over our business for the upcoming week. Thank you for your support." She sent the sales staff home at 4:30 p.m., the regular hours of a Sunday show home.

Chloe has drawn new documents over the last half-hour. Car lights catch her eye on the security camera feed on the big screen, it's Suhki. Chloe scans the all-white office and decides it's clean and organized. She closes her eyes and reminisces about taking the stage for the first time, in the Moulin Rouge in France. She was nineteen. *I kept it together for one of the most scrutinized shows in France for six months, I will keep this act up until I get through this development's sale over the next few months. I have a perfect stage, with all the actors. I'm the star of this show; I will bring down the house with this act.*

Chloe steps from behind her large, solid, white desk, and heads to the foyer door. She's locked the door for two reasons, only one being security. Suhki arrives at the door before her, and gives the door's handle a light pull, it's locked. He notices Chloe walking to the door, her left hand up and a finger in the wait motion. Suhki is taken aback, *How does she look that good today, it's only been two days since Tony was killed. She's flawless.* He takes in the all-white pantsuit with a pleat down the front touching the top of her white high heels. Her coat is buttoned to the top of her chest, her platinum blonde hair hanging straight, with bangs falling across the tops of her eyebrows. Her makeup is flawless. *Man, Tony was a lucky guy. She must have been to the spa this morning. She's a boss. This is all going to work out. I wonder how much she knows about my deals with Tony?*

Chloe opens the door and stands framed in the opening for two seconds, "Thanks for coming, Suhki. I've drawn up a contract I believe is satisfactory; will you please follow me to my office? We will discuss our options."

Suhki's eyes widen, "Yeah, it's your show."

Chloe turns to walk away, she says over her shoulder, "Would you lock the door please?" Suhki obeys. Turning to lock the door, he peeks over his shoulder and pauses to take in Chloe's alluring walk. Chloe watches discreetly in the reflection on a display counter;

giving Suhki a chance to show her he's a regular man is the second reason she walked over and let him in.

Chloe is sitting behind the desk when Suhki walks in; her head is down on the documents, but her peripheral picks up that she is being watched. She has one personal thought before the conversation begins. *Suhki is a beautiful man, he is so alpha male. Such a gentleman as well. His wife is so lucky to have him.* "Suhki, I know about that contractor, the one who ran off with the draw. He's your cousin. I know you and Tony made that deal to keep the Polish contractor's draw, and you've been paid for that portion. The courts have locked up another one point nine million of this company's capital while they decide if the Polish have a case against the developer. And currently I'm the developer."

Suhki flatly asks, "So this is the room the police had wired for the assault sting, right?"

Chloe smiles knowingly; her voice is a little uncomfortable,

"Yes. After the sting, I had to oversee the police technical team while they took it all out. When they left, the electrician you met at our anniversary party last year came in and checked the place out, from the power box to every outlet. This place is clean."

He believes her. Suhki loves the prolonged eye contact,

She is a confident business person, I wonder what the papers are for?

"Suhki, I would never ask for a favour in a business deal. I've drawn up this offer for you, so we have more than just a verbal agreement." Suhki's face is neutral; Chloe can't read him at all. She carries on as if she has a thousand other audience members that she has to please as well. "I need you to get the Polish guys to drop the case. If they do, and the one point nine million is released, I can offer you one of the properties on this development with only a vendor-supplied mortgage on the land; the building will be totally paid for."

Suhki has to school his face; this is the most money he's ever been offered in a single deal. "Why do I have to have a mortgage, can't you sign the land and the building over to me?" he asks with a playful smile that is nonetheless serious.

Chloe has been a realtor for three years. She's gained a lot of knowledge fast, mostly due to participating in all of Tony's deals, from ground breaking to occupancy permits. She's fully qualified to have this talk. "Well, let's add all the hard costs: the land is from the investor, not the company. Eighty percent of the building material was supplied by the company, and the remaining twenty percent was supplied by the Polish contractors. They also supplied the labor. So the company, as in myself, can give you a building, but not the land. You'll be earning it by getting the capital released by the courts."

Suhki is ready to accept the deal, but has gone for the whole prize out of habit. "What if I do a bunch of heavy stuff to these Polish guys and they don't back off the court case?"

Chloe had directed the back-up dancers in her shows, and had fired many girls. The last two years she's been leading a team of realtors; she knows how to motivate staff. "Let's highlight the percentages; there's one point nine million locked in the courts, and your group has already been given two hundred and fifty thousand dollars for the disappearing construction manager act, and I'm to provide you with a house with a cost of approximately five hundred thousand dollars from this company, you will have received over seven hundred and fifty thousand dollars of the one point nine million in the courts. I strongly suggest you put your best efforts into this job. You might have to drop another job that's paying you less to give this one more attention. Tell me right now your initial feeling about you backing the Polish off? If you're not comfortable, I understand, I do have another option I can try. Will you do this job?"

Suhki's blood is getting hot. *This little girl thinks she's my boss?* He sits glowering at her. Chloe locks eyes with him, her head tilted enough to inspire his answer. Suhki nods as he accepts she's not a little girl: she has the Italians behind her. Plus that thug who Tony grew up with, Dean Schmitt, and his crew, and who knows who else. Sukhi laughs and puts some bass in his voice, "Look at me, I'm built for tough jobs. I already threw their boss so hard on his head he passed out, and his crew stood there shaking in their boots. I'll chase them out of this country. Forget the case. They will be done."

Chloe smiles and nods gently, as if accepting his word into her mind-castle. She turns the paperwork around in front of her and gets the third act of the night going. She stands and turns on the desk light to illuminate the papers. Chloe bends forward; her straight hair hangs to the top of the page, not blocking anything as she points out where he should sign. She had been to the spa this morning: her gel nails are perfect, her hands are moisturized, and a light flower scent radiates off her as she leans across the desk.

Suhki is trying to pay attention to the contract for purchase and sale, and the side agreement for the capital being released as the trigger that finalizes his house purchase. With a quick glance at Chloe leaning across, with her fresh scent, her pink nails matching her pink lips… Suhki holds back a smile.

A beautiful angel is giving me a mansion.

As they get to the last page he grins. Chloe recognizes the signs of a happy new home-owner, so she reminds him of the essence of the contract. Leaning further across the desk, with her face about two feet from his.

"So the date the money is released is the date this contract comes into play. If the case goes to court and we win by a lawyer's hand, no house either. Only if the Polish drop the case."

Suhki confirms, "Got it."

She notices his face going flush with colour again, but not in anger this time.

Act four is about to begin. Chloe reaches out her hand for a handshake. As he gently takes her hand, she says, "Thank you for coming tonight." She stands tall and looks to the foyer, then back to Suhki. "Will you join me in the demonstration area for a coffee or a tea?"

Suhki nods yes, as he believes his voice might shake.

Chloe opens the glass office door and walks across the minimalist white showroom. There are two desks by the front frosted-glass wall, and the refreshment counter is on the opposite wall of the room. Between the two is a sturdy white counter on chrome legs, bolted firmly so clients can lean on it while talking. Chloe goes to the hot beverage machine, and Suhki leans on the white counter, facing her, with his hands and legs crossed in front of him.

He wants me to lead; he isn't asking any questions or making any advances on me. He's smooth, She opens the cupboard above the beverage machine and takes out two white designer mugs. She peeks over her shoulder, "Would you prefer tea or coffee?" To her disappointment, he isn't watching her backside.

Suhki makes eye contact. "Tea please. I'm working tonight. Going out to a club with my boys to find those weak ass truckers."

Chloe knows this man from his actions. He has a beautiful wife at home who's educated and as perfect as him. He is here for business. But a man is a man, her roommate in France had taught her. Chloe was an extraordinary ballet dancer, and just eighteen when she arrived in France. Emma was twenty-three, and invited Chloe to stay with her until she got on her feet. Emma had all these men buying her things; they would moan so loudly from her room. At first it was funny to Chloe, but after the third guy in one week she would hold the pillow over her head to sleep. The men were all gentlemen, and would invite Chloe, in their casual French way to join them. But Chloe was determined to be a star and to marry a rich man, not sleep around for shirts and other items.

Emma had told Chloe, "When a man is smart and married, you have to crack him. Haha, you know what I mean?"

Chloe had no idea; she was pretty, and guys wanted her, but that was all she knew back then. Chloe asked, "Emma, please tell me your bedroom secrets, and I'll use them to catch the richest man."

Emma giggled. "There is hope for you yet, little Canadian."

She remembers those lessons as she smiles at the man in front of her. "Suhki, you were doing other things with Tony. Do I have to guess or will you tell me?"

Suhki smirks, and he moves to a parallel stance, with both feet facing her. He keeps his hands clasped. *This woman is on the ball. I spill my guts or lie, and she catches me. Too funny.* Suhki starts slowly. "Should we talk about trucks? Would you like to talk about cars? Or restaurants? How about money owed?"

Chloe turns and pours the hot water into the cups, "I picked these tea selections from a store in Chinatown, Emperor's Choice. So let's assume that you're the emperor today, and you have the right to say and do whatever you want." Chloe turns with style and heads over with his teacup. *He is a rock, he's all business still.* She arrives in front of him with the white teacup. With both hands Chloe lifts his cup to her lips. She stops about an inch away, and theatrically blows on the hot tea. "Let me cool this for you, sir." She jokes as she blows hard enough to send the hot ginseng steam, up to his nose.

Suhki inhales a small whiff, then inhales like a race horse.

"There you go sir, your tea is ready." She is playfully batting her eyes as she turns to walk away. Suhki is quiet. She goes on, "I'm mostly interested in the hundred kilos of coke that Pacific to Atlantic Trucking lost three weeks ago." At that, she turns swiftly, letting her hair fan out and settle luxuriously over her shoulders.

Suhki talks slowly through gritted teeth, "Do you know how much I'm owed by P and A Trucking from that stolen blow?"

Chloe does know, "I believe it's for ten kilos; bricks is what they're called though, right?"

Suhki's blood boils; he drinks the tea with a long sip.

"Yes. Five hundred grand on the street."

Chloe displays an exaggerated frown, "How do you think the other investors feel about the other ninety bricks?"

Suhki decides it's time for straight talk. "Tony was the one who gathered all the investors, including me; I don't know them all. Five bricks went to one guy, I hear. Fifteen to another crew. I'm going after the P and A Trucking company president, they had the load in their possession. I don't give a single fuck what they say, I'm going tonight to hound their boss at the bar he hangs out in. I've been on them for weeks. Word is he is fucking one of the waitresses"

Chloe has her hands hanging at her sides with the palms forward. *Time for the final act.* She looks at Suhki with her head tilted over her shoulder, her mouth slowly opens. "Do you mind if I take off my heels? I'm so much more comfortable with them off."

Suhki puts his cup down, leans back, "Of course, please be comfortable."

Chloe stands on her left leg and lifts her right foot behind her bum, then reaches back with one hand and undoes the straps. She lets the shoe fall. She lowers her foot so slowly that Suhki lowers his eyes as she places the ball of her foot on the floor. She keeps her body on the ball of her foot; when she lifts her other leg behind her bum to release the shoe, her head stays at the same height. Bringing her second foot down, she notices Suhki isn't talking anymore.

All men take pleasure from a stripping girl. Emma had told her so long ago.

"Suhki, the money that's owed to the investors is in a list I have. I believe with Tony not here for them to focus on, we will keep most of that money for ourselves." She's pointing one hand at Suhki and her other hand at herself. He rubs his hands together.

"Millions in cash, between how many people?"

Chloe lowers her hands gently as she saunters toward him. "If nobody but you and I know who gets paid, and I create a grey area with your support, I think at least three million at the local street price of fifty thousand a kilo could be ours. Can I count on you to support my every move? I'll support you in every way; lie, blame. I'll meet you at your new house to go over how we spend the money." Chloe is within arm's reach of Suhki. She hears his excitement, the way he's breathing through his nose. The big money windfall in front of him is charging Suhki up.

Chloe can feel he isn't over the line yet, though. Emma's sultry voice comes into her mind. *Do it, be a bad girl, tell him dirty secrets.* Chloe asks softly. "Suhki, are you down for this change in business?"

Suhki answers confidently, "For sure."

"Can I depend on you to do whatever I need?" She turns sideways, getting closer, she wants him to whisper in her ear.

Suhki leans forward to accommodate her. "Yes Chloe, I will handle whatever you need."

Hope blooms in her. "Suhki, no one will ever know our secret, right? Whatever we do will never get out, okay?"

Suhki moves off the table, and as he does her hand is right where his hardening penis lands. He doesn't flinch.

"Yeah, we'll keep all our business private."

Chloe grasps his shaft as she turns back toward him. *He's so big.* She gets a good grip. He smiles, knowing women always get a little surprised when they touch him. Emma's French accent whispers in her mind again. *You fuck him the first time, don't even let him do one thing he wants.* Chloe drops to her knees in front of him and pulls his designer jogging pants down; Suhki leans back on the table to see what she'll do. Chloe grabs the long thick phallus and glances at Suhki for two seconds. Keeping eye contact, she spits onto the end and rubs the head. Suhki is surprised by the move, and smiles.

Chloe isn't done yet; she places her lips on the end and takes him into her mouth until her nose is almost touching his belly. Suhki's eyes go wide. She pauses there looking up at him, with his massive phallus in her throat. And then moving in and out a half inch. Suhki leans back in passion, *Holy fuck this is what a deep throat is.*

He stares down; Chloe keeps eye contact as she pulls it out of her mouth, takes a gasping breath, and goes back on it. This time she has a tear in her eye as she bobs her head back-and-forth, only a half-inch, to keep the deep throat going.

When she pulls out this time she begs, "Hold me and fuck me with my feet on the desk behind you? We don't have to use a condom, I'm on the pill." Suhki is pulling her up and nodding.

As she stands her pants drop; she has no panties on. She holds his cock with her left hand and unbuttons her coat with the right, exposing the white lace camisole that's covering her small perky tits. She jumps knowing he will catch her, Chloe lets him push into her fast. But then she puts her feet on the table and both hands behind his neck and orders, "Hold me; I'll fuck you." He accepts the order, and squeezes her ass with both hands as she uses the table to go up and down his shaft; they both moan. When she grind's on him to get her climax going, he begins to climax. They both stand in the showroom under the few LED lights that dimly glow, moaning and yelling as they cum together.

I.H.I.T. HEADQUARTERS, 6:15 P.M.

Sara watches the screen of her laptop, which has the feed from Air 1 playing live from the show home. The green Lamborghini and the purple Hellcat Charger sit out front. The helicopter arrived fifteen minutes ago, after Sara got the message that the signal from Chloe and Suhki's phones indicated they were meeting alone in the show home. Sara had a feeling right away; these two must be up to something. First, it's tea, then Chloe appears to instigate sexual contact. Air 1's camera has zoomed in through the front doors; the picture is crystal clear as if the camera is in the room. The lights are dim so the officers have it set on night vision, the footage is green. We have a video of consensual sex between the widow Fukadero and a married Suhki Trivedi, the head of a large Indo-Canadian family with a history of violence.

Sara wonders, *Did these two murder Mr. Fukadero? Or is everyone having sex?* Sara types on her laptop: "End of her operation for Air 1. Thanks for the quick response." The screen goes blank.

The live communication responds to her from the turbine helicopter. "Just doing our job. Let us know what other windows we should train our camera on. Goodnight."

She lets out a short laugh, *Well, this job is going to be talked about for a while.*

17

E DIVISION, SURREY,
MONDAY, APRIL 9TH, 8:15 A.M.

The Wolf is sitting behind his desk vacantly staring out his office window. It's going to be a sunny day. He wonders what his wife is doing this morning. *Did she leave early enough to pick up the kids at the airport? It's always hard traveling with a toddler. My daughter is tough and cheery, she handles the short flight from Alberta with ease. I'm so glad her husband has that good job on the oil rigs. I couldn't be happier with that marriage. I would have enjoyed visiting, but his work didn't allow him to come here for my wife's birthday party. I'm glad he works so hard, we'll see him in the summer.*

Knock knock. The Wolf heads to his office door, he pulls the door open and flashes a genuine smile of welcome for his guest. He speaks as he shakes the attorney's hand. "Mr. Livion, thank you for coming to my office on this bright day."

The Fukadero attorney smiles back and walks into the office. "Mr. Wolvsmere, I'm here for my wallet that you took for evidence at Mr. Fukadero's house on Friday. Your officers couldn't find it after you left. I got the call yesterday to come and get it at this time. From you."

The Wolf smiles. He stops walking and turns to Mr. Livion to speak directly to him. "When a person is murdered we're cautious with evidence from the crime scene. The mix-up with your wallet isn't a personal matter, and I'm giving it back to you right now."

Mr. Livion quickly changes his tune. "Of course Mr. Wolvsmere, it's a challenging time. I'm glad you took the time to call me to help me get my wallet back."

The Wolf heads to his chair on the other side of his desk and gestures with his hand for the attorney to have a seat. "Call me Bill, Mr. Livion."

They look at each other for three seconds. The Wolf starts his inquiry, "Can we help the Fukadero family in this trying time?"

Mr. Livion keeps his face controlled, "I have not been given any instructions from my client to initiate a conversation."

The Wolf begins his standard pitch for this type of attorney. "The RCMP and your client have enjoyed a mutually-beneficial relationship for close to twenty years. You tell them that we're here with many resources to assist in taking their enemies to jail. We are on their side; they've proven time and time again that they're law-abiding citizens, and have used the special knowledge they've gathered through unknown forces to help us successfully arrest many criminals. We take it very personally when our friends get murdered, and we want to help the family. Do you have any leads?"

Mr. Livion sits looking at the Wolf, his face composed. Bill can't make any assumptions form the poker face. "I'm glad you called me. Options are important for people in tight positions, and you are a man with a lot of resources. I'll pass on your offer to my client. Can you give me an idea of who we suspect?"

The Wolf keeps his face schooled, "We can't discuss an active case. You need to give us the leads, then we work them. I'm sorry, Mr. Livion, but our appointment was for eight a.m., and your late arrival has cut the meeting short. I'll see you to the elevator."

"No, no, Bill, I'll find my own way. Thank you for my wallet." At that, the attorney reaches onto the desk, grabs his wallet, and stands to leave. After extending a friendly handshake from his seat, the Wolf turns to his computer and begins to type.

8:25 A.M.

Sara watches Mr. Livion walk out of the Wolf's office from a desk on the other side of the room. She studies the attorney. *Just another day at work for him, eh? Well, my appointment with Bill is for eight-thirty. Should I head in early? Yes, it's only five minutes, I'm going over.*

"Knock, knock," Sara announces as she heads through the door without slowing. The Wolf's head snaps up, he starts to stand, but Sara holds her hand up in the stop motion, "Please stay seated, I'll sit as well."

Bill obeys with a smirk; he isn't used to being told when to sit and stand in his office.

I picked the right person to help this department. Then he asks, "So how has the weekend been going? Any leads?"

Sara knows he's been following her emails and requests. "There are three insiders: one criminal agent, one good-citizen agent, and one desperate agent. I have their codes, but I can't see their identity because of security blocks. Could they be of use to this case? Should I access these assets?"

The Wolf smiles faintly, "You know how important information is. You can surmise how important these three agents are."

Sara answers back with an affirmative nod, "Yes sir."

Bill goes on. "These assets have certain protocols for contact by their handlers. First, you read the file on the handler and the way they regularly communicate with the agent. Then, if you think they can be utilized, you file a request explaining how you would use the agent and how it conforms to the handler's methods of use. Then I give you permission, and we release the names."

Sara has already read the handler's reports on each agent. She explains her case to Bill. "The criminal agent who's been working in the Fukadero organization for five years is an official member of their drug and street crew, the Grim Sinners. His handler contacts him on his mobile device under a code name. We meet him within twenty-four hours after a request. He has been eighty-percent reliable, and all his contacts are available to us. We don't bust anyone he knows unless they're proven to have a violent tendency or brazen lifestyle. This agent provides us with vital information about the gang's interests and moves.

"The good-citizen agent is part of the Indo-Canadian family that has Suhki at its head. She's reached through a school-liaison officer at the school she works at. She is contacted any day at her school. This agent has only been able to confirm gang movement and current feelings toward others that she gathers from the family's conversations. The soft intelligence she provides only gives us an idea of the movements of Suhki and his family gang.

"The desperate agent is inside the Polish group, Trowel. He was caught drinking and driving, and had three grams of cocaine in his pocket that appeared to be for personal use. He led us to his dealer; that gave us a small bust. Since the Fukadero assault case, we've used him to gather info on the group's general plan. He's contacted by his cell phone, and his handler makes an appointment. The agent is always trying to delay the meetings and is uncomfortable talking to us. Threats of charges and the loss of his driver's license seems to keep him in line. His handler has worked to bring him to heel by tracking the agent's phone. When he left a bar at eleven-thirty p.m., his handler pulled him over and had him blow a breathalyzer. The agent failed, and new charges were drawn up, but not filed. The agent co-operates reasonably again."

The Wolf upgrades Sara clearance. "Good work. You may contact the handlers at your convenience. I'll upgrade your authorization." Bill leans forward, and neither officer speaks as he types for five minutes. Sara's phone email alerts her. Bill uses his eyes to motion for her to check her phone. She does, and in the email is the clearance for the three agents; her heartbeat increases slightly. *This is for real. I have to use these assets properly, or they get exposed or killed. Their police handlers would hold a professional grudge against me forever, too.*

Bill sees her skin change colour and associates it with the pressure of the agent clearance. "Sara. I asked you to help because you make good choices. Do what comes naturally; doctors lose patients all the time. All the agents chose in some way to participate. You will be responsible and utilize the handlers' knowledge and protocols. You will do better than most."

Sara believes him, and nods affirmatively.

LANGLEY, 9:30 A.M.

Sammy and Naomi are walking Patch along Derby Reach, on the Fraser River. The low clouds are burning off, exposing a blue sky. The air has the crisp moist smell of the fresh water from the river.

Naomi has on the unofficial mom's uniform. Her long copper-red hair is in a high pony tail, she has a sport bra under her brand name yoga sweater, and tight form-fitting bright blue yoga pants leave her firm butt on display. The blue pants make her luminesce white skin even lighter. Naomi has a slim, athletic build at 5'6" and 125 pounds.

Sammy asks, "Can Patch run off leash?"

Naomi shakes her head. "No, the off-leash area is the other way, this trail has too many people running by. Patch scares joggers when he runs to sniff them as they pass."

Sammy is grinning proudly as his daughter gives him the local rules on dog handling. "So on this forest trail we have to keep a dog on a leash because people running by are scared? Poor Patch."

Naomi changes the subject. "Dad, do you think Damon would cheat on me? He keeps such a strange schedule. He always chalks it up to work, but... What do you think?"

Sammy is wearing his faded light-blue jean jacket and matching jeans; he has the sleeves of the jacket rolled just below his forearms. Sammy has known Damon since before he married Naomi, through Damon's father Leo. Sammy is positive that Damon is falling back on old habits to make ends meet.

Sammy digs a little deeper, "Does Damon ever tell you about his extra work?"

Naomi has the dog-leash in her left hand, and the dog is pulling her toward the river on her left side; she has to turn back a bit to look at her dad. "No, he never tells me anything. Should I ask? I feel he's not open to talk about his routine."

Sammy knows for sure that Damon is taking on con-tracted hits for the extra money he needs. If it was less serious Damon would talk about it with Naomi. Sammy knows how to calm his daughter about an affair, but he doesn't know how to even attempt to calm her about her husband killing for money. "Hun, Damon has never been the cheating type. I knew him when he was in another long-term relationship before you. He never talked about side women; his dad told me many times, 'Damon isn't like me, he stays with one woman. He's sort of crazy I think. I don't know how he stays with one woman, he's a monk.' I've known his family for thirty years. Damon is *not* having an affair. Just trying to make a living, and it's hard out there. He doesn't want to worry you."

"Has Damon told you he's in trouble or needs help?"

Sammy watches the big white dog that's pulling his daughter. Naomi plants her feet and with two arms yanks the dog.

"Heel."

Patch stops and turns his big head towards Naomi. After, Patch walks with a slack leash.

Sammy admires his daughter. *Good work hun, you have a good handle on that big dog.*

Naomi asks again. "Dad, has Damon mentioned anything to you? He's been really distant since we got into the new house."

Sammy is nodding slowly. He understands more about the new house, the notary, and the Polish barbecue. "No hun, Damon hasn't mentioned anything that's alarming. If he needs help he would come to me for sure. But hun, he was raised to take care of things by himself. You know I've always handled things alone as well, right?"

Naomi stops; Patch halts. "Dad, I'm old enough to hear it from you. There were always rumours when I was growing up that you were some sort of dangerous person. I never saw a hint of it. What does everyone mean when they say that you're a person that nobody should mess with?"

Sammy laughs, and his eyes sparkle as the spotlight shines on him. "Ah, hun, those are old stories, back when guys fought it out with their fists. Old news, not exiting at all really."

Naomi stares at him intently, "Seriously, give me an example. Damon is always insistent, 'Nobody messed with your dad back in the day. Even my dad knows Sammy is bloodthirsty!' Damon's dad was in the news as a murder suspect when I was a kid! And *he's* saying *you're* dangerous! Give me an example right now, it's us two walking alone on this trail. Go ahead, start. I'm listening."

Sammy is rocked by his daughter's interest in his violent past. But he decides it's all really harmless and old news, so he takes a breath. "Well, let's keep walking and I'll tell you a good one that's pretty mild." Naomi bites her lip and turns to walk; Sammy places his Ray-Bans over his eyes and puts his hands in his jacket pockets, as he falls in beside her. He chuckles a bit as he begins, as if he is recalling fond memories. "So when you were a baby and we had that house in Abbotsford, I used to ride a rigid-frame Harley."

Naomi highlights, "Of course, I remember the bike in the pictures; you sold it to buy us a cabin later, right?"

"Yea, that one. Well, I was at a party in Surrey one weekend and this group of six guys roll in on their choppers; they're known as the local tough guys. The big guy in their group tells me, 'I can get you a front tire and install it for two hundred dollars, but you have to give me the money now.' I knew it was a risk, but it was almost a hundred under a bike-store price, so I did it.

"Two months later, the big guy wasn't answering my calls, and everyone was telling me how he rips people off with this scam. I was told how tough he was, and 'I'd better just forget it.' My bike's bald front tire was about to pop, and I didn't have an extra two hundred to throw out. We were living cheque to cheque back then."

A train on the North side of the river blows its horn. Naomi and Sammy look across the river to see the red train engine heading east, pulling rail cars. A tugboat is heading in the other direction with a load of logs dragging behind it. Naomi lets Patch edge closer to some rabbit trails he has sniffed out, staying near enough so Sammy doesn't have to raise his voice. Sammy fixedly stares up the trail and tells his tale like he's watching it on a screen that's hovering in the centre of the trail; the three walk on.

"It was a hot August night; I had worked all day putting rebar in a tower in Vancouver. I had been riding the chopper to work every day. Your mom knew I'd given the two hundred dollars to the big bully in Surrey for the new tire deal; and the big guy won't even call me back. I decided on the spot to go find him and demand an answer. When I got to Surrey I went to his house in the badlands; it was this old two-story, with three concrete steps heading to a small stoop under a faded yellow-and-white-striped tin awning.

"I turned my bike off and ran to his front door. I knew all the way over how this would go down. The big bully opened his door snarling, and yelled at the top of his lungs, '*What* the *fuck* do you want?' I never flinched. This big bully was at least 265 pounds, with a massive gut. He came about two feet from my face after he shouted that at me. I calmly asked, 'Hey, you have my tire ready?' You see hun, I knew when I came out he would ask one stupid question, then as someone answered the question he'd start swinging. I knew how he worked because he'd done it so many times, and I'd heard all the stories.

"So, at the moment he was pretending to think about giving my tire back to me I popped him with everything I could muster, a left uppercut. He never saw it coming, he was so focused on his prep to hit me. This big fat biker crumbled onto the little stoop with both knees going to jelly. I had smoked him with a solid uppercut in his eye socket, and he was walking into it so I had real heft. Then I grabbed his shirt and jumped back off the steps, pulling the big bully onto all fours in front of me.

"Big fat bully couldn't move fast on all fours. I started feeding the right side of his head, in the ear, with right hooks. This big guy was yelling about me 'being dead' and when he 'gets his hands on me' I'm a 'dead man.' Of course I was asking about the money and my tire, while delivering shot after shot.

"In the end, all the neighbours had come out and were yelling, "*Give* it to him." I had a cheering section. I was a twenty-seven-year old with the classic demon biker rings on. The rings had these horns and fangs back in the day. I had turned the rings over, so the points were facing towards my palm. I started clawing his back in big round wind-ups with my arm going straight up and back down, raking across his back."

Naomi notices Sammy is breathing heavy, but they're walking slowly, the dog is peeking back and stopping often.

Sammy never stops his tale. "I raked his back with the sun setting, my bike right there, local people cheering. I must of raked his back twenty times, at least. That was after fifteen shots to each side of his head. His fat head was pouring blood. I stood tall, and looked down on the broken bully; the crowd went quiet. I shouted, 'You gonna give that money back or put the tire on my bike?' The big guy wasn't trying to get up, he kept going on about my 'future demise.'

"I yelled loud enough that it would wake him, from the head shot haze, 'You either say you'll pay me before midnight, or I start from the beginning of the beating, you goof thief. Which is it?' The bully broke. He stared at the ground on all fours, his belly almost touching the ground and said, 'I'll get you your money, no more. please, I'm sorry.' I never missed a beat; I yelled to the crowd to tell whoever shows up that, 'I'm at home waiting for my money to be delivered.'

"I went and washed my hand in a sprinkler that was going back and forth on the lawn. My demon rings had peeled off thin lines of skin, and as the blood washed them off I had to pick the fresh-raked strips of skin out of the claws on my rings."

"Dad, that's disgusting!" Naomi yells in an over-dramatic way. "You could have stopped at, 'I'm at home waiting for my money,' that last part is so gross. You're lucky you didn't get hepatitis."

Sammy has his palms up in a defensive position. "What? What? I don't get it, you said you wanted a story!"

Naomi speeds up the walk, and Patch notices and steps quicker, with his eyes forward.

Naomi calmly walks forward and asks without looking at her dad, "Did the bully pay you that night?"

Sammy puts his hands in his pockets as he laughs. "Yeah hun, two of the crew rode to our house. I was ready for anything; your mom wasn't happy with how it was going. So one guy comes to my door, the other stays at the bikes on the curb. I asked in a calm voice, 'Did you bring my money?' The guy reached in his vest and pulled out a pile of twenty dollar bills. 'Two-hundred dollars.' Was that story a little gruesome for a father daughter walk?" Sammy tries to peek at his adult baby girl's face.

Naomi turns enough to not let her face show, "That's a happy ending. That situation could have become a lot more serious, fast. Good work, Dad." Naomi turns to show her dad a big smile, "Everyone knows you've always been the fairest guy in your Union. I have thirty years around you. This bully must have been such a piece of shit. I have never seen you get that mad in my life. Don't worry, I'm sure that guy deserved it ten years sooner."

Sammy snickers, "That's the cleanest story I have."

Naomi spins and charges her dad with a fast-punching attack. Patch turns and jumps straight at Sammy to get there first. Sammy lifts his hands to protect from the incoming punch and back-peddles so Patch does not jump him.

Sammy and Naomi are dissolved in laughter within three steps.

18

Suhki has slept in again. His mind is gripped by a hang over as well. He takes a shower and dresses in his room's walk in closet, on the top floor of the family's 8,500-square-foot house. Hunger is dragging him to the kitchen before he leaves for the day. He steps out of his room. He hears the chatter of more family than he expected to be downstairs, and wonders, *Is today someone's birthday? Do we have family in from out of town? I'm supposed to know these things. I run this family now.*

Suhki stands on the top of the stairs and listens, with his mouth a little open and head tipped to the side, to hear better. From behind, he feels a hand on his ass; Suhki jumps a little and laughs at the start it gives him. He continues to peek over the railing, "Zarita, who's in the kitchen?"

His wife answers in her calm, knowing voice. "Our family is having an impromptu meeting." She waits for the news to land.

He turns to her with pleading eyes. "I can't go in there and start explaining all the hassles I'm dealing with. They'll tell me to stop. It's all for our family, you know that right babe?"

Zarita's long, thick, curly black hair drapes over her shoulders and back. Her skin is light brown and as smooth as silk. Her almond-shaped eyes are deep brown, and her oval face features a straight, pointed, sharp nose. Suhki loves her in this colourful, blue, sari that one of the aunties brought back from India. His chest flutters as he notices her eyelashes reach out to him like butterflies, *Every part of her is natural, even her hourglass body is perfect.* He wants to grab her ample breast in his hand and kiss her, but he doesn't dare disrespect her in a public area of the house.

Zarita is a tall woman at 5'11", but she's petite next to Suhki. She takes his hand reassuringly, as she lets out a relaxed breath, "I waited for you to wake up. I know you're working hard for us all. My dad is down there, and you know he has your back." Suhki's shoulders relax a bit. Zarita goes on. "Over half the family in the kitchen has your side; you officially run the house. Relax and assure them all that you're working on a plan for all of us. Okay?"

Suhki smiles big and leans in for a kiss. Zarita lets him kiss her, but only kisses back half as much; she keeps her eyes on his the whole time. "Are you hungry? Let's go eat with the family." She turns and walks away; Suhki follows and reaches for her hand. She looks away, but gives his hand a light squeeze.

As they get to the main floor of the shared house, where twenty family members live permanently, Suhki hears the dim chatter getting louder. He picks up a few sentences that reassure him of the upcoming conversations. "What is this, Uttar Pradesh? Will we run our enemies into the ground?" is one angry question he hears clearly. Then another. "You think you know what's best? Say it to his face." The family all knows what he has been up to.

Zarita sings lightly, a spring folk song, while they walk down the hall. As they get closer to the kitchen, the chatter goes quiet as they hear her singing. Suhki and Zarita walk into the kitchen, and her singing is the only voice in the air. She keeps the song going as Suhki goes to his seat; his mom has a plate next to the stove, waiting for his arrival, and she loads the dish up as the song carries on. Everyone loves Zarita's singing voice. She sings songs at every occasion. The single toddler in the room stares in wonder as she walks; Zarita finishes the song while petting the little one's curls. The family is smiling as Suhki takes his first bite.

Suhki has no intention of talking between bites, so they occupy themselves with casual conversations about work and upcoming marriage plans for a cousin. Suhki is lost in his thoughts as he eats in the sunlit kitchen. *I wish my dad was still here, everyone trusted his plans. He was so strong and confident. How could his heart go on us all?*

Zarita notices that Suhki has almost cleared his plate and asks him, "Would you drink a cup of chaas?" Everyone looks to Suhki with wide eyes.

Suhki laughs, "No thank you, sweetheart, let's save that for our aunts and uncles. This coffee is perfect." Everyone shakes their heads at her little poke. Most of the younger generation doesn't drink the traditional buttermilk. Suhki knows this is her cue to get the questions started.

"Suhki, the family has a few questions about some of the rumours they're hearing in the community. Do you have the time to hear them? Maybe a few answers?"

Suhki drops his spoon on his empty plate and smiles genuinely. "We are all family, I'm glad we're all here. I'm always happy to talk with the family."

Yadva is an aunt on his father's side, and she gets right to the point. "Suhki, I heard that you're chasing a drug debt? With violence? Please tell me this is not the case, so I can go back and say my family would never be in the drug business."

Suhki's heart sinks; his dad and Yadva were very close. This is what his dad would have said, as well. He scans the room again, measuring everyone's faces. The count is as his wife had told him; over half of the room is onboard, and the other group is devastated. Suhki's face becomes stern. "As the head of this family, I have to work the best angles to make all of us, and our family back home, the safest. Safe means more money. I will earn more money from a single collection than twenty of us will working for a year. The money from this collection will be used to bring over more cousins and uncles and aunts from back home. This will then give us a bigger labour pool, which means we will do bigger jobs for cheaper, and secure more stable jobs for our future generations."

His aunt Yadva levels with the room. "See, it's true. He's turning our family into thugs." She glares back at Suhki. "You must stop this, we have enough. We have built it already, legitimately, with pride. We are Canadian; this is not a slum back home where we have no doctors, and anything goes. We all have more than enough. Stop it, Suhki. Make smart choices, your father used to."

That is the knife in the heart he was waiting for, and he retaliates, unruffled. "I was back in Uttar Pradesh after Dad died. I lived with his brother for three months. They are still in the slums. The little we send them just keeps them afloat. The rest of the family wants to come here, and I'm going to bring them. There will be enough from this collection to bring fifteen families here, right away. Do you want them to have no chance? You want to fly over and tell them that you would not let me collect one point five million? And *not* use that money to bring family over and set them on solid ground. I'll get you a plane ticket, if you want to tell them in person, auntie."

Yadva isn't done yet. She narrows her eyes, "Suhki, do you have younger boys delivering drugs around Surrey?"

Suhki's stern face turns cold. His aunt changed his diapers when he was a baby, and he knows she isn't out of place, so he is honest. "Auntie, I have to do everything possible for our family. I don't judge any method of profit as good or bad. We need to help the whole family come to Canada, and have money to send them all to university as well. I went to UBC, and I want all our relatives to go as well. We take that dirty money and bring good people over, and they get good jobs and bring in good money for the family. It's okay if you aren't comfortable with the way I do things. We'll have great success while I'm head of the family."

Suhki re-examines the room; a couple people have changed their demeanour. More people agree with Yadva now, even his little brother Naresh. Suhki stews, *I don't care about hurting feeling, I'm the leader. The family will get all the benefits. When I'm old, this will all be a distant memory.*

Naresh lifts his hand halfway up in the air; Suhki nods politely for his younger brother to add something. Naresh is two years younger but has been raised the same as Suhki. Naresh has a lot of extra muscle and is only a few inches shorter than his brother, at 6'3". Naresh is also university educated, and Suhki loves and respects his 'little' brother. Naresh speaks while staring at the centre of the table, picking the skin off his fingernail. "Suhki, I love and respect you. Auntie Yadva has some valid concerns that I share. I also see your side of this, we all do, I'm sure. If you do this big collection you're talking about, and sell the rest of any illegal drugs, then will you think about stopping the illegal stuff? You will bring many new families over from UP and secure a better future for many families. I think that's a good plan to keep the family name clean as well."

Zarita has been feeding her cousin's toddler and keeping him quiet while watching her husband field all the inquiries from her family. While Suhki begins his long-winded answer to his little brother, her mind drifts. *Suhki changed so much after his dad passed away and he went on that long trip to visit his dad's brother in Utter*

Pradesh. Suhki came back so driven to make this big name for himself, in the guise that it's for the family. He's so power-hungry. I know Suhki killed that wrestler in a public match by accident. The family over there treat him like a god, and he wants to bring them all here. I want the family to get over the sea as well, but drug dealing and beating people for money? I can't believe this is the sweetheart who I loved so much when we were younger. My father swears Suhki is the greatest man in the world, and wants us to have a baby so badly. But I need Suhki to stop dealing drugs or no baby, they both know this. I must stick to this private protest. Please god, let him come back to me; he seems to be possessed by evil. He lies so much, and I think when he's out 'searching for the thieves that stole the Fukadero money,' he's on drugs and has sex with other girls. He always showers and does not come to me for love when he gets home. I just want my loving bear back.

Suhki wraps up his apologetic explanation to the family. Yadva comes back strong with, "You are brilliant Sukhwinder. You finished top of all your classes. Stop being so stupid."

Zarita stands quickly from the toddler, walks around the table, speaks firmly while

watching Yadva,

"Suhki, I hope you've enjoyed a meal with your family. We all understand that family comes first. You be safe today and know we all support you. We know you have to go to work now." Suhki smiles to his perfect wife and stands. Zarita adds in a wishful tone, "I also pray that after these big wins that you have arranged for our family, that you will focus on a more stable business that we can raise a family in, and be proud." The room freezes; no one has ever heard Zarita speak against Suhki in public.

Suhki's shoulders sink, he opens his eyes wide.

"Okay, my love, I hear you. After I finish this collection, I'll get us out of the drug business as well." The room almost bursts into cheer. Everyone keeps their cool, although the joy in the room is tangible.

Zarita's father, Zoltan, stands and asks Shuki, "Do you have a minute to go over the security crew's schedule from the construction site?" Suhki nods a yes as he heads to the door.

Naresh asks, "Should I not be in on this conversation, since I've been running the construction while Suhki has been so busy?"

Zoltan shakes his head. "This is a little thing."

Suhki compassionately looks at his little brother, "Thank you for taking over the family business while I've been preoccupied. You have been doing a good job. I'm happy with your work little bro. We will be working together again soon."

Yadva starts to say something; Naresh cups her arm on the table and nods to her. Suhki sees the move and is proud of his little brother, and embarrassed about the way his auntie is glaring him at the same time.

Zoltan walks out first, with Suhki following. Suhki is uncomfortable with his wife's dad. The man is bald on top, with buzzed hair on the sides and a short temper. Zoltan works out on the weights and has years of boxing training since childhood. To top it off, Suhki can't legitimately fight back against his elder, unless it's apparent the man is wrong. And nobody would ever think Zoltan is wrong. He's a shrewd businessman who plays everyone straight and never misses a beat. Zarita is his only child, and he had worked out the marriage with Suhki's dad as soon as his daughter was twenty and Suhki was thirty. Suhki had all the right boxes checked, and Zoltan wanted him as a son.

Zoltan stops a 100 feet from the purple Charger, which is parked where Suhki's dad had parked during his life; the only spot that's covered, right beside the huge house. Zoltan starts right away. "Smart, you were honest in there. You left out the house offer though, eh?" Zoltan is smirking ear-to-ear.

Staring at Zoltan. Suhki firmly responds, "I want to live there with Zarita." Suhki wants his father-in-law's respect.

Zoltan answers, "I've always told you that you have two fathers. I will cover for you when the time comes that you want to move to that house. We can play it any way, maybe as a gift from me?"

They both laugh, but Suhki frowns, "Oh, you want to be the hero forever eh? No, no, we will come up with a better reason than that."

Zoltan laughs. "Okay, yeah, that's down the road. So one point five million, eh? From the white girl, I guess? You wear a condom when you fuck her?"

Suhki curses his brother-in-law Jagen, who was with him last night while hunting the bars for the guys who stole the coke; he must have overheard Suhki tell Devan or Ravi.

Suhki can't lie too much to Zoltan, the man seems to find out everything,

"Yes, of course. Come on, I'm not stupid. I only did it to keep her in line."

Zoltan had hoped his son was wrong. The admission from his son-in-law turns his stomach to liquid. His daughter is too good for this disgusting treatment. But he keeps his cool as he continues, "Hey men are men, but you better not give Zarita any sexual disease, she will leave you for sure. I need you to run my business with my grandkids when I'm old. Use a condom; you hear me?"

Suhki squints from the pain his father-in-law's words are causing him,

"Yes, of course, please talk about something else."

Zoltan knows he's going to get what he asks for. "Suhki, you suggest we will bring fifteen families over at least, right? Okay, I'll need ten of them for my construction company. It doesn't matter really, because I'm leaving everything to you and Zarita, so it's a win for you either way."

Suhki is still reeling from the browbeating about the out-of-marriage sex, but he answers back, "That won't add up, some will be women, a few kids probably. How about half the working men for your company and the other half for my family company?"

Zoltan hugs him, "That's the deal then. You are a good negotiator, I'm proud."

Zoltan keeps talking as he comes out of the hug. "The drug money that's left over must be used for a job that both our companies and all the family will share; and then you will get your dream house and make a baby for us all, okay?"

"That sounds fair, Dad. Thank you for helping with everyone. I've gotta go, Devan and Jagen are waiting at the gym for me to pick them up for lunch."

His father-in-law grabs him by the shoulder and locks eye contact, "By the way, I spoke with one of the uncles from that thieving truck company, Pacific to Atlantic, at the temple last week. They want me to tell you 'they will all take a lie detector test to prove they didn't steal the hundred kilos of coke.' Should we get the lie detector out?"

Suhki rolls his eyes. "No way, not a chance. It's insured by them because they had it. I don't care if they didn't steal it, they're paying. It was stolen from their warehouse. I don't care, and neither should you if we want that one point five million. That's common street law, you take it, you pay for it. They get a thousand dollars a kilo to move it in their trucks to Toronto, and they lose it? Fuck them and anyone who stands with them. Who is the uncle who talked to you? I'm going to beat him until he tells his family to pay. Who is he? Call him and tell him I want to talk."

Zoltan is smiling; nervously, "Suhki, they have people too you know."

Suhki tips his head back and laughs. "They're running and hiding all over, I can't get them to come to meetings since I beat two of their toughest guys at the same time. It was a close fight for a couple of seconds when one went for my legs. He only got one leg, so I was still standing firm on the other leg. As the second guy ran in, I gave him a straight right. With all his forward momentum, he flipped back so hard onto the ground I thought I had killed a second guy by accident. The other clown had my leg, but seeing his pal go down hard and fast, he started to let go of my leg to retreat. I grabbed him by the back of his sweater, right in the middle of his back, and he just covered his head. He knew it was over, he knew it, Dad. I got a clear shot on his left ear with a hook, then stuffed him face-first into the ground as I sprawled, hard."

Zoltan listens with wide eyes. "I heard about it from my Jagen. He said that the guys were a couple of semi-pro MMA fighters or something, and you destroyed them in one move each. They will use guns, you know that, right?"

Suhki stares down at his father-in-law, "We have guns too. When we see them we'll try and talk, and if that doesn't work I'll beat them. If they pull out guns, we will too. We need that money, and it's rightfully ours by the order of the widow Fukadero."

Zoltan grabs Suhki by both wrists and locks eyes, "Less alcohol, no drugs. Just focus on the two jobs. The Polish will resist, but I bet you're close to breaking them. The P and A truckers will fight now. Be aware and you make the first kill. don't get yourself killed. We can bring more guys in to help you, maybe?"

Suhki shakes his head. "There's not enough money to go around. I will do this with our family crew."

Zoltan nods in agreement as Suhki walks away. "I gotta go pick up our guys and get to work for 3:00 p.m. at the show house. Love you, goodbye."

19

RICHMOND, YVR, 12:00 P.M.

Damon waves goodbye to his in-laws as they walk into the Vancouver airport domestic departures doors; he's parked in the drop-off area right out front. A parking monitor is walking toward him to remind him that all vehicles must move as soon as they drop off. Damon notices the man in the fluorescent-green vest coming toward him and waves him off politely as he quickly heads to the driver door of the white Caravan. The attendant gets the picture and stops heading over, but watches until the van pulls off the curb.

Damon casually notes, *No texting or last minute calls before driving out of this drop-off area.* Damon judges the security level here is polite, but extremely high-level. *There has gotta be a sniper that covers this driving area. Good on them. I hope they get to blast a terrorist one day. Putting in all the work to learn to shoot and all the protocols. I bet they pray for the day when some lunatic pulls a knife.*

The person watching the camera announces something along the lines of: "Shooter one, we have a knife out by the doors of domestic, do you have a shot?" The shooter answers, "Affirmative, black jacket going towards a family. I have a clean shot, may I fire?" The controller answers immediately, "Fire at will." The shooter pulls the trigger on their government-issued firearm, and a terrorist's head explodes. Instant hero.

So many good jobs where you get to shoot people, and there's a pension and support crew. Should I try and get a government job?

The Simple voice in his head laughs. *Yeah right, haha. Oh my God, are you kidding? Those people were raised by people already in the government. Most of them were volunteering at city hall when they were teens. Where were you when you were a teen, eh? Come on, where?* Damon smiles a bit and remembers hanging out at corner stores with the other kids who had no after-school programs to go to. Fighting kids who got off the bus near them. Late night parties down in the inlet of Confederation Park.

Damon answers back to his Simple voice. *Why don't you think of a better plan? Instead of making fun of us. If it was up to you, we would be dead or in jail. You have any good plans? Huh? Oh, quiet now eh? Just shut up unless you add something useful. Got it? Shut up, you wasted years of my life.* Damon is at a pause in his angry rant at the Simple voice in his head when his Coach pipes up. *ENOUGH, listen to me. We are almost done this job. We have naturally logged the schedule of Suhki from following Fukadero. This will be easy because we've already done so much surveillance. You've done the work. This is a dream job. You have two spots Suhki keeps to like clockwork. What are we doing right now?*

Damon relaxes as he listens; this is what he needs, a positive outlook on his dreary life. Damon answers with a calm and confident thought. *We're going to grab the vehicle that the Polish supply, get the gun, and go check on the 3:00 p.m. Suhki schedule.* Coach answers back fast. *Yes, you have a busy day and nobody is going to pick up the slack for you. Focus on the things that work, not what you wish would happen. No more questioning your duty. Keep your head focused and work. Okay?*

Damon concentrates on the road ahead as the weight of the job settles on him.

The long days of transferring vehicles, unpacking the firearm and putting it away when I don't get to use it, the costume changes. I don't even get a day off. I went to the range and worked light drills, met the notary, and I'm back on a hunt. Holy shit this is never-ending. I wish I had some help. The Coach speaks in a reassuring and definitive voice. *You have a lot of help, think about the help you get from me and the others. The help you've gotten over the years from well-timed training. And last but not least, the messages you get from the universe that always keep you safe. You're not alone, you just don't have a sign on your head that reads, "I'm an exceptional hitman who has never failed." But you don't need the sign because the world knows it, that's why you don't get days off. Do you believe that you have many people seen and unseen helping you?*

Damon answers, *Yes, I do.* And he means it.

SURREY, 1:00 P.M.

Damon parks his white Caravan on a side street in Surrey and walks a block and half; he steps through the bush and views his new getaway vehicle. A white Safari van that must have been painted at least once, but the black steel rims have no rust on them. Common, clean, white work van.

Good work Yakub.

Damon grabs the key off the back tire. He opens the door and turns it on. *Starts smooth, let's check the lights.* Damon checks all the turn lights and the brake lights. High and low beams work as well. He turns the old Safari van off and on again, to see if it has any starting issues. *Runs well enough.*

SURREY, PORT KELLS, 1:30 P.M.

Damon steers the Safari van into the parking lot behind an old commercial building. He gets out and inspects the blue shipping container in the back corner. *More rust and bit more moss on the side.* He peers over his shoulder as he opens it. No one is watching. Even if they are, he's just another guy in blue Levis and a white t-shirt. He steps inside the old container and shuts the heavy swinging door behind him. There's a hanging LED lantern that he clicks on. The light shines on a worn wooden workbench, piles of old boxes along the other wall. Damon walks to the middle of the wall of boxes and pulls cartons down, one by one. He opens one of the boxes from the middle, it's filled with old white rags. He reaches into the rags and pulls out a vacuum-sealed bag with a Heckler and Koch USP Tactical .45 semi-automatic pistol, that has been waiting for him.

Damon piles the mildewy boxes and moves to the end of the trailer; there, he pulls more boxes down. Choosing another box, he digs into the dirty rags. He pulls out another vacuum-sealed bag with five magazines in it. Damon then heads over to the worn workbench and puts the two vacuum-sealed bags on the counter. Pulling the bottom drawer out of the bench, Damon pries the false wood floor and grabs the two boxes of .45 ammo that's been hidden there.

As Damon places the ammo on the counter, he recalls how he picked this ammo from a list the internet said worked well in the USP Tactical HK .45 pistol, with a military grade commercial-made silencer attached. *It's crazy that a civilian can search specs for a gun suppressor on the internet, easily as how to save money on a flight. Thirty years ago the only ones who would have been able to properly utilize a suppressed pistol would have been government employees. Because they legally kill people, quietly. But regular citizens aren't supposed to. Down in the U.S.A they sell the suppressor to civilians, ones who are allowed to use lethal force on their property. I guess the U.S. government is polite enough not to want all that defensive shooting bothering the neighbours. Maybe I'd be a better American?*

Damon reaches up to the shelf and pinches the white rubber gloves out of their box . He slips a knife out of his waistband and slices open the bag with the pistol. Reaching into the plastic vacuum-bag, he grabs the pistol by the grip with his right hand and finger off of the trigger. Once the pistol is out, he keeps it pointed to the wall in front of him and rolls his hand counter-clockwise; grabbing the slide with his left hand, he pulls it back and tilts the firearm into the light, confirming it isn't loaded.

Always check if a weapon you pick up is clear. That's the first thing you do every time you hold a gun. Every instructor and gun handling book insists this is followed, so Damon follows it out of ingrained habit. He aims the gun with a two-hand grip, and dry-fires it to drop the hammer. "Every time you dry fire is another chance to practice proper grip and trigger pull," one of his world-class instructors had told him once. He pulls the slide back and locks it open, placing the unloaded pistol on the bench with the breach facing up.

Damon slices open the other vacuum-sealed bag and dumps the five magazines onto the counter. They fall in an unorganized pile. The light from the lantern is more than enough for this work, but it casts long shadows to the back of the trailer. The collection of magazines casts a shadow about twelve inches long, When Damon touches anything with his left hand, it casts darkness to the end of the bench. He turns each magazine over and finds their numbered markings; these tell him which order he has chosen for them when he had taken this gun out to his testing ground. One to five. He had started with seven magazines ; two caused jams so he threw them out.

While opening one of the .45 ammo boxes, he recalls how much work acquiring this specific gun and noise suppressor had been. Dozens of hours training with it. This gun is his best piece of equipment; he isn't happy to be using it on this job, since it means throwing it away at the end.

PITT LAKE, 1 YEAR AGO

The mountain valley rose sharply to 4500 feet from the creek that Damon stood next to. The mid-morning air was damp; the shadow from the mountain on his right was still at the top of the other hill. Nobody was around for 10 kilometres at least. He had directed a small boat with a twenty-five-horsepower motor to the back of Pitt Lake, and hiked over a mountain to test run his newest piece of equipment: the USP Heckler and Kosh, .45 tactical with a factory suppressor.

Obtaining the gun had cost him time, and favours, from a smuggler who worked a route from Los Angeles to British Columbia. The guy had asked, "Why would you want to pay so much for a gun?"

Damon stayed positive, "You only live once, and this is a dream gun. How much?"

His pal typed on the encoded blackberry. After the message was sent off, he peeked up and asked, "I assumed a .22 caliber is the best round for a hitman, what do you want the .45 caliber round for?"

Damon had known this man for a long time; he had done two hits for him. This was a casual conversation, nothing more. Damon explained, "A .22 caliber is great for close range and surprise, but a .45 round is great for serious combat. The suppressor helps you have a short shooting spree and not alert the whole city."

The smuggler's blackberry chimed, he typed in the access code. His eyes went wide. "Dude, this gun and the government-quality factory-made silencer goes for ten G, delivered here."

Damon knew it would be about five G for the factory suppressor, but five G for the gun was too much, so he countered. "Tell him to add in ten magazines, and it's a deal."

His pal typed in the counter offer, "You know a large-frame pistol is two thousand, three tops. Do you really want this factory silencer?"

Damon shook his head, "Not a silencer, a suppressor. It only suppresses the sound. Nothing silences a round, a little quieter at best. And yes, I really want this setup."

The encoded blackberry binged its alert and the smuggler read it out-loud, "He only has seven magazines with it."

Damon agreed with a smile. "Done."

Damon turned to leave. The smuggler wanted to assure Damon of the timeline, so he began to explain. "Just so you know, we're loading the—"

Damon raised his voice to cut the guy off. "Hey, I don't need to know what truck or train or whatever is going into your business. I don't care if it's in a load of coke or in a backpack of some berry-picker who'll walk across. You know when shit goes bad, and the load's *missing* or stolen, everyone sits around asking, 'Who did I tell.' Next thing I know, you guys are goose necking my way. Call me when it's here and I'll bring the ten grand. We'll meet for lunch. Okay?"

The smuggler laughed, "You sure know how to stay out of trouble."

When the gun landed in Canada, Damon had brought it out to Pitt Lake to practice. He stood in the crisp morning air with the HK USP tactical laying in front of him on a little blanket, with the seven magazines and 1,000 rounds of .45 ACP. He had been dreaming about this gun since he was a kid. It was one of the most tested in the history of the planet. Some called it the Colt 1911 killer. It was reported to work with sand in the slide, under water, or frozen. All Damon wanted was it not to jam. Then he would have his ultimate war pistol for a critical situation that required more substantial firepower and less noise.

He put on fresh rubber gloves, hearing protection, and safety glasses, and loaded the seven magazines. With the slide back, he pushed his first magazine into the base of the pistol and released the slide. Getting a proper two-hand grip, he lifted the gun and aimed at the target he had at ten yards. He pulled the five-pound trigger and…*click*. Nothing but a dry hammer drop.

His heart sank. His Simple voice was disappointed, *Ten grand for a dud gun. go back and shove it up his ass. Damn it.* For a moment, Damon agreed. Then he remembered to go through some troubleshooting. Holding the gun in his right hand, with his finger off the trigger, he rolled the weapon to his left hand and pulled the slide back enough to see if a round was chambered. *The hole is empty, so a round never came out of the magazine. Take that one out and insert a fresh mag. See what happens.* This was his own conscious mind, which had spent hundreds of hours around ranges with instructors and doing the drills in private as well.

He hit the magazine drop button for the first time, and the full mag of ten slid out fast, due to the weight of the bullets. Damon placed it on the top right of the little blanket. Loading a new magazine in the bottom mag well, and cycling the slide, he lifted the pistol to aim and fire a bit quicker this time. *Pow.* The echo in the valley was amazing; Damon stood there and imagined how far that might go. *Not ten kilometers,* he told himself as he lifted and fired four groups of two. He dropped the magazine so that there was still a round in the hole. He remembered that he was testing all the magazines first, so he aimed and fired with one arm. All ten shots were in a group the size of the top of a coffee mug. Damon felt warm, the gun had a tendency to group the rounds tight, whereas his Glock had huge groupings the size of a dinner plate.

Loading another magazine and closing the slide, Damon lifted the gun with another perfect two-hand grip. He pulled the trigger, and *pow pow*. He fired five two-shot groups, and the slide locked open. Dropping the magazine, he picked another. He inserted it and quickly lifted the gun with the two-hand grip, *click*. This time he dropped the magazine and grabbed another and inserted it. Before he closed the slide, he reached down and grabbed the dud magazine and placed it beside the other dud. He closed the slide and grabbed the pistol, *pow pow*; another five two-round groups were fired off. Damon speed-dropped this magazine and worked through the remaining three. All worked without a hiccup. So he tried the first dud again, after taking the ammo out and reloading. Still a flop. He tried fixing them both, but the two mags never came around. He put them in his garbage bag.

He screwed the suppressor onto the .45 ACP tactical and removed his hearing protection. Damon loaded the five magazines while his heart pounded with excitement. He loaded the first magazine and dropped the slide. Damon had to take a breather, holding this dream gun in his hands,his heart is pumping quickly. He lifted it and fired two shots as quickly as he could pull the trigger. *Pop, pop*. He listened for an echo in the hills.

Almost no echo, this is a real suppressor. Damon unloaded the rest in a three-shot burst to have the slide lock on a predictable count. He unscrewed the suppressor, smiling like he just had sex for the first time. He placed it on the blanket, opened the slide of the pistol, and laid it gently next to the long suppressor tube. *Let's set up some targets and get to work doing drills with the new gun. Let's move the target out to twenty yards and another out to thirty. We'll put one out at sixty yards as well.* Damon was talking to anyone who was listening in his head; none of them could run a drill session, so he never asked for help. During drill practice, he felt every voice in his head was observing the training. Damon took long deep breaths, to keep his muscles and eyes oxygenated during the drills; lots of oxygen meant better muscle control and better eyesight. Any situation that required shooting also required long deep breaths, he had decided years ago.

After setting the targets up, Damon loaded the five good mags. This time, when he loaded the first magazine into the pistol's grip, he released the slide and loaded a round, dropped the magazine, and with the barrel down range placed the loaded gun on the blanket. Picking a single round up and pushing it into the dropped magazine, he then reinserted the magazine with eleven rounds in the gun. He will shoot five two-round groups, and when he dropped the magazine there would be one in the chamber. Essentially saving three to four seconds on a reload. All proper shooters practiced this, and Damon had been more than happy to work this drill for the last ten years.

With all the mags loaded, he brought out his shot-timer and hit the start button; it started its three-second countdown, *beep, beep, beep, beeeeep.* At the final long beep Damon began his drill work on the three targets he had put out: two rounds on each target, *pow pow*, at twenty yards. Reacquired at forty yards, *pow pow*. Reacquired at sixty yards, *pow pow*. Damon dropped the magazine and pulled the slide back to remove the round from the chamber. With the slide open, he put the pistol down.

He picked up the shot-clock and checked his time for the three groups at three different ranges. *Nine seconds. Well, that sucks. Let's go see if we even hit anything.* As he approached the first target, at twenty yards, his heart warmed. *Two rounds in a two-inch group.* As he got to the forty-yard target, he was happy the group was under five inches. Getting to the sixty-yard target, he knew it would be bad, and it was: an eight-inch group. Shooting to sixty yards and above with a pistol took years of practice; he wasn't going take any sixty-yard shots if he could avoid it.

Walking back while wearing the ear protection and the eye protection trap heat, and his glasses started to fog. Damon pulled them down his nose a touch so the air would clear them. He always shot drills with them on his face, purely from habit. Much the same as all good shooters, he had grown accustomed to working around the foggy lenses.

Resetting the timer and putting a new mag in, he had eleven rounds in the gun. He did that same drill for 100 shots. The next exercise was similar, but without the sixty-yard target. A row of three targets, two twenty yards and a thirty yard in the middle. For 100 rounds he shot it left to right, for the next hundred he shot it right to left. The next 100 he started in the middle thirty-yard target, and then went left then right on the twenty-yard target. All the while timing with the shot-timer.

Damon reset the targets so they were all fresh. He pulled a burrito out of his bag took a big bite, cleaned his glasses, and drank water. With all his mags loaded and new targets, he ogled the unloaded gun. The gun hadn't had one jam in 400 rounds. *This is the German engineering I've always dreamed of. But in untrained hands, it wouldn't matter. A race car in a new driver's hands. When you put a professional driver on the same track versus the untrained, the trained driver will win every time. This is how the elite special forces train, at the range more often, better drills, constant improvement. Lots of guys have guns, not many can use them properly.*

Damon frowned, remembering that an untrained monkey could shoot a gun. *We train and stay alert to acquire targets first,* his Coach reminds him. Damon nodded and stood to get back to work.

Time to go through all five magazines, with some movement and cover practice. With the gun in his hand in front of him but pointed at the ground, he listened to the shot timer count down, *beep beep beep, beeeep.* Damon lifted the gun as he acquired the two-hand grip and fired two shots on each of the three targets, starting in the middle. But from there he kept going, beginning on the left at the middle target. He had fired his tenth round, so he dropped the magazine and installed the next; with a round already in the chamber he fired two shots immediately at the third target. He kept firing, until all five magazines and fifty rounds were run through. He placed the gun with its open slide on the blanket and checked the shot clock. *Thirty-five seconds. But it felt like two minutes to shoot fifty rounds.*

Damon walked over to count the holes in the three targets while they only had the fifty rounds fired at them. *Bullet groups are all averaged at under six inches. But I only count forty-eight.* He counted again and still only found forty-eight holes. The targets measured eighteen inches across, so a couple of flyers was okay. *Those two bullets could be the deciding factor, and they're gone, that's not good.*

His Coach spoke to Damon in a conversational tone. *We're only here to check that the gun works, go to the range and refine pistol habits later.* Damon nodded and went back to the blanket bench rest, where he began reloading the five magazines. *Five hundred and fifty rounds left to drill and to get comfy with this gun, this is a long day. I've gotta push through fast and move on. I've spent two-and-a-half hours already so I'll be another two-and-a-half minimum once I start the concealed-draw practice with the suppressor on.* Damon had been shooting so long that this was work, not fun anymore. He remembered, *The results are measurable, it's all on the internet. How well a top shooter in the police does, how well a military guy does. Then it gets crazy when they give you a glimpse of certain government secret service guys shooting. One group hits a playing card from any position with a .22 caliber at twenty yards, even hanging upside down from ladder rungs. That's the level of drilling I should be aiming for. But I'm not going to get to there, no time or budget for that kind of focus. Back to work.*

He strapped on the chest-mounted holster that he'd created to hold the suppressor. He'd built it in his garage with adjustable straps and a traditional holster with its bottom cut out so the longer suppressor stuck out the bottom. The magazines would be mounted on his belt across the front of his belly. His costume would always have to accommodate the chest holster. Drawing the weapon from there wasn't traditional, so instead of his average one-point-five-second draw it took approximately three seconds, including undoing whatever coat he had on to cover his chest from top to bottom.

With the magazines across the front of his belly, he would easily grab them as long as his coat was open. He zipped his jacket and went for a walk around the hillside. Sitting in some spots, laying on his back, laying on each side; Damon even climbed a tree to see how the loaded gun and magazines hung in their new home.

After an hour of this he decided that he shouldn't lay on his stomach and still be effective. Laying on his belly at all was out of the question unless it was for a short time and he would support his weight on his hands. Sitting on his bum with legs out was a possible drawing and firing position, but the magazine pull for reloading was slower. The best positions proved to be standing, and laying on the right side once the gun was out; the magazines were trouble-free to grab in those positions. Kneeling worked well as long as it was right knee up and left leg down. Running was fine with the strap on the gun holding it in. But if he were close to a target, he would want that strap undone. With the belt undone he had to stabilize the gun in a run so it wouldn't bounce around in the holster. Overall this was a great set-up with the suppressor on the .45 ACP.

While wearing the gun, Damon walked out and changed the three targets to new paper. He took one of the twenty-yard targets back out to sixty yards so there were three at three different ranges again. When he got back to his firing line, he placed his safety glasses back on. Damon picked up the shot-clock from the blanket, stood there and took three long breaths, and then pushed the button. *Beep beep beep beeeeep.*

Unzipping his coat, he drew the gun and suppressor out slowly, with his finger off the trigger and the barrel directed away from his torso. He already knew that when he drew the weapon out of the chest holster it came out at eye level, which was actually perfect. Damon had to change how his left hand met the pistol's grip, to acquire the solid two-hand grip he needed. With the gun drawing out of the holster at chest height, it's right in his line-of-sight as the suppressor cleared the chest holster; he kept it up there and brought his left hand up to meet it.

The sights on the USP H&K tactical were mounted higher to clear the suppressor thick dimension. He aimed at twenty yards, *pop pop*. Forty yards, *pop pop*. Sixty yards, *pop pop*. He placed the loaded gun back in the holster, put the strap across the pistol's wide grip, and headed down-range to see the groups.

Tightest groups of the day; the longer barrel gave better accuracy. *If we ever use this gun, it'll be a massacre. We'll have this piece waiting for a time when a group is on a rampage, and we get them all together.* Damon's confidence in this gun was at 100 percent. He walked back and checked the timer, for a baseline on a slow draw-and-fire. Next round would have a magazine change, because he put it away with only five left in the gun, so two groups of two then a magazine change. He would run through the draw-from-concealed drill on the three targets until the last 450 rounds were gone.

SURREY, PORT KELLS, 1:45 P.M.

Damon has changed his clothes and has the chest holster on already. He puts the four magazines across the front of his waist. Damon grabs the blocky .45 ACP and slides the last magazine into the grip, hitting the slide release. Once it loads one round from the magazine, he drops the magazine and pushes one more round into it to make it ten. Sliding the mag into the gun, it holds the max of eleven shots. He stares at the weapon's black finish in the dim LED lantern-light of the damp, cool trailer, and his head is lightly spinning as he lets his mind ask him a question to clarify some grey areas. *Will you shoot if he has one friend with him?*

Damon robotically answers, "Yes." *Will you shoot if there are three of them?* Again he answers out loud, "Yes." *Will you open fire if there are four of them?* Damon elaborates this time. "I will shoot as many as I can and still safety escape and evade. If they are all his crew, and I've got the drop on them, I'll shoot ten of them." Damon has always thought, *When I have to use this weapon, it will be as close to total war as I can get.* He's sick of this job and these thieving assholes.

Damon zips up the blue coveralls he's wearing today as his costume. The worker coveralls are perfect because they're baggy enough to cover his chest holster; plus he's playing the part of a contractor on a site. *A perfect situation,* he notes. *This will be a quick job as long as Suhki keeps his schedule for 3:00 p.m. at the show home.*

The garbage from the .45 ACP ammo and the vacuum seal is in a black garbage bag. Damon peels his gloves off, tosses them in the bag, and ties it off. He turns off the LED lantern; it goes pitch-black in the metal container. Opening the door slowly, the sun's rays pour in. He's spent an hour in the dark with the single lantern, so his eyes need time to adjust.

When he steps out, he hears a voice yell over to him, "We haven't seen you in a while. How's things?" It's the old groundskeeper who lives in the back of one of the commercial bays. He watches this place while he drinks at night. That's why Damon has this container here: safe long-term storage with an old friend watching it. *Another perfect situation.* Damon locks up and walks over in his blue coveralls, with his gun loaded and holstered under his coveralls.

Let's go talk and see if he looks at me funny.

The old man doesn't bat an eye while they talk.

20

Driving toward the show home, which is only twenty minutes from Port Kells, Damon accepts the good fortune he's received: the new target drives a bright purple muscle car, and often revs his engine to get attention. Thinking of his past surveillance while he drives helps him be present.

The enormous brown guy had one guy with him most often; some of the time he had two guys with him. The extra guys might go in for a few minutes to use the wash-room or something, but they always came back to the car to text or email on their phones. About three weeks ago it appeared the extra crew was always two guys, they had pistols.

Damon is only using his judgment to determine that they had guns each time he saw them. But thanks to many years of reading about how the secret service protects dignitaries, and watching guys who are hiding a firearm on themselves, the body tells made it clear these guys have guns. Civilians who carry a gun for the first time act like a pigeon with their chest pumped out. They tend to stare out far, waiting for an arriving army to draw on. But the best tell is to watch their hands. *They have to touch it, their new dick. 'Yup still there; oh yeah there it is.'* They usually don't have a proper holster, so the weight of the gun with bullets makes it shift in their belt, or in their man-purse.

With Suhki's guys, it appeared one had the gun in his man-purse, because when he stood guard he would adjust it, so the zipper opening gave his right hand easy access to grab the pistol's grip. Purse Man would make sure the purse hole was always where he needed so he could draw quicker. The second guy seemed to have his pistol in his belt. He would always grab the top of the pistol handle that was sticking out, or the whole thing, and adjust it.

Damon had laughed while he watched. *These guys are trying to emulate cartel or militia men to impress the realtor girls. Haha, lookin' good for the ladies while you wait to get shot or shoot someone on camera with eight witnesses. Smart.*

I'll watch from my spot when Suhki goes in for his twenty-five minutes. When he's exiting, I'll start my walk over. The two might notice me, but most likely, they'll be texting or joking with each other as Suhki comes out. They always drop their guard when he gets back, he makes them safe. I'll slowly unzip the coverall and get a grip of the handle of the pistol. By then they'll be alert to me moving in. As the gun becomes visible, one of the two will make a move. Pop pop, *he's first; then number two will make his move, while standing firm and giving a quick-draw a good try; or he'll be running for cover.* Pop pop, *either way. Realistically, Suhki could draw first if he packs a gun on him, but he's always in those fancy jogging pants, and unless he's wearing a proper belt and holster against his skin, he probably doesn't have a gun.*

So after I drop the two guards, I have to believe someone in the glass-walled showroom will be on the phone to 911. I'll have about a minute to corner the big guy in a game of hiding-behind-the-car. I'll win that game. If I don't waste any rounds, I'll still have six in the magazine and one in the chamber. Such a waste of all these extra mags sitting in their holsters.

SURREY, 1:30 P.M.

Suhki watches as Jagen, his brother-in-law, eats the last bite of his chicken quinoa salad at their favourite chain restaurant. Out of the silence Suhki asks, "Jagen, you think I love your sister?"

Jagen's face goes red; he knows that his dad, Zoltan, said something about the white girl. Jagen explains, "I know you do Suhki. I was just speaking about how you roped the deal in for us. I wasn't trying to make you look like an asshole. You know Dad and I will never say anything to Zarita. We're family." Jagen and Suhki have known each other since elementary school, and have worked out with each other since high school. Jagen was the best man at Suhki and his sister Zarita's wedding. This is a touchy subject on many levels, so Suhki is on his best behaviour; as is Jagen.

"Jagen, you can't go telling the family about all of the actions we take to make it all work. It's too disturbing for everyone."

Jagen flashes a condescending smile, "I'm sure it was 'disturbing' to get a French dancing girl to deep throat your big prick."

Suhki laughs. "It's not funny, Jag. I'd be destroyed if your sister found out. I love her. Keep your mouth shut about these types of things. You'll be married one day, and you won't want rumours getting back to your wife."

Jag wraps it up and gives Suhki a warning. "My sister is young still, no baby. Zarita could find another husband. I won't say anything, but you better not get caught, either."

Suhki is furious—everyone at the table feels it. But he would never attack his family over a talk, so they all keep smiles on their faces. Even Suhki accepts the humour in it.

Devan, changing the subject, clarifies, "How much of this one point five million will we get, since we're doing the work?"

Suhki is happy for the change of topic, "Well, on top of the one point five that the widow Fukadero says we'll earn from the collection, from the thieving truckers who lost one hundred kilos of coke. Ten of those kilos were mine. I paid twenty-five thousand wholesale for each one, and they go for about fifty thousand on the street, right?" Jag and Devon both nod affirmatively. "Since I'm getting the house out of the Polish deal, you two will split the five hundred thousand from the ten bricks of coke when we recover it from the truckers, okay?"

Jag and Devon are beaming with joy; they're both thirty-one years old, and this is the most money they've ever been offered.

Suhki adds, "You two have to piece off anyone else in our family who helps on this collection."

Devon is small compared to Suhki, but he's still a large-framed man who benches 300 pounds a couple times. "We'll do this job on our own." Jag nods agreement.

Suhki knows his father-in-law wants the drug money to go toward a family deal. Zoltan will convince his son and Devon to build a house or something. It will be win/win. The guys have a long lunch, with plenty of jokes while they try and impress the pretty waitresses.

Suhki stands, "It's two thirty, let's head over to the show home to make our appearance. Then we go turn up the heat on the Polaks and find those truckers."

SURREY, 2:10 P.M.

Damon has his blue hat and his sunglasses on as he drives along the two lane country road, toward the new development. This is where the show home is for stage two of the three-stage development that the Fukaderos have planned. *I wonder if they will carry on with stage three with the Fuk dead? Time will tell. If the show home is run right and the rest of stage two sells, the investors will probably keep going. Oh, wait, not if there's a multiple murder in daylight at the show home. Not my problem.*

Why doesn't everyone play fair? Big guy always has to abuse the little guy, the oldest story in history. Robin Hood probably wasn't stealing anything. The sheriff was likely stealing and had better PR.

I'm so glad this show home isn't near phase one. That neighbourhood will be on high alert after the Fuk got taken out on his lawn. This area is all fresh and new, with new construction crews. Sure was easy to replace the Polish contractors with brown guys. New homeowners will be getting all comfy, not knowing each other yet or the pattern of the construction crews. I'm a ghost on this construction site.

Damon holds in a smile so he doesn't attract any attention, but he wants to grin as he remembers his good luck stalking the show home while hunting the Fuk.

Day one, I found active construction of five houses, right across from the show home. It was so easy to blend into the scenery while watching the show home. He recalls how, over the two months of stalking, he would clean the work sites slowly and methodically until the crews were reliant on him to clean up.

SURREY, 5 MONTHS AGO

When a busy carpenter came over and asked who he was with, Damon had acted slow in the mind as he answered. He kept reaching for off-cuts and putting them in the big, thick garbage bags he had brought, "Hi, boss, I'm trying to get in the big guy's good books by keeping the site clean. You tell anyone that asks that I'm good at clean up, okay? I gotta keep going. I'll sweep later, don't waste your time, boss. Ah man, do you see the dog shit over there I'm going to pick that up right away." Without ever stopping or looking at the busy carpenter, Damon kept bending and picking up debris. The guy walked away, smiling, happy with the situation.

Once the building was having its wiring and air conditioning installed he switched jobs, and costumes, to blend in further. The finale had been after the doors had gone in and the locksmith showed up; Damon had unloaded his hand tools and electrical meter and walked past him. Down in the mechanical closet, Damon took a panel off and got his meter out. Damon walked past the locksmith a couple times and cursed his luck. "Jeez man, these thermal exchange valves keep locking open, I've gotta get this done before anyone finds out or I'll never get another job outta these guys. Will you be here for a few hours?" Damon knew the locksmith was almost done.

The locksmith asked, "Who gave you access to this building?"

Damon took a leap of faith, "Tony. He runs this place."

The locksmith came along nicely, "Yeah, Mr. Fukadero has a lot going on. I'll give you a key if you will drop it off at the show home after? I'll tell them I gave the air conditioning guy a key. They'll expect it back later today, okay?"

Damon was nodding. "Of course, that's great, I'll need the key to the garage as well? I'm going to sync the thermostats."

The locksmith instructed, "Same key for all doors."

Damon tested the key in the door. "Okay, I'm leaving my tools here and heading to the refrigeration supply store before they close. Thanks."

Damon drove straight to a hardware store, that copies keys. Later in the day he walked into the show home and dropped the key with the receptionist, "Great, we've been waiting for you. This makes a full set of four keys."

Damon had been able to park his little blue getaway car in the locked garage and sit in a window in an empty, heated house during the winter while taking in all the comings and goings of the regulars. Lime green Lambo, Purple Charger Hellcat, the realtor girls. But throughout the two months he regularly watched the show home, Tony Fukadero never came on any schedule. The Fuk knew his ticket had been punched, so he kept a wanted man's schedule; erratic, even at his own show home.

But all that effort has led to what should be a smooth hit on big Suhki and his crew.

SURREY, 2:15 P.M.

It's ordained. All in your path shall fall. Damon shakes his head. *Swim back in, you're in the deep end with those thoughts.*

Damon drives into the alley of the executive development; it appears the houses have folks living in them. *Shit, what if someone is in the house I use? I'll have to play it by ear. Maybe park in the alley?* His coach speaks in a direct tone. *Change the plan if you have to, don't start inventing plans that we don't need.* Damon agrees and cheers up. He gets out of his van and strolls to the back of the big house; he holds his hand tools. No one in the house; bare floors still. *Thank God.* Damon turns and walks to the garage while pulling on his thin leather work gloves. He unlocks the man door and hits the garage door opener on the wall.

After pulling the white Safari van into the garage and shutting the door, Damon grabs his hand-tool kit and a toolbox. Damon goes straight to the mechanical room and takes a panel off of the air conditioner. To be engaged in a job is a good cover if anyone comes in. Nobody asks a tradesman too much. He then heads up to the spare room at the front of the house; his folding beach chair is still in the closet. *This is insanely easy. All that time watching The Fuk has made Suhki's hit a breeze.*

He opens the chair and sets it six feet back from the window, so only his head is visible through the window, from the street. He begins his lookout at 2:35 p.m., and gets his head into the timing of today's assassination. *Purple Charger arrives. Suhki and guards get out. I visually verify it's him. Which is easy, he's a mix between a linebacker with the style of Usher. I examine his guards for a moment to judge their demeanour. Fold chair and carry it to the room across hall, place it in the closet. Walk to the basement and shut the panel on the air conditioner. Carry my tools out to the van. This takes six minutes at a fast pace.*

I'll walk to the side of this house, and on one knee I'll look at the drain-spout that hangs down the front corner of the house. I'm in position seven to eight minutes after the purple car arrives. I'm in my hold spot. I'll catch my breath at the drain inspection spot; nobody gives a second thought to a drain spout inspector on a vacant house. Suhki walks out and I start my walk over, which takes twice as long as his walk to his car. They'll probably notice me, but I'll be shooting at that point. If by a miracle they get in the car, it'll be easy as shooting ducks on the water.

Turn and walk back to the getaway van, start the long drive out to the hills; then eat some hot pho for dinner. Damon replaces his work gloves with white rubber gloves and begins to take long deep breaths as he relaxes and watches the showroom.

SURREY, 2:55 P.M.

On cue, the purple Charger turns the corner. Suhki parks right beside the slime green Lambo and gets out quick. He scans the entire area like a bull moose as his two guards get out and copy him. Suhki walks away before they're even half-done their scan. Damon can't shake the feeling that Suhki is more prepared than most gangsters. *He transitions from vehicles fast. Does he know that a sitting car is a perfect ambush? Does he carry a gun?* Damon's Coach comes in clearly. *Agreed, lets adjust the shooting order and carry on as planned.* Damon nods in agreement and makes a note to keep a close eye on Suhki during the pistol draw. If Suhki moves his hand towards a quick draw, he'll be the first target.

Damon watches the two guards as they settle into their routine. Guard one, with the man-purse, adjusts it so he can do his version of a quick draw. Guard two is adjusting his pistol at his waistline. They're both texting, and laughing occasionally. *These two really think they could get away with a broad daylight shooting? What are they laughing about? I'd bet money they're from good families, and this is their first time being in a war.* The Coach is sharper in demand. *The time, damn it, watch your time. Tighten up. Mission critical timing.* Damon checks at his watch; it's been four minutes since they parked.

Damon stands carefully and folds his beach chair. He takes one last examination of the guards as he turns to walk the chair to the other room's closet. After placing the chair he heads out in a light jog; hitting the stairs, he begins to skip steps to save time. As he hits the bottom step, he notices the back door is wide open; Damon freezes. He hears a man's voice beside him, and has to use all his will not to quick-draw his suppressed pistol.

"Sir, what are you doing in my house?" the man asks. Damon hears a toddler and mommy patrolling the house as well.

Damon falls right into tradesman character. "Good afternoon, sir, I'm here doing last-minute double-checks that our apprentice was supposed to do. May I show you how to operate your heating system?" The Indo-Canadian family stares at him blankly. The man is a young professional, maybe an attorney; his wife appears university educated and dresses like an attorney as well. Their toddler is wearing a Chicago Bulls outfit, with Jordans on his feet.

Damon starts to sweat. *How close are these people to the Fukaderos? Are they suspicious?* Damon carries on. "This is a no-charge visit. We've had an issue with a young apprentice not doing start-up testing, so the company's dispatched a journeyman to each job the kid signed off on in the last six months. All's well here, I can prove it with some demonstration tests if you have a moment?"

The young homeowner has overcome his surprise at finding a man jumping down the stairs of their new home.

"No, no, we trust you. Is that your white van in the garage?"

"Yes, it is. I'll pack my tools and get out of your hair right away, about six minutes."

The couple glance at each other, clearly annoyed. But the husband politely replies. "That's great, I'll have to move my Bimmer when you leave. Who gave you a key?"

Damon throws in a much needed grey area. "I grabbed them off the apprentice when we let him go last week. He said the locksmith gave him a set when he was working onsite during construction. I'm sure I should leave you the spare key."

The new homeowner smiles. "Yes, of course, thank you." Damon heads to the basement to gather his tools and leave quickly.

SURREY, 3:00 P.M.

Suhki is sitting in Chloe's office while she speaks on Shari's phone, on speaker, with a disgruntled client. "Yes sir, I'll send you an email right when we hang up confirming the pool-house rain gutters are covered by the warranty… Sir, I'm absolutely positive the drains are sized correctly for the coastal region. I'll send an email over to you for your records… Okay, yes, with the warranty verbiage highlighted and indicating the company that covers the deficiency lists. Thank you for your call. Shari is more than capable of handling all your questions. Also, I'm here for you. Bye for now."

At that, Shari, who's hovering above the phone with her bright red hair and matching pant suit, grabs her phone and takes it off speaker; she leaves the room with the phone to her ear, "You see, sir, we keep a close eye on our business. The whole team is here for you."

Suhki is staring at Chloe. She has no jacket, a royal-blue silk t-shirt decorated in embroidery that covers her chest and shoulders. Her hair is straight, as usual. Her nails are light blue, but her lipstick is dark today. Suhki notices she doesn't seem affected by his presence. And he playfully makes note, *Next time I do the fucking, and you'll remember me.* Her desk is covered in active files.

Chloe notices Suhki observing her desk, "You see how much effort I'm putting in on my end, I hope you've made some progress."

"Whoa, wow, not even a hello?"

Chloe smiles back, "Oh, well, hello sir, may I get you a tea?"

Suhki is taken aback by the change in her character. *She can be so bossy and sexy. She's perfect. Tony didn't deserve her. This woman is the head of a family.*

Suhki gets to the point. "I'm here to see if you need anything? I've got Pacific and Atlantic's Trucking guys on the run, and the Polaks are almost done. The truckers have passed word through the family that they'll take a lie detector, to prove they didn't steal the coke." Chloe is unsettled, and Suhki reads her mind and laughs, "I reminded them, 'You get paid to move a load safely. You lost the load of coke, you pay. Fuck your lie detector.'" Chloe warms with the news.

Shari's high heels clicking on the engineered wood floor approach the office at full speed. Suhki and Chloe turn and wait for the announcement of the newest emergency. "Chloe, sorry to bother you. The Pandeeps took possession of their house yesterday. They went there today, and an air-conditioner mechanic was in the house with the furnace panel open."

Chloe grasps her chest, "When did this happen?"

The tall realtor answers, "They're over there right now. The mechanic just went into the basement to grab his tools."

Chloe lowers her eyes, "I really don't have time for babysitting today."

Suhki asks, "I can go over and see what's going on? I've built houses with my family over the years. I'll make the new owners happy and check the air conditioning guy out."

Chloe smiles, "Perfect. If you need me I'll be here. Suhki, I'd rather you direct all plans to Shari, my assistant. I have an email to compose about a pool house gutter warranty. Thank you." Chloe turns her focus to the computer. Suhki pops out of his chair with the new mission to calm the homeowner's worries.

LANGLEY, 3:05 P.M.

Sara lifts the phone to her ear. "I'm calling to check if my email request was viewed?"

The voice on the other end answers, "Yes officer, we received your request to have surveillance on the Fukadero show home and to make a video log; we can be onsite for fifteen hundred hours. and must leave by three twenty. Will that work for you?" Sara agrees and thanks the Air 1 flight organizer before they hang up. She turns on her investigation laptop and logs into the RCMP helicopter's live-viewing camera mode. As the computer boots up, she wonders who's going to be at the show home in daylight hours with Suhki and Chloe.

An idea comes to her that she almost missed; she emails communications, "Get me every cell phone ID within 500 yards of the Fukadero show home from 2:30 pm to 3:30 pm." Sara leans back to watch the live feed from the chopper,

We'll catch these murders.

21

Damon is putting his nut driver back into his tool pouch, and clipping closed the lid of his black plastic toolbox, as he thinks about the ramifications of these people seeing him here at this time. *If I kill Suhki here, at this 3:00 p.m. hunt, these folks will remember me for sure. Do they have a dash camera? Do they have video of the getaway van?* Damon hears footsteps coming and sees brand-new Nikes and fancy jogging pants on the steps. His heart freezes. *Holy hell in a handbag, it's Suhki.*

Regardless of getting away or not, this has become life or death. Damon carefully places his tool bag and toolbox down, and with his left hand reaches for the zipper on his jumpsuit. *This is what the extra magazines are for. Breathe deep, we do this here.*

Through the pounding of his heart in his eardrums, he hears a woman speaking over a toddler who's whining to his mom. "Thank you for coming over to see what your trades are doing here. I don't want any bills for service appearing. And I don't want any more tradesmen walking into our house. Your company is paying for new lock-smithing of our choice, or my husband and his father's law firm will make suing you guys their new hobby." Damon knows right away this isn't a death squad. Suhki is here to appease angry homeowners for the Fukadero group. He stops unzipping his blue coveralls, *This is a new way to fuck up a job. Or is this helping me in some way?*

Suhki's thick hands hang off his dense arms, as he introduces himself. "Good afternoon sir, I'm sorry your schedule overlapped with these clients taking possession of their home. The Pandeeps have a few concerns I believe we should document right now, to help them feel at ease. Do you have a moment to answer a few questions?"

Damon nods, "Yes, of course. This is all my company's fault. I should have checked with the builder before coming to run a final system check. This visit is so we can supply a proper warranty document to the builder."

Suhki smiles; Damon can tell Suhki wants to appease the homeowners, not make trouble. Suhki asks, "How did the system check out?"

Damon had actually tested the system a few times over the months he had been using the house as an observation post. So he gives his verbal report. "All pressures on the air-conditioning side are normal. The condenser fan, on your outdoor unit, kicks on and off precisely on cue. The T/D, temperature difference, at your evaporator, which is your indoor coil, is measuring accurate. All the thermo-stats call at the same time for cool and heat."

Suhki cuts him off, "How many degrees does the ther-mostat have for separation?"

Damon draws a breath and nods, "Two degrees."

Suhki laughs, "So the sytem is exactly as it should be. Do you have the keys on you?" Damon pulls out the single key; it's on an orange tag that has the house address written on it. He hands it over. The meeting ends, Suhki, who's assuring the homeowners that the locksmith bill will be taken care of as they all walk upstairs. Suhki turns to Damon, "Sir, would you mind putting your tools in your truck and coming to talk to my boss about the schedule? So we don't have any more mistakes."

Damon is heading to his tools; his heart sinks as he speaks over his shoulder. "Of course, my pleasure. I feel so bad that these lovely folks have any discomfort on their first day in their home." When Damon gets to his van, he notices the new homeowner's BMW sedan is parked right behind him, outside the open garage door. He quickly runs through options.

Shoot them all, and move the BMW? Then the world news is spot-lighting Surrey, again, for the killing of inno-cent civilians.

Damon's Simple voice chimes in, its tone mocking. *You said no mercy. This is the perfect situation for NO MERCY. Then you're done. One day of work. Great success for us. Bad news for Surrey.*

Damon stands still for two seconds, *Even if this job is that important, we don't know if they took a picture of the getaway van. The police would be at the Polish cli-ent's doorstep quick. Then we cross our fingers and hope nobody points our way. Bad move tactically."*

So instead Damon turns, and follows Suhki along the side path between the houses. The day is bright, with high clouds. Damon stops and looks up to Suhki, "Hey man, I gotta be straight with you."

Suhki is grinning and nods slowly while looking down at Damon.

"Go ahead"

Damon clasps his hands behind his back, "I owed my pal a few hours work because he helped me at my cabin, installing a heat pump. He gave me this address and asked me to come to check the start-up. I don't work for the Chilling Corp."

Suhki smiles, "There it is, I knew something was up. The company that did these installs were all…" Damon and Suhki say it at the same time, "Chinese." Suhki adds, "Hey bro it's no problem, we all gotta get the job done. I'm only bringing you over so the new homeowners think we're reprimanding you. It's nothing, come in and use the bathroom or make a coffee and leave, okay?"

Damon smiles and nods. "Thanks, big guy."

Damon is following about four feet behind Suhki as they come around the side of the house. Damon sees that the guard with the man-purse is leaning on the purple Charger. Watching the two of them as they come into view, *This is about when I'd be making my attack. And instead I'm being led over by Suhki for a cup of coffee. I wonder what I'll get out of this little visit? Last time I was this close to the showroom I received 'the message,' although it was vaguely hidden, it had been screamed into my ear. This day won't be a waste.*

As Suhki approaches the leaning guard, Damon categorizes him as a professional bodybuilder and has to be 240 pounds. "Hey Jag, I'm going to get this guy a coffee, and update Shari on their client's issue. I'll be out in five minutes, then we'll take off to the truck yard."

Damon is watching the front door, but he feels Jag's eyes on him as he answers Suhki. "Okay bro, everything all right over there?" Jag stares at Damon and does the mandatory purse adjust to make himself feel useful. *Maybe he might need to blast a trades guy,* Damon snickers.

Suhki answers off-handily, "Just some trades finishing up, scheduling overlap. Let's get outta here before we have to build these houses."

Jag laughs, "No doubt. I've had enough time on construction sites for the rest of my life." Damon watches the guards reflection on the glass door as he walks up the stairs to the front of the showroom. *You three won't be on any construction sites soon.*

The hairs on the back of Damon's neck stand up as he hears the dull whine of Air 1's turbine engine flying up behind him at about 600 feet, and slowing to a hover. Damon doesn't turn. He practically lived at the local airport when he was younger, and after you hear it fly past a couple hundred times you can hear the high-pitched whine of Air 1 in any weather. As he pulls the door open, he hears one of the guards, "I think that's the cops bro, up there behind the house. What do you think they're doing?"

The other guard's head swivels, "Where do you see it? I think I hear a jet engine."

The door to the showroom shuts, silence. All the realtors zero in to see who follows Suhki in. When the pack of hungry saleswomen see a blue coveralled tradesman wearing a hat and rubber gloves, they all go back to their screens or close-talking with each other.

Suhki leans close to Damon and whispers, "Hey bro, the bathroom is to the right, coffee and tea is over there against the back wall. We'll leave in five. Okay?"

Damon knows it's an order, not a question, and answers appropriately. "Yes, of course, I'm really sorry about any hassle I've caused."

Suhki smiles, "Equipment all works, who cares if they're a little upset about seeing a trade guy in their house. It's fine." At that Suhki turns toward the middle row of tall white tables with steel legs attached to the ground; he takes out a notepad and starts to write. Damon heads to the bathroom.

In the bathroom, Damon pulls the rubber gloves off and puts them in his pocket. He turns on the tap and washes his hands. *I've lost my watch post. The targets close up viewed and interacted with me. I'm caught on the show home video at the regular time I'm hunting. The cops flew over, when I would have been shooting. Why me?* Just the sound of water and the drain answers him. No advice from his Coach or his all-knowing ancestor. *Is this it? Is my lucky streak officially over? I work off effort and timing and a touch of miracle. How could this get any worse?*

Damon shuts off the water, dries his hands, and grabs the door handle with a paper towel. He tosses it into the waste bin as he leaves the bathroom.

Suhki is talking to a red-haired realtor in high heels. He's pointing at his note page. The tall woman glances toward Damon, and Suhki's eyes follow; Damon reads Suhki's lips. "Yeah, that's the guy. Just finished the start-up." Damon can tell that she's uncomfortable with her new duty. She simply nods a yes, takes the paper from Suhki, and tucks it into her file. Damon relaxes, he'll be walking out of here soon. Then he hears the thunder from the downwash hitting the glass wall on the front of the building as Air 1 does a low hover over the front parking lot.

Damon keeps casual and walks over to the tea station. Everybody else stands and heads to the window to see the low-flying bird. Damon is breathing heavily but controlled as it settles on him that he has a loaded suppressed gun on him, and he's the murderer the police want to arrest.

Damon grabs a cup and begins pouring hot water from the red tab while keeping one eye over his shoulder for a rushing police ERT team. His torso breaks into a sweat, and panic hits him; his vision is blurring, and everything becomes silent. Damon turns to face the back wall and automatically rips open a tea package and drops the bag into the hot water.

He asks a futile question. *Should I try shooting my way out? Fuuuck, of course not. I'm on camera, no chance of a getaway. They storm in, full body armour with assault rifles at the ready, covering every inch of the room. I'm the only guy in here that needs a gun pointed at him, besides Suhki.*

It's over. I put my hands up and lay on the ground. When they politely ask me if I have any weapons, they'll be shocked to hear, "Yes sir, a suppressed .45 caliber autoloader with one in the chamber in a holster on my chest, with fifty rounds. It's safe, sir, just unclip the holster and keep your finger off the trigger while you draw it out." After that, I can't say another word until my lawyer has briefed me. At that point, I'm just a tradesman that's a gun nut, not a financially-motivated hitman. At the end of this thought, his sound and his vision return with a jolt, with the same feeling of snapping awake after accidentally falling asleep while driving.

Damon feels calm again, with a plan for the new events unfolding. He turns to see all the realtor girls and Suhki still gawking out the window. There appear to be five girls working here today, all dressed to impress. Damon wonders if Fukadero's staff follow the dress code chain restaurants maintain? Heels, skirt, low-cut blouse, suit jacket, nails and hair, with stage-quality makeup. He has become comfortable watching all the woman from behind, when he stops on the one with the straight, ashy blonde hair that he knows so well. *Chloe, when did she walk in this room?* Damon's calm is rocked again. He's staring at her tight black-silk pants that hug the crack of her bum, when she turns and catches him in the middle of an up-and-down look. He's been caught with his eyes on her bum, and they both know it. Damon turns his head and takes a sip of tea.

Damon would rather be outside in front of police, than have Chloe recognize him with Suhki here. Damon knows he can't just leave; he's Suhki's duty. And Suhki told him *'we leave in five minutes.'* So Damon can either walk over and politely say goodbye to Suhki in front of Chloe, or wait until he's waved over to leave with him. Damon choses to avoid Chloe and wait for the wave.

Chloe calls the girls off the windows. "Ladies, the police are letting us know they're here for us. I have their boss's number. Don't gossip about the helicopters at work on social media, please." The women all nod politely and head back to their pastimes. Chloe walks over to Suhki, never taking her eyes off Damon. She gets close enough that it's a private conversation without being intimate, "Suhki, who's the construction worker in my show home?"

Suhki gives a short version of who he is. Chloe stares at the man in blue coveralls. Damon is pretending to read a pamphlet from the counter, after finishing his tea. His attention is on Suhki and Chloe, and her eyes are drilling a hole in him. *Will she remember what she did? If she does, will she blow her top and command Suhki to kill me with his bare hands? Haha, no, of course not. She might imagine the connection, I hope it's too far-reaching.* But that's what 'the message' always is when it's delivered to Damon from his higher power. *She couldn't grasp it this fast.* Damon watches as the two chat casually. His mind goes back to the last time he was at the show home, and how desperate he had become to get a lead on the Fuk.

Damon remembers the day 'the message' was delivered. First, he noticed the window to Chloe's office was open from his lookout across the road. *Why not try listening at her office and see if anyone mentions the Fuk's schedule.* So he walked over and brought his hand tools, and took the inspection panel off the outdoor unit for the air conditioner. Damon had his pressure gauges for the refrigerant lines, so he screwed them on and took out his notepad to jot down some pressures the unit was putting out. He sat cross-legged behind the air conditioner, right under the window. After five minutes, Damon realized this had zero chance of working. The A/C was too small for the big show house, so it was always running loudly. He couldn't hear a thing over it.

Laughing at the desperation and uselessness of the attempt, Damon thought about disconnecting the fan unit to overhear better. But he knew the temperature would rise fast in the building, and the real technicians might get called out quick.

Just then, Chloe had come strutting around the corner, standing ten feet away from the A/C, in front of her green Lamborghini. She was in an impressive red pantsuit with red heels. The air conditioner was against the wall, and Damon was sitting on the other side of it.

Chloe started to pace back and forth in front of her car while holding the phone to her ear; she was nodding quickly waiting for her turn to talk. When it was her turn to speak, she let it fly. "You fucking pedophile, she just turned nineteen, and her dad is your dad's friend, an uncle to you. You stupid pig. You've embarrassed us so big this time. Oh, yeah...oh yeah, right. Listen to me; you're my husband. I'm your wife, and we are going to make this work... Fuck that, you stupid pig, you think that because you fucked our house assistant, you can hire another little whore to take out our garbage? Who, by the way, told me she was a virgin six months ago. Try and grasp what you've done to our relationship with that side of your father's friends? Anyway you filthy pig, you take the garbage out tomorrow... No, no, don't ask anyone to do it, you pull it out at 9:00 a.m. Then bring me a muffin at work, like you used to.

Before you started fucking a teenager."

Chloe hung up the phone, cursing, after the last comment. Damon had stayed frozen, staring at the gauges with his notepad and pencil, writing random numbers. Chloe noticed him and yelled, "What are you doing to my air conditioner? It's always hot in there!"

Damon scrambled up and laid on the technical lingo so she would storm off. "Ma'am, the three-ton unit that was installed is undersized, but its pressures are correct on the high and low side."

Chloe shook her head franticly, "Tell your boss to replace it at his cost. Go now!" Damon lowered his head, got on a knee, and started to put the inspection panel back on as Chloe walked away.

———————————————

That was the last job's little miracle, delivered to Damon personally by the Fuk's angry wife. *These guys really do it to themselves; every person around them is usually disgusted by them. But they all want something from the monster that seems to have all the money. The greedy sickness that catches whoever tastes a bit of the dream.*

This afternoon, Chloe and Suhki are talking about the serviceman. Suhki appears to be blowing it all off and trying to move on. Damon feels her eyes lock on him. She cranes her head back a touch, the way a bad smell hits an unsuspecting victim. Damon knows this situation just changed. *She remembered the last time she saw me. I know she has a temper, I've seen that.* Chloe looks up at Suhki and whispers, without losing eye contact with Damon. Suhki is nodding and agreeing with her. Chloe turns and heads to her office at the end of the showroom.

Suhki watches her walk for ten steps or so, clearly enjoying the view. Damon runs through a best case scenario. *If Chloe has put it together, and made a plan with Suhki, they'll try and set something up away from here and all of these witnesses. I know how it will sound when Suhki comes over. "Hey bro, it's all good. The boss needs you to check another house out down the road that has no tenant yet, they're coming soon so it'll help if you can check it right away.* Damon's heart feels light at the possibility of these two giving him an address to a quiet house and then coming there to 'get him.' *This will be such a good day if he comes over with a set-up the two of them just slapped together.* Damon's adrenaline begins to pump; he has to take a long deep breath and hold in a Joker-size grin while Suhki walks over to him.

Suhki explains quickly, glancing over his shoulder to where Chloe is sitting in her office. "Hey bro, the boss is mad about the subcontracting thing you and your pal worked out. I told her it's normal on construction sites for the guys to trade work. She wants to hold the journeyman who sent you responsible in some way. I'm sorry for this hassle, bro. She wants you to stay here while she calls Chilling Corp and gets their list of staff from this job. Bro, she's way too mad about this, but she's been through a lot. Would you sit on that couch and have another tea while Chloe sorts this out? I've gotta take off, I have my own work to get to."

Damon is nodding. "Of course, I can wait. I'll go sit on the couch. Thank you for your efforts. Have a good day." Damon turns and walks to the couch that's against the glass wall to the left of the doors. Suhki strides over to Chloe's office, pops the door open, says a few things, then turns and heads to the front door to continue to his next appointment.

Damon has gone through a rollercoaster of emotions since Suhki told him about keeping him as a willing prisoner, then in the following sentence hearing that Suhki's leaving. Damon sits back, he hears the Hellcat's engine roar to life; a couple revs of the engine and the car backs out and pulls away.

Nobody in this office can force him to stay. Damon checks his watch and starts timing how long it will take to walk across the street and get in his van to leave. When it's been double the time it will take to walk back to his van, Damon stands and heads out the door. He's sure on two levels that he won't be stopped; one being that Suhki is twice the distance it takes to get away; two, Suhki might not come back if Chloe calls about a service guy leaving.

Damon keeps his head down trying to avoid all the cameras. Once off the steps he takes a long breath and lets it out with some sound. The extreme dissatisfaction of this hunting spot being ruined settling in Damon's mind. This just became another long job.

E DIVISION, 3:30 P.M.

Sara is reviewing the faces that were at the Sunday Trowel barbecue that she can connect with a name. Most of the men have a file because of the assault and extortion case that their boss Kuda earned. After Kuda stated, "There are many more than just us," on the assault video. The RCMP created a large file on the group. Sara notices their informant was at the barbecue as well, and puts a request email to his handler to talk with him about the case, or at least to provide a list of questions the handler should ask.

Sara studies the picture of Yakub and his unseen friend. *Why was that guy under the gazebo standing with his head in the roof for fifteen minutes? Was he trying not to be seen by the helicopter? The only reason to hide would be guilt.* Sara zooms in on his shoes and pants and snaps pictures; she gets a picture of a yellow gold wedding band on his left hand. She makes a file and moves on.

The showhome photo shoot today was more eventful, that's for sure. With a few clicks, Sara opens the file. The pilot had asked her over the secure connection, "We have limited time for surveillance at this site. May I suggest a manoeuvre that makes everyone look at the camera?

We fly so low that nobody will miss us." Sara knew what this meant, fly so low that people think it's landing. She thought about it and decided it isn't a secret that the police are around the Fukadero murder.

"Yes, Captain, I authorize a low and over for this surveillance."

The show home flyover had been fruitful, except that the worker who had walked in the front door earlier never came over to the window.

He must have been on a ladder or something.

She smiles at the photos of the realtor girls and the three South-Asian men all gawking at Air 1.

Are they looking at a UFO? Wide-eyed and slack jawed, Chloe and Suhki standing right next to each other. They sure seem to be tight; sex, and meetings with guards outside.

Sara reads the cell phone record she requested for this afternoon around the show home. *Perfect. Suhki, Jag, Devon. Chloe and her realtor team. All of the neighbours around the area. Wait, the photo of Jag and Devon... There it is, they're both holding Blackberries, but their phones are registered as iPhones. They must have encoded phones as well, or burner phones to text from.*

These could be any of these straggler phone numbers that we netted. I'll scan the next area they're in and pick up the same numbers. Then we'll know their burner numbers as well.

Sara knows it's not admissible in court, but this is a murder investigation, so any way to gather evidence is acceptable. *We will find a way to blend it into a confession later.*

Sara types in a request for a meeting with the Basmati group informant. She's a school teacher, and is officially recorded as an extremely helpful personality.

HIGHWAY 15, 3:45 P.M.

Damon is driving the white Safari van northbound, back to the steel bin, to put his costume and firearm away. His mind is numb from the turn of events. He had spoken to a few targets over the years in passing, but it never ruined his chances at a location. It had always made them more accessible, because then they were relaxed when they saw him again. *This is a bad situation. Chloe is investigating me. I left before I was cleared by her, and Suhki will care about not being obeyed. He had been polite, I was rude by leaving. He knows something is wrong with me; if he sees me again, he will not be polite. My watch-house is gone. My cover is blown. Damn it, these coveralls conceal the suppressed pistol perfectly.*

Damon's Simple voice tears into him. *You're a liar.*
You hugged Yakub and told him 'no mercy,' and your lie
just cost you this job. Damon has been waiting for this,
and lets out a single laugh before answering back. *Killing*
Suhki and two young parents would only inflame the situ-
ation. His two guards would swear revenge. The police
would get an unlimited budget because of the innocent
casualties. The Fukadero family would carry on with the
case because they would hide behind it all as victims.
How can you be in my head and be so stupid? Seriously,
what the hell is wrong with you?

The Simple voice responds like an angry teen. *We'll*
never know if I'm right because you did nothing back
there. I'll shut up because you never listen anyway.
Damon taps his fingers on the steering wheel.

I can only dream you'll be quiet.

Damon has an idea for a hunting location. It will be a
totally different costume, but the same plan.

Shoot Suhki and his guards: Jag, and the other
tag along.

22

Dean Schmitt uses his key on the front door of the show house then locks the door behind him. He does a quick step-change and heads to Tony's office. Dean sees Chloe behind the desk, his heart skips a beat. *I guess this is Chloe's office now. This is fucked up. Is she going to ask me for the sixty-two thousand dollars I've got out on the street with my dealers? Do I really have to give that to her? This sucks. Who knows, maybe it's good news.*

Dean knocks as he opens the door. "Hi Chloe, what's up? You sent me a text message with the emergency code."

Chloe sees Dean and smiles, *Good old dependable Dean.* White skate sneakers, light blue designer jeans with thick stitching, and an expensive designer shirt with a bloody white bear on it, plus his gold watch. He does a couple cycles of steroids every year, he's solid as a tank, about 220 pounds. Chloe comes around the desk and wraps her arms around Dean, then turns and goes back to the other side. Chloe has noticed that since Dean began having sex with her younger sister, Amber, he doesn't get uncomfortable around her anymore. *My sister must be convincing him he's great in bed, his confidence is up. I'll take it from here, sis, I need this man as well.*

Chloe drops the news. "Dean, I think I have Tony's killer on film here today." She lets it sink in for ten-seconds while watching his face. For all she knows at this point, Dean had Tony hit.

Dean falls heavily into the chair facing Chloe. He wasn't expecting this topic, and is walloped. Dean asks in a hushed voice, "How?"

"He was sneaking around in the last house we sold, messing with the air conditioning. When he was brought over here to be questioned by me, he took off. Nobody knows who he is over at Chill Corp, and that company did all the installations of the heating and cooling." Chloe points the remote at the screen and displays the best still photo she captured of the worker in the blue coveralls.

Dean almost jumps out of his seat and yells, "Holy shit, that's the Cooler. This big shot I was getting bricks off of, has him on his payroll. That guy is definitely a hit man. I shook his hand once. I was grabbing a brick one time, but ended up drinking all night with the big shot. He says to me at five a.m., 'Hey, you gotta meet my air condition-ing guy.' I told him, 'I don't have an air conditioner.' He laughed, 'I'm kidding, the guy is a top-level hit man, he trains and hunts. I call him the Cooler. He's coming here tomorrow to for this crazy gun he had me bring up from the U.S.' Sure enough, around ten we were still drinking, and in walked this guy in blue jeans and a white shirt, with a black hat on. My bro introduced us. His name is Damon. Then they walked off together."

Chloe's mouth hangs open. Dean stares back with his eyes wide and nodding, "Yeah, this is fucking crazy." They both sit back in their chairs and take a couple breaths.

Chloe grips the arms of her chair, "Will you come over to the house with me? I've gotta give you something." Chloe stares at Dean, and Dean stares back. The only sound is the click of the security motion sensor in the corner of the room.

Dean is unblinking. "Yeah, I'll come back to the house with you."

SURREY, 6:30 P.M.

Chloe arrives home first. She walks up to the front stoop and turns around, surveying her street. *I was here when this was a cow field. I watched them survey the lots, dig in the underground services. It's all so different without Tony. He did make it safe for me, even if he was a lying cheater. This is my show now. The players Tony had are my players. I'll wrap up all the loose ends while getting as much pay as possible. Then live here and have a great life. Mom said I'd never get out of the trailer park. Wrong. It's her who still lives in the trailer park. Tony bought her that brand new trailer. It was really for us, so we didn't have to bear the thought of her in the old moldy one she'd been renting for the last ten years. I'm so glad*

I took off to France when I was eighteen. I'm a winner. I'm a leader. The proof is in my address, and the size of the deals I'm working. Ah, here's Dean. I wonder why he stopped at the gas station on the way here? Probably to buy more perfumed body spray. He should clean that car, it hasn't been washed for two weeks and it's been sunny for five days.

Dean's white Chrysler 300, on the twenty-inch rims with chrome five-star mags and dark limo tint on the back windows, pulls into the driveway with an upbeat bass line reverberating out of the car. Dean pops out of his car, does a quick step-change, and skips up to the stoop.

Chloe scrutinizes him for any changes since they left the showroom an hour ago. If she spots something he has tried to improve, she has him. If he's thinking about sex, Chloe will steer him all over the place and make all of his dreams come true in about fifteen minutes.

There it is, his blonde frosted-tip hair has been gelled at his last gas station stop, freshly slicked back. Ah man, if he did a line of coke then he just took a poo at the gas station. Her sister Amber, had told her all of Dean's habits.

' Dean stays awake for two days and nobody even notices because he keeps his hair tight. He's so smart! He also keeps spare clothes in his trunk, including socks. To stay alert for meetings, Dean keeps some real clean coke with him all the time. He keeps Viagra in his wallet as well, because he stopped getting regular hard-ons a few years ago. I know him so well. Why won't he marry me?' Amber had confided during an afternoon lunch with Chloe and their mom. Chloe had felt bad for her dumb little sister, who had worked as a high-end escort out of a strip club in downtown Vancouver. Amber had decided to stop going on paid 'dates' when she was twenty-four; fewer men asked for her, so her boss started to send her with drunk frat boys instead of the wealthy businessmen who tipped well.

Chloe told her sister that to get a husband, "You need to land them when they're in the excitement of a new relationship. You need to find a husband somewhere else. Dean won't marry you.

You screwed Dean at a West Vancouver party in an infinity pool on your first date, with thirty people walking around. How do you top that?" The two sisters and their mom laughed at the memory.

Their mom had bragged. "That's my girl, she knows how to party."

So Chloe concludes that Dean has probably used his 'meeting coke', fixed his hair, and had a poo; maybe he ate a Viagra, too. Chloe is far too good an actress to let her disgust show. When Dean gets to the top of the stairs, Chloe smells the fresh body spay.

"Dean, you're one of Tony's oldest friends and were the best man at our wedding; you're the only one I truly trust. Whatever happens in here, you can't tell anyone, okay?" Chloe watches as his mind races.

"Whatever we do will stay with you and me."

Chloe sees the joy in his eyes, *He is totally picturing using his little dick in me.* Chloe pulls out her house keys, turns to the massive red door, and slips her key in. As the door opens she locks eyes and bows her head.

"Follow me upstairs."

When the door shuts it echoes around the lower floor of the house; the automatic lights come on and illuminate the spiral stairs. Chloe heads to the stairs and listens as Dean locks the door, then follows her. He step changes before he starts to move, he falls in close enough to watch her move. His eyes lock on to her ass as her cheeks change shape with each step.

Dean decides she's wearing a G-string, or no underwear. His thoughts get away from him after three steps. *She smells so fresh. Tony said she gets waxed all the time.*

She must be so lonely to be taking me home this way. No, scared. That's it; she's worried. Amber says Chloe is a goddess who's always two steps ahead. Oh well, whatever happens, I ate a Viagra twenty minutes ago.

Chloe hasn't turned around once; as Dean follows, she's sure he's watching her and thinking dirty man-thoughts. She opens the door to her Chanel walk-in dressing room. She did her stretching routine in here this morning. She manually turns the lights on and off; she enjoys hearing the click of her crystal light switch from France.

Dean lets out quick breathe and shakes his head. The white ceiling and dark cabinets have a cooling effect against the black and white checked floor, but it's the open closets that grab his attention. On his right is a rack of sexy, skimpy underwear that hang below a chrome bar in front of a perfectly clean mirror. When he turns, Chloe is watching him with a neutral expression he can't read, she gives a light order, "Come over to the other side of this bench." Dean walks over to the other end of the two-foot-high cushion seat in the middle of the room; it's six feet long. Chloe bends over and puts her hands on the bottom on her side. Dean is waiting for his next order. Chloe smiles, "Bend over and grab the bottom; you'll feel two screw-heads. Push them in with your fingers."

Dean obeys; as soon as he pushes the two screw-heads there's a small click, and the bench becomes light in his hands.

They lay the soft bench over to the left. Chloe walks around to the middle, and reaches into the open hole. She grabs the lone case that's there. "Come sit on the bench with me and look in the case." Dean is all ears, and does what she asks. They sit on the bench they've moved, with the case between them. Chloe dials the code into the briefcase and the locks flip open.

Dean is expecting what's in here; he has seen Tony's emergency case before. He just didn't know where it was hidden. Sure enough, there is Tony's chrome 9mm pistol with two loaded magazines; five bundles of $100 U.S. bills for a total of $50,000; fake passports for Tony and Chloe; and a few pill bottles and a vacuum-sealed eight-ball of coke.

Chloe takes one of the stacks of hundreds and counts fifty; she hands the fifty $100 bills to Dean. She picks up two other $10,000 bundles and hands them over. "Twenty five thousand dollars each. Tony would want you to have this."

Dean feels an overwhelming rush of emotion and has to stand to take a moment, looking away; Tony's death seems fresh again.

When he looks back, Chloe is standing with the gun in her right hand, pointed to the ground beside her. Dean freezes for a second, "I know what you're thinking. I'll get on it."

Chloe gives a heavy order, "You go after this Damon and shoot him right in the head with Tony's gun."

Dean is walking toward her, waiting to see when she'll start to cry. He notices, *She isn't emotional about this conversation. She's putting on a perfect front.*

Chloe continues, "Dean, the man who hired Damon is probably the Polak, Yakub. Will you also shoot him for us?" Dean watches her for a moment and decides it's time to close the distance; maybe she will crack and they'll start making out in this dream-room. On the money.

As Dean walks closer, Chloe puts some bass in her voice, "Will you kill them? I need to know it's me and you. Then I'll give you what I brought you here for. Will you kill for us?" Dean's heart speeds up as she says *us*. He realizes in Chloe's mind it's the two of them versus everyone, if Dean will kill for her. He smiles as fantasizes about Amber coming over here and them all drinking in the bar downstairs, naked.

"I'll put the word out for his address tomorrow. I'll go right to his house and shoot him in the face. We already know where Yakub lives, so once his hitman is dead I'll go over there and shoot him in his fat gut." Dean walks over and slowly reaches for the gun.

Chloe lets him take the pistol from her hand. She tells him, "Put the gun in the case," He does. She grabs her

$25,000 and the fake passports out. She snaps the case closed, "You keep the case and the rest of it."

Dean inches toward her ever so gently, like a teen boy going for a kiss.

"Dean, go over to the lingerie closet and bring all the pieces here, and lay them on this bench."

Dean's heart is beating at 150; he knows he's about to get treated to one of Chloe's amazing performances that Tony had told him about so many times. He turns to the closet, and tries to decide which one he'll ask her to put on if she gives him a choice. Grabbing all five of the expensive pieces of lingerie, he settles on the red set. He walks back over and delicately lays them in front of her. Dean stands and makes eye contact.

As soon as they make eye contact, Chloe directs him. "Go back and reach up with both hand and grasp the bar."

Dean's mouth goes dry, *Oh my God, what is this girl into? I'm in, no matter what it is.* When both his hands are on the bar, Dean is breathing heavily, "What next, mistress?" with a bit of a laugh.

Chloe explains, "Grab the bar at both ends and turn it forward, then push up."

Dean follows her order, and the bar comes off in his hands. He turns to look at her, but she has moved over by the three big mirrors.

"Bring me that bar."

Dean is a little uncomfortable; he doesn't want to hit her with a bar or anything weird. As he walks, he decides, *I don't know if I need this French sex that Tony talked about.* He hands the bar to Chloe.

Chloe stands staring at him with the bar in both hands. "Are you ready for this, Dean?" Dean keeps eye contact, waiting for her to whip the end of the bar at him in some dominatrix game; he decides he doesn't like this act.

He whispers, "I'm ready Chloe."

She turns and places the bar horizontally onto the left of the centre mirror; Dean hears a big click. The mirror, which is framed with dark wood , swings open like a door. Dean sees cocaine bricks stacked like Fort Knox, in the hide.

His eyes bulge out and his mouth gapes, "Holy shit, Chloe, whose is this?"

Chloe seductively grins, "Mine and yours, Dean."

Dean gawks at her with his new bulging eyes. "No really, whose is this? Somebody must own this."

Chloe lets the cat out of the bag. "I'll give you the short version, you tell me when you get it. The Pacific and Atlantic trucking Company lost one hundred kilos of Tony's coke, right? Suhki is chasing them for it as we speak. All the investors expect P and A truckers to pay them back. It's right here. Tony stole his own load; he was going to make the P and A president pay it back."

Dean hugs himself. "Tony wouldn't steal from his boys. He's our leader, we all work together."

Chloe grabs his shoulder. "Dean, it's insured by P and A Trucking's president. Suhki has money in the load, he will collect the whole amount from the truckers. When P and A pays everyone back, we keep one hundred percent of the coke sales."

Dean smiles. "Who else knows this is here?"

Chloe is watching his face, which shows no signs of sex. " Me and Tony. And now you and I are going to split this fifty-fifty, okay?"

Dean grabs her, and kisses her on the lips like a gold miner, when they find a strike. Then he lets her go and runs into the coke pile hiding-spot. Chloe rests her hands on her hips. "Dean, what did you think I was inviting you here for?"

Dean answers with his eyes wide, "I thought we might fuck." They both laugh.

"I'm sorry, but this is way better than any sex we could have had; thank you for this, Chloe. We're million-aires, right?"

Chloe confirms with a nod, then gets back to business. "There's a lot of juggling for us to do, with everyone watching how the truckers will sell the coke they 'stole.' We can't just start dumping this coke quickly. I've gotta steer Suhki all the way through the collection, that way we pay everyone; then nobody will be looking for this coke anymore."

Dean is smiling from ear-to-ear. "I sell eight to ten a month on the street. At fifty G each, minimum. That's four to five hundred thousand a month we'll be making, clear of any debt." Dean looks to Chloe; she's already nodding.

"You have to kill those guys so word on the street is we're strong."

Dean glances at the coke piles, then Chloe. "I want to kill Tony's killers."

Chloe is worried about herself, "I need you to focus on this Damon; why was he in my show home today?"

Dean becomes serious, "I'll kill them, so we're safe to spend this money. And maybe have sex."

Chloe rolls her eyes. "Oh Dean, you're like a brother."

"But if I kill them both, can we have sex, just once, on this pile of coke?"

Chloe smiles, they burst out laughing, and she concedes, "If they're dead, then we don't really have any worries, one good go at each other on our pile of money will be okay, partner."

Dean yells, "*Yes*," and punches the air above his head. He's picking up piles of bricks twenty high and laughing hysterically. They enjoy the obvious great future they have for a couple minutes. Chloe is happy with Dean's reaction, and to have someone she trusts who will pull their own weight to help her seal this deal.

APRIL 10TH, SURREY, 10:00 A.M.

It's raining outside. Sara is in plain clothes: blue jeans, dark blue shirt, and a black tactical raincoat. Her badge is hanging on a chain, and her sidearm has a magazine in the hole and two spares on her belt. She's sitting in the high-school liaison officer's private office. "Please call me Sara, thank you for your work at this school, Officer Mundy. Have you had much luck reaching any of the kids before they start getting violent?"

Officer Mundy replies with a courteous smile that says, 'you have no idea how much I have to deal with to even make a dent in these Surrey kids.'

"Call me Ruth." Ruth gets the details of Sara's visit out of the way first. "Yadva Trivedi is a well-respected teacher at this school. She teaches grade nine math. It's a tough age, and she's dealing with disadvantaged kids. Yadva will give us whatever she knows, to help stop any violence. Her only motivation is to be a good person. She's giving info on her family, so she requests that her name is never on an official file. Yadva only wants to keep the RCMP up to speed to avert violence."

Sara nods, "I'll be completely respectful of Yadva and her wishes."

Ruth leans back in her chair; she's wearing full uniform. Dark blue pants with the gold strapping up the legs and a ballistic vest under her grey shirt. Her police-style hat is on a hanger behind her chair. Ruth explains school duty. "Kids react quicker than adults, and have no idea of long-term ramifications from their actions. A boy will grab a girl's bum at 8:30 a.m., her brother and his friends will swear a beating for the boy by lunch. The parents might even support the beating.

"We continuously find knives and machetes hidden around where fights are supposed to happen. Good thing most of the kids' parents know each other; their support is enormous. At this school, we all raise the kids. Imagine if I arrest a straight-A student who utters threats. Does he become more tame if we take away his chance at a good university? No. So instead we talk them down and get them to say sorry. The kids I help the most hate me. I hear them talking loudly, using the only insult I should charge them with." Sara cringes as Ruth whispers.

"Pig."

Sara leans forward, "I'm really sorry you have to tolerate that; I'd throw the skinny pricks through the wall."

Ruth smiles. "You see, that's why I'm here, and you're out doing your duty. My job is long-term care of these kids, so hopefully, you or a gangster doesn't shoot them when they run their mouths out there in the real world. If I can save them, they'll thank me when they're adults... I hope." Sara and Ruth lock eyes, both knowing they will be friends.

Yadva knocks on the door and opens it, "Hello Ruth, I see you have a friend for us to talk to." Sara stands and introduces herself. And thanks Yadva for her assistance. Yadva is serious as she speaks about the business she suspects Suhki has been up to. Sara takes notes the whole time and has a recorder in her pocket for personal review later.

When Yadva is done, Sara speaks. " Yadva, you're being exceptionally caring in the way you're trying to avoid any violence in our community. I'll be making a detailed note on your contribution to our city; you are truly a community caretaker. Thank you. I have to clarify a few things before I go, do you mind answering a few questions?" Yadva offers her hands with open palms.

Sara continues. "Thank you. This collection that Suhki spoke of is for 1.5 million; did he mention any specific people he is working for?"

Yadva shrugs. "No."

"Do you have any idea who Suhki is after for the drug debt?"

Yadva looks back and forth between Ruth and Sara, "I'm sorry, no."

"Do you have any names of the kids he has dealing drugs around Surrey?"

"No, but he said, 'I'll stop dealing the drugs soon,' he admitted it."

Sara allows what she has heard during her conversation with Yadva to settle in the room.

Mainly, Yadva doesn't have any facts. Yadva becomes panicked, "Suhki killed a man with his bare hands." Sara knows Suhki has no murder on file with the RCMP, so her ears perk up.

Sara prompts Yadva, "Please go on."

Yadva checks the clock; she has less than ten minutes remaining to chat, so she plans on telling the short version. "When Suhki's dad died a couple years ago, Suhki went to India, to know his father's brother, my brother. While there, my brother kept taking Suhki around to all the local wrestling clubs to show off his big nephew from Canada. Suhki is an extremely well-trained fighter, and also has a natural size advantage. I think he started doing steroids while over in Uttar Pradesh. Anyway, the city was all talking about this Canadian who is undefeatable, so all the local big shots arranged a 'friendly' match in a local stadium. Suhki has fought in many tournaments here in Canada and has said, 'Nobody in Uttar had a chance, they don't have as many instructors and good eating I have always had. It was so easy to win over there.'

"The night of the wrestling match, the stadium filled to its max of twenty thousand. My brother had every person from our region there; the local champion had his followers. Many politicians and police were on both sides. Apparently, the local fighter knocked Suhki down and was standing straddling him, and throwing big punches to finish Suhki. Then Suhki grabbed his ankle and did some kind of a lock; I was told it broke the local man's ankle.

"Suhki rose and was walking around with his arms up. Suhki's one eye was swollen shut, and he had a fractured jaw. But the referee did not stop it. When Suhki heard the crowd going crazy, he turned around to see the local champion on his feet. Suhki went to shake his hand, however the man charged on his hurt foot, slapping Suhki in the ear. Suhki told us, 'I saw his one good leg, so I drove in low and grabbed it. I knew he couldn't defend with the broken ankle. I dragged him to the ground in a single leg pick up. As he fell, I let go of his leg, then soccer-kicked him once in the side of the head as he was falling. I backed up, and didn't look away from him. I knew before anyone in the stadium that I had broken his neck. His eyes just stared at me, with no life.'

"Suhki has never been proud of that fight; he rarely talks about it. The local officials in Utter Pradesh judged it an accident in a fair fight. The crowd chanted Suhki's name for twenty minutes. My brother made him a legend in India. He returned home, and wants to bring all the family here." Yadva is content that she has given the police an idea of how dangerous Suhki is with this last story, "I've got to go to class, call me if you need anything else, officers." At that, she leaves the room.

Sara's mouth is slightly ajar. Ruth speaks up first. "Yes, we have quite a few talented MMA fighters in this school. It used to be boxing for their dads, nowadays it's Jiu-Jitsu and Muay Thai."

Sara has regained her composure; she stands. "Thank you officer, you're doing a great job here. This meeting really helps us better understand Suhki and his group." Sara turns for the door.

FORT LANGLEY, 1:00 P.M.

Dean is driving to the smuggler's house where he first met Damon. He's thinking of all the ways to convince Chaz to turn over his hitman. *I can straight-up threaten him. 'He killed my bro. I'll kill you if you don't turn him over.' Nah, Chaz has tons of connections around Canada and the U.S., I definitely need him. I'll tell him, 'Oh man, it's not me, my guys are gonna kill you because you're friends with the hitman who killed their leader.' I gotta be smarter than this.* Chloe and Dean drank until 1:00 a.m., planning and laughing. She made him go to bed in the spare room and woke him at 7:00 a.m. Chloe brought him some of Tony's casual clothes: Hugo Boss jeans and a matching black t-shirt. When she dropped it on the end of the bed, she said, "We have a lot of work to do for the next little while, lay off the party and get used to being a boss."

Dean feels the power his new-found wealth is going to provide.

He drives up to the front of the country estate just outside of Fort Langley, overlooking the Fraser River. The camera at the gate is monitored; whoever sees the white Chrysler 300 opens the gate. Dean and Chaz have known each other for ten years. Chaz was either supplying Tony with bricks of coke or vice versa; Dean was always the guy doing the pickup and delivery between the two.

Dean sits in his car for a minute, thinking. *Okay, Chloe said to stay off the party and get used to being a boss. How would a boss handle this? Think, think.* Dean is holding his steering wheel and thinking hard when he hears the loud tap of a heavy gold ring on the window. It startles him awake. Dean grabs his door handle without checking who knocked.

Chaz is the only guy with heavy gold rings around here. He's the last of the early 90s big shots; he made lots of money when locally-grown pot was selling for $3,200 a pound, and turned the loads of fresh green he was sending down to the U.S. into coke for the drivers to bring back up to Canada. He's about fifty years old, with slicked-back grey hair, thin lips with crooked yellow teeth. The dude is 160 pounds soaking wet. Chaz is dressed how he always is: shorts and sandals and a button-up surf shirt.

Chaz takes a step back as Dean gets out and makes big gestures with his hands that say, 'the show is about to start.' Chaz is smiling from ear-to-ear. "Ah, Dean. Dean Dean, the party machine. I'm so glad you're here. I've been partying since last night, but the girls I had over left this morning at seven. They've come over at least once a month for the past three months. Two twenty-four-year-old blonde yoga instructors, man. We were eatin' ecstasy last night, then they got crazy in my bar. They worked the dance pole, and we all got in the steam room. Oh, Dean, you're twelve hours late, man. I asked them to stay for the day, but they said, 'You pay our bills and we'll stay.' I said, 'Ladies, have a good day at work.'" At that, Dean and Chaz laugh hysterically.

Dean gets into his new job. "Hey, Chaz, can we go for a walk and talk? It's work related."

Chaz tries to be serious, "Oh yeah, Dean, serious work happening around here. Let's go to the gazebo. I've got a drink over there. Oh wait, you need a drink?" Chaz points at Dean with two gun-fingers.

Dean smiles. "Not today bro, gotta keep working when I leave here."

Chaz nods and heads to his gazebo; it faces north over the Fraser River. He picks up his drink as he sits. Chaz appears sober and gives Dean his full attention. Dean locks eye contact, "Chaz, you've always been really cool while I worked for Tony. I've taken over a route that Tony had going, it brings up five bricks a week of high-heat blow. I'll give you the first five for wholesale, no markup. Thirty thousand dollars Canadian delivered here."

Chaz replies right away. "Five kilos of coke that tests higher than ninety-six percent pure for thirty G each?" Chaz lets his last comment hang. Dean nods while keeping Chaz's eyes contact. Chaz loses all cheer. "What do you want?"

Dean holds his eyes on Chaz. "Damon's address."

Chaz throws the drink out onto the grass in one quick flash. "What the fuck are you talking about? Oh, oh, I see, do you think Damon killed Tony?" Dean confirms with a nod. Chaz goes on, "Who hired him is more important. He doesn't go around killing guys for looking at him sideways, and he's not in the coke business. Who hired him?"

Dean nods. "We have a lot to do, I just need his address. I don't want to get into too much with you. I will give you one more brick at wholesale each week, until this route changes. The supply could go on for years though, right?"

Chaz stares at his feet, even though they have a commanding view of the river flowing by. "I need Damon. Can't you skip him and go for the guy who hired him?"

Dean's eyes dart around. "No, my contact for this route insists we kill the hitman *and* the guy who hired him."

"When do the first five bricks arrive?"

Dean holds his excitement in. He knows Chaz has the $150,000 here. This is pocket change for him.

"Today or tomorrow, the ride we're using won't tell us the exact day, so he won't catch heat."

Chaz nods, "Smart. You bring me the five bricks, I'll pay you thirty Gs each. I'll also give you his address." Chaz extends his hand to make it a deal. And they shake.

Dean throws a good idea up, "When the yoga instructors come back, call me."

Chaz beams, "That's a deal too."

As Dean pulls out of the driveway, he wonders if Chloe will be upset that he's sold five bricks for less than market value, or see it as the significant move that it is. Dean is smiling as he drives. *Seventy-five G for each of us and Damon's address. Being rich is easier than being poor.*

23

It's pouring rain. Damon sits in his garage with his favourite twelve-gauge shotgun, a Mossberg 590, on the counter. He's wiping and lubing its matte black body. He has installed a dedicated Sure Fire fore end, with a light output of over 200 lumens at fifty yards; it only takes fifty lumens to fully blind a human. He recalls an opportunity he had to hunt with this shotgun. *I really thought a deer was going to flip over when hit by a two-and-three-quarter inch slug at fifty yards. But it just made the fur around the penetrating slug react with a shock wave. A rifle bullet seems so much less invasive. That deer weighed in at 170 pounds, if it didn't do a dramatic movie-flip, neither would a human.*

The thought still makes Damon sad; he had really wanted to see something straight out of a Hollywood action movie, from a shotgun blast.

Damon is trying to distract himself from the dire circumstance that might be unfolding on him as he sits here. *When Chloe called the air conditioning company to check on me, for sure they denied knowing me, because they don't. Suhki told me to my face, 'You sit, until Chloe checks you out.' They have a full picture of my face in the show home from yesterday. This sucks.* His Coach chimes in. *Probably time for some hiking with the dog, in the rain. Go to the top of that hill and back, under the power lines by Rolley Lake.*

Damon knows that the power-line trail will be empty in this rain; the 2,000 foot incline up the service road will have rivers running down it. He notices his Under Armour waterproof trail runners and his soft-shell raincoat. He decides it's best to have a good run. Damon opens the garage door to the house, calls to his wife, and lets her know he will be back by dinner.

SOUTH SURREY, 5:00 P.M.

Dean is driving in the downpour that started around 2:30 p.m. in Surrey. His white Chrysler 300 is all-wheel drive, but he's driving at three kilometres under the speed limit. Dean's mind is racing. *Drexel will do what I've been doing for Tony, and I'll do Tony's stuff; which apparently is driving around making a hundred G a day. Holy shit, as long as nobody ever finds out about Chloe and I slowly unloading the stolen coke, that's it, I'm a millionaire. The Grim Sinners are all going to make more money off this load. We'll attract more big dealers with our cheaper high-test blow. Then we keep ordering more at regular wholesale pricing. This is so easy, Thank you, Tony. I wish I could repay you. I knew you'd help me get rich somehow.*

Dean pulls up in front of the Grim Sinners main house, which Tony rented to them last year. The place is a castle near the U.S. border on 8th Avenue in South Surrey. The land is a five-acre parcel with a huge white barn that had been filled with a #150 light grow-op before it was busted. It's all cleaned out, the doors locked tight; members only in the barn.

The house is about 4,900 square feet, an executive house built with a mix of horizontal white-plastic siding and river-rock trim around the windows and arched doorway. The basement had also included fifty 1,000 watt lamps to grow pot. It was converted into an after-hours that the Grim Sinners throw wild parties at; the longest party so far lasted three days. Tony had rented the house to the Grim Sinners after the bust because the city had marked the house as a marijuana grow house, so it was land value only or rent it out.

Dean tries to get his crew to stop partying on the second day, because guys start to kill each other after two days awake. Dean knows that Drexel and his tight crew have been awake partying since yesterday night for Amber's birthday. Well, since Amber is Chloe's sister, Drexel made the party about Amber.

Dean struts to the front door and stands for a minute, listening. Bass from the speaker inside is vibrating the brass door-knocker in a rhythmic beat. Dean tries the doorknob. *Locked door and music on full blast, what's going on today?* Dean pulls his key out of his pocket. Every member of the Grim Sinners has a key to this house. They all pay the bills, and they all party hard as well.

Dean swings the door open and looks down the hall to the kitchen. *Holy fuck, the place is a mess. Why have the new guys not been cleaning as the party's going?* Bottles and half-empty cups cover the entire counter in the kitchen. There's a stack of ten empty pizza boxes on the dining table, and paper plates all over the house. Dean closes the door behind him. Nobody notices him yet. He walks to the stereo and turns the volume too low for the party atmosphere, but now he hears how many people are in the house. It's full of all-night party animals. At least seventeen people are chatting away loudly. When the music stops, they all stop as well.

One voice shouts from the living room. "Who the fuck would even think about messing with my girl's playlist?" Dean recognizes Drexel's voice right away. Dean waits in the kitchen with the stereo next to him, smiling at his music-off prank. Two substantial kids with barrel chests are in the kitchen with Dean, but they don't know him. Dean figures it's their first time at the party house. They look nervously at each other when Drexel yells; they watch Dean with kind of a half-smile that says, 'We're just minding our own business over here by the beer fridge, with this dinner plate of coke in neat little lines next to a straw.' Dean can tell by how healthy they are that they don't party much, but they want to.

Drexel comes into the room with his eyes blazing, Dean takes in the big, baggy white shirt with gold Chinese writing on it and the enormous baggy jeans over white skate-shoes. The gold bracelet is new; it's designed is a motorcycle chain. Dean is taken aback by how much muscle Drexel has lost over the last two weeks. He wonders if Drexel has this party under control, or if he's off the rails. Dean yells, "I turned that shit off."

Drexel heard the fight bell ring. His eyes go as wide as saucers and his head whips to Dean. Dean is smiling at him, but Drexel doesn't smile back; he immediately walks over with his face all screwed up. Drexel still has enough of the semi-pro MMA fighter left in him to be very intimidating. "Drexel, don't you think the guys want music with some testosterone?"

Without changing his screwed up face Drexel asks, "You want testosterone, eh Dean? I've got some extra I'll give you right now." Drexel stops in front of Dean with his nose almost touching Dean's. Drexel grabs Dean around the torso in a bear hug and yells, "Man, I'm glad you're here, now we'll get this party going."

Dean switches the music to a 90s playlist, and they walk off to the living room together. Drexel's arm is around Dean's shoulder, he tips his head over and leans his weight on Dean. The living room has all the old vertical slot blinds closed, and all the lamps are on to give off a desired degree of light. Amber sits next to Shelly, Drexel's woman, along with a group of four guys Dean doesn't know. Drexel points at them with the hand that's wrapped around Dean's shoulder. "Those guys are from the crew up in Trail."

Dean's eyes snap wide open, Drexel smiles. "Yeah, they like *my* idea of their crew joining us and getting better pricing on blow. Smarter than their boss was."

Drexel runs over to the group of four guys and puts one of them in a standing rear naked choke; he never tightens it. With that screwed up face, he hisses, in a rhetorical way, "Who wants to leave, uh? Who? Lights out, bye-bye."

The four laugh nervously. Dean hears a familiar voice beside him; it's Rocket. "Yo, Drexel, keep your hands off our new guys' throats, they know what you's all about bro. I'm putting another gram through a strainer in the kitchen.Who wants a big line to get this party going again?" The four from Trail follow Rocket; the two girls have their own little silver plate with a white pile about two inches high on it. Amber does a small pinch on the back of her thumb, then slinks over to Dean.

Dean has to hold back a laugh as he notices the state Amber is in. *Her hair is blown out like she was on the back of a motorcycle, her eyeliner is all over her face, and her clothes are baggy from wearing them for forty hours. Ah man, she wants to kiss me. Not going to happen.* Dean turns his head as she comes in for a hug. "Amber, what are you doing hanging here for so long?"

Amber whispers in Dean's ear, "Keeping an eye on the Grim Sinners for my sister and you."

Dean smiles. "Don't worry about that, have fun. Take Shelly in the kitchen for me?" Dean notices Shelly squinting at him. He locks eyes with her; with a little chin-up nod he asks, "How you doing, Shelly?"

Shelly rises slowly with her elbows pinned to her ribcage and forearms pointing straight out, fingers clawed. "Oh fine Dean, thanks for asking. We don't do anything without your approval, right?"

Drexel's jaw drops, "Shelly, come on, play nice." Dean feels they've been talking behind his back.

Shelly carries on. "Drexel, you going to pretend to care about Dean's feelings? Is he your boss today?" Dean grits his teeth as he looks back-and-forth between them.

Drexel holds his drink in his mouth, by pressing his lips together as he jumps forward and grabs Shelly by the arm. "Babe, you're insulting, go with Amber and Rocket to the kitchen, do a line to chill out." Shelly turns away from Dean and heads to the kitchen with a smirk on her face. Drexel and Dean laugh and shake their heads at Shelly's crazy attitude.

Once they are alone, Dean asks Drexel straightaway, "Why the fuck is the dead guy's crew here?"

Drexel hits his chest, "They know I'm the shit, and they want to work with me. The word up in central B.C. is the Grim Sinners have this crazy hitman who will choke you to death in front of fifty people and not get caught. So they all want to work with that insane hitman—me."

Dean is staring at him shaking his head, "You gotta stop talking about killing that kid up there. And having his crew around ours, while people are still talking about the murder, isn't a good idea."

Drexel laughs. "Scarface gutted Rabenga in front of the whole camp. He was fine."

Dean knows this guy is off the rails on day two and making no sense, so he keeps it light. "Does Shelly know about you killing that guy?"

Drexel raises his arms straight to the sides. "Bro, everyone knows I choked that idiot at the rave. Everyone knows we own the area now. No one saw me do it. It was pitch-black out. They saw us walk off together, Rocket had his crew on our blow, rippin' rails. An hour later they find their fearless leader out cold. Actually, I sent Rocket over to get the guy's bankroll, his guys had just paid him. Rocket took nine G out of his jeans."

Dean is both happy and sad about this monster he's created. He found Drexel up in a little town in central B.C., fighting at a sanctioned MMA fight with striking and submissions. The open-weight-class tournament was an eliminator. Drexel beat three guys that night. At the after party, Dean and Drexel hit it off. Drexel was selling three ounces of coke a month, by the gram, to his work crew and other friends. *Man, Drexel has changed so much. He was working a day job and banking money from his little side dealing. One hundred and ninety-five pounds of solid muscle, hair always trim on the sides and short on top. Nowadays he's closer to one hundred and seventy-five pounds, cuts his hair maybe once a month. And he spends money as fast as we make it. He's been spending ten to twelve grand a month on partying and clothes for him and his girlfriend. And she's a real catch. He'll have to clean up his act if he wants to take my old job running this crew.*

Dean asks Drexel, "Can we sit on the couch and talk?" Drexel smiles and turns to the sofa. Dean follows; they sit next to each other. A classic 90s mosh pit song blasts on the stereo, and the two guys start to nod their heads and smile. They both start to sing their favourite line together; the second course is yelled. "Gather round the family! Fists full of hell. *Gather round the family, Fist full of hell!*" They are pumping their fists in rhythm, then suddenly both are grabbing each other in a wrestling match. Dean is stronger, but Drexel has his purple belt in Brazilian Jiu-Jitsu. The music stops, and the wrestling match stops too. They let go of each other and shake their heads, both guys are sure they would have won the match.

They hear Shelly talking over everyone in the kitchen about the music. "We'll have good music on, my music. Go tell Drexel that my music isn't good, than. Yeah yeah, just stand there looking dumb. I don't care who put the last songs on. My man runs this place, you know that right?"

Drexel shoots Dean an apologetic look. He starts to stand and go say something to Shelly, but Dean grabs his arm. "Don't worry about her running her mouth, it's all-right when she explains that to the new guys. You're running this place bro, but I need you to do more than you're doing. Can you help me?"

Drexel is relived to hear Dean admit that he is running the place, because he's been telling guys this since Tony died; he could feel Dean was going to move up the ladder soon. Drexel clenches his free hand, "What more can I do? I kill guys for us to get more workers. I put on parties almost every night to attract more workers. What else do you want?"

Dean puts his arm around Drexel's shoulder, leans in, and speaks quietly. "I need you to sober up. Will you party less? I have more work for you, more money."

Drexel was pushing a white-powdered line together on the table in front of them while Dean was talking; now he stares Dean in the face. "You think I can't handle myself?"

Dean thinks he's kidding, and pushes Drexel's arm gently. But Drexel hits all the bottles off of the table in front of them as he jumps to his feet. Dean finds himself nose to nose with a furious day-two coke head MMA fighter.

This isn't Dean's first rodeo. His stare goes steely as he slowly stands, eyes locked on Drexel. Dean sees a bit of wind leave Drexel's sails; the coke head is used to everyone being afraid of his new-found high rank in the Grim Sinners, but Dean had found Drexel, and might send him down the road with nothing.

The two are standing nose to nose when Shelly yells from the doorway, "Kick his ass, babe! Show him how you roll."

Dean turns and points at her.

"*Get back in the kitchen, Shelley!*"

She turns to Drexel for direction, who nods and waves his hand for her to go. Dean leans a little closer his left eye flickering.

Drexel regains his composure and bows his head, "Bro, I'm sorry. I have a bad temper. I'd never fight you."

Dean keeps his eyes locked on Drexel. "Let's go for a walk to the barn."

As they walk out the front door Dean recognizes that Drexel believes he's better suited to run the Grim Sinners, because he killed a weak punk. Dean decides to give Drexel something to think about. Dean heads to his 300's trunk and pops it; he grabs a black gym bag then closes the truck.

Drexel is blinded by the daylight, but revived by the fresh air. *Man it's so smoky in there. Dean's right, I gotta straighten up. I'm so close to my brown belt, I should get another fight going. I'll show all my brothers in the Grim Sinners that I'm not afraid of anyone. I wonder what Dean wants me to do?*

Dean opens the door to the barn and hits the light switch. A black '69 Camaro convertible sits there, with spoke wheels, white wall tires, and a white interior. Dean walks past it, "We gotta get this car over to Tony's dad, Tony Senior. It can't stay here unless you buy it." Dean glances over his shoulder at Drexel, who's staring at the car and practically drooling.

Drexel grumbles, "Yeah right, I don't make that kind of money."

"You do now. I got me and you bricks for sixty thousand on the arm, and fifty thousand for cash."

Drexel looks over at Dean to see if he's kidding. "What do you need me to do?"

Dean is blunt, "Sober up, and start going to the gym twice a day again."

Drexel becomes sincere. "There's so much change going on, I'll do it. I'll stop partying for thirty days while I get back in the swing of training. This is it, eh? I'm really in! Those are boss prices. Who are you getting the bricks from?

Dean almost laughs, *Yeah right, I tell you who my connect is, and you and Shelly will run this all, eh?* "Don't worry about that. Listen to me. Do not repeat what I'm going to tell you, okay?"

Drexel nods solemnly, "I'd never betray you, bro. I'm a vault."

Dean crosses his arms. "I'm going after the hitman who killed Tony. I need you to keep this street stuff safe while I'm working on the big stuff, okay? I'm going after the Polish guy who hired him, too."

Drexel asks, "You need my help, right?"

Dean has him right where he wants him. "No Drexel; you fight the street fights, I go after the heads of the opposition."

Drexel takes offence. "Bro, I killed the leader of the crew in Trail with my bare hands. You know this is what I train for."

Dean tips his head down and to the left, "Grabbing an untrained kid in the dark and slapping a rear naked choke on him from behind isn't the same as what I'm going to do." Drexel opens his mouth, but Dean cuts him off. "Not this time, bro. This guy is mine, he killed my family. If I need your help with this, I'll ask. I need you to sell bricks, sober."

Their hand shake grows into a hug.

Dean opens the black bag and pulls out two white rectangles, about four inches by eight inches and an inch-and-a-half thick. Dean lays out the good news, "These two bricks are ours for sixty thousand on the arm."

Drexel recalls high school precalculus, "We've been paying sixty-seven thousand five hundred, so we just got a thirty-seven hundred and fifty dollar profit on each one, eh? That's over fifteen G more a month, each, if we only move eight bricks a month. I just got us Trail, they move two a month, so we are selling ten kilos a month going. This is crazy. I'm going to shut this party down."

Dean throws both hands up, "I'd need a few drinks before this party ends."

Drexel looks to the sky, "Oh yeah, lean Dean the party machine is in the house."

Dean is all smiles, "Will there be any blow left in there or should we break one of these bricks open?"

Drexel ponders, "We have four ounces in there, or at least we did last night at eleven." They put the two kilos in the cupboard and head in for a few drinks. As they walk across the yard, Drexel attempts to clear up a point. "I didn't grab him from behind, bro. I hit him in the jaw with a quick left jab, then I pulled him into the rear naked choke."

Dean stops walking, "Seriously bro, stop talking about killing that guy." Drexel nods, he'd forgotten. They carry on walking to the house. Dean gets back on track, "Bro, I feel like I haven't drank in weeks. Did the new guys stock the bar with the Grey Goose?"

"Yeah, but we drank it all last night; we're onto rum."

"I'll send those two big kids to the liquor store for more Grey Goose."

Drexel adds, "Great plan. They'll get me two packs of smokes as well."

24

MISSION, 6:00 P.M.

Damon stands in the rain at the top of the power-line service road. Stave Lake is roughly a mile away as the crow flies, Hayward Lake is to the south of Stave, and Alouette Lake is at his back about four kilometres off. The rain falls hard and long in this part of the Lower Mainland. It's still daylight, and with the cloud cover it will be bright for a few more hours; lots of time to get back. Damon steps under a tree with a big overhang that creates a six-foot dry area around the trunk. Patch sits beside him, only slightly more comfortable than out under the downpour. A short-haired boxer, Patch has the shivers already.

Damon lets his thoughts come to a head as he peels his Mandarin orange. *Almost certainly this has become open warfare. It's my fault. I should have taken Suhki out in the house with that couple.* The Coach speaks up quick. *Too many variables in shooting Suhki and the two witnesses. Open warfare is fine, it's part of the job. You shoot faster, and you were born for this; they make it up as they go.*

Damon recalls one of the examples from his past that shows what 'winning' an open war results in. One of his mom's boyfriends, Jack, had gotten into a beef with some other neighbourhood guys in East Vancouver. Jack had said, "Come to my house you pricks; the door will be open." The two pricks did come that night—with baseball bats. They pushed open the slightly ajar front door. Reached for a light, but it didn't come on. Jack had removed the hall lightbulbs. As the second prick entered the house, Jackstarted firing his hunting rifle at the them. Two shots, two kills. Jack got a life sentence for premeditated murder, and did twelve years of his life sentence inside.

At least he got a good education and became an engineer while he was inside. Jack was only twenty-five when he went in, back on the street by thirty-seven. I'm forty.

Damon eats the last bite of his orange, and notices Patch is trembling heavily beside him. He feels under his dog's armpits, running his hands down the dog's body and wiping the water out of his fur like a window squeegee. *Patch is fine, he's warm.* Damon reaches into his pocket, pulls out his water bottle, and drinks half a litre.

His Simple voice is staying positive. *Look, this is it. We're backed in a corner. Just be on alert and start picking targets as they present themselves. Right? You train all the time, you'll get them first.* Damon nods affirmatively, but he's unconvinced. This isn't a time to pretend that it's all okay.

His Simple voice jumps in. *Hey! Sell the Polish guys out? They're on the ropes anyway. Speed it up and we land on our feet as well.* Damon smiles as he answers the Simple voice. *We start selling out, then we don't have clear targets anymore, right? You get it? What do you think will happen once we sell out our employer to a bunch of thieves who are capable of murder? They kill us as soon as they can put a price on our head. No, we pick a side. Take clients' money and push their goals. That's why we work for people we like. Or at least people who have clear issues.*

Damon is done speaking to his Simple self. When he hears his own voice, it's foreign in this rain fall.

"Fuck me." *It is always too much money when a job goes smooth, and not enough when it goes wrong.* This is a truth that he'd forgotten until his own ass landed in this war.

This is it. The Polish know I won't stop, because I'm personally involved. They're in this financially and personally. Now I am too. I have one Indo-Canadian gang of fucking giants that have seen my face close up. Plus whoever else Chloe pays to come after me. This is fucked. The money I've made on this isn't enough for this shit. Damon is shaking his head, looking at the ground.

Damon's Coach gives some useful orders. *Stand tall. Keep your eyes open. Look out as far as you're able. Look for movement, keep doing that. Don't start whining. You're lucky to have as much as you have. You must defend it. As soon as they show themselves, it's total war. We'll go to their houses, it's full attack. Whoever is left alive can put up their hand and you will send them to hell, until either they stop thinking about you or you're dead. Right?*

Damon lifts his head and stares out, taking in the view and scanning the service road for movement. It's only for practice, keeping watch, his Coach is right. 'Keep looking.' Damon answers his Coach with his teeth gritted and squinting. The rain is dripping over his head. *I'll be on full alert. I'll go after intel this week on Suhki's location. I'll keep my hunt going; I can only hope they come to me.*

Damon bends over and pats Patch; his dog intuitively knows they're leaving, and bounces up to kick Damon in the chest with two paws. Damon isn't ready for the ninety-pound dog's kick. He laughs, "You little devil."

He runs after the dog, reaching to grab him with two hands. But Patch tucks his tail and runs fast enough that Damon over reaches and stumbles. Damon is laughing hard as he regains his balance, and Patch comes back at him, he might do it again. Then the big dog turns off and runs ahead, down the steep service road. Damon feels good, laughing, and begins drawing in big breaths of the crisp, fresh air. Refreshed, he happily walks along in the downpour.

APRIL 11TH, VANCOUVER, 9:00 A.M.

Sara is sitting in an unmarked black Ford Explorer police cruiser. It's pouring rain. The car is running, the wipers set on intermittent. She's logged into the cruiser's laptop, reviewing the notes on the Trowel informer.

Peter Nowak, forty years old. Born in Vancouver, only child to two Polish immigrants. He went to school at Sir Charles Tupper. Drinking and driving charge at seventeen years old. Second drinking and driving at twenty-one years old, this time with the addition of a verbal assault charge directed at an officer, which was later dropped. Drunk and disorderly at the fireworks in English Bay at twenty-five years old. His record is littered with drunk charges. *Peter isn't a criminal. Just a guy who can't handle his booze.*

Then a few months ago, one of Sara's members caught him with a couple grams of coke while drunk driving. From Officer Ponzi's notes, Sara reads, "Peter had recently started a job with a delivery company driving a five-ton cube truck. When I pulled him over, he blew over the limit on the breathalyzer in the work van. I searched his pockets before putting him in the back of my duty car. Peter sobbed, 'I'll do anything, please, Officer, please, I can't lose this job, my girlfriend is having a baby.' I asked him what he could possibly do to stop me from proceeding with the drunk-driving charge and the controlled-substance charge.

"Peter mentioned the Fukadero case and the extortion gang that had beaten Tony Fukadero in his office. 'I know the Polish community, I'll keep you informed about anything they plan on doing to the Fukaderos. We all get together, I hear things. I knew they were going to the office that day of the beating, I could have told you guys that.' I called our on-duty supervisor and got approval to give Peter a pass."

Sara reads on and concludes that this informant hasn't given them anything useful yet. Officer Ponzi asked him about the Fukadero hit, but Peter just said, "I'll ask around," and came back with nothing. *I'm going to see if I can straighten him out and get him working.*

Sara notices Peter coming towards her cruiser as the windshield wipers clear the rain away. She performs a visual judgment of him as he walks. *Shaggy brown hair under a hat, pale white skin. Old black Adidas tracksuit, faded and worn out material. Worn out sneakers. This guy is a mess. He probably eats once a day, maybe twice. Drinks at work, for sure.*

Peter opens the passenger door and narrows his eyes, expecting to see Officer Ponzi. "Who are you? I don't have time for this, I'm busy with my job. Tell Ponzi to call when he wants to see me." Sara starts to speak, but Peter slams the door with a smirk, knowing he is cutting her off.

Sara's blood boils; she flings her car door and slams it as she runs over to Peter. He hears the driver door slam and turns to see what the female officer is doing. Sara is already grabbing his left wrist with her right hand. She yanks his arm straight to the ground like a whip. Sara knows this will pull his weak shoulder socket, and give his scrawny elbow a shock as well. She lets the wrist go; Peter opens his mouth to start bitching, but Sara is an inch in front of his face. "Listen to me, you make one more rude comment or action and I'll throw you on the ground and cuff you. You will be charged with drinking and driving and possession of the drugs we found. I'll also add resisting arrest." The dense rain creates a private environment in the middle of the parking lot. Sara is in a full black uniform, with a utility belt. Peter looks her up and down, and Sara observes his demeanour change.

"Sorry Officer, I've had a long week. My head is foggy. Let's sit in your car and talk? We're getting soaked out here."

Sara has a cream-cheese bagel from Tim Hortons sitting between them. As they get in, she notices Peter spot it, so she offers it as a peace offering. "Peter, I have an extra bagel here. It was for Officer Ponzi, but he has a family emergency and can't be here with us. Please take the bagel, I can't eat two."

Peter gleams, he's won a small lottery; he grabs the bagel, and takes a big bite. Sara decides Peter lives moment to moment, and has no plan to deal fairly with the RCMP.

Sara asks, "Peter, what have you heard about the Fukadero hit?"

Peter pauses, chewing; his head turns toward the passenger window to hide his reaction. He swallows the bite in his mouth and sits staring out the window.

"Peter, you've produced nothing for us to solve any crimes; we'll have to charge you soon for your offences." She's speaking kindly. "Peter, do you understand that's how it works? If you can't come through on your end, we have to proceed with the charges that Officer Ponzi wrote up that night in your work truck. It's not personal, it's our job. You suggested helping us out, remember?"

Peter's head swivels back to Sara with tears in his eyes. "How long until you guys charge me? I'll lose this job. We just had our baby last week."

Sara shows a hint of compassion, "I decide after this meeting if any information you have is of use. If not, then we proceed with your charges. If you tell us useful information, then we drop the charges."

Peter folds the wrapper around the half-eaten bagel and puts it in his jacket pocket. He places both hands on his thighs, and stares out the front window. "Okay, I was at a family barbecue last Sunday." Sara's heart races; she knows he was there, they have his cell phone onsite and a photo of him from Air 1. "Everyone was there to have a good day. Lots of the people there have been ripped off by that Fukadero guy, so they're happy about his death. I've heard that some of the badass guys there have something to do with it."

The windshield wipers clear the window at the end of his sentence.

"You tell me the names of the guys that are involved?"

"No, I don't speak Polish, everybody talks in Polish about family stuff. They don't really talk to me, they only talk about work. They never party. They treat me like a lowlife."

Sara persists, "What do they look like?"

"They hired this badass guy, he was there. I don't know his name, I only saw him from far away. He dresses like the rest of them, work clothes. I'll go to the Polish community centre and all the events, please trust me, I need my job. I'll get his name, he's a killer for sure. I'll get his address by the end of the week, okay?"

Sara knows this is as good as she will get from this guy. But she keeps the heat simmering. "Okay, Peter, if you get his address by the end of the week, I'll help you. If you can't, Officer Ponzi will submit your charges. Call Officer Ponzi when you have something, he'll contact me. Thank you for taking time to see us today, and congratulations on the new baby."

Peter quickly rubs his face with both hands, then he solicits. "Thanks for the bagel, I'm on it. When I give you this guy's address, I'm off the hook, right?"

"You deliver us a murderer, your record is clean, for sure. We'll help you in other ways, as well. We help those who help us keep the streets safe."

Peter nods and slinks out of the car. The wipers clear the window, and Sara watches Peter take out the bagel and take a huge bite as he walks away, shaking his head.

LANGLEY, 9:00 A.M.

Naomi knocks on the garage door as she opens it. "Damon, you've been in here all morning, are you all right?"

Damon is at his workbench cleaning his twelve-gauge Mossberg 590. He swivels the chair, "Yeah hun, just thinking about the best way to spend this week. Lots of balls in the air again."

Naomi frowns, "Are we okay?"

Damon's heart sinks, knowing he's put his family in danger again, and can't tell her.

"Oh, hun, this is normal. We keep our heads up, and we'll be ok."

Naomi stomps her foot, "What does that mean? Are we in danger? What's going on?"

Damon stands and locks eyes with her from across the room. He smiles.

"Listen hun, the world is full of dangerous people. We're part of the world. Anyone comes by here and they're done, I'll go deal with whoever they send to talk to me. I don't hide. I don't make deals with bullies. I'm just playing along the way they choose to play the game."

Naomi shakes her head. "You're crazy. Not everyone is thinking about having to kill or be killed. You know that, right? You should be doing different things with your efforts. I don't know what you're doing half the time, but I hear rumours from people. How come other people know you and your family better than me?"

Damon laughs and waves 'them' off, "All rumours, hun. The people who talk about us are just gossiping. You can't think for a second that if I was killing someone I'd leave a witness or brag about it. So all we have is a bunch of gossip."

Naomi's hairs on her neck stand up, "If we're in danger, you tell me, and I'll leave with our kid until it's over." Damon has considered telling his family to go away for a while. But it's no use, these problems never go away. You have to make them go away. Damon intends to make them go away very soon.

"Naomi, we're fine here. Just keep your eyes open for any strange cars around. Tell me what and when you see, I'll sort it out."

Naomi takes a moment to think, "Great family environment you've made." She shuts the door quietly, as she leaves.

LANGLEY, 10:30 A.M.

Damon hears the familiar knock pattern on his garage door, he hits the open button on the keychain. It's his dad, Leo. Leo is sixty-one years old, with a bald head and the nice tan of someone who's been out boating all summer. Leo always hit the weights hard when he was younger. Now that he's older, he does more cardio, but is still in great shape. Leo usually has a new girlfriend with him; his girlfriends' ages haven't changed since Damon was a kid. Twenty-four to thirty-four seems to be the range of girls his dad will date.

Leo comes in from the rain and smiles when he sees his son sitting at the workbench next to the twelve-gauge. He raises his eyebrows, and he gestures with one fingertip to the pump shotgun. "Whoa, you going bear hunting?"

Damon doesn't laugh. "If one sniffs around here, I'm ready to shoot it."

Leo waves the answer off; his face goes sour as he responds. "Damon, nobody will be coming here."

Damon raises his eyebrows, "How can you say that? You don't know how work has been lately."

Leo flicks his hand toward the street. "You wanna go for a quick walk around the block and chat? I've got a date with me so I can't stay long."

Damon nods, then he places the twelve-gauge in a tin safe by the garage door and locks it. He pulls on his black raincoat and hands his dad a spare green raincoat; the two walk the driveway. Leo waves to his blonde date. When she grabs the door handle to jump out, he gives the one minute sign with his finger, and she smiles and nods happily. Leo tries to share his joy with his son, "Great house you've had built. Amazing, eh? Who would have guessed that the kid who got kicked out of two school districts would be having a house built? I tell everyone about your house. You should throw a party and have everybody come over."

Damon puts his hands in his pocket and rolls his eyes. "No."

Leo rubs his clenched fist. "It's your house, do what you want. Remember all the parties I've thrown over the years. Nobody ever came to my house looking for me, more than once. Let them come."

Damon won't argue with his dad. It's been a headline in the news since Damon was a kid: 'Notorious hitman working with high-level gangster brought in for questioning on...' The police have been knocking on their door at least once a year for as long as Damon can remember. Damon and Leo once counted eight police visits to the house for different murder investigations. Other times the police called Leo to come to the station for questioning.

Damon explains, "I try and live differently. I don't want partying around my family. Everybody is crazy."

Leo smiles and shoves Damon's shoulder, making him stumble. "You're a good dad, but you gotta relax. Do you ever see me walking around all worried?"

Damon kicks a pebble off the curb. "No I don't, but you're always coming from a party or going to one with a hot chick."

"Exactly; relaxing. What do you do to relax nowadays?"

Damon goes through his list. "The range for pistol practice, rifle practice. Hiking, a little weight training. Trips with my family."

Leo nods, "Sounds like a good life. So why are you so tense? You have a great house as well. You must be making tons of money, right?"

Damon throws his head back. "That's just it, I'm working my ass off, but I can't get ahead. I might have to sell the house if I don't finish the job I'm doing."

Leo taps Damon stomach with the back of his hand. "Why are you whining so much? Who do you think is going to save you from your problems? You made the problems, right? You took some job, it's harder than you thought, and now you wish you hadn't taken it, right?"

Damon surveys ahead and counts only local cars as they turn the corner. His dad notices him check the street. "Is it that bad? Are people really scoping your house?"

"Yeah, I got made on camera and I was talking to them all. My story was picked apart, I barely made it out before a shootout started."

Leo cringes. "You have any money at all for help with the job?"

"You're hilarious, Dad. I have to hire you? Really?"

Leo smiles. "You know I'll help you, but if it's a paying job, I'll need half."

Damon loses his composure and does a chop in the air with his hand. "Half eh? I got paid the house. So you think I'll give you half of my house to help me?"

Leo stops walking and stops Damon with gentle hand on his bicep. "You see Damon, you chose this. You've been paid. You don't want to pay a partner. I'd finish the job and forget all the 'maybe' stuff. Get a list of guys and their addresses and go take care of them. I know it's time-consuming and expensive but unless you want to sell your new house, you better get to work." Damon has already come to terms with this. He nods politely. When Leo finishes they turn and walk.

Leo asks about his grandkid and Damon's wife. After Damon talks about family stuff, he asks Leo about his schedule. Leo lights up, he's been waiting for the question. "Man, you would not believe it, I met these two girls at a party, they travel around doing this duo act in real fancy strip clubs. They knew me from stories that other girls have told them. They took me to their hotel, and we had this crazy three-way till nine a.m.; the room had a jacuzzi tub. They were twenty-five years old, and they treated me so good, I never paid for anything the whole night."

Damon has tuned him out and is simply nodding along. They come around the last corner and Damon scans the street, "So you've been doing the same thing you always do?"

Leo claps his hands, "Yep, you know me. I'll never change. Why would I?"

Damon shakes his head, "I don't know, only you pull that off. People pay those girls to hang out. But those girls pay you to hang out."

Damon looks into his dads eyes. "Do you have a deal with the devil?"

Leo grabs him in a hug. "No son, just having fun. I gotta go. Do you want to meet Kristen? She's so hot." Leo hands Damon the borrowed raincoat.

Damon marches up the driveway, his eyes forward, "No, you have fun. I'm going to clean my shotgun."

Leo waves and before he gets in his F-350, yells to Damon, "Relax, it always works out. You'll know what to do. Love you."

Leo starts his huge pearl-white truck and drives off . Damon stands vacantly staring out his double garage doors, as the rain comes down in buckets.

25

Damon is in his garage, having finished his workout routine. Today he followed a plyometrics DVD, also known as jump training. *I wonder how I would do in one of those boot camp classes? I've been doing these workout DVDs for two years. It's getting boring.* Damon's Coach reminds him of the situation. *You have one South-Asian gang after you. Who knows who else. How could you watch your house and still train if you were the one keeping a schedule at a gym? You work out at home for two good reasons. No schedule to be had by some unknown murderer, and you get to be right beside your gun, waiting for the next great murderer. It's win/win for you here.* The reminder refreshes Damon.

Naomi opens the garage door, "Good morning hun, I heard your workout end. Are you going to shower and leave?"

Damon is drinking a cup of room temperature water; he stops to answer her. "I'm actually going to be around the house today, what's up?"

Naomi beams, "There's a local fair with kids rides and carnival games after Benji gets out of school. Can you join us?"

I can't go to the three p.m. for Suhki, I lost my watch post, and they're aware of me around there for sure. I should hang out around here today and keep an eye out. Damon notices Naomi looking for eye contact.

"I'm so glad you told me, I definitely want to hang out today."

"Should I put eggs on while you shower?"

Damon cheers up a notch. "Perfect, I'll come in and have a protein shake as well."

SOUTH SURREY, 10:30 A.M.

Dean is in the kitchen of the Grim Sinners' house. They have not stepped back outside since Drexel and him spoke in the barn last night. He watches the new guys clean. *These two guys had it so easy before they came here. Up in Trail, they were the big shots. They used to play on a football team. They're too healthy for regular party guys; trim waistline, hair is tidy. Now they work for us, they'll be the heads of the Grim Sinners in their home town, Trail. We need to get them on the party right away.*

Dean is smiling, with a red plastic cup in his hand, "Guys, did you think we would bring in a maid to clean all the cups and spilled drinks? Cool, free drinks and blow, and we'll clean up for you too. That would be so great, eh?"

The two guys, Steve and Dave, are smiling and shaking their heads. Dave plays along, "No, we have no problem cleaning after a party. You guys have been so good to us. This party has been awesome. After we clean the kitchen we should go to bed for a few hours before we hit the road."

Dean smiles ear-to-ear, "Who said the party is over?" Dave looks at Dean to see if he is kidding, but Steve knows it wasn't a joke. Rocket told him that new guys are the last to leave a party. Dean raises an eyebrow, "You two have a change of clothes?" Steve is holding the black garbage bag as Dave empties cups and bottles and throws them into it. Steve answers, "Yeah, we came down for two days. This is day two, and we haven't slept yet, so our clothes are still in the bag."

Dean explains the situation, "With you guys being the Grim Sinners new faces in your town, it's important that you really know our main headquarters. Then when you two bring your guys down, you show them around this place."

Dave nods, "Totally bro, what job should we start after we clean this mess in the house?"

Dean yells, "Rocket, get Drexel in here and bring us a plate. Break open another O.Z."

Rocket pops his head into the room. "For sure bro."

Dean observes Dave and Steve.

Last night I thought I'd have a couple drinks, now I'm training the new guys after we've been up all night. I was born for this. Will they make it through the day or will they tap out? If either one quits, he's done. I'll forever ride him like a rented pony. Dean pours another drink. "Do either of you know where the mop is?"

Dave and Steve say, "No" at the same time. Dean notices they are still optimistic.

"Have either of you seen the toilet cleaning supplies?"

The two guys freeze for a second. Dean sees them resist the natural reaction of disgust. Again they answer in unison, "No."

Drexel walks in with Rocket right behind him; Dave and Steve both stiffen as they become aware they're on centre stage. Drexel demands,

"Rocket, grind some fat lines, these guys are gonna need them."

Rocket rubs his hands in front of his face.

"Oh yeah bro, training day has begun."

Rocket is 165 pounds, but he's known for fighting anyone who bugs him. He's always with his bros from the Grim Sinners, and his confidence is higher than his fighting abilities. Everyone knows it, even Rocket. Rocket defends himself by saying, "I'm with a crew so I can throw my weight around." The guys always agree.

Dean explains, "Dave and Steve, all the chores you will do today have been done by all of us in the past, okay? You'll help your guys do chores when they come down. We all take our turn." Dave and Steve relax a bit. Dean continues. "We'll keep going until we run out of things the three of us think of for you guys to do. You can leave at any time, you understand? You grab your stuff and go and never come back, whenever you feel like quitting." Rocket laughs and focuses on crunching the little chunk of coke with his credit card.

Dave and Steve look at each other, Steve affirms. "We're not going anywhere, bro, we're Grim Sinners, we're here until we're dead."

Drexel hollers, "Woo hoo! Good man."

Dean tips his chin to Drexel, "Does the riding lawn-mower have fuel?"

Drexel makes known, a small part of Dave and Steves new schedule, "Enough to start. One of these new guys will go buy some gas. That chore will be the break."

Dean asks, "Does the pressure-washer still work?"

Drexel looks up and left, "We'll see, when they try and start the dammed thing."

SURREY, 1:05 P.M.

Chloe asks Suhki to close the door as he walks in. Suhki notices the blinds are shut behind her desk. She's peering at him with ice in her eyes.

"What's up Chloe? You look pissed about something."

Chloe is unblinking. "Do you know a hitman named Damon?"

Suhki stops smiling. "I've heard he works for cartels and the government. I hear he appears outta nowhere."

Chloe is content that Suhki doesn't actually know Damon, only rumours. *Thank god Dean has a lead on Damon.*

"You walked him in here yesterday."

Suhki grasps the arms of the chair and leans forward with a whisper-yell.

"That fucking service guy? He works for you?"

Chloe has not thought about pretending to have Damon as back-up; she's amused at how easy it could be to claim that a notorious hitman works for you.

"No Suhki, he's been snooping around for months. I think he killed Tony."

Suhki is wearing a loose long-sleeved white shirt and dark designer joggers; he sits back. "When did this come out?"

Chloe has no intention of telling anyone that she yelled Tony's schedule right in front of Damon the day before he was killed, and then he was executed at that exact time.

"We have a lot of people working on finding Tony's killer. I can't get into it."

Chloe notices how Suhki has become another man; full of rage and violence. Suhki asks, "Where do I find this little piece of shit?"

Chloe has always held a soft spot for the kind side of him, but now she's a little turned on by his alpha side. Chloe tells Suhki, "You have two critical jobs on the go; the Polish and the P and A Trucking collection. Millions are riding on your efforts. We have other guys working on Damon. You can't stop working to get the Polish to drop the case, and we're all depending on you getting the truck drivers to pay back the load they stole. You don't have time to chase a hitman."

Suhki proclaims, "When I finish with the Polaks and the trucker thieves, and your other guys haven't finished this Damon off, I get to do it. I'll strangle him with my bare hands, right where I find him."

Chloe takes a long breathe. "I have something at my house for you tonight. Be there at six."

"I can't come over tonight, it's my wife's birthday, all the family is going to a rented restaurant at eight o'clock for dinner. I'm driving my guys. Zarita is taking a limo to the restaurant."

Chloe adds more bait. "Bring your guys. This is work-related."

Suhki's curiosity has him. "Okay, I'll be there at six with Jag and Devon."

LANGLEY, 3:30 P.M.

It's a sunny day, with blue skies and big fluffy white clouds high in the sky. The fair is set up on the Langley Events Centre fields. Benji's riding a small carousel, and Naomi is trying to get a perfect picture every time Benji comes by on the giant white rabbit. Damon waves his arms to get Benji to look, but the boy is totally enthralled with the white rabbit ride. After capturing serious-faced pictures by the fifth rotation of the carousel, both parents fall apart laughing.

Damon asks. "Should I go get some cotton candy?"

Naomi pokes Damon's belly. "I know that you want it, don't pretend it's for us."

Damon waves her off and smiles. She knows he can only handle a few bites of the fluffy sugar. It's definitely for Benji.

Damon is standing in a short line when he notices a familiar face, the designated driver. The kid sees him as well. Damon puts out his hand to the twenty-year-old, and he accepts and laughs while shaking his head. "Oh man, you embarrassed Chase so bad at the grocery store, we still bug him."

As the kid finishes talking an adult with him turns around with a smile.

"How did you embarrass that kid? He's usually embarrassing himself."

Damon sees right away this woman is all business. He's quick to judge and decides she's either active military or a cop. The kid announces. "Aunt Sara, this is the guy who talked Chase into shutting up in front of a grocery store." Sara reaches out to shake Damon's hand, Damon accepts.

Damon and Sara lock eyes. She tries to read him. *Is he a cop? A martial arts instructor? Maybe he's in the military?* Damon sees her trying to get a read on him, so he gives her something. "The kids were just hanging out. The one boy, Chase? He was just testing, nothing serious. Your nephew was their designated driver that night, he told me."

Sara smiles. "Are you here with your family?"

Damon turns and points to his wife, who's meeting little Benji at the exit of the carousel. Sara takes a double take;

something about the woman makes her senses tingle. Sara profiles Naomi quickly. *Early thirties, eats well, clean, tidy clothes. The child is in clean, tidy clothes. Mom and son's hair is healthy. How could I know her?* Sara's eyes follow the ground back; as she gets back to Damon, she notices his shoes are black with bright orange trim and laces. Nikes. Her mind flashes a matching pair of shoes from last week. *The Trowel barbecue.* Sara's heart speeds up, but her logical mind tells her there's little chance of this being the guy under the gazebo.

Sara views his pants. *Black tradesman jeans.* Then up to his wedding ring; she almost grabs his hand when she sees the yellow gold band. Her mind races. *Is this the guy who was talking to Yakub? No, can't be.* Sara's eyes find Damon's; he's staring back with a look she can't place. She's attaching different motives to his facial gestures.

Before suspecting that he was a Trowel member, he gave the impression of being a good citizen. Now he appears to be Polish mafia.

"So Sara, what do you work out so hard for?"

Damon is looking back and forth between her and her nephew. The nephew smiles and turns to Sara.

"See Auntie, it's obvious you're a fighter."

Sara smiles at her nephew but doesn't answer. So Damon digs a little more.

"Woa, an MMA fighter? For hobby?"

" RCMP officer, general duty, so I stay fit."

Damon's heart warms; he knew it right when he saw her. Civilians train hard for marathons, pedal biking, maybe bodybuilding. But this woman is in top physical condition; Damon notices her neck and back attach to her shoulders, as well as her thick legs. Damon shrinks a bit, knowing how easy a woman this strong can 'man handle' him.

"I see you take your training seriously. There are woman similar to you at the Jiu-Jitsu gym I train at once in a while; they beat me in every level. From standing, they have solid throws, but on the ground they're stronger and faster. What type of martial art do you focus on?"

Sara stares into Damon's eyes.

This guy is getting a lot of info on me, my turn.

Sara clasps her hands in front of her belt. "I dabble in Judo."

Sara's nephew shakes his head. "Dabble is how you describe a black belt?"

Sara smiles at her nephew. "So what's the name of your gym, Damon?"

Damon stands a little taller. "Repetition. Lots of pro martial artists there, I just do it for some exercise."

She pries further. "What do you do for work?"

As she finishes the sentence, Naomi walks over. "Hi, what's going on? The line is gone. You all come to the consensus that nobody wants cotton candy?"

Sara freezes as Naomi speaks. *The red hair, this is definitely the woman and child from the Trowel barbecue.* Sara notices the candy concession has no line.

Damon introduces his wife to Sara. "I'm an air-conditioning mechanic. It's been nice talking to you both, let's get this cotton-candy-line moving." Damon makes a hand gesture for them to turn and get the candy, Sara pinches her nephew's shirt sleeve and steers him away.

After Damon purchases his family's cotton candy, he explains to his wife how the kid remembered him from the night Damon had gone to get his in-laws from the Vancouver airport. Damon gets a couple butterflies as he remembers that the day he spoke to those kids at the grocery store was only hours after he had shot the Fuk.

What a small world, a cop's nephew is the third person I spoke to after pulling the trigger on the Fuk.

Naomi grabs Damons sleeve and gives it a tug. "Earth to Damon."

Damon snaps out of the thought. "Let's get Benji on a few more rides, then I've got to go work on something tonight."

Naomi holds Benji by the back of his shoulders. "Come on Benji. Let's go have some fun." Naomi glances at Damon with a forced smile.

SURREY, 5:30 P.M.

The sun is still putting off heat. Damon parks about a kilometre down the road; there's a commercial truck-park on this Surrey farmland road, and the white Safari van is parked there. *Only people I've seen since I parked have been brown. They're in every house; all the workers in every yard appear fresh off the jet from India. This neighbourhood is blueberry fields and commercial truck-parks.*

The houses are either sixty years old or massive thousand-square-foot multi-family castles. There it is, Suhki's house. Blueberry fields cover the acreage. You never know if a family worker is sitting in one of the rows of blueberries watching.

Damon tries to blend in with a brisk walk speed. He absorbs the area for his next visit, he notices movement in the yard.

A limo, eh? These people have something big to celebrate. Or is it Suhki and his crew, just bar hopping? Damon has his hat on low, big sunglasses, and an old black jean jacket. From far away, he is another trucker.

He examines the street and can't help but remember what he had been told at a sporting goods store that sold firearms. "Oh man, this older East-Indian guy came in the day after the long-gun registry was cancelled and asked, 'How many SKSs do you have in stock?' So I told him we have two pallets. The guy never batted an eye, he just says, 'I'll take them, both pallets.' We loaded them right into a five-ton cube truck out back for him." Damon has always thought that these farms in the Lower Mainland are strongholds.

What can you do against twenty SKSs firing 7.62 rounds? How about if they shoot you on their property? They would bury me under a blueberry bush. It's all family on these farms. Damon surveys the area to make sure they aren't surrounding him. *This is crazy, I can't stake this place out. So many workers and kids that know all the local traffic.*

Damon walks to the end of the long two-lane country road and turns around. As he passes by Suhki's house again, he notices that five ladies in stunning, long, bright-coloured dresses are running to get into the limo.

Must be late for dinner?

He decides that since he has the Safari van out and the .45 autoloader with him, he better go check another place for Suhki. At least the purple Hellcat stands out in a parking lot. The bright paint compliments finding Suhki.

Damon watches the last lady get into the white limo in her vibrant red sari. He notices an old pick-up truck with no licence plates, workers piling in with yard tools in hand. The truck has five guys in the back and two in the cab. Damon watches it back out of a field and turn around on the concrete driveway near the limo.

Odd that a work truck near the end of the day can't wait for a limo to leave. Maybe the guys' wives are leaving and it's a goodbye?

Damon takes the first long breathe, as the truck crawls to the end of the driveway and sits there. The driver and all the passengers lock onto Damon. The truck's broken muffler is all Damon hears. *Rar Rar Rar Rar*. Then *Rrrrrrrrr* as the driver hits the gas. The truck turns onto the public street and pulls over in front of Damon.

The crew are in dusty work clothes, and their thick black hair is thoroughly caked in dust as well. Each guy has a pick or metal rake; three leap out of the back and go to the bottom of the six-foot-deep ditch and two stay up top. The driver and the passenger get out and head to the other side of the road and point into the ditch. Damon's blood freezes. All the workers have their eyes covertly on him.

Damon is satisfied with the .45 ACP across his chest under the jean jacket. Yet Damon feels overwrought. With seven guys all over the place they could rush him. Damon heads to the middle of the street the way anyone would do to avoid a work site. The two guys on the other side of the road look fixedly at Damon.

Damon takes a long breath in and determines that if they stop or rush him, he'll use evasive techniques and draw the .45 ACP and fire. He's content with the idea of shooting this group. *These are Suhki's closest people. They benefit from his bullying and theft. They will die today, if they try and stop me.*

Damon stares at the two workers who are beside him, and gives them a big smile and wave. The two dusty farmers shrink as Damon directs his full focus on them, and they wave back weakly. Damon heads to his Safari van.

As he drives away the seven farmers, slowly working, hold their eyes on the white Safari van. Damon silently curses as he passes their prying eyes.

26

Chloe is in her immaculate and modern kitchen when she hears the doorbell chime. She checks the screen in the corner of the room and sees Suhki, with two guys, at her red front door. Chloe hasn't changed out of her work clothes. Today, she wears a black pantsuit with gold pin-stripes, and a classy eighteen-carat gold chain with matching earrings. She runs barefoot to the front door to let the guys in. She knows they can't stay long.

Suhki walks behind Chloe, and Jag and Devon follow him. Devon, who hasn't been in the kitchen, exclaims. "Wow, you really went all out in this property eh? This kitchen is exquisite. Who did the finishing work?"

Chloe and Suhki smile. "The first contractors we hired did this kitchen." Devon bites his lip and nods; he just realized it's the Polish crew's work. Chloe asks if they want a beer. She has a fresh pizza on the counter ready for them.

Suhki shrugs, "We might as well have a drink, we're going out later." Chloe gives all three men Budweiser bottles. They politely decline the pizza.

339

Chloe has the massive white-granite counter to separate her from the guys. She cuts to the point. "Suhki, I've taken over a small route that Tony had been running for years. I know your guys on the street must be low or out of coke. I can loan you one kilo of high test for fifty thousand dollars on a pay-later plan. I might be able to get you one every week. Does that help?"

Suhki jumps at the chance to have a product in hand for no money up front; since the truckers took the ten kilos he bought, money and bricks of coke have been scarce. "When can I get it?"

Chloe opens a drawer, pulls out the coke brick, and puts it on the counter. She slides it over to him.

Suhki stares at the brick. "Jag, you and Devon take this and stash it, I'm going to stay here and talk to Chloe about the house her company is building for me, come pick me up after." Suhki throws Jag the keys to the Hellcat.

Jag catches the keys out of the air. "You're going to go over house plans the night of my sister's birthday dinner?"

Chloe's stomach sinks. *No, no, Suhki is making me out to be his side piece of ass. I never wanted his family to know about us.* She interrupts. "I agree with Jag, Suhki. It's been a long day. Let's work during the day so we can call the trades." Jag is rigid and looks at Suhki, who's opening the fridge to grab another beer.

Suhki turns with his fresh beer and cracks it. "Jag, I just want you to go stash the brick, and call the guy to grab it tonight. I'm going to give Chloe some instructions she will work on in the morning. I don't want to hang out in the office too much."

Jag frowns as he sends a text. "Yeah, sure Suhki. We'll be back in less than an hour."

When they leave, Chloe stays on the opposite side of the centre counter. Suhki stretches his hands high. "Why don't you come around this side?"

Chloe doesn't smile, "Jag is your wife's brother, and you make him leave us alone on her birthday? Have you lost your mind? Your family will kill me."

Suhki's loins are stirring. " I'm crazy about you, Chloe."

She blushes and smiles. *Is it too soon to replace Tony? This will never happen in the condition I'm in. Shut him down easy.* "Suhki, you have a wife. You work with your family. You can't get a divorce."

Suhki places both hands flat on the counter. "Then we must carry on this affair in secret."

"I'm going to display your house design on the TV in the kitchen. We're going to sit at opposite ends of the table and go over designs until your brother-in-law gets back."

Suhki smiles. "That sounds nice, I'll play along."

Chloe pulls out her laptop and syncs with the big screen in the kitchen. Suhki asks, "How about a glass of wine?"

Chloe types on her laptop; she won't return eye contact, but she's smiling. "No, thank you, I'm not drinking alcohol." Chloe loads the digital architectural drawing of the house that Suhki has the contract on. She focuses on the TV.

Suhki pulls a chair next to her. "Is it possible to change the size of the front doorframe still? Or have materials been ordered?"

Chloe knows this could be the start of an avalanche of requests that would increase engineer budget and build costs, so she gives her carbon-copy answer. "The house you've purchased is already budgeted for this architectural design; you can add interior changes, but then you'll see the cost rise or fall based on your choices. The price we agreed on for your house is the base price for our executive build. My house is at the highest level of upgrade, and it's an extra $700,000 on top of the base price."

Suhki watches her talk; he knows all of this. His family has built many houses. The Fukadero development used high-end build supplies and classic Italian finishing. Suhki gently rests his hand on Chloe's back. "I'm cool with all the materials, I don't think I'll change anything." Chloe doesn't pull away, so Suhki rubs his fingers in a small clockwise circle on her upper back.

Chloe warms to his touch, "Suhki, if we go upstairs, will you be gentle with me?"

Suhki is feeling the two beers he drank. "I've been thinking about pulling your panties off, opening your legs, and slowly rubbing your lips. After you're real wet, I'll be gentle and quick."

Chloe stands, "Let's go upstairs."

Suhki scoops her up, and they both laugh. They head out of the kitchen and get to the first step of the spiral staircase when the doorbell rings.

Chloe jumps out of Suhki's arms and clutches onto him for safety. "I'm not expecting anyone, and your guys have only been gone for a few minutes. I'm going to check the camera in the kitchen." She runs off on her tip toes, not making a sound, toward the kitchen.

Suhki stands on the bottom step of the spiral staircase, fuming that his little sex holiday got canceled. Suhki yells toward the kitchen. "I'll get the door."

Chloe balls her fists. "No! Suhki, we don't know who is out there." But he is already pulling the big red door open.

Suhki knows right away he's been set up.

"Zarita, I'm glad you're here. Come in."

Suhki's wife is standing in the doorway in the bright red dress she bought specifically for her birthday dinner. She has been to the spa to have her body waxed and her hair done. Suhki is doubly shocked, first by her sudden appearance at Chloe's house and with Zarita fuming in the doorway.

Chloe is half-hidden behind the door; when she sees Zarita in the doorway she knows this woman is no fool. She has come here at this time on purpose.

Chloe turns on the charm. "Zarita, it's a pleasure to finally meet you. Suhki said it's your birthday today. Happy birthday! Please come in and see what we're working on." Chloe walks toward the door while she's talking.

Zarita smiles in the pleasant, polite way a princess might if she was in the company of a lord she can't stand, but whose support her family needs.

"Chloe Fukadero, such a pleasure. I heard about the tragic loss of your husband. I'm so sorry for your troubles. My husband tells me he has become the champion for some important business that's up in the air. I hope my husband is doing a good job for you."

Chloe is shaken by this woman's composure, and wonders how much Zarita knows already. She extends her hand, but Zarita steps in and hugs her instead. Chloe hugs back as she and Suhki make guilty eye contact. Chloe lets go first, and begins her case. "I know it's your birthday, I see you have a limo waiting, but please come see what we're working on."

Zarita batts her eye lashes while evaluating the foyer. Chloe sees the body language and turns to walk into the kitchen; Zarita accompanies her, and Suhki shuts the door and follows.

Zarita sees the TV on and the architectural drawing of her house on the screen. She evaluates the blue designer kitchen with the white trim.

Four beers drank, one for Jag and one for Devon and two for Suhki, and an untouched pizza. The house is quiet; this girl has no family. How is she be handling all this with no mother or father, no uncles, no aunties? She must be so desperate. Giving away houses for favours? Only a desperate person would do this. Alone with my men doing business over beer. She would be treated very poorly back in India.

Chloe and Suhki stand stock-still. They watch Zarita; Chloe knows she's not admiring the kitchen. "Zarita, I need to let tell you something. I've been leaning on your husband for my business; I hope the house is good remuneration for you. Suhki has been a gentleman. Now that you're here, I want to be honest with Suhki.

I'm pregnant.

Tony and I were waiting until we got through the first trimester to tell everyone. You are the first two people that I've told; this has been such a scary time."

Chloe breaks into tears; she finishes her sentence balling.

"Suhki has been so kind to my family, thank you for allowing him to be in this mess. I'll pay you more, just don't leave me."

Zarita runs forward and grabs Chloe in a firm hug. "We are here for you, you are not alone. Calm down, sh sh sh, we will all get through this."

APRIL 13TH, LANGLEY, 9:00 A.M.

Damon sits on his living room couch, the horizontal blinds rolled open enough that he can see the street, but not enough for a clear view in. The sun is beaming; a strong wind towards the West has cleared all the morning cloud away. Damon is in black jogging pants, with no shirt and no socks. He's been out of bed for twenty minutes, and has his first coffee in his hand.

Damon spent the evening between the restaurants and bars that the big shots in Surrey frequent. He could not walk into each bar; Suhki knows his face. Damon was just searching for the purple Hellcat, then ambush Suhki on the spot. He had his suppressed .45 caliber with him, the custom holster on his chest, and a couple of decent costumes to blend into a crowd. No purple Charger last night. Damon had kept a sharp eye out for the limo he had seen at Suhki's house as well. Nothing.

The 9:00 a.m. news begins, so Damon settles in for the night's gossip that the press has covered. A story about a car accident or knife fight at a bar is all the news usually reports at this time of the morning. His heart skips a beat as he sees a building on fire in the clip of upcoming stories. *It's my mind playing tricks on me, I'm tired from getting in at three a.m.* The news has an early morning helicopter-view of a small commercial building fire.

The announcer explains what's on the screen, and the backstory they've been fed by some news reporter. "This warehouse is owned by the same people who were charged in an extortion sting last year. The main victim and witness was killed in a targeted shooting on his lawn two weeks ago. There is speculation of a tit-for-tat gang war underway."

Damon lifts his coffee to his mouth and takes a big sip, hoping to shake off the sleep in his mind. His Simple voice comes into the quiet opening. *So, still happy about the mercy the other day? You going to give the money back and quit? Ha, haha.* Damon sits still and continues watching until the screen changes to a lady who's trying to save a bird's nest that's in a tree near a construction site; he hits mute.

Damon has only drank a third of his coffee, but he knows what this fire at the Polish warehouse means: open warfare. It's his fault; getting made at the Fukadero show house sent Suhki and whoever else over the edge. Every rookie gangster on their side will beg for a chance to get revenge. The fire shows the basic level of their strategy. Damon's hand shakes as he lifts his coffee to his mouth.

Damn fools, so weak. They burned the spot they should have found their targets at. So it's amateur hour. The police will be on full fucking alert. While some rookie is going around throwing a tantrum and lighting fires, the police know this is a great chance to catch somebody in action.

Damon stares at the TV with the volume on mute. Naomi calls from the kitchen, "Hey honey, what are we doing this weekend for Benji's friend's birthday party? Are we going to drop him off? Or are we going to hang out there for the afternoon?"

Damon cringes inside, "I might have to work, how about you go hang out at the party, and if I can get out of this job, I'll join you."

"It would be nice to hang out while the party is on, like a date. We could visit Fort Langley or something?"

Damon walks into the kitchen for his second cup of coffee. He sees that Naomi is wearing her red hair in a ponytail, her bangs neatly cut, makeup on. He puts his cup on the counter, "I'm here right now, this is like a date." Naomi laughs and keeps prepping the chicken for the slow cooker. Damon pours his coffee, "Okay, so if I can get outta work on Saturday, we will do whatever you want. Hang out at the party or go for a day date. Does that sound nice? I'll do what I can to get out of work." Naomi bats her eyes. Damon offers, "I'm going to the garage for a workout. If you have the time, I'll meet you in the bedroom before I shower for a little morning glory."

Naomi giggles and with her eyes wide, "Why would I want you near me before you shower?"

Damon flashes a big grin, "I'll lick you slowly then I'll pull you on top of me. You'll ride me, we'll shower together after."

Naomi shakes her high ponytail. While smiling, she gasps, "How can you talk that? Oh my god, Damon. Go work out, I'll be in bed when you're done."

He grabs his coffee with a smile, then heads to the garage to work out.

SURREY, 10:00 A.M.

Sara sits on the long couch in the Wolf's office as the sun shines through the glass wall. She's in black cargo pants and a grey short-sleeved t-shirt. Sara wears a full utility belt with her gun and three magazines, handcuffs, and flashlight. Her badge hangs around her neck. When the Wolf walks in, Sara feels underdressed; he's in full uniform. She notes his four spare magazines; she's always curious what he's prepared for. His uniform is perfectly pressed. Sara wonders, *Does he have four sets of uniforms? Does he always have two out to dry clean?*

As he walks in, the Wolf states, "This must be big if you can't just email me a question. I don't want to be short with you, but I'm short on time. Please begin."

Sara hops up as he passes and follows close on his heels; she veers off and sits in the chair in front of his desk before he hangs his hat on the hook behind his seat. "From review of the surveillance video from the Trowel barbecue last week, and a video from the Fukadero show house, I believe I may have found the shooter." Bill locks onto Sara, and nods once for her to proceed. Sara summarizes Naomi being at the barbecue with the boy Benji; how Damon was wearing the same shoes and pants and wedding ring; and furthermore, how at the Fukadero show house there had been a serviceman that Suhki was walking in who was wearing white gloves.

Bill confirms, "No facial picture either time Air 1 recorded either of the two sites?"

"That's just it, everyone gave us straight profile angles to photograph, at the Fukadero show home. This one service guy never came to look at the low-flying attention maneuver."

The Wolf plays devils advocate, "Maybe he was on a ladder, working?"

Sara swallows and refers to the Trowel barbecue. "Everyone there, except one guy, reacted normally. This guy kept his head rubbing the top of the gazebo for twenty minutes."

"Maybe a bad back? Had to stand for a leg cramp?"

Sara brings up the chance meeting at the fair; she ran Damon's plate when he left. "Sir, this guy is the son of one of the lower mainlands most notorious hitmen."

The Wolf asks quickly, "Which one?"

"Leo Harpole."

The Wolf's heart speeds up. "I see why you would connect the case to them. You've been immersed in the case. You have a Trowel informant giving you an address in a few days, correct?"

Sara nods. Bill goes on. "If it is this Damon's address, Sara, you have unlimited resources to follow that lead. I will put a request in today for Leo's schedule from phone resources and his car tracker."

Sara's eyes go a little wider, obviously wanting more explanation on how the Wolf already has a tracker in Leo's vehicle.

Bill just smiles. "Sara, we keep a close eye on a multitude of criminals. I've personally been on three murder cases where we suspected Leo. You call me with any lead that points to them, understand?" Sara stands, a head rush blurs her vision. She thanks the Wolf for his time and turns to exit.

LANGLEY, 10:30 A.M.

Damon is drying off after his shower with his wife. He tells her he's going to the garage to work on something. Naomi calls out from under the water, "I'm leaving for the day to go help garden at a friend's house. I'll pick Benji from school at three, then we'll come home."

Damon flatly answers, "Sounds good." He dresses in his blue Levis and a black shirt; once in the garage, he puts on his black runners. Damon pulls the sheet off the rifle on his counter; it's the SKS that's customized to be a halfway decent medium-range rifle with a 3-9 power scope on top. He glances on the shelf and sees his five magazines for the rifle. In Canada magazines for rifles can't hold more than five rounds. So those five magazines only have a total of twenty-five shots in them. But at these ranges from the garage to the street, Damon doesn't think he could miss a man-sized target, even if the person was running flat out. Under 100 yards a torso is huge in a scope.

Damon has shot a few different wild game that were in a full-panic run at seventy yards. *Once you shoulder the weapon, the game is locked in the cross-hair. Just pull the trigger.* The matte green rifle's bolt is open and facing up. Damon turns on the desk light and examines the rifle to decide what kind of cleaning and maintenance he should do. This is the best way for Damon to spend spare time. *Feels good to have a freshly greased rifle in my hands.*

LANGLEY, 11:15 A.M.

Dean is driving along, following his handwritten directions to find Damon's house. He's driving Steve from Trail's truck: a black Dodge half-ton pickup with the stock chrome five-star mags.

Dean is giddy, thinking about his new position in the Grim Sinners. *I'm leading them, and I'm the new supplier for every one of my guys in B.C. At least I will be once I under-cut everyone's prices from my new stockpile that Tony left Chloe and me. Once I kill this hitman, I'm on easy street. Drexel and the rest of them will be blown away that I took out such a dangerous guy. I'll be the legend in this crew, not Drexel. Oh, I can park here.*

27

Damon hears a sharp ring of a metal object tapping his newly-painted garage door. He grabs a magazine, quietly slides it in the SKS, and pulls the bolt back. While holding it from slamming shut, he slowly eases the bolt closed and watches as the round gets fed in. He checks that the safety is off and lays the gun on the bench facing the garage opening; then he pulls the thin sheet over the gun with his hand on the stock and his thumb wrapped around it. With his finger on the trigger, Damon hits the garage door opener.

As the door opens a few inches, Damon sees the shoes of the unrevealed door knocker. The feet are in purple slippers, with light brown nylons that don't cover the blue veins and stout ankles of an eighty-year-old grandma. He decides right away that this is an old lady, not a meth-head hitman. Damon takes his hand off the rifle and snatches a book off the workbench. He opens the book as the door raises to the lady's head level.

The aged lady is wearing a flower-pattern muumuu, and has a metal cane with four legs in one hand. She sees Damon reading. "So, You have time to read a book, eh? Well, then you have time to clean my car."

Damon smiles. "Hi, I'm Damon. I own this house. How can I help you, ma'am?"

"I'm Alice, I've been on this street since the houses were new, in 1981. Your dusty dirt lawn blows all over my house and car. I understand you're trying to get your property organized, but I'm driving to pick up my son at the airport later and my car looks like I live in the desert. Will you come to clean it or not?" Alice leers at Damon, "This is the crossroads sonny. Friend or foe?"

Damon is ashamed with the mess he's making around the block. He jumps up and grabs his wash bucket and some car soap; he grabs the car wash brush hanging by the door. Alice smiles and turns to lead the way.

Damon pulls her hose off the hanger and sprays the car. Most of the loose dust is washing away. He sprays the water into his orange five-gallon pail. After adding the soap, he uses his long handled brush to mix the water.

While scrubbing the roof of the car, he notices a guy in a black jogging suit with white skate shoes stalking along; the guy's hood is over his head. Damon's heart skips a beat; he shields his face behind his arms as he continues to scrub the roof of the car, for longer than needs be. He nods to Alice, who sits on a lawn chair, reading a flyer.

Damon studies this person carefully. *Is this just a crackhead thief? It's so hot I'm melting in this t-shirt. Why would a guy have his hood up? Or even be in a sweater?*

How the hell am I over here when my gun is over there? This is ludicrous.

Damon watches as the man in black scans the addresses; then he does a little hop with a step-change then strolls up the driveway to Damon's house.

Mother fucker. Should I go to his getaway car? I've got a solid folding-knife in my pocket, I'll pretend I dropped something and when he gets close enough I'll bury the blade in the first fatal target I see. Damon rinses the car; his back turned to give the assassin a feeling of privacy. He sees the man in black, moving around in his peripheral vision.

Well, he knocked twice on the front door, I hear his footsteps from here. That little step-change hop he's doing when he changes direction is familiar. This guy is going for it, eh? Just walk around back, eh? It's that easy, huh? Maybe he'll shoot and kill me while I play with my kid?

Damon's Simple voice comes in hard and vicious. *Run over, enter through the front door, and get your rifle. Go, go now. The timing is right.* Damon considers taking a dead run to his rifle, but he can't, it will draw attention to him. And supposing Damon emerged a moment later, running with the rifle in a ready position, and fires a perfect hit in the centre of this dummy's back, he'll be going to jail. He peeks over to Alice, as she rips a coupon from the flyer.

Damon answers his Simple voice. *I agree, it's possible. But I have an idea of who that guy might be. We have a lead. This old lady's dirty car just averted a shooting on our block.* The man in black is coming back around the front of the house. He has his right hand in the kangaroo pocket of the sweatshirt. *He's right-handed. This is the guy who the Fukaderos had coming and going from both the show home and the stone house. He has a white 300 Chrysler. That long surveillance was fruitful, this guy just stumbled into my lap.*

Damon bends over to wipe the bottom of the car's door. He spies over his shoulder as he scrubs.

The man in black eyeballs him, and Damon smirks.

Oh I bet you'd like to come over here and see if this man across the street, that sort of looks like your target, is your target. But you won't do it. Ha ha ha, I'm coming for you now. You stupid piece of shit.

The man in black does a step-change hop and heads off the driveway. Damon watches as the man lowers his hood about four houses down.

Too hot, big guy? Better to be caught on a home camera than to have a bead of sweat run down your cheek. This guy probably lit the fire at the Polish business. This is a big chance to show everyone how crazy he is.

He's not crazy; he's ignorant.

FRASER RIVER, 2:00 P.M.

Damon calls Naomi and suggests she go to her sister's house for dinner after picking up Benji at school. She likes the idea, and agrees. Damon is on the Fraser River in a twenty-eight foot aluminum jet-boat. His friend Nick has a sturgeon-fishing business, and is on the river almost every day. Nick wasn't surprised to hear Damon's voice or his request for a ride.

Damon hops off the boat and pushes it off the dock. The captain lays into the throttle, lifting the bow, the boat heads east. He stands tall and ponders the owner of this estate. And how all these full-time hustlers keep themselves alive. *Does this guy have any real friends? Since I've known him, he's survived the rise and fall of three different street crews. So many guys believe that once you meet the main man, with all the connections, that he will have a safe-haven with some secret table where everyone is friends.*

Damon draws a long breath of the fresh, crisp air off the river.

This dock is on the south side of the river, just outside of Fort Langley, and has shade from the tree-line on the bank. Damon stands still, with his hands in his black jean-jacket pockets, and his mind wanders.

If the church was aiming to exorcise a demon, the owner of this house would be a prime candidate. Greed clouds the minds of everyone who meets him, as they wonder how they'll get some of the wealth. Gluttony is prevalent in everything around Chaz; his parties never run out of booze and drugs. Envy is created by his house, which is a palace; all his cars are exclusive and rare. Lust is dripping from his words, and the constant sexy women he has parading around.

Pride is the mainstay of all gangsters; it's closely tied to wrath. I've been his tool for delivering his wrath.

Sloth is all Chaz ever exhibits in his day-to-day display of beach life, with his shorts and sandals. What does this make me? If I don't have those sins, but I associate with the sinners, could I be the wrath of God? He gets me close enough that I cut the core out of these evils?

A bald eagle soaring at tree height along the shoreline, stalking the water for its lunch. He shakes his head and smiles.

Take it easy. We're all just hunting for our next meal. Same as every animal on earth. When that eagle sinks its talons into a fish that was minding its own business, no god notes a minus in the fair-play chart, for eagles.

Damon turns and walks tall up the commercial-grade aluminum ramp. He walks with his head up, across the manicured green lawn to the back of the house, and taps the kitchen door with the back of his knuckles. Chaz opens it with the phone to his ear. He's drinking a smoothie that his maid prepared for him. He notices Chaz freeze for a split second, but quickly gains his composure and waves him in. Damon steps into the kitchen and sits at the live edge table that presents a commanding view of the Fraser River out the floor-to-ceiling windows.

Chaz says his goodbye on the phone, then asks Damon. "Should I have Jenny pour you a smoothie before she leaves for the day?"

Damon keeps his eyes on the soaring eagle as it turns downwind and gains speed.

"Sure, that sounds nice."

The maid pours him a tall milkshake-glass full of smoothie. As Damon drinks it, he notices the maid pouring the remainder of the jug down the drain.

Chaz sits at the head of the table. But Damon has another plan. "Let's go for a walk outside. We need to go over something we're working on together."

Chaz woke at 10:00 a.m. today, and is feeling fresh. He furrows his brow and shakes his head, trying to wake his mind. *I haven't talked to Damon about any work in over a year.* Damon stands and opens the door for Chaz to go out. Chaz's mind races. *Damon let the maid go, so he's probably not here to kill me. Or he has, and they came in the front? No, Damon is a survivor, he knows I'll pay anything and help him. This game is always the same, I don't even have to leave my house, they all come to me.*

Damon is uncomfortable with conversation; he knows that Chaz has a financial interest in all these players. The trick is going to be in making a deal that Chaz will bank on in the future. They walk toward the gazebo.

"Chaz, you trust me. I've placed my life in your hands for work in the past. I need you to give me information that will clear an issue I'm having."

Chaz takes short breathes. *Supposing that Damon knows I gave Dean his address, and he's just fucking with me, I'm dead for sure. What was I thinking siding with Dean? That damn fool has no future.*

"Damon, tell me what you're thinking, I'll help you in any way. Just spit it out."

Damon stops Chaz with the back of his hand on Chaz's chest. They're eye-to-eye. "What's the name of the guy who drives the white Chrysler 300? He was a friend of that land developer."

Chaz's guts turn to liquid. Chaz talks fast, "Look man, Dean came by here and said he would kill me if I didn't tell him where you were. He's the head of the Grim Sinners. You know those street gang guys are nuts, running on speed and booze."

Damon chuckles. "What? What are you talking about? Dean is the name of the guy with the white 300? And you told him where I live? Is this a joke?"

Chaz cringes. *Faack*. But he holds it together.

"Dean came by here with four guys, they had guns in their belts. He told me he remembered meeting you here once. They threatened me. It was two days ago. I've been too scared to call you. I was going to call today, I really was. Right after I drank that smoothie, I was calling you."

Damon isn't surprised at all. Every hustler who lives in these castles is a conduit for everything that is happening on the street.

Damon's jaw is clenched. His eyes locked on Chaz's. Damon is confident how this will unfold. "Yeah, I know, Chaz. Work gets pretty tight sometimes. You're going to help me in more ways than one in this situation, okay?"

Chaz nods. He crosses his arms, then uncrosses them 2 seconds later.

"I'll need Dean's address and his most frequent daily locations. You say he's in that street crew, the Grim Sinners?"

Chaz spills the beans, "You know how those types roll, whoever has control of the connections for the supply is

the leader. With Tony dead, Dean inherited his connections, so he has the power for now."

"Was Tony the head of the Grim Sinners?"

Chaz updates Damon, "No, he'd been supplying them,
so Dean was his distributor. Somehow Dean has a supply
coming in from somewhere. With no Tony, Dean is the
main man."

"If Dean is gone, will you be able to supply them
with coke?"

Chaz relaxes, "Damon, you're making a business plan
for me. You sure you don't want to be my partner? Ya,
of course, I'll have whatever they need. It's not just blow
nowadays. They need perks, fentanyl, party drugs like
ecstasy. Meth is huge. I'll keep them rolling, don't worry
about that. It's harder for me to get rid of dope than it is to
get it into Canada."

Damon's eyebrows force together. "I'll need the address
of the Grim Sinners' main headquarters as well, I'll get a
bead on them."

Chaz nods blankly. Damon wants to grab Chaz by the
arm, pull out his folding knife, and chase him around
stabbing him while Chaz yells. 'No, no, please no.'

Damon closely watches Chaz. "I'll need some regular
spots that Suhki hangs out as well."

Chaz's eyes go big, now he knows Damon is swimming
in the Fukadero war. Chaz brightens up. "He's making a
lot of trouble for a trucking company I use for transport,
Pacific to Atlantic, beating them in public and demanding
payment of some bullshit debt. I'll get whatever details
about him, for you."

Damon works the angle. "So, you're still going to make money with Dean gone. You're going to have a smoother operation with Suhki gone. You sold me out; I have to work on this crap. Since you're being paid and you don't even have to leave your lawn, I'll need fifty thousand dollars, now. This will help with all the costs you've dumped on me." Damon strung this plan together when Chaz said he needed Suhki taken out of the game.

Chaz opens his mouth, then closes it. He feels a chill when he locks eyes with Damon. *This guy hates me. I need him happy now more than ever, or I'll land on his list with Dean and Suhki.*

"I've only got thirty thousand cash here. I'll get you the rest next week?"

"Sure, I'll take your gold chain and rings as collateral."

Chaz chuckles. "I can make up the difference in U.S. cash if that's okay?"

Damon nods. "I'll wait in the gazebo for you."

Chaz returns fifteen minutes later. He hands a cheap purple backpack to Damon.

"Thirty thousand Canadian, fifteen thousand U.S. I wrote Dean's info as well. I'll contact you with Suhki's info shortly. Do you have any help with Suhki? P and A Trucking brought this stone killer in from India. He's been driving around in these cloned cars, hunting Suhki. The president of Pacific to Atlantic makes the cars in a secret shop."

Damon peers in the backpack.

"I'll be okay. With my good friends helping me."

"Hey bro, I'm really sorry I was forced to turn on you, I was scared."

Damon gazes at him, "Chaz, you know I'll be here after they're all gone and the next group rises up. I know you'll be here. Just call me sooner next time, okay?"

Chaz reaches out and shakes Damon's hand, "Done."

Damon stands and makes his way to the dock, and Chaz follows. As they saunter down the large aluminum ramp Chaz spots the jet boat waiting, and the boat begins to head over. Chaz sparks up, "Hey, is that Nick? I was out in his boat with some pals last year, he's a great guide. We caught three huge sturgeon."

Damon pats him on the back. "Man, you know everyone, eh?"

Chaz brags. "I don't try, it seems everyone comes through my gates. It's all real easy bro."

The boat arrives and Chaz grabs the side rail. Damon gives Chaz a one-arm shoulder hug then jumps onboard.

Chaz shakes Nick's hand.

"I'll call you, and we'll get a day booked for Damon and me! I've got these two hot yoga instructors who love to party. Do we have to wear clothes on the boat?"

All three laugh, and Damon dilutes his response, "I'll let you know when I get some free time." Damon knows he'll never make time for a party day. He's happily married, and his free time is spent with his wife and son.

Nick yells back to the dock. "Hey, you tipped so well last time, clothing is optional for you, Chaz."

All three guys laughs as the boat idles away from the dock.

FRASER RIVER, 2:40 P.M.

The Fraser River is the main river that pours out of the southwest of B.C. The river is affected by the Pacific Ocean's tidal schedule. Sometimes the river flows out to sea as the tide goes out, very fast. A few hours later it is a slack tide, where the water is flat and almost stagnant. The jet boat is cruising at twenty-five kilometres over a flat still river, heading west to drop Damon at the dock at Pitt Meadows airport.

Over the drone of the low rpm inboard engine, Nick asks. "How long have you known Chaz?"

Damon focuses ahead, watching for logs. "A few years. How about you?"

"I took him out once, sturgeon fishing on the Fraser. He and his pals were going on and on about loads of drugs they move and guys getting arrested. I felt like I was going to get arrested after hearing it all." Nick nervously laughs, waiting for any comment from Damon.

Damon scans the water ahead. "Chaz has a way about him, that's for sure. He's always the same."

Nick is eyeing Damon. "What are you doing around him? You don't move any drugs around, do you?"

Damon purses his lips and shakes his head. "Chaz is a person that always has some sort of work; if he doesn't have work, he knows where to find it. I'm just a worker, trying to stay afloat."

Captain Nick surveys forward, and can't think of a way to ask, *Are you his hitman?* So he nods. Nick has known Damon for over fifteen years; they met through a mutual friend. He has heard stories about Damon being a hitman. Nick has never known a hitman, so each time he's with Damon, he tries to get a piece of info that would confirm it. Nothing strange yet.

Damon recognizes Nick's expression.

Here come twenty questions.

"Wow, sure is great on the water, I'm going to sit on the bench and enjoy the view." Nick is used to clients wanting to have private moments on the river, he nods and gestures toward the bench that protrudes out the back of the hard cabin.

Damon sits heavy to test the seat. *This boat is solid.* Right away, his all-knowing voice comments tenderly, *You did it. You followed the clues right to the answer again. Do you feel better?*

Damon's head shoots up, his eyes wide. He hasn't heard from this voice since the day he took Fukadero down.

Why are these the clues I'm left with? Guys make fifty grand in one stock trade. How come I have to risk my life and those around me? You know I don't like all the time these jobs take, right? Damon bows his head and stops whining. No answer from the calm all-knowing voice.

Damon sits steady, and his own thought answers him instead. *Somebody has to do every job. Don't take it so seriously. It's natural. Some guys have an eye for laying tiles straight with no spacers.* Damon shakes his head and looks up. *When will this end? Each hit leads to more murder. How will I step away?*

This time his Coach answers. *Are you done thinking about things that have no tactical value?*

Damon knows this is a rhetorical question. Plus, his all-knowing voice and his Coach are in his mind at the same time. This is the beginning of a big game.

The boat swerves to miss some debris in the river. Damon allows his body to sway as the boat glides smoothly to the right, then back to the left. His Coach comes in, confident, with a current de-brief. *We have an Indo-Canadian and his crew/family after the Polish, and probably us. We have the leader of the street gang the Grim Sinners trying to make a name for himself, coming after us. Both groups have lots of human resources. We know the main kind of help they have; young guys who are new to gang life and are dying to make some solid street credibility.* Damon chuckles at the emphasis Coach places on 'dying.'

Coach pauses while Damon laughs; Damon composes himself and goes back to listening with a grim face. *Chaz will win, regardless of whoever wins this little war. We die, he has Dean as his new tough street guy. We kill Dean, we're grateful and more trusting of Chaz. Chaz's issue with Suhki is a nice surprise, that's the main reason he will help us and not double-cross us. If Chaz will tell his transport guys that he took Suhki out, he'll have a more secure ride for his drugs in their trucks. In actual fact, we have two active contracts on Suhki. One from the Polish and one from Chaz.* Damon pounds his fist on the side of the boat.

I should have asked for more than fifty G for my hassles. Chaz would have paid double that for a Suhki hit.

The all-knowing voice drifts in softly. *Chaz already knows you have a hit on Suhki, you told him. The fifty thousand dollars is for giving your address to the Grim Sinners. Don't get greedy. The help you needed came with a paycheque. Be grateful.*

Damon feels he's cursed, not blessed, in this moment.

Do I work for good or evil? The all-knowing voice asks. *Can evil be done for good?*

Damon withholds a big eye-roll and head-drop.

That's nice. A good riddle. I don't deserve a straight answer.

Damon checks out of his Coach's seminar and uses the last few minutes on the boat for his own thoughts. *Is Chaz my friend? I know him better than most know him. He knows more about me than almost any person, unless they've employed me to do their dirty work. Would I trust him with my wife?* Damon laughs out loud and slaps his knee as he stands. *Nope!*

The aluminum jet-boat arrives at the North shore of the Pitt Meadow's float dock. Damon hands Nick a hundred for the ride. He almost says, *Don't worry about it,* and hands it back. Damon didn't go into Chaz's with a bag, but now he has one. Nick concludes, *Damon can afford it, he's Chaz's hitman.* Nick laughs as he pockets the hundred; he has no evidence at all that Damon is Chaz's hitman, but he can't wait to tell their other pal.

Damon went in with no bag and come out with a bag. And Chaz offered to supply women and a day trip for Damon. This is surely good talk over a couple beers.

Damon jumps off the boat; it drifts away as he yells, "Thanks Nick, Lets get my kid out on the water one day. I'll call, we'll book it once he's old enough."

Nick hollers back, "Call anytime, I'm always on the river."

Damon strides up the dock's ramp toward the locked gate that leads to the parking lot, happy with the future of this little war. Then he contemplates a serious question he can't answer. *How are Yakub and the other Poles handling this assault? Are they okay? Even worse, have they taken the matter into their own hands? I don't want to be tripping over them; they told me no one would attack the Fukaderos or their people as long as I'm working on the job. I really hope they all stick to this plan. I hope to hell that Yakub is alert to the Grim Sinners joining the fight.*

28

Dean stalks the sidewalk in front of a row of tightly packed older houses in East Vancouver. The houses on 14th Avenue, some as old as 1925, sit on lots that average 5,000 square feet. Dean was born out in the Fraser Valley; he's only visited East Vancouver a handful of times throughout his life. He can't believe how many Asians live in this area.

Dean's black hood is up as he walks casually as possible. *I have to bury this guy. I've been back here twice. The drive is killing me. Being away from the action in Surrey isn't good. Drexel is throwing a party tonight. I'll be there by nine at the latest. This guy has to be home. If not I'll whip by Damon's house in Langley on the way to the party. I will blast these bastards later this week, no matter what.*

Dean sees Yakub's house, and Yakub's truck parked right out front. Butterflies erupt in his stomach as he scans the street from under his sweater's hood, without turning his head too much. *Seems quiet around here.* The sidewalk stretches out in front of him, leading to Knight St. Dean

369

pauses in front of the gate; he listens for five seconds. He turns quickly and reaches over to unlatch the old-style lever that holds the bolt, and begins wiggling it free so the gate will swing open. It takes a firm wiggle to free the pin. The gate opens, and he heads up the stairs to the front door. Dean's heart is pounding so hard he imagines they might hear it in the house. He knocks loudly four times.

Dean hears no sound, so he heads down the stairs and takes a right on the thin concrete path that leads around the back of the old house. Dean had been around back two hours ago; the corner has a tall hedge that seems to reach over the path and touch the house. He feels much better going around this time, knowing what he's going to see.

He stops at the back gate. The garage light is on, and the small white man-door is wide open. Polka music is blaring out.

Dean smiles and pulls the chrome 9mm pistol out of his waist line; his finger on the trigger. Dean holds the gun against his leg, pointing down. He reaches over the gate to unlatch the old bolt. Breathing carefully so nobody hears him. He never takes his eyes off the garage door.

VANCOUVER, EAST END, 5:05 P.M.

Yakub's wife comes running out to the garage and whispers quickly. "He's back. The man in the black hood is at the front gate." Since the Fukadero issues began last year

Yakub's wife has been sitting in the window sewing, to keep an eye out. Since their workshop burned down this week, she has been on full alert.

Yakub furrows his brow, he drops his tools on the bench. "Go in the house and lock the door. Call our uncle to come here. Talk casually on the phone." Yakub's wife turns on a dime and leaves. Yakub cranks the music and runs out the door.

Earlier his wife had told him about the man in black creeping around. Yakub runs on his toes over to the side gate and stands stock-still against the wall.

With the high police presence, he can't have guns around, so he has nothing but his hands. Yakub hears light footsteps coming down his path. He has lived at this address since he and his family came to Canada. He would recognize the neighbour's cat walking in his yard. Yakub takes in long deep breaths to feed his muscles for the upcoming fight. He inhales four full breaths. He sees an arm reach over the gate his father built to keep him and his brother in the yard when he was a toddler.

The fence is about three-and-a-half feet high, made of wood, and even after all these years of Vancouver rain it still has a perfectly flat top. The arm in black reaches down to find the bolt that secures the gate shut. Yakub lets the hand find the pin; he watches as the mysterious hand fumbles to get a grip on the old latch. Yakub knows the man is focused on the garage or he would have peeked over to inspect the lock.

Yakub identifies that a left hand is reaching into his yard. Yakub's traditional Judo training provides him a plan. *Uponzi Unogi to the left; this will make his other arm, which is most likely holding a gun, flail uselessly as he flies over my shoulder. Then as he hits the ground with his head and shoulders, I go right into a Juji Gitami.*

Yakub draws in an ultimate long breath, then exhales as he grabs the intruder's left hand as gently as possible. He lifts the arm as he spins around and tucks his other arm under the uplifted arm. During this movement, he pulls the man's body onto his back. Yakub feels the full weight transfer onto him, pulling the man in black over him in one motion.

The man in black expels two words in one breath as he leaves Yakub's back upside down. "What-the!"

The throw is swift. If an onlooker had seen the man in the blue jean jacket grab the man in black's arm, then quick as a wink the man in black flipped over the other man's back.

Throughout Yakub's Judo training, he's been careful to always keep the roll going, so his opponents' heads were pulled through the throw up to safety. This one time, Yakub doesn't pull the roll all the way; he lets gravity stop with the man in black upside down. Yakub keeps the arm, though, and directs the man's body-weight directly onto his head and shoulders.

Yakub receives a shock to his calm. As he controls the assailant, a single gunshot goes off wildly with no aim: *bang*! The round explodes some wood off of the frame of the garage door. As soon as the attacker lands on his head, Yakub spots the gun in his other hand, finger on the trigger. The throw results in the attacker's gun hand being slapped on the ground, and the man in a complete daze from the full-weight throw directly on his head. The gun bounces out of his hand as Yakub pulls the arm of the semi-conscious man in for Juji Gitami.

Yakub has never broken someone's arm with his training; nevertheless, he's in a blind rage after hearing the gun go off, and he grunts like a bear as he pulls the arm to his chest. It breaks easily. The man in black wakes up once his arm breaks. Yakub drops his knee, and all 250 pounds of his weight, onto the top of the man's neck, right were the skull connects. The ground and Yakub's knee make the man in black's eyes roll up.

Yakub is done with techniques and drops onto the man in a straddle. The broken arm is between Yakub's legs, and the attacker's other arm is pinned to the ground. Yakub grabs him around the neck with two hands; he feels the man's windpipe pinch shut. Yakub knows he has at least one of two arteries that feed the brain blood is pinched off as well. Yakub stares at the attacker's face as he squeezes as hard as he can. After nearly fifteen seconds, Yakub calms; he knows the man has no chance of recovering from his death grip. Spit hangs from Yakub's mouth and he shakes from adrenaline, *You piece of shit, want to steal from me, kill me. Kill me at my family home. We are going to kill you all very soon. Your friends are coming to join you in hell soon, get the table ready.*

Yakub lifts his head after fifty seconds of squeezing the artery and airway of the attacker; his wife is standing there with a big kitchen knife, her long flower-print dress hanging still. Her scared face tells him everything, 'I came out to help you, but now I wish I had never come out.'

Yakub lets go with his support hand; the other easily continues to restrict the air and blood in the neck. He softens his eyes, "Go back in, send Uncle Gabriel out when he gets here. It's okay, I'm fine. Please don't come back out." He waves her off nicely. She nods with pursed lips, pivots, and leaves.

After another fifty seconds to be sure, Yakub gets off the body and stands while listening to his surroundings. The tall cedar hedge his father planted thirty years ago blocks the visibility into the neighbour's yard. Yakub glances at the shivering body as he walks away. Its jaw is opening and closing, and both eyes are slowly closing then snapping open. He runs into the garage and grabs an orange work tarp. Unfolding it as he walks, he pulls it over the twitching body. When he broke the arm, he had recognized the man as Dean. He has time to think. *This was the Fuk's friend, who always came around the site dressed like it was a night club, in designer jeans and sparkly shirts with designs on them. Jesus Christ, how many people are trying to stop us from getting our money? Why do they think we don't need it?*

Forty-five minutes later, Yakub hears the familiar sound of his Uncle Gabriel walking the side path, lightly humming an old tune. Yakub watches Gabriel examine the tarp, then he points and scrunches his brow. Yakub explains.

"It's okay. We're going on your boat tonight. To feed the crabs."

VANCOUVER, EAST END, 5:05 P.M.

Dean reaches and finds the latch he used earlier in the day; he keeps his eyes on the garage door.

With that music on the fat man won't even hear this rusty latch open.

Dean's fingers have just gotten a use-full grip on the latch as he feels someone touch his wrist. He changes his focus from the garage door to his arm, and sees a huge blue jean jacket spinning in front of him. Right away he recognizes the Polish contractor's coat. *I don't know why he's lifting my arm, but I'm going to.*— At the moment Dean lifts his gun-hand, he finds his feet leaving the ground. He quickly notices where he's heading; about five feet into the yard.

I'll shoot him when I land.

But as the throw speeds up and Dean is upside-down, he yells uncontrollably, "What-the—"

He slams into the ground, dazed.

Did I hit him with that shot? Did I hit myself? Am I moving? There's something heavy on my side.

Dean's arm breaks. *Motherfucker, that fat fuck just broke my arm. I'm in a fight! When I get back on my feet...* At this point, Yakub drops his knee with full weight on Dean's neck and skull before spinning onto a high mount. Dean sees a bright light flash; as he becomes aware again, he sees Yakub staring at him with black eyes, spit hanging from his gritted teeth and lips.

Dean's final thought is, *This fat fuck is going to pay when I get that gun back in my hand. He's so heavy I can't move an inch. Oh no, this is it. He's going to kill me. No, no, okay, okay. No...* Dean strains through blurred vision into the blank stare of a woman in a flower-print dress and a knife. The light goes dimmer, and dimmer. Blackness. Silence.

29

Damon jogs with Patch around his neighbourhood. He had a light sleep as he always does during an ongoing war; each sound makes him open his eyes and evaluate if the sound requires him to grab his twelve-gauge and investigate. Damon sleeps well enough with Patch in the house; his dog is always on guard.

Damon is being extra vigilant, thanks to the black jogging-suit guy running around his house. Damon continues to evaluate the clues he gathered from watching the Fuk for so long. *I noticed Dean's little step-change hop at the show home. That house I watched from gave me this info. I got the Fuk from sitting beside the air conditioner, I got to see Suhki and his guys' body language and gauge their competence levels. All from that empty house. It doesn't matter that I got made there. With Chaz's help, these guys are all going to be dead soon.*

They're all busy with their schemes. Dean with coke to sell and a gang to run; he'll be a part-time hunter at best. Suhki has a big family to participate in. Both have so many enemies. Me, I only have them to think about. All day, all night, until they're dead; then I'll never think about them again. The situation is always the same. This is always the pattern. The one main greedy narcissist has a group of wannabes around him; they don't know half the shit their leader is into. When the leader dies, his evil spirit breaks into pieces and flies into those who surrounded him. They all start jockeying for whatever it is the main narcissist left behind. They always overlook that someone so mad killed the last asshole.

They become possessed with greed; all they see is the large house and beautiful clothes. Their minds are instantly clouded by whatever evil puked out of their leader when he died. When these two guys are gone, the darkness will be watered down again. I've never heard of more than eight guys needing to be put in the ground to end a war. I'm ready to shoot as needed. Can't put a number on it.

Damon is lightly jogging merely to pass the time. He glances down for a second when he sees Patch's head perk up, and pulls the leash taut. Damon sees someone leave a house in a shiny grey suit with skinny pants, a thin tie over a bright green shirt.

"Easy Patch, you can't eat a salesman this morning."

LANGLEY, 9:00 A.M.

Sara sits on the reclining armchair in the Wolf's office for two minutes before the Wolf walks in. He points at Sara as he passes. "I see our Trowel informant gave us an address last night. Did you believe him when he gave it to you?"

Sara has never noticed the Wolf show emotion during a case before. *This assassin is very important to Bill. He is taking this personally.* Sara leans forward. "The informant is afraid of losing his job. He was crying when he handed the warehouse address over, saying, 'I grew up with these people, and you make me betray them. Now I'm nothing. You have destroyed me.'"

Bill stares at Sara, trying to decipher if she believes the informant or not. Sara schools her face, trying not to commit. But the Wolf wins, "Bill, in my opinion, the informant is desperate enough to give us the intel to get his record clear. His emotion appeared authentic. He is devastated by the situation."

The Wolf sits back in his chair, turns toward the window, and crosses his hands in his lap. He lowers his chin and stares out the window. After ninety seconds, he turns to Sara. "Get full surveillance on the warehouse address for two weeks. Give the Emergency Response Team the case info and have them ready to raid the place."

Sara stands. "I've already prepared the ERT report, and the request for surveillance is in draft form. I'll submit both in the next ten minutes."

Bill smiles ear to ear. "You know how to keep the ball rolling. We might catch some real killers on this one; good work Officer."

LANGLEY, 5:00 P.M.

Damon is surprised at how fast Chaz comes back with intel. The text from Chaz's burner phone is clear enough. "Come by my house. I have the parts in for the furnace."

Damon's chest tightens when he considers a reverse set-up in Chaz's yard. *Chaz needs me. Dean is the replaceable head of a loosely organized gang. Chaz also needs the transport company running smooth. Chaz will want to show them he's more than a guy who just needs some bags of dope moved around; he's their protector as well. I'm heading over, the information might be time sensitive.*

Damon is sitting at the dinner table with Naomi and Benji. When they finish, he puts his plate in the sink. "Benji, pull out your math practice book and do two pages. If your mom says it's okay, you can play on the computer after."

The boy pushes the chicken drumstick with his fork. A frown grows on his little face. "Okay."

Damon looks at Naomi; she has her eyes pinned on him. Damon explains, "I've got to go work. When I leave, I don't want you answering the door unless you're expecting someone."

Benji's head swivels back-and-forth between the adults. "Why? Who's coming over that you don't want in the house?"

Naomi bites her lip and pinches her nose. Damon tries to give an age appropriate example, "Benji, we have a door on our house to keep the cold out. The door is also made to keep strangers out. People act like animals. Do you think a lion would steal another lion's food if he could?"

The boy flashes a huge grin. "Yeah, lions eat the other animals."

Damon smiles. "We have a door on our house to stop animals from eating our food. With the door shut and locked, they can't get in." Damon forms his right hand into a lion mouth and comes at Benji fast and grabs his tummy.

Rarr Rarr

The boy shouts as he tries to block. "So don't open the doors or a lion might run in and eat our food!" All three of them laugh. Patch jumps from his bed by the back door, and stands on his hind legs to join the game, lightly pushing Damon.

Damon has to pet him, "Good boy," to calm him down."

FORT LANGLEY, 5:45 P.M.

Damon drives up to the gate and hits the buzzer at Chaz's house; the large iron gates swing open. *The concrete that holds these gates probably cost as much as the foundation on my house. I'm glad I get along with this guy.*

Chaz walks to the front of the house, and over to where Damon will park. Damon steps out and scans the house's enormous front windows. But the tan tinted windows keep inside private; you can't see in unless it is night, and then only shadows.

Chaz nods towards his orchard. "Let's walk." Damon feels the other man is really nervous, the way people behave when there's murder in the near future. It actually makes Damon relax a bit. *This is how Chaz acted last time he gave me the exact time and location to hit our target. This job will be done soon. Thank God.*

Chaz hands Damon a small folded paper in the way kids pass notes; he keeps it low and moves his arm as little as possible. Damon takes it the same way, palming it. They walk close together, Damon in his black jean jacket and blue jeans and Chaz in his Bermuda shorts and button up surf shirt, grey hair slicked back with the sides shaved.

Damon asks, "Do they have guys after Suhki?"

Chaz drives his pointer finger into the air in front of them, pinning the info to an imaginary wall. "That's the mustard right there. They have a solid killer from India after him, and they're searching for Suhki day and night. The president of P and A doesn't want to share any intel they have. I told them to give me one good spot. I told them I wouldn't waste it. I have my best guy on it."

Damon is shaking his head. "This sucks, Chaz. I have to trust a bunch of South-Asian gangsters with a single location hit? They could have a deal with the cops. Or they could have already blown the spot and Suhki will be ready. One place isn't suitable for me."

They walk along, not talking. Damon notices they're walking towards an apple orchard, with nine trees, three rows deep. Damon stops; he's not letting Chaz lead him anywhere. Chaz keeps an eye on Damon, trying to read the outcome of this meeting.

Damon crosses his arms. "I gotta go, I don't think I should use this. Thanks for trying, Chaz." Damon walks away.

Chaz raises his voice. "Hey, Damon, when this is over let's go downtown and have a night out with some fun Chinese girls I know. The whole night will be my treat."

Damon turns and walks backwards. "Maybe, when I have nothing to do. You sure have all this life stuff figured out, eh?"

Chaz beams. "Yeah, I don't give a single ounce of fuck." They both politely smile as Damon turns and puts his hands in his pockets.

FORT LANGLEY, 6:30 P.M.

Damon drives his white Caravan along the two-lane back roads of Fort Langley en-route to the gas station on exit 232, off Highway 1. He drives a couple kilometres under the speed limit while thinking. *This is out of any perimeter of safety. The Polish know I'm after Suhki, Chaz knows I'm after Suhki, even Suhki knows I'm after Suhki. The chance of a smooth ending is slim-to-none. I can't even stop the job at this point; Suhki will be joining Dean in the hunt for me soon, if he hasn't already.*

Walk a thousand miles to avoid a fight, but once one starts don't give an inch. Who said that? Damon crosses the highway on an overpass, and into the gas station, then parks at a gas pump. He grabs his stainless steel water bottle from the cup holder, twists the cap off, and takes a mouthful from the one litre jug.

Chaz isn't double crossing me, I've proven too useful to him. The truckers shouldn't rat me out, they're drug smugglers who want Suhki dead. Even if they work with the police in pointing out competitors in drug deals, they're not talking to the police about their plans to kill guys. It's all a risk I signed up for; this is precisely what the money is for, not the killing. The money is to ease the burden of people hating you. This is it, I'm already fucked. I'll scout the one spot Chaz supplied, now.

Damon's Coach joins the conversation. *This is open warfare, if you don't attack, you will be attacked. Let's go over and see how to plan an ambush. The site will tell us a lot.* Damon draws the note out of his pocket and reads it.

Great, the Little India part of Surrey. Damon turns on his van and puts it into drive. He knows this area of King George is filled with industrial buildings that comprise of every type of building contractor, Indian food supplier, dressmaker, chai tea supplier, and even gold salespeople. This is the heart of the South-Asian business centre of Surrey.

SURREY, 7:50 P.M.

Damon drives Westbound along 88th Avenue, past Bear Creek Park, and takes a left on King George. After a couple blocks he turns right. Driving into the busy South-Asian community, he remembers a stat he read: "Over forty percent of the immigrant population in Surrey is South Asian. This area is the epicentre of their community." Damon feels a heavy weight on his shoulder. Attacking a famous gang leader in front of his community is not in his original plan. Damon pulls into an industrial building and parks.

Exiting his white Caravan in his work clothes won't raise one eyebrow in this area. Many trades work out of small vehicles around here. Damon pulls his black hat on and walks out of the industrial delivery truck loading yard, to the sidewalk.

He takes note of the regular activity around the street. *Old F-two-fifty with three brown guys on the bench seat, the back loaded with a new bathtub for install. The traffic is moving slowly on the congested side street. In each car there's a brown person of different employment status. First a young woman in a five-year-old Corolla, holding her phone and talking with it on speaker. Next car is a white Chevy van with dents all over, with an old grey-haired guy with a young helper in the passenger seat, both covered in drywall dust. The next car is a perfectly clean Mercedes, all black with tinted windows, driven by a mature business-orientated lady who could be a politician. Every person is eyeing the white guy walking along. I feel they all know each other.*

Damon's Coach speaks calmly. *You feel that, eh? Well, why don't you note cameras and places to park? You don't have time to imagine what's going on in every car that drives by.* Damon has been trying to get a feel for the area, not imagining what each person around him is thinking, but he doesn't have the energy to argue with a voice in his head tonight.

As Damon turns into the big India-themed complex, he wonders what he's getting into this time. *Is Suhki high up in this community? Does his family own this complex? Is he some South Asian general's kid, in charge of importing heroin from India? Will this death start a massive blood feud with Surrey's entire Indo-Canadian community?*

The Coach's yell bounces off Damon's skull. *You want to die? You're in an ongoing war. At this moment, you're in active surveillance of a violent and prepared target. You continue imagining, you're going to be dead for real. Pay attention to this location.* Damon becomes present and answers. *Yes, of course. Thank you for reminding me.*

Damon initiates an efficient monitoring of the complex; he takes a seat on a bench and pulls out a magazine. He faces the magazine, but his eyes scan the parking lot. And he makes mental notes on the level of awareness of the people walking around. *These people are from a country rife with violence. This neighbourhood has issues with violence. Every single person is alert. Everyone has a casual eye on everything. I stick out like a sore thumb. White, sitting, doing nothing but reading. It's obvious that a white guy sitting for more than five minutes will draw attention around here.*

Most likely they think I'm a cop, or an insurance inspector trying to witness a car insurance claimant lifting more weight than they said they could. 80th and 128th has scored one of the highest accident claims in the lower mainland.

This job has so many unknowns. I'm going to assume the intel is 100 percent solid; I know how I'll do it tomorrow. One good push, bang, *done.*

LANGLEY, 9:00 P.M.

Sara sits in a grey jogging suit, with her blonde hair in a low ponytail. On her back deck, she scans her work laptop while sipping from an iced mug filled with Guinness. Sometimes she will have one tall can at the end of a long day. This investigation is cutting into all her spare time. Sara has thought more than once, *Lucky the overtime pay is so good, I might get to rebuild my deck this year. If I keep working at this schedule, I could get an above-ground pool as well.*

Sara's husband pokes his head out the back door and asks, "Are we going to watch that Netflix series tonight?"

Sara lift her head to show a dramatic frown. "Ah, I love it too, but this case is in real time. I have to schedule the teams for tomorrow."

"How's it going? Will it end soon? Any leads?"

Sara knows her husband wants time with her; he doesn't care about some criminal land developer getting justice for being murdered, or stopping an Indo-Canadian from being killed, or catching the Trowel group. "This is a single extra duty case, it has a time limit. I'm getting somewhere." He nods as he pulls his head back into the house and slowly closes the sliding-glass door.

Sara has been reading the current reports on Suhki and his crew. It seems he's in the middle of collecting a drug debt from a trucking company that lost a load of cocaine. The load is said to be Tony Fukadero's. Sara's stomach is upset, reading this. Is she supposed to find a murderer who killed Tony for the money he stole from the Trowel group? Or the missing cocaine? She sits back and takes a long pull on her iced mug of beer, drinking a third of it and brooding. *Jeez, this guy had it coming from all directions. How do we make things right when everyone is so wrong?*

Sara shakes her head, puts her beer down, and opens the laptop. She is determined as she types tomorrow's orders for everyone.

I have a job to do. Let the judge decide what to do with everyone. I've been given a broad scope to work with. This Fukadero investigation has led to a cocaine smuggling ring and a new murder plot against Suhki from the trucking company he's after. Tomorrow I'll have our team watching the hitman's warehouse. We have eyes on Suhki. We'll monitor Chloe Fukadero. I've put the request in for the Grim Sinners' informant to tell us what Dean Schmitt is doing, and his location. We have all phone locators for Trowel being tracked.

Sara leans over her laptop typing directions for each team, ensuring she tells them that if any contact is made in regard to the Damon hitman issue, she is to be alerted within two minutes. Sara reasons, *Because Bill wants to know within five.*

30

Damon stands in his metal shipping container with the little LED lantern on. It's damp and musky smelling; he forgot that he intended to bring another light, so the harsh shadows cast by his body wouldn't be as prevalent. *It's functional. Keep your eyes out of the shadows and focus on what the light is illuminating.*

Damon walks to the pile of damp cardboard boxes, and lifts a few down to access one. He reaches inside, withdraws a tied-off garbage bag, and carries it over to his workbench. Opening the bag, he takes out the black wig, a jar with makeup, and an applicator, as well as a mirror. Damon ordered this face-makeup from a movie company over a year ago; the wig was purchased locally at the same time.

Damon previously watched a YouTube video on face-makeup application. It takes almost thirty minutes to get it all smooth. He puts the black wig on. The little mirror in front of him reveals a South Asian man looking back at him. The cream foundation is a few shades darker than his own skin, so he's a light-skinned brown guy.

I hope this make-up is spread evenly in daylight, I'll double-check it in the Safari van vanity mirror.

Damon dresses in the rest of today's costume and packs all the remnants of evidence for disposal later. He clicks the button off, on the LED lantern. And opens the metal door on the metal shipping container; the light beams in, blinding him for a few seconds.

Damon advances from the metal container, his head straight while eyeing everywhere at once. As he drives out from between the two rows of light industrial two-story buildings, he notices a white work van sitting at the far left end of the parking lot. Damon takes a mental note to see if this new vehicle is around later.

Probably a delivery van.

SURREY, LITTLE INDIA, 12:30 P.M.

The sun is hidden behind a solid layer of high cloud; it's bright and warm out. Suhki blasts India FM on the radio; an Indi pop song's upbeat base line emanates from his Hellcat. He taps the steering wheel and sings along while bobbing his head. Zarita isn't impressed.

She wears a loose-fitting black jogging suit, her thick black hair in a wide ponytail. Her makeup is casual. She doesn't get overdressed to go to the salon, since she visits each week. Suhki makes it a date for the two of them, with lunch in the little India plaza after, but Zarita isn't enjoying these dates anymore.

Zarita sees they're nearing the plaza, so she turns the music off. "Suhki, this used to be a proud day for me, coming here to our community's upscale spa. You bring my brother along as a bodyguard."

"Hey, I can hear you. Nice to see you too, lil' sis."

Zarita waves at Jag with a smile. "Everyone in the salon acts nervous around me. Why? Why are they scared?"

Suhki's stomach flips while she talks. He is out of room to B.S. anyone in his family. The talk of open fighting is in the air of their community. He takes a big breath in. "Zarita, we are a strong family. You don't have to worry about everyone's strange looks. Once all this work clears up, people will forget."

As Suhki talks he scans the street for parked cars, that could hold possible get-away drivers. He notices every movement from across the street to the walkways in the plaza.

Just another normal day. Suhki looks in his rear-view mirror; Jag stares back and nods.

"All good bro."

Suhki parks in front of the spa, and Zarita gets out without kissing him. Jag watches the parking lot while his brother-in-law watches Zarita go around the front of the purple Charger. Suhki rolls his window down. "We'll be back in two hours. Try and have a nice time. I love you."

Zarita knows that someone in the spa might be watching them, so she walks back over and kisses him for two seconds. His heart pounds.

SURREY, LITTLE INDIA, 12:30 P.M.

Damon watches the purple Hellcat drives into the plaza. He holds a broom and is sweeping the curb across the street. Damon knows that these buildings employ cleaning companies, but sweeping the street, nobody will notice.

This is it. Damon almost cheers. The intel was good. Suhki will return for her in two hours. Then they will go eat in the traditional diner in the plaza. Damon isn't going to wait until they go to lunch. When Suhki comes back, Damon will be close enough to the door to ambush them all.

SURREY, E DIVISION, 1:00 P.M.

Sara's work phone rings. "Hello, Sara here."

The officer on the other end introduces himself. "Officer McNab here, I'm with the surveillance unit in Surrey. We have Suhki Trivedi at the spa with his wife, and possibly another man in the back seat. We have two watch posts here with three officers. When Suhki drove off we spotted a lone subject watching him; the single man hasn't left yet. He's not shopping and continues to watch the spa entrance."

Sara questions, "Is it Damon?"

"No, we have a South Asian man of interest here."

"Are you wearing your vest, Officer?"

The officer has heard that Sara is alpha in her approach to policing, and he's onboard. "Yes, and the other two officers; we have field rifles as well."

Sara is pleased. "Good to hear. You three stay close enough to intercept the hitman, we want to catch him in the act. Don't go over to him. Let him close on Suhki, then apprehend."

The surveillance officer is ecstatic, "Thank you, Sara, I'll prep my team."

SURREY, LITTLE INDIA, 2:30 P.M.

Damon is in his old worn-out blue work coveralls. He has headphones on and is bobbing his head as if the music is on, specifically to stop people from speaking to him in some South Asian language. Damon began a prolonged approach to the spa after Suhki pulled out. First using the broom to sweep the sidewalk for an hour. Then swept around the back of the building for half an hour. For the last half hour, he's been sweeping the front of the plaza storefronts. He has timed how long he needs to clean each store front to arrive at the spa's front door at 2:30. He's at the next unit.

The purple Charger turns into the parking lot. Damon hears the base from the stereo playing over the engine purring. Damon sweeps as he peeks over his shoulder again.

Wait, that van is on my *schedule.*

The phone company van that is parked on the curb at the far end of the sidewalk starts its engine and crawls forward. Damon feels a tingle in his spine. *That van has been here as long as me, I never saw anyone get in or out. The Hellcat's arrival and the phone company van moving; is it a coincidence?*

SURREY, LITTLE INDIA, 2:30 P.M.

Suhki spots a janitor sweeping as he turns into the parking lot; he turns the music down and speaks to Jag, who is in the back behind the passenger seat, "Yo bro, you see this janitor sweeping near the spa?"

Jag already has his eyes locked on the sweeping janitor. "Yeah, I noticed him when we turned in. Should we park on the other side and Zarita can walk over to the diner?"

Suhki's face twists in disgust, and half-turns to look down at his brother in law. "What's wrong with you? That's my wife, your sister. We pick her up at the front door. Get your gun out. Keep it ready to pop off, if this guy moves."

SURREY, LITTLE INDIA, 2:31 P.M.

"Unit Two, I have the Charger coming into the lot, I'm going to move my position to the business next-door to the spa."

Unit Two confirms the plan. "We have him, Charger drove past us. We have a clear line of sight on the guy that is waiting in the gold Mustang, and the Charger from this location. When Suhki stops, I'll get out the passenger door with my rifle hidden behind the door. It's only ninety yards, I'll cover you completely from our position. On your signal, we'll advance to you."

SURREY, LITTLE INDIA, 2:32 P.M.

Damon is at the edge of the spa unit; his head is down watching the broom. He notes the two guys in the other van by the road that pulled in after the phone company van. His mind races. *Three white guys in two vans. So there are four white guys in this South-Asian mall, and we're all scoping the spa. This is an unnatural feeling. Why is the phone company van parking on the curb? There are spots to park right beside him, and he's not unloading anything.*

Damon decides to wait until the wife is on the way out before he makes his move. The notion comes to him, *Maybe I don't make a move. I'm working off dirty intel. I have no idea what I've walked into.* Damon's eyes scan back-and-forth between the vans. The target rolls up behind him. He knows where the Hellcat driver is sitting. No need to check that.

SURREY, LITTLE INDIA, 2:33 P.M.

Jag confirms, "I've got one in the chamber bro, but he's right in front of the spa. Zarita will be out any second."

Suhki stares at the white guy in the van that has pulled in front of him; the driver is staring out into the parking lot.

"Don't you dare point that gun at my wife."

Jag has taken his seatbelt off and has his back against the car door on the parking lot side. He's holding the 9mm pistol in a two-hand grip, aiming it low in the car. Suhki dials his wife's phone number. "Zarita, where are you?"

"Hi sweetie, I'm in the line to pay. Over here! I see you."

Suhki grips his steering wheel. There she stands in the front window, smiling, eyes bright and cheery. Zarita flashes her hands, wiggling her fingers. Suhki notices her nails are a lighter shade of pink.

Suhki whispers, "Zarita, something is going on out here. Go to the back of the spa."

He watches as her joy fades; and a deep frown with furrowed brow appear.

Zarita's grim voice broadcasts over the Hellcat's speakerphone.

"Do you really think people have come to hurt us here?"

"Please Zarita, go in the back. I'll call you when it's clear."

Zarita moves a bit to keep a clear view as a janitor sweeps in front of the window. Her voice is stony.

"This is it, Suhki. I'm never coming here again. I'm never going anywhere with you again. You leave, I'll catch a cab." Zarita doesn't hang up, but she turns away from the window and takes her place at the counter as the next customer.

Suhki begs, "Zarita, just go in the back, please."

Suhki sees her pull the phone away from her ear.

"Total up what I owe. Cancel next week's appointment and call me a cab. Thank you."

Suhki hangs up. He watches the van park right in front of him. A white guy gets out and stands still behind his driver's door, watching the parking lot like a hawk.

Jag sees an opportunity. "This guy with the broom isn't sweeping very well, his eyes are all over the place. Once he sweeps a little further he'll be away from the front window, I'll have a better shot at him."

Suhki slams the Hellcat in reverse, and presses the gas heavy enough to make Jag brace himself against the passenger seat as his weight is thrown. Suhki purses his lips and shakes his head. He won't risk his innocent wife or the workers of the mall to take out a hitman. Suhki shifts the car into drive and gives the engine enough fuel to make the engine roar, but not enough to make the tires smoke. He passes the van door by inches. The white guy doesn't even look at him.

Suhki makes eye contact with Zarita as the car races away. A new reality lands on him. *Zarita watched me run away, leaving her with nobody to protect her. I hope she knows it's me they want; with me gone she's not in danger.*

Suhki slams the steering wheel with his flat open palm. *Fuck*

SURREY, LITTLE INDIA, 2:33 P.M.

Officer McNab puts the van in park. Glancing at Suhki; he sees the other man staring at him. The officer discreetly grabs his mic button. "Cover me. The suspect in the gold Mustang is getting out of the driver door."

The officer draws his pistol and opens the driver door. He steps out with his gun in a two-hand grip.

The South Asian guy has his door open, and stands beside his ten-year-old Mustang; on the far side of the parking lot. He will have to walk past one parked car to get next to the Purple Charger. Officer McNab suspects the guy is wondering if he should ignore the phone repair-van and start his walk over to shoot up the Charger, or leave.

The Indo-Canadian man and the officer lock eyes for three seconds. The man jumps in his golden Mustang. At that moment Suhki's car reverses. Mustang guy watches the Hellcat take off; his head on a swivel.

Officer McNab grabs his radio. "Suhki has left. I'm going to read the plate on the Mustang."

Leaving the door open, Officer McNab takes two steps across the parking lot's road. The Mustang engine fires up, and emergency-reverses, the tires screech from getting too much fuel.

Officer McNab turns and runs back to his vehicle. He slams the door, and reports to his radio, "I'm following a suspect, you stay here and wait to see if Suhki comes back."

SURREY, LITTLE INDIA, 2:33 P.M.

Damon sweeps the broom past the front window, two feet from a tall Indian princess. *I think this is Suhki's wife; why is she staring out the window? She's so emotional.* Damon discreetly glances over his shoulder to see what she's focused on, rechecking the white van as he looks. He knows instantly when he sees the white guy getting out of the van that his only defence with this undercover cop guarding Suhki is to continue sweeping, and hope no one notices him.

Damon hears the Hellcat rev into gear; he turns slightly to his left to see the car's back end drop as the engine roars.

Damon's body turns slightly to the right as he sweeps, he keeps his sight on the driver of the phone repair van.

Where is he walking? Whoa, why is that gold Mustang in such a hurry? Does Suhki have guards posted? Are these cops breaking up his security?

Damon sweeps as the phone company van takes off in hot pursuit. His Coach whispers. *There is too much going on here, keep sweeping. We'll go to the end of this strip mall. This place is crawling with adversaries.*

It takes an hour to sweep the length of the plaza at the same snail's pace Damon had started at. He does see the beautiful Indian woman get in a cab twenty minutes later; her shoulders are rounded, her hair over her face.

I'd bet money she was crying as she got in that cab.

Ten minutes after the wife leaves, the other white van in the far corner starts its engine and pulls away. Damon is glowing inside with this new information.

Suhki has police crawling on him. I could not have found out more reliably. I will make my next plan taking into account that he has a police presence around him. I wonder if it's to protect him—or to catch him? It's so hard to know if a guy is an outlaw or a police agent nowadays.

Damon had devoted over seven hours today to the hunt. *"No kill. No next location."* He heads for his metal container in Port Kells, *I'll have to try his house. The show house at 3:00 p.m. is probably still good. If I can't find him by next week, I'll try the spa again. Suhki will get it soon. I feel it. He's on borrowed time. Anyone who goes to the spa during a war is either confident or ignorant. Suhki is ignorant of how committed a real assassin is. Because he doesn't know any real assassins.*

Damon feels cheery as he surmises his target's understanding of the situation.

SURREY, 2:34 P.M.

Officer McNab pulls out of the parking lot in time to see the gold Mustang driving straight across the two-lane road into another industrial building yard. He calls in the pursuit on his radio with the direction of travel, then puts his foot down in his phone-repairman undercover vehicle. The white van blasts out of the brightly painted plaza, two cars slam their brakes to avoid T-boning the van.

McNab races his white van through the open gate of a chain-link fence. He sees the gold Mustang turning right at the end of the white two-story building. McNab peruses at top speed to the end of the unit. He turns right, tires let out a wailing screech. He slams on his brakes as soon as he sees the Mustang's driver door open, and the single occupant bolts toward the back chain-link fence.

McNab pulls his seatbelt off; grabbing his mic button, he jumps out.

"Suspect on foot, wearing black pants and black long-sleeved shirt. South Asian skin colour. Heading east, over a fence." The guy dashes up the ten-foot fence swiftly as Spiderman and jump-drops off the top into a forward roll. The officer watches to see how the landing roll turns out; the suspect keeps his momentum, rolls onto his feet and is off at full speed.

"McNab here, I'm out of the foot chase. I will secure the scene."

SURREY 3:55 P.M.

After Sarah received word of the short pursuit after the gold Mustang, she immediately left the E Division main headquarters in Surrey and traveled to 80th and 128th.

She studies the license plate on the gold Mustang.

This is a perfectly cloned counterfeit license plate.

They run the plate, and it's identified as belonging to a sixty-two-year-old lady in Prince George who works at the library. When they contact a local RCMP officer in

Prince George, he says he knows the lady and the car. "I saw her car parked at the library two hours ago."

Sara takes a picture of the VIN number in the window; it matches the Prince George car.

This vehicle was created to commit a crime in. This took time and money. Someone has the mechanical know-how. Is this how Damon works?

Sara calls McNab over. "Good work today, Officer. I strongly believe you and your team averted a public shooting today. You almost caught the guy red-handed."

McNab shakes his head. "I should have gone over to this car sooner and checked it out, I might have caught him."

Sara defends the team's process. " You could not have detected this counterfeit job. The car would have come up clean, and you would have driven away. Now we've seized an expensive and time-consuming getaway car. We might have a picture of this guy on one of the security cameras. Most importantly you caught on before there was any gunfire. Again, good work."

McNab is stoic, lips pursed with his hands clasped in front on his belt. McNab asks. "Will we take prints off this car?"

Sara has been wondering how to utilize this counterfeit car.

"Someone put a lot of money into this getaway vehicle. Yes, we'll try and get a name from a fingerprint."

PORT KELLS, 4:15 P.M.

Damon decides that while he's in his South Asian costume, he'll park a few blocks away from the warehouse and metal storage container. Damon can't shake the feeling the cops are everywhere. He remembers an excerpt from a Vietnam-war biography by a famous Special Forces guy. "We are in their territory, so we have to suspect they know where we sleep. So we come and go from our base as if the way in and out has been booby-trapped."

Damon knows this is no time to take a breather. The authorities on all levels have their eyes open. Damon parks the white van about three blocks away. He eats the bagged lunch he prepped in the morning: black forest ham and cheese with tomato and lettuce, a huge red apple, and three chocolate-chip cookies.

Damon steps out of the van in his South Asian makeup.

Let's have a nice casual walk around for a few hours and get a good view of our home base.

LANGLEY, 7:00 P.M.

Damon is in Benji's bedroom. The boy is standing on the bed with a pillow held above his head, ready to swing it at his dad; Benji is laughing uncontrollably. Damon tries to be serious with the eight-year-old. "Benji, it is bedtime. Don't swing that pillow. Just lay down, we'll pillow fight tomorrow."

Benji lunges swinging the pillow like a sword; Damon grabs it with his left arm and yanks the pillow, which makes Benji fall into his dad's arms. Damon can't resist this opportunity for some revenge; he holds the little guy down and tickles him mercilessly.

"Okay, okay. Hahaha, I'll stop, please stop tickling me. Hahaaaa."

Naomi enters with a knowing smile. "This is not how you calm him down for sleep."

Damon stops, and Benji jumps off the bed, laughing, and tries to run past his mom. Naomi catches him with one arm around his chest. "I'll take it from here, you go put tea on for us."

Damon smiles. "I almost had him under the covers." He rubs the boy's head as he walks past them.

31

Damon leaves his white Caravan at the park three blocks away. He walks along, reminiscing about how he misses all the mixed-Asian neighbours he went to school with in this East Vancouver neighbourhood.

Damon sees the work truck parked in front of Yakub's house, and he relaxes a bit. *Glad the drive and walk isn't wasted. It's so hard to meet people to talk with cops everywhere.* He stops in front of the old wooden gate and examines the well-kept house. Damon pulls the gate's bolt over; he has to wiggle it. Once he's on the porch, he rings the doorbell and knocks. Damon stands so whoever is inside will see his face.

People get so paranoid in a war over money, these people are getting it hard.

Damon rings the bell again. He cups his hands on the door's window and leans in. Behind him he hears the sound of a single piece of gravel crunch under a shoe and he smiles as he turns. Only the house's owner walks that quietly. Yakub is in a light-blue cotton work-shirt and clean jeans.

I knew it, poor fucker can't even go to work.

Yakub has a polite smile for Damon.

"Let's go around the back and talk in my garage." Yakub turns and leads the way, Damon hops quickly down the stairs to follow.

When they get into the shop, Damon reveals the story about Dean at his house and how he figured out that Dean is in the Grim Sinners. Yakub sits on a tall metal stool, and listens with his hands crossed in front of him. His thick face is a stone, nodding along enough to be polite. Damon sees this fight is taking a significant toll on this working man, whose brother and cousin are in jail from this; all his work capital is tied up in court. Now Damon is telling him one of the province's most significant street gangs are gunning for them, along with Suhki and his crew.

"Yakub, has anyone come to your house yet?"

Yakub's poker face makes Damon uncomfortable. Damon is taken aback by this new demeanour.

"Yakub, are you okay? Is your family okay?"

Yakub finally breaks his silence. "Damon, you said to me before that after 'it's done' we never ever mention 'it' again."

Damon tips back on his heals. *Oh shit, Yakub is going to mention the Fukadero hit. Is he a rat now?*

Damon's voice hardens. "Yeah, and nothing has changed on that front."

Yakub leans in. "Dean will not be back. I heard he left town."

Damon pulls his head back and squints. "What are you talking about? Who have you been talking to?"

Yakub clasps his thick hands and gives them one high shake. "Dean is not coming back. He is 'gone.' Okay, Damon? You know how sometimes someone is just 'gone?' Well, that piece of shit is gone from this city. For goodness sake."

Damon is lightly shaking his head. Then the slang registers with Damon.

Does he mean dead?

"There it is, you get it now,"

Damon's eyes flash big; Yakub nods slowly.

Damon racks his brain. *Who killed Dean? What situation? Who knows? Where's the body? Were there witnesses?* While he's thinking these questions, Yakub studies his face. Damon quickly realizes that he doesn't want any of these answers, any more than he would want to tell someone about his murder details. There are only two people in a good murder; one is dead, and one did it. No story time later; they always end up in police recordings.

Damon and Yakub both slowly smile.

Damon suddenly feels less useful.

"I was close the other day."

"Say no more, my friend. I know you work as hard as we do. Will you come in and have a snack and coffee? My wife wants to say hello, I'm sure."

Together they walk to the house. Yakub twists the tarnished door nob.

"June? June, we have Damon here to have a coffee. Will you come to say hello?"

Damon is taking his shoes off when he sees June come around the corner. The dark bags under her eyes make Damon do a double take. He looks over at Yakub for support. He points to the dark wooden table.

"You two have a seat, I'll pour the coffee. Would you rather have a tea, June?"

June lifts her sorrowful head. "Coffee is good. I need a wake up."

Damon stands at a chair waiting for June to find a seat; he sits as she does. She shows gratitude to the chivalry with a gentle smile. Damon attempts to pick up a clue that will tell him why June has become so downcast.

Her hair is combed and neat, her makeup is taken care of. Her pleated flower-print dress is clean.

Yakub comes over with three cups of coffee on a tray with honey and cream; he sits at the head of the small kitchen table.

"June is strong, but this week she had a traumatic experience. Well, to tell the truth, we both did."

Damon reaches for the honey-dipper. His hand freezes on the thin wooden handle. *Yakub's wife has been part of the murder in some way.* Yakub nods quickly without looking at Damon. Damon lifts the stick out of the honey; it is one of those little honeycombs that you have to drip the honey off of. His heart feels heavy.

Nice people are so upset by murder. Will June recover from being part of a murder?

Damon knows that Yakub needs some help with his wife. They can't tell anyone about what happened, yet they need someone to talk to.

Damon stirs in some cream. All three finish their own unique coffee-making ritual. Damon doesn't beat around the bush when he knows it's serious, so he talks direct. "June, I heard your family has been through so much in this century. All of your family that lived through World War Two. Everyone who immigrated and struggled so hard to have a good life in Canada. This generation has a tough fight going on." Yakub focuses on Damon and listens with a polite smile. Damon sees June is all ears, so he carries on. "Yakub is a perfect man. I've seen many types of men who use violence to get around in the world. Yakub isn't one of them. In a fight, you have to win. Your family is the winner. When attacked, smart and strong people defend themselves. You, good honest people, are being attacked on many fronts. Yakub and I and the rest of your family must defend. The bullies can't take our lives, if they try to then we take theirs."

At that last sentence, Yakub clears his throat, grasps his wife's arm.

"Sweetie, are you okay, do you want to lay down for a bit?"

Damon feels his face flush, maybe he went too far with his little *kill them all and let God sort them out* speech.

June closes her eyes and draws in a big breath, but after she releases. "No, I'm okay. Damon is correct in his evaluation of our situation. I just don't know how we go back to enjoying life again now that it's gone this far."

Damon smiles. "Oh, don't worry about that, we're humans. We've been doing terrible things to one another since before the written word. When this is over, and the judge makes good on a decision for your company, the bullies will move on to their next victim. If we let them." All three have a playful laugh. "June, if I had been faster, you and Yakub would have been safer." Yakub exaggeratedly shakes his head in the negative.

June defends him as well. "Don't think that way, Damon, these thieves are running wild. Nobody can control them."

Damon takes a sip as she speaks, then he adds to her comment. "We'll help them find new places to live, forever." Yakub holds in a belly chuckle at Damon's little inside joke referring to Dean 'moving.' June sees her husband smile for the first time this week, and she relaxes. Finding June becoming more herself, Damon offers further comfort. "You care about others, and that's a good sign. Don't stop caring about good people. The bad ones are weaker, good always wins. Well, that's assuming I'm good."

June is keeping solid eye contact. "You're as good as they come, Damon. Thank you for coming by here today. You make this crazy world seem less crazy."

Damon deadpans. "When you want to talk about crazy, I'm your guy." June laughs for real this time.

A knock at the front door stops the laughter. *Tap...tap tap...tap.* The second time the pattern repeats, Yakub and his wife relax and became visibly happier. Yakub stands. "Uncle Gabriel has used that knock on doors since I was child."

Yakub comes back into the room with Gabriel right behind him. Damon stands to greet the older gentleman. Gabriel's eyes come alive with joy and surprise. "What a surprise, oh my, god does love us. I walked from Alexi's office over on Commercial for an unplanned visit with my family, and I find a friend as well. Let's sit and have coffee together."

Damon sits in unison with the other three. Gabriel smiles at Damon as the three get the conversation going.

VANCOUVER, EAST END, 11:30 A.M.

Yakub walks beside Damon on his side street. Damon casually mentions that with Dean on holiday, his crew will search for him at his last locations. "Street gangs make a lot of decisions at four in the morning. They do the drive-by shootings, burning stuff. Stay off the open streets in your natural areas."

Yakub nods along, and spins one finger in the air . When Damon finishes his soft warning, Yakub turns to him. "Damon, this is the lowest our family has been since we came to Canada. We have never had to murder anyone before. Our whole family has historically saved money and worked hard. My father always worked for a wage; I'm the first one to try and do business. Tell me the truth. When this is over, either way, are we ruined in the business world?"

Damon shakes his head while Yakub finishes his question. Damon smiles, "Yakub, the whole Lower Mainland knows your company was robbed. Anybody who knows your company's issues with the so-called extortion is silently rooting for you guys. People know those cocky thieves deserve the grave. Regular people walk away and hope karma gets them one day. We're making your karma; karma wants your money back, too. Good people will work with you. Anyone scared of being killed if they rip you off, you don't want to with."

Damon sees Yakub cheer up. So he backs away, "I'm going to plan a holiday for a friend."

Yakub squints one eye, and Damon smiles and waits for Yakub to remember the 'Dean on a holiday reference.' Yakub's brow relaxes, he is happy as he turns to walk slowly home.

SURREY, 12:00 P.M.

Suhki and Jag sit on the stools at their gym's juice bar. Devon sits casually at a table against the back wall, with his eyes locked on the front door and a 9mm in his jacket's inside pocket, ready to draw. Jag asks, "How's it going with my sister?"

Suhki shakes his head while drinking his post-workout protein shake. "Not good, bro. Since you sent her over on her birthday to bust me, Zarita has been ice-cold. Then leaving her with a hitman." Suhki laughs and bows his shaking head, "This collection has to end quick." Jag goes to defend himself again for telling his sister that Suhki and Chloe were alone, but Suhki holds up his hand bashfully, "You're a good brother to your sister, I'm going to be a better husband." Jag warms with relief at the news.

Then Suhki turns to Jag with fire in his eyes, and Jag stares back with butterflies brewing in his stomach. Suhki asks, "You know what I heard? The president of the P and A Trucking company is hosting his sister's wedding at the hall this week. Let's go to that wedding."

Jag relaxes, Suhki is thinking about putting pressure on the trucker for the missing coke. Jag takes a pull on his protein shake straw, then asks, "How badly do you want a fight? Every tough guy in their family will jump us."

Suhki exclaims, "Oh, I hope so. I think we'll keep it respectful and ask a handful of them to come out back to talk. When they come out, we'll go bonkers and start swinging."

Jag knows it has to come to a head sometime, "Okay bro, when this is done, we just chill and go back into construction."

Suhki vows, "I'm going to make a baby with Zarita, she said once the drug dealing stops she will do it." Jag and Suhki bear hug.

SURREY, 2:30 P.M.

Sara sits taping her foot. Reading the report from the surveillance team on the warehouse where the hitman was reported to be working out of, according to the Trowel informant. Sara reads the activity report.

"A few lone occupants coming and going from the front door on different schedules. One guy parks where the surveillance team can't see. He keeps the oddest schedule. I'll focus on him for the remainder of the surveillance timeline. Less than ten days left in the budget."

Sara reviews the newest Grim Sinners agent report: Dean Schmitt has not been seen or heard from for days. Drexel is stepping into leadership.

Sara has a brief on the Basmati group as well: Suhki's phone and that of his brother-in-law are together every day. Sometimes they have a third and fourth associate in the car as they cruise around Surrey. His only pattern is the gym and show home visits.

Trowel's report is straightforward: Yakub is located at his house nearly twenty-four hours a day, always with his wife.

And Chloe: Chloe goes to work every day at the show home, then straight home. Suhki goes to the show home consistently each day at 3:00 p.m.

What are these people doing? It can't be good. I have to see what we have for information on the trucking company, Pacific and Atlantic. It's reported to be transporting drugs and owes the Fukadero group for a lost load of cocaine. P and A Trucking are a more prominent player than Dean and Chloe. Suhki is in a perilous position. Is he the one who stole the coke and killed Tony?

Sara rubs her eyes. *Stop guessing. Rely on facts. Find someone to tell you exactly what went on and what's going to happen next. Dig into the trucker employees, someone might already be on our information program, if not, make someone join. Facts will come from there.*

Sara agrees with herself and nods.

LANGLEY, 2:45 P.M.

Damon drives slowly around his neighbourhood when he gets back. Starting about three blocks out, he drives up and down every street scanning for any car that doesn't belong. *I love this area, each house has four spots in their driveway, so out of every ten houses, there's only a car or two on the street. A getaway car will stand out around here.*

Damon parks in his driveway and gets out of his car. He stands viewing his raw dirt yard as a light wind kicks up a cloud that blows over toward him and his white Caravan. He hurries to his house to get out of the path of the dust cloud. Damon opens his garage with the keypad that's on the doorframe.

As it opens he sees Naomi inside breaking down a big box for recycling. He greets her with a kiss on the cheek and a bum grab. Naomi tries to read Damon by his body language, *He considers crazy things as normal, so why would his body language change if something crazy is going on?* She shakes her head as she places the cut cardboard into the yellow city recycling bag.

Damon notices her shaking her head; he's afraid to ask her what's wrong because he knows it will be a long answer. Instead, he smiles, "I got some good news about work today." He's thinking about Dean being dead; the house is safer without him snooping around.

Naomi asks, "Like we're safe forever? You'll do normal stuff for work that we can post about on Facebook?"

Damon turns to face her with a big smirk. Naomi quips, "Yeah, I didn't think so."

Damon changes the topic, "Where's Benji?"

"With my sister and her husband on an after-school walk at a lake over in Maple Ridge." Damon asks about dinner, and Naomi sighs. "I haven't thought about it yet, what should we eat?"

"How about we go out for an early dinner? Four-thirty? We can pick Benji up after from your sister's house?"

"Can we talk about our plans?" Naomi asks. "When will the yard be planted? The dust is smothering. Also, what will we do with Benji this summer?"

Damon nods dramatically, "Oh yeah, we'll have a riot going over all the small details."

Naomi frowns. "This is our family, we need to go over the details. Who will if we don't?"

Damon is a little embarrassed he mocked her family-planning dinner, "You're right, I'm a caveman. Go get ready. It'll be fun."

Damon walks over to his workbench and sits on the stool. "I'm going to hang out here for half an hour or so, then I'll start to get ready." Naomi smiles; as she turns to leave her red hair fans out from the fast head turn. She hops off her back leg as she leaves the room.

Damon hears the house access door close behind him. He reaches up and unlocks the cupboard door, reaches in, and pulls out his twelve-gauge Mossberg. He puts the code in for the trigger lock and pulls it off. Opening a drawer, he pulls out nine shells, four slugs, and five double-zero bucks. His favourite loading pattern is a double-zero buck and then a slug, repeat.

Damon stands and leaves the loaded twelve-gauge on his bench; he covers it with the light sheet he keeps on the counter for this reason. Gazing out at his yard he notices the clouds have condensed and a light rain has begun. *Nice, this will keep the dust down on my lawn. Also, this will make a would-be assassin rush to not get wet. I'll let him walk right into the garage before I let him have it. Tomorrow I'll go by the gym. Suhki will be ready there, but he does keep a schedule. He's proven the routine twice. Once at the show home, and once in that South-Asian mall in Surrey. I'll nail him and his crew within two weeks, for sure.*

Who will the evil infect when Suhki and his crew are in the ground? Does he have a brother who'll hunt the Polish? Eventually, the darkness will change its direction. Murder will still be at the front of someone's mind. Only the targets will change.

Damon sees his neighbour, whom he hasn't spoken with, getting into his F-250 red crew cab truck. The man is a South Asian Canadian with a caucasian wife; they have a little girl who's about two years younger than Benji. Damon crosses his arms. *I wonder why that family is so private? We're all the same age, and with kids. He should have looked into my open garage and given a friendly wave; but no, they're always head-down. Oh well, we'll know each other one day.*

32

Damon sits in the white Safari van and watches the gym that Suhki frequents. He uses 10x42 binoculars. The white Safari van is parked across the same four-lane highway where he had parked to watch the Fuk's schedule. *That guy's erratic schedule kept him alive for a few extra months.*

Suhki's purple Charger Hellcat sits in its usual parking area. Damon smiles and feels lighter, because the unmarked Ford Explorer with the two police officers in it are watching Suhki's car as well. Damon surmises, *Suhki will see them, The police will see Suhki see them. Everyone will know the police are at the gym watching Suhki. Suhki will feel safe and come back tomorrow, but the police won't. I'll be here as well.*

Damon holds his post. When Suhki and his two friends come out, they spot the police. The police stare back. Suhki leaves; the police leave twenty minutes later. Damon places his binoculars in their case and starts his van; he slowly drives off.

See you tomorrow, Suhki.

APRIL 18TH, SURREY, 11:00 A.M.

No purple Hellcat. Damon sits stewing. *This is the beginning of five months more work. Naomi will not be happy if I'm on a year-long job. I'm going to drive by the show home. I'll park on the street around the corner. When Suhki arrives, I'll get into a good position for an ambush with cover. I'll pick them off from twenty-five yards out.*

Damon rests the binoculars on the seat and pulls a newspaper over them. He takes out his bagged lunch. *Let's see what extra goodies Naomi put in my sandwich today. Oooh jalapeño peppers with turkey, crisp lettuce on sourdough bread. This is so good, I love roasted turkey.*

As he eats the sandwich, he digs in the lunch bag. *Jackpot. There they are.* Damon pulls out the Ziplock bag with four homemade chocolate-chip cookies. The cookies had been in the freezer, they're perfectly chilled and soft.

SURREY, 3:10 P.M.

Damon walks by the show home dressed in his red tracksuit; today he is Ali G with bright white shoes on. A guy who wants attention; this is hiding in plain sight. This style of disguise is only good for a few passes a week.

There's the green Lamborghini. The other realtor's BMW. No Hellcat. What is Suhki doing? Shit, is he over at Yakub's house today? Damon passes the front of the show home. He doesn't even glance at it. He turns the corner and walks to the end of the block before turning around to pass a second time fifteen minutes later. *Still no Suhki.*

Damon's Simple voice whispers. *Chloe knows where he is, she keeps a regular schedule. Ask her, then pull the gun out of her mouth and let her answer.* Damon is back in front of the show home, walking at a casual pace. Damon considers. *I can't think of a reason she's still alive. I'm going to think about this. Maybe I'll get Suhki to come to her if she calls asking?*

Damon's Coach states the outline of the plan that has arisen. *Kidnap Chloe, call Suhki and ask him to come to meet her.* Damon gives an unthought answer. *Let's meet Chloe.* As Damon approaches the corner that the white Safari van is parked around, his mind races with scenarios of how he will grab Chloe.

Maybe cutting the head off and killing the muscle at the same time would be the fastest wrap-up.

Damon starts the white Safari van and drives off slowly. He decides, *I'll do the rounds this week, gym, show home; also, the South-Asian plaza in Surrey for his wife's spa date. If there's no action by then, I'll grab Chloe and end them both at once.*

SURREY, E DIVISION, 4:00 P.M.

The surveillance team has a loose schedule for the suspected hitman. Sara decides, *I'll have to execute a warrant before the end of next week on the hitman's warehouse. With the active surveillance, this is the safest time to go in. After last night's showdown, this guy might disappear. Early next week, probably Monday morning. Yeah, I'll send the request now. ERT will plan their raid with lots of time then.*

LANGLEY, 6:00 P.M.

Damon sits at his dinner table with Naomi and Benji; Patch lays beside him on a dog mat. Benji asks, "What are you staring at, Daddy?"

Damon clears his throat as he refocuses in the room from his deep thought. "Oh, I have an idea of how to spend a few weeks this summer. We should go down the coast to California, stop at beaches, and do a day or two in Disneyland." Benji listens blank-faced, but beams when he hears Disneyland. Damon reaches for Naomi's hand. "A few days at Huntington, Crystal Cove, wherever else would be nice, eh?" She grabs back with both hands.

Naomi can't contain her smile, "Will you have cleared your schedule by then?"

Damon pledges, "I'll give it my all to be done by the end of May."

LANGLEY, 9:00 P.M.

Damon sits in front of the TV; he and Naomi are going to watch Netflix and chill. She sits as the news begins; he grabs her arm to alert her to his attention to the news, so she'll keep quiet. Naomi is in purple-silk pajamas. She places a tray of hot cheese nachos on the table, quietly.

"Here on Local News, we've been following a story since last night, when a South Asian wedding that included the President of Pacific to Atlantic Trucking Company turned violent. Two men are dead, two are in hospital. The story is not yet entirely clear, but we do know that the deceased were under active monitoring by the RCMP. Suspects are being questioned."

Naomi asks, "Friends of yours?"

Damon shakes his head, "I don't hang out at Indian weddings."

The news camera goes through a series of video clips. One of a purple Hellcat with the door open; a blanket over the slumped driver, lying face-down on the front seat of the car. Blood soaking through the white sheet. His fancy black jogging pant legs are on the wet street; his brand-new bright-blue Nikes have blood on the bottom of one shoe. Damon knows for certain this is Suhki.

The other video clip is of a body under a sheet over by the entrance of the hall. Shiny dress shoes are exposed, and the blood seeping through the white cloth indicates many wounds in the chest of the face-up body.

The news continues. "A witness who has chosen not to be identified claims that they saw the whole incident unfold. Allegedly, four uninvited men arrived at the wedding. Fifteen to twenty of the men attending went to ask them to leave, and a fight quickly ensued."

The feed switches to the witness, his face blurred out. "One of the uninvited dudes was throwing guys to the ground. Anyone who came near the huge guy got thrown or hit. His three friends were kicking tables and chairs. Finally the huge dude started yelling something, I couldn't hear what. That's when I heard the gunshots. The big guy got hit in the arm and ran outta here."

The newscast cuts back to the reporter. "It seems a gunman from inside the hall followed, shooting the victim in the back as he was attempting to escape in the purple car. One of the victim's associates pulled a gun from a bag he had hanging around his chest, and shot the gunman who had come from the wedding hall. He stood above him and fired bullets until the gun jammed. The three remaining attackers fled. No one at the wedding knew the assailants. Police have descriptions, and are actively searching for them."

Damon sits back and reaches for a nacho chip; he dips it in the guacamole Naomi has made. She asks, "You still want to watch a movie?" She studies his neutral face again, trying to decide how he could have any connection to a South Asian wedding shooting.

Damon jumps up and heads out of the room, "First, I need to grab some water and go pee. You pick the movie, something funny would be cool."

Naomi sits back and grabs a nacho, dips it; she's content believing that the news has nothing to do with them.

Those communities are always fighting, of course Damon doesn't know them.

Damon returns and suggests, "Does Amy Schumer have anything new? She's so crazy that she makes me feel normal." They both laugh.

APRIL 19TH, LANGLEY, 5:30 A.M.

Damon is in his garage with his coffee on the workbench next to his Mossberg pump. He initiates the cardio plyometrics DVD; it's a sixty-minute workout. His mind is always the clearest when he pushes his cardio to the limit. He follows the instructions on the DVD on autopilot as he contemplates, *Okay, let's get warmed up.*

Dam it. I'm not responsible for Suhki's death, I'm not going to get paid. That asshole went to the wrong party. Now I have a street gang after me and no contract on them. Fuck. The DVD changes exercises every thirty-seconds. *Let's get those hamstrings ready to work.*

Obviously I'm not giving the deposit back to the Polish. That job is over. The South Asian crew will be after the truckers full time. The Fukadero collection will be forgotten by Suhki's crew for sure. The evil that infects the greedy still has a murder going on, now it's aimed at the truckers from the wedding. Actually, there will be more murder in the air. The truckers lost a man in front of a hundred witnesses. They'll be screaming bloody murder. The darkness that hovers over us always finds and creates more deaths. There is no end to bad blood. You can't kill your way to peace.

The DVD allows a thirty-second break after the warm-up. Damon drinks a big sip of his coffee. The warm-up doesn't accelerate his heart rate. Damon tries to imagine who in the Grim Sinners will grab the reins. *So does the new leader need to prove his worth by going after a hitman? Or is this person all about the money? Damn it. I don't even know these guys. Most likely, some kid who wants to make a name for himself is going to stick his neck out for a dead thief. What a waste of time.*

Well, with Suhki gone and no clear targets, I'll check if anyone has called my air conditioning business line. The exercise DVD gets a little more intensive, with a move that requires bending his knees and touching the ground, then jumping and reaching for the sky. Damon checks the clock. *Holy shit, this is a long work out, forty-five minutes left.* He stops thinking about work, to focus on the drills.

LANGLEY, 10:00 A.M.

Damon sits in a coffee shop in Langley. He pulls out his cell phone and turns it on. Listening to the banter around him and watching the rain pour outside the window, he daydreams. *These folks in here seem stressed in their little conversations. Are they worried about a gunman running in here and shooting them? Or if their car mechanic is telling the truth?* He smiles as he lifts his tea and takes a sip.

If I never had one worry about who's trying to kill my friends and me, what would I worry about? Maybe my new home roof warranty would keep me awake at night? The phone on the table lets out a ding. Damon checks at the work phone and shakes his head.

I really have the best luck. I always receive work leads.

He reads the text message. *"Hi, our air conditioner isn't working. Will you come and fix it? Summer is coming, so the sooner the better."*

Damon lifts his green tea and takes another sip. He plans the next few days and decides it will be best if he works this job on Monday. Damon types his schedule. *"Good morning, send me your address and I'll come by on Monday at 10:30 a.m. Can you send me a picture of the air conditioning unit, so I know what to bring?"*

Damon has a cheese quiche on a plate that he let cool. He picks small bites off with his metal fork. As he eats the last bite, a text returns with a picture of the five-ton air conditioner, an address, and a message, *"Thank you, you are a lifesaver."*

Damon sends another text message back. *"NP. I'll text Sunday night to confirm with you."*

His phone dings right away. *"Thx, c u sn."*

SURREY, 1:00 P.M.

Chloe sits in her office with the glass door shut; her curtains are drawn. The desk is clear in front of her. She asks her assistant, Shari, to hold her calls unless they're critical for closing a property sale.

Chloe is deep in thought. *Dean hasn't been heard from for almost a week. Last I saw him he came to grab two kilos for the dealers in the Grim Sinners. Would someone there kill him for some reason? Who got the kilo would be a good start. Did Dean tell anyone about the hundred kilos we have from the missing load? If he did, I might be killed at any moment.*

Suhki, oh, Suhki. I'm so sorry for what I did to you. He died in the street; a common thug. Suhki was so much more than the street stuff he was killed for. All the time, university, physical training. He was so honourable. Will his wife hold me responsible? I wonder if I should go to the funeral? I have to, I need that crew to keep after the truckers...for the debt.

Chloe's arms hang beside her with her hands on her lap, fingers lightly intertwined. She's staring at her empty desk when Shari opens the door, "Excuse me, Chloe, there's a Drexel and Shelly here to see you. Drexel says you and him have some business?" The last statement is said as a question. Chloe snaps to the present as Shari says the name Drexel. Dean had mentioned him a few times. 'Hothead street dealer' was how Dean had described him.

"Thank you, Shari, show them in."

Chloe views them through the glass wall; they're standing around gawking like they're in a spaceship. Drexel is in pair of dark-blue baggy jeans with thick stitching. He has a baggy white shirt on with no insignia. The woman with him has put more effort into coming to the show home; Shelly has black high heels on, a white skirt that's cut above the knee, and a red silk thin-strapped top. Her hair is feathered.

Chloe stands and greets them at the door of her office. She shakes both of their hands and gestures to the seats in front of her desk that they are to sit in. The girl, Shelly, tries to achieve prolonged eye contact with Chloe as they pass. When Chloe doesn't reciprocate, Shelly turns her head to Drexel with a huff. Chloe doesn't notice, too focused on the lobby of the showroom and who else saw them come into her office. Her heart aches. *The whole staff watched these two gangsters come into my office.*

Drexel had been at the gym this morning, and every day this week. After Dean spoke to him about the upcoming future that included more money and more responsibility, Drexel has been on the wagon. He wipes his clammy palms on his jeans while watching Chloe. *Wow, this girl is super-hot. She's flawless, from her flat ironed hair down to her perfect nails. I'm going to send Shelly to the same hair and nail place Chloe goes to; that's a good way for them to be friends, since we all work together now.*

Chloe lays her hands flat on the desk; she leans forward off the back of her chair. While staring right in Drexel's eyes, she asks, "Where is Dean?"

Drexel maintains eye contact and doesn't flinch at the question; he spits out what he knows. "He told me he was going after Tony's killers, a hitman and the guys who hired him."

Chloe hits a button on her office phone, "Hi Shari, Come in here for a second." She sits back in the chair, resting her elbows on the armrests with her fingertips all touching in front of her face. Drexel and Shelly glance at each other for support in their mutual confusion.

Shari opens the door and walks over to stand next to Chloe, facing Drexel and Shelly. Chloe's voice is cheery, "Please take Shelly and show her the full presentation on our company's plan for our next home-building phase. She'll be shopping for a house soon I'm sure, and should lean on our operation as a baseline for her future house shopping."

Shelly kisses Drexel as though she's been given a house. Her eyes wide as saucers, Shelly stands. "Show me the way. Drexel, I love you. Chloe, you're the best. Let's have a few drinks soon." Shelly leaves the office before her new realtor.

Chloe refocuses on Drexel, "Please shut the door, Shari." Shari nods as she walks to the door with her mouth slightly ajar. When the door is shut, Chloe tells Drexel one of her rules. "Please don't talk about crimes in front of your girlfriend with me, ever again."

Drexel holds his mouth shut, as it dawns on him that Dean tells him the same thing.

"I understand, I won't do it again."

Chloe asks, "What is it you've come here for?"

"I'm not sure what's happened to Dean, we're looking into it. Grim Sinners take care of each other. But, like, on the money side of it. Where I am now, is the head of all our dealers. Do you know that?"

Once more, Chloe is so disappointed with this whole situation; it's as if Tony died yesterday, she feels so alone again. But Chloe is a survivor. "If you're the money guy, where's the money from the last two kilos Dean took?"

Drexel leans back and puts his hands behind his head. "I've got the hundred and twenty thousand cash in the car. Should I bring it in here? It's already counted. The only problem is, there's about fifteen grand in five dollar bills. Is that okay? Dean usually makes us drive around and get them turned into twenty dollar bills."

Chloe feels a little spark of light inside her chest. *'One hundred and twenty thousand dollars.'* That means Dean gave the Grim Sinners the street price. Chloe answers him, "No, never bring any of our business to this business, okay?"

Drexel holds one finger over his lips, "Got it."

Chloe becomes worried about getting killed in a robbery and decides to have a get-together tonight at her house with her sister and her mother for dinner, "I have some people coming over tonight, you come by at seven and we'll go to the home office and count the money, then I'll tell you who to call for two more kilos. Okay?"

Drexel lightly slaps his hands on his thighs, "I was hoping for four kilos, or we'll have to meet twice a week."

Chloe closes her eyes and shakes her head. "We can't get more than two bricks without paying in full for them."

Drexel nods in agreement. "Yeah, that's right; then we pay fifty grand for each in cash."

Chloe smiles, "That's right." But then her eyes go wide.

Drexel observes the colour drain from Chloe's perfect face. He turns and his gaze becomes fixed.

Man, did this guy just walk out of an old Italian mobster movie? Long tweed overcoat, three-piece suit with a matching hat. He even has a guy dressed like him watching his back. Holy shit, this must be...

Chloe stands as the man opens the door without knocking, "Mr. Fukadero, what brings you into the office today?"

The older gentleman with the white hair inspects Drexel, who remains seated when he enters, "Friends of yours, Chloe? Am I interrupting?"

Chloe feels her cheeks flush, "No sir, we're finished here. Drexel, would you go join Shelly in the presentation?"

Drexel stands and extends his hand out to Mr. Fukadero. "Drexel, of the Grim Sinners. I'm here to help you in any way, sir." Chloe's stomach turns at the sight of these two talking.

Mr. Fukadero shakes his hand, "Thanks kid, I might call you some time. I'll get your number from Chloe. Nice meeting you."

Chloe goes around the desk reaching her arms as she walks to hug her father-in-law. He pats her back; then with his hand, he gestures she go sit behind her desk; he takes Drexel's chair. Mr. Fukadero Senior levels with Chloe, "Too bad about Suhki, he was solid. No word from Dean lately either, eh?" Chloe solemnly listens; her head is still. He pulls his hat off by pinching the top. "I know how my son worked. So, Chloe, where's the coke hidden?"

33

Damon carries his tools to the side of the house. *This day came fast, it's strange to never really get a day off. The hours I put in, I should be rich. But I get more troubles than they're worth.* He sees the air conditioner on the side of the house, halfway toward the end of the wall; it's the same distance from the front to the back. On the other side of the wall, inside the house, is the mechanical room for the home.

Damon assesses the yard. *The cost of these big yards has skyrocketed; it's three hundred yards to the fence from each side of the house. Enough tree and bush around to give the impression this house is alone. Well, might as well text them then take the inspection panel off.*

Damon pulls out his phone, then he suddenly hears heavy feet running from behind him; he sees a flash of light as he is hit from behind. When he regains focus, he is on the ground being held around his neck from behind.

Damon looks up and sees two heavyweight, mid-twenty year old guys staring down at him. With two hands

Damon grips the arm that has his neck, but he has no control of the choker who has him; the arm is a vice. He's securely held from behind, in a solid rear naked choke. Damon's consciousness begins to fade to black just as the choker's arm relaxes; Damon gasps for air.

The voice of the choker in filled with rage. "Where is Dean, motherfucker?"

Damon tries to move, but feels the choker has both his legs wrapped around Damon's legs, and is yanking them apart like two hooks. Damon is too afraid to let go of the choking arm to even consider using his hands to free his legs, he can't stop another choke either. So Damon answers. "Dean who?"

The choker laughs ruthlessly. "Dave, Steve, watch how fast I send this weak-ass hitman to his grave." Damon feels the choke arm tighten slowly like a snake. The choker hisses. "Tap if you want to tell me where Dean is before you die."

Damon taps out by lifting his finger up and down on the choke arm ever so lightly. As the arm lets loose, Damon's hearing is cutting out, and his surroundings are blurry. *No blood to the brain is worse than no air.* Damon's Simple voice urges him. *Look at the guys standing above you. Hehehe.* Damon replies out loud. "No."

Drexel tightens the choking arm. "What's 'no' mean?" He shakes Damon like an alligator, and Damon's hand is whipped off the choke arm. Damon wants to look at the guys standing close by, but the attacker holds him facing the air conditioner as he sqeezes the full choke on Damon.

Damon feels a splash hit his ear. The choker rolls onto his back, which drags Damon to view the guys who are standing; only one guy is there. Then the choke arm loosens, Damon gasps for air. Out of habit, Damon counts in his head after the first splash of blood hit his face and the wall beside him.

One, two, three. Bang.

This time he's forced to watch a hole appear in the centre of the forehead of the other heavyweight; the back of his scalp flies up like a shirt on a clothesline hit by the wind. Another spray of blood blows out of the entry hole and covers Damon's face. The choker lets go and log rolls away, then flips up and sprints, going left and right in steps of three. Damon sees the running pattern and knows Gabriel will see the pattern as well.

Bang.

The round catches Drexel in the right shoulder, and he stumbles while running around the corner of the house. Damon is coughing and choking from the death choke, but he manages to draw his suppressed .45 pistol from under his coveralls and scurries to the corner of the house. Drexel is going out the front gate; there's no clear shot because of the cars parked in the driveway. Damon goes back and grabs his tool bag; he has a brief look at the two corpses that had been standing above him twenty-five seconds ago. *"Both headshots, the exit wounds on both guys are a seven-inch mess that were the backs of their heads. Damon makes eye contact with one of the bodies, eyes frozen in an unblinking stare. With a volcano of brain and skull splattered for fifteen feet. Time to go.*

Damon gets into the white Safari van, more distraught at seeing the strangler run away than he is worried about the gunfire. He throws his tools on the floor on the front seat. He keeps his pistol on his lap in case anyone wants to have a gunfight. Backing up nice and slow, he heads down the driveway. At the gate, he has his hand on the HK .45 ACP, but no one is around. He pulls out and leaves at a regular driving speed.

ABBOTSFORD, 11:15 A.M.

Damon is on Highway 1, heading to a spot where he will get rid of his clothes and wipe the van down. He has time to reflect. *It really was only twenty to twenty-five seconds before Gabriel aimed the first round at the guys trying to kill me. It felt like an hour. I'm glad their first ambush was reversed. I would have needed old Gabriel watching my back for months. Now he's free to go back to his quiet life. I'm sure by the way Gabriel was raised in Poland, he's having no trouble with his own escape and evasion plan.*

So that's it, the Grim Sinners are after us still. They do know who we are. This is the most useless fight ever. These kids are defending a dead thief, and they'll want justice for a few dead would-be murderers.

Nobody has studied anything about making money, obviously. We are officially fighting over nothing but revenge. Revenge stacked on revenge. The dark demon is having a heyday. It has Suhki's crew locked in a death match with the truckers, and a street gang after me and the Polish. How can this end well, does anybody care about calming this situation down?

PORT KELLS, 11:00 A.M.

Sara is in the Port Kells warehouse; she executed a warrant on it this morning at 9:00 a.m. They have a mid-thirties man in custody. He's not saying anything, but his ID reads Paul Warshouski. He emigrated to Canada from Poland ten years ago. The surveillance officers say this is the guy they've watched come and go from the warehouse.

Sara has been moving boxes with the other officers, searching for anything suspicious, for the last two hours. Nothing yet. Her phone rings. "Sara here."

It's Bill; he sounds calm, but she hears a little bit of shakiness in his voice. "Sara, come to this address, I'll text you. It's a double murder. I'm on scene now." Sara was going to tell him she's in the middle of a search at the suspected hitman's warehouse, but decides that nothing of importance is happening here. She strides over to the most senior person in the room, quickly explains why she's leaving, appoints them in charge, then lightly jogs to her police cruiser.

SOUTH SURREY, 12:00 P.M.

Two Grim Sinners have been shot and killed, so Sara and the Wolf walk around together to cover some ground while surveying for evidence at the double murder property. Sara explains how she's lost in her investigation of the Fukadero murder. Bill stops and turns toward her, but he doesn't touch her. She looks up to him.

Bill is compassionate in his explanation, "Sara, people have been killing each other since before the Bible was written. We try and keep it to a minimum. Listen to me; I asked you to take on the Fukadero case because it's really just the tip of the iceberg. The Tony Fukaderos of the world are embedded in so many layers of criminality, we stay close and catch them as they pop up like whack-a-mole." Sara has to suppress her smile when she hears the Wolf use 'whack-a-mole' as a reference. He grins. "You ever play whack-a-mole? " She smiles.

Bill directs his talk to the business at hand. "We have a Grim Sinner in the hospital with a rifle wound in his shoulder, he's in surgery now. The doctor reports that Drexel should live. Possibly lose his arm. We have an all-out war starting in the South-Asian community. We're calling in our deep informant in the Grim Sinners today. Officers brought in Sheldon Smith, aka Rocket; he will be our murder witness. He's also been supplying and buying drugs for three years. I'm going to the office now, I got a call from the attorney, Mr. Livion. He's bringing Mr. Fukadero Senior to my office for something." Sara listens intently, feeling foolish being so out of the loop in this investigation. Bill smiles, "Meet me back at E Division. We depart now."

Bill shouts to a uniformed officer, "We're leaving, send someone over to continue the search in this area."

SURREY, E DIVISION, 2:00 P.M.

The Wolf sits in his office with two gentlemen in front of him, one in a crisp grey suit with a red tie, classic politician. The other in an old tweed suit that's pristine. They had shaken hands at the door.

Bill is leaning back in his chair, "Thank you both for coming here, it means a lot to us."

Mr. Livion lays his hands on the desk. "My client says that you have a record of his family helping the RCMP; Mister Fukadero has decided to work with the tradition."

Bill leans forward, "Yes, of course, how can we help each other this time."

Mr. Livion explains the prepared offer. "Mister Fukadero has recently become aware that his daughter-in-law has come into possession of some cocaine. Being young and naive, she tried selling it to Dean Schmitt, who then sold it to the Grim Sinners. Chloe also gave the gangster Suhki and Jag a couple of kilos of this cocaine. Mister Fukadero is suggesting that if we tell you the location of the remaining cocaine, you might be able to forget Chloe's involvement. You see, Bill, Chloe is four months pregnant with Mister Fukadero's grandchild. So her freedom is of the utmost important to the Fukadero family."

The Wolf sits at his desk, leaning off the back of his chair with his hands folded on top of each other. The three men have no problem sitting in silence for a few moments, while the Wolf absorbs what he's heard and makes a plan. Bill mulls, *I can't tell them about our Grim Sinner informant being brought in today. Mr. Fukadero figured out that his daughter messed up before we arrested her, well played. This family has been making deals since his kid was a teenager, I trust him to keep his word. I'll get another informant in place with the Fukaderos, since we're bringing one in today.*

The Wolf asks, "Who would you give the cocaine to?"

Mr. Livion has an answer ready. "A Grim Sinner named Drexel."

Bill smiles, "That won't work, he's in the hospital with a rifle wound in the arm." Mr. Livion and Mr. Fukadero glance at each other. The Wolf asks, "How much cocaine do you have in your possession?"

Mr. Livion clears his throat, "Ten kilos is all that Chloe has left of the twenty kilos she found after Tony Junior was taken from us."

The Wolf plants the seed for the next case. "Would you hold them for a week or so, then pick a Grim Sinner to give the ten kilos to?"

Mr. Fukadero shakes his head, "Come on sir, you-a know if-a we hand over ten kilos to some kid and he gets busted right after, everyone will know we're workin' with the police."

Bill quickly nods, "Of course, Tony, that's why you should give him two at a time. Until the ten are gone. We'll arrest him discreetly after a few months on some other evidence. We'll flip him onto the good guys' side, then you and Chloe are free from us again."

Mr. Livion gently asks, "How about the money from the drugs?"

The Wolf confirms, "You mean the evidence? Turn it over to us, of course."

Without hesitation, Mr. Fukadero agrees, "Of course."

"Can we do this, Mr. Fukadero? Without any trouble?" Mr. Livion asks.

Mr. Fukadero runs his hand through his white hair. "We're in trouble right now, ya buffoon. Of course we'll make-a this plan work; Bill is a smart man. We-a will-a listen to him." Mr. Fukadero stands and extends his hand; Bill stands and shakes it. Mr. Livion is waiting to shake hands next, but Bill moves around the desk to open the door.

The Wolf holds the door for the two men; he smiles and reaches his hand out to the attorney to shake. Mr. Livion gratefully takes the officer's hand. When the door shuts, Bill saunters back to his desk. And in a quiet voice that's lower than regular conversation, "Sara, come to my office for debriefing. End recording."

Sara sits in the control-room on another floor, listening to the meeting with two male officers. She stands to leave. The officer she was sitting next to asks her, "How are you enjoying working with the Wolf? Do you think you have kept up?"

Sara stands tall. "Nobody keeps up with their teacher in the first class." She cracks a big smile. The two male officers agree with knowing smiles.

SURREY, E DIVISION, 3:35 P.M.

Sara sits at the desk in the open area outside the Wolf's office. She writes a file essay for the RCMP long-term records. She had a thought about the Trowel informant, Peter. Sara sends an e-mail to Peter's handler: Peter has lost his opportunity to clear his drinking and driving record. The address he supplied for the suspected hitman was a dead end. The Polish man who works in the commercial unit in Port Kells is an industrial plumber with rock solid alibis for the day of Mr. Fukadero's murder. *I'll personally go to Peter's work and tell his boss about the impending loss of his driver's licence.*

Sara gets back to making an in-depth report about her overall perspective of the Fukadero murder case.

APRIL 24, NORTH BURNABY, 6:45 A.M.

Sara drives away from the ragtag cube-van delivery business located in a light industrial area south of Brentwood mall. The road is so old it is gravel in some areas. Sara sees Peter step out of a bus 300 yards from his work.

Peter pulls his sweater's hood up to hide from the rain. He's wearing a grey jogging suit with red Adidas cross trainers. He keeps his eyes on the ground as he walks.

I'm glad those cops are done with me. It's better to have no licence and not have to go to court as the guy who fingered Damon as Yakub's hitman. I'm sure the boss will let me wash trucks or something until I get my licence back.

———————————————

NORTH BURNABY, 7:30 A.M.

Peter shakes and sobs. He sits across from his boss in the seventy-year-old office space; the room is swaying, Peter's stomach is turning.

Peter's youthful fifty-five year old boss with his blonde hair and baby face. The boss speaks kindly and quietly. "Listen Peter, I'll tell you what I was told, and what I must do to protect the company. A real serious police officer was just in here, she told me you lost your driver's licence last night due to drinking and driving. She also said the RCMP have been dealing with you since the murder of a prominent business man. I asked her if you're involved with a murder and she said. *'All I can say is, Peter is close to the murder by association.'*"

Peter bawls. "Was it that bitch? The one who acts like a man?"

"I'm not allowed to talk about the officer. Her being here was confidential. I want you to know why I'm letting you go. I'm going to pay you for ten business days, but you have to leave the property today."

Peter stands and spits on the floor, then points at the boss. "You fucking asshole, I have a baby at home. I'm not in a gang. I never killed anyone. You going to tell everyone at work that I've been 'dealing' with the police? Huh? Is that it, I'm being fired for being a rat? Or a murderer? You're the rat! You work with the police. You fire me for them. Fuck you!"

The boss stares at his desk; trying not to inflame Peter. He calmly requests. "Would you please leave?"

Peter storms out of the office and runs down the stairs; halfway down to the main floor he stops to weep. He's five-seconds in and remembers he has a twenty-six-ounce of vodka in his locker. He lifts his head and, without wiping away the snot or tears, storms into the lunchroom at the bottom of the steps and opens the lock on his locker. Peter reaches in and grabs the bottle; it's already a quarter empty. He free-pours it into his mouth for eight-seconds.

A co-worker's voice interrupts him from behind. "Peter, I hope you're not driving today drinking that way?"

Peter lowers the bottle and answers calmly while facing in his locker. "I bet you don't, Kurt. You and the boss can't wait till I go eh? Stupid drunk rat me, eh?"

Kurt is used to Peter being a little buzzed and saying absurd things, but this is reaching. "What do you mean, rat? What do the boss and I think?"

Peter turns around with a sawed-off double-barrel twelve-gauge in his hand. Kurt raises both hands. "No Peter, I'm sorry. No, no."

Peter lets him get through the shop door, then he pulls the fire alarm. The small cinderblock lunchroom has a fire bell on the wall; it's deafening in the tiny room. Peter takes a couple steps over to the stairs to his boss's office. *When my boss gets to the bottom of the stairs he's getting a slug right in the stomach.*

A hand reaches in the door of the lunchroom and grabs the shotgun from the side; a round goes off while fighting for the sawed off shotgun. *Boom.* The hand lets go, and Peter swings around and aims at the worker who grabbed the gun. Peter angrily pulls the trigger, *click*. His co-worker is back-pedalling fast, his eyes fixed on Peter in horror.

Peter stumbles backwards and remembers he has to switch the barrels on this double-barrel shotgun. He fumbles while looking down; as he flicks the switch over, he's alone in the lunchroom. He only has one shot left.

Peter turns the barrel towards his right eye and pulls the trigger as soon as the barrel touches his eyelid. The back of his head paints the green lunchroom fridge and the white cinderblock walls behind him in thick red splatter.

34

Six days later, the newspapers and television news break the latest biggest story on the local gang turf war.

"Jagen Singh charged with the murder of Rangeet Amble. Jagen Singh left the country the night of the double homicide. He is believed to be in India at this time. The violence broke out at a wedding that included a trucking company executive that has been implicated in national drug transport. Jagen's brother-in-law Suhki Trivedi was killed at the scene. Also killed was a cousin of the trucking company president, Rangeet Amble. The police have arrested Devon Bhandari and Balginder Padmanabhan. The suspects were eye-witnesses, and arrived with Suhki and Jagen moments before the shooting began. Both are facing criminal charges, and neither is co-operating with the police about the night of the violence.

"In other news, there has been a double-homicide of two low-ranking Grim Sinners. Known to police, the victims are connected to a man with a severe gunshot wound that cost him his right arm; Drexel Davies, from

451

Trail, had a bullet in his arm that matched the ones that killed two more in a yard in South Surrey. Drexel Davies is not cooperating with police at this time.

"A high-ranking member of the Grim Sinners, known only as 'Mr. A,' is ready to testify against his former drug partners.

"One case that we may finally see closed. The murder of a young man from Trail who was strangled to death at a rave party in Trail, last year. 'Mr. A' claims he was an eye witness to Drexel Davies choking the young man last year, and states the murder was over who was to run a local dial-a-dope business. That business was reportedly bringing in fifty to a hundred thousand dollars a month in illegal gains.

"This long-term informant inside the Grim Sinners will be shedding light deep into the heart of the criminal underworld of the Lower Mainland; how the gangs interact, who is running them—"

Damon watches the news report with a coffee in his hand, wearing his black jogging pants with no shirt on. He watches a work truck park in front of his house; a dump truck is backing up as well. Damon doesn't pay it much attention; he reasons a neighbour must be doing some work. Then he's alerted by a knock on his door. He hops up and peeks through the blinds; he recognizes one of the crew from when his house was being built standing on his doorstep.

Damon opens the door and stands aside. "Come in Olek, it's been a long time."

Olek points at his boots. "I'd rather just start, I think we'll be done in two days."

Damon asks. "Do you want a coffee?"

"No, thank you. Yakub says we're to flatten your yard and put rich topsoil down, plant some good grass, then build you a concrete barbecue slab off your back porch. Is that okay with you?"

Damon is surprised. "If Yakub sent you here, then go ahead. I'll leave the back door open, you guys use the powder-room by the kitchen for the toilet, okay?"

Olek smiles, and they shake hands and depart. Damon calls over to Olek. "Hey, where can I find Yakub today?"

Olek scratches his chest. "He is with Alexi in Vancouver, you know the office?"

"Thanks Olek, would you lock the back door when you leave if we're not back by then?" Olek nods and waves goodbye as he walks away.

VANCOUVER, 11:30 A.M.

Damon reverses his parking pattern this time. When he arrives in Vancouver, he parks at Trout Lake and walks over to the notary office. Damon breathes in the warm air and acknowledges the big fluffy cumulus clouds that are blowing out to the East. He turns the corner on 12th and sees Yakub's work truck; that brings pep to Damon's step.

When he walks into the office, Olga comes around the desk and wraps her arms over Damon's and squeezes.

Damon feels the love in the hug and knows that the Fukaderos have paid back the money.

Yakub comes out of Alexi's office. "Damon, thank you for coming today, my brother." Yakub gives the same embrace as Olga did, but with a bear hug that makes some air squeeze out of him.

When Yakub puts him down, Alexi is waiting and take Damon's hand in a two-handed shake, and kisses both his cheeks. Damon smiles bashfully, "So…what changed?" Everyone in the office laughs, including Damon.

The three men go into Alexi's office. Yakub explains how Fukadero Senior's attorney contacted their attorney and said, "Case is over, we are sending a cheque." Yakub holds up a copy of the cheque. "It's real, we already cashed it. We are back in the black."

Damon doesn't want to mention that he didn't help with Suhki, but Yakub does. "Damon, I know you were trying to clear it up. That's how that street gang started to chase us. You stuck it out and helped clean that mess." Alexi pulls out the contracts he had drawn up and Damon had signed. Damon sees them. His heart sinks; he wanted to finish the job to get the rest of the contract paid out. Yakub watches Damon's lifeless eyes on the contract.

Yakub keeps his smile in check, "I sent the guys to pour you a twenty by twenty, four-inch concrete slab to barbecue on, and a few steps for out of your back door. We want you to have the twenty-five thousand dollars that's in the contract, in a cheque."

Damon's eyes come alive, a glowing smile appears. Old Alexi knows it's a deal and holds the old contract over the shredder. Damon exclaims. "Shred it. You guys have a deal. You both know you don't owe me anything. I even needed help to—"

Yakub holds his palm up flat. And with a confidant smile adds. "Let's move on without going over old friends' travel plans."

Damon is a little embarrassed that his client had to remind him to shut his mouth about the recent murders. Damon is humbled. "Of course."

Yakub slaps his hand onto his thigh, "Damon, did you hear the news about Peter's suicide at work?"

Damon nods, mirrors Yakub hand slap. "You never know where someone's mental state is."

Yakub keeps focused on his old uncle as he informs Damon of a couple details. "Damon, it was reported by Peter's boss and his co-workers that he was yelling about *'being a rat.'*" Yakub goes on to mention a friend's shop in Port Kells that was raided by police a week ago.

Damon's lip curls up for a second. "Yeah, that makes sense. I noticed some extra guys in vans hanging around for too long and at strange times, so I got a new place to put my tools last week," Damon eyes the two men, "When we stand by the fire, we might get burned. I know you guys did nothing wrong. Close calls are normal. You guys are golden in my books."

Yakub asks Damon. "Can you do a furnace install on my new construction job ? I'll pay for material if you'll carry the labour until the building sells. Will you do that for us?"

Alexi smiles while he watches the kids play nice. Damon answers cheerfully. "Holy moly man, you are all business. Yes, it's my pleasure to be on one of your sites."

SURREY, 5:30 P.M.

The show home parking lot has all ten spots filled, and the front door is locked for the private meeting taking place inside. The two groups are on either side of the tall table that runs down the middle of the show home, and all the lights are on. Some have tea or coffee, a few have water bottles that display the Fukadero logo on the labels.

On the side that faces the glass wall is the Fukadero group: Tony Senior, his brother Robby, and two other younger men stand back by the coffee machine holding their coffee cups, looking morose. The two older Italians wear almost identical tweed three-piece suits with polished black shoes.

The group that faces the back wall and have their backs to the front glass wall are Suhki's family: this includes his father-in-law Zoltan and Suhki's younger brother Naresh. This family also brought two other men; both are grey-haired gentlemen who arrived in a new BMW X7. Everyone on this side is also dressed with respect for the meeting, Naresh in a two-piece suit and the three adults in three-piece suits that they had custom-made back in India.

Wearing a baby-blue pantsuit with blue heels, Chloe stands at the end of the counter, her eyes fixed on the centre of the table; no refreshments in front of her, she holds a file with a thin pile of documents inside.

Everyone had shaken hands and completed formal introductions as the refreshments were handed out by the two younger Italian men, who are both over forty-five years old. Mr. Fukadero Senior starts the meeting. "Please, allow-a me to give our deepest condolences for the loss-a Suhki. He was a young man, I admired him and wanted to see-a him rise in this world. I believed in him. He used to hug me and I'd kiss-a his cheek."

All of Suhki's family nods lightly in agreement. Zoltan places his teacup down as he speaks. "Mr. Fukadero, your family tried to make a deal for us to prosper together. You lost your son in all of our ambitions to get ahead. The Trivedi and Singh family send our deepest regret for your loss."

All of the Italians gently nod. Mr. Fukadero stared at the table as Zoltan spoke; he raises his eyes. "Thank Zoltan, this is a tragic time. But we, the living, have to carry on, agreed?"

The older South-Asian men are slowly nodding in the affirmative. Zoltan moves along, "We agree. What are you thinking, sir?"

Mr. Fukadero has both hands on his hips as he speaks across the table. "We've dropped the case against the Polish. We have already paid them out as well. That is over, for now." The Italian group watches the Indian group get hit with this information. All at once they retract their heads back with wide eyes. On cue, they all gain composure. Tony Senior gently nods.

This family is close, they all react the same.

Tony moves his hands off his hips, and clasps both hands together level with his belly button as he delivers the next news. "Suhki and Chloe made a property deal for the end of the court case against the Polish being instigated by Suhki. It was not, I paid to end the fighting. Do you all agree to void the contract that Suhki and Chloe were working off of? Or are you going to take us to court?"

Zoltan and Naresh glance at each other. Naresh answers, "Mr. Fukadero, it's only fair to void the property agreement under these circumstances." Tony Senior looks to Chloe; she unfolds the file in front of her. She writes VOID in big letters across the page with the signatures and the cover page. Mr. Fukadero had taken a long breathe in while listening, and he lets it out while explaining, "I'm glad you see it this way. We will need to sell that house to pay the Polish contractors."

Zoltan has both his hands on the table, his head faces the ground as Chloe writes the void note on the contracts. He lifts his head, staring at Chloe, "The collection for the hundred kilos; how much did you tell Suhki we would get?" All the South-Asian men give Chloe their full attention.

Tony Senior raises his tone. "We know she promised Suhki half-a da profit." Chloe stares at the ground, silent. Tony Senior goes on. "Chloe has been though a lot. She is-a four months pregnant with my dead son's-a baby, you know that?"

Zoltan nods, "My daughter Zarita and Chloe became friends a while back, Chloe told her the news at that time. Now both of you are widows." Zoltan shuts his eyes to fight back some tears that suddenly appear. Then asks a little harsher then he intends, "Do we get to keep half of the collection Suhki died for? We want to make them pay still."

Tony stands silent for a moment, until Zoltan turns his head to him. Mr. Fukadero replies, "Of course we will-a make it work, I need-a to make a deal with the guy who sent it to us. They understand wars, they'll help us all make it work. They already sent me a few kilo of the coke to keep the business going. I'll deliver them wherever you need. Same deals as Suhki was getting."

Zoltan feels better after hearing the older wise man help everyone move forward. He opens his mouth to talk, but Suhki's younger brother Naresh jumps in. "Hold on, that was Suhki's business plan, not mine. I run what's left of my house now and—"

Zoltan touches his arm gently, "It's an open offer, we are friends here. Opportunity is good."

Naresh turns to gauge the older men they have brought, both are nodding in agreement with Zoltan. Naresh proclaims, "We need to keep our contractors working first, period."

Tony Senior nods, "Your father did a good job with you and Suhki. I see how similar you both are. I don't hold you to any deals your brother made. I want to support your family. We will make sure to call you, Naresh, with construction quotes, okay? Does that help you-a?"

Naresh, who has always kept calmer than Suhki, watches the old man's face,

"Okay Tony, thank you. I never want to talk about drugs again, okay?"

Tony nods, "Anything for you-a."

Zoltan ends the meeting, "Tony, I think we are done here. I'll call you this week, you and I will go over some details alone."

Mr. Fukadero comes around the table and, starting with Naresh, gives everyone a hug with cheek kisses before they leave. Before they exit, Tony Senior announces. "Oh yeah, nobody is-a to contact Chloe about anything. No drug talk, no collection talk. She is done with that life. She is-a mommy soon." Everyone in the room turns their eyes to Chloe; she meets the stares and bashfully smiles as they nod and exit.

Tony turns around and asks to his two younger associates, "Would-a you two wait out front?" They put their cups in the trash and walk out silently. Tony Senior takes off his blazer and lays it on a chair. He walks over to the side of the table that faces the wall, while his brother stays seated in the middle of the long table facing the glass wall.

Tony has compassion in his voice, but this is clearly a one-way information session. "Chloe, our baby in your tummy is all that matters, capeesh?" Chloe lifts her head, locks eyes with her father-in-law for mercy, for all of her plans that failed. "Me and my brother will take the coke-a from the house tonight. We will deal with all that now. With no Dean, it is only us three that know about the stolen load of coke-a, capeesh?" Chloe's eyes overflow while nodding in agreement with her best honest face.

Tony Senior is just getting started. "We are selling the house you are in to cover the Polish debt, it's still a win. They are owed the money. So it's just no free house for you and Tony." Chloe's mouth drops open; she has envisioned raising her child in that castle. Tony Senior comforts her, "It's for the best-a, that place will be falling apart in fifteen years, how you gonna keep-a house that big, with no man?"

Chloe almost blurts out, 'I'll have another man by then who will pay for it.' But realizes how bad that sounds under the circumstances.

"Where will I live?"

"Sweetheart, you're still going to run our sales here at the show home, you will be a realtor to anyone that you rope in as well. But its best-a to keep costs-a down. So you will go to stay in the place you and Tony bought your mom."

Chloe bursts out, "It's in a trailer park!"

Tony Senior gently touches her shoulder with the tips of his fingers, "It's-a fully paid for, it's-a beautiful place. I went and looked when-a I saw it on-a the company books. We are family Chloe, you-a will never go without. We gotta keep-a tha costs down while we weather this tough-a time. You make-a good-a money on each sale of a house. If you-a want to save some down payment, we will help you with financing. Okay? Capeesh? That's done." Chloe shuts her mouth and stares down the centre of the table into her empty office.

Tony Senior lays his hands flat on the table, "I called the car dealership about the Lamborghini. They say-a if-a we give them-a twenty thousand dollars they will-a take car back as is. My brother will-a take it back in the morning. Capeesh? That's done too. Over, no more worries."

Chloe asks quietly, "What will I drive to work and to baby appointments? Alone."

Tony consoles her, "You are not alone-a, little girl-a, we are a family." Chloe's tears are pouring; Tony Senior closes on her quickly and gives a tender hug, "Don't worry about a car-a, relax-a stay calm-a, remember the baby. We have-a my brother's wife's Corolla you-a can drive."

MAPLE RIDGE, 6:00 P.M.

Sara is in black BDU pants and a grey shirt, with a bottle of Budweiser in her hand; she sits at an old wooden picnic table with her husband. She watches Bill take the sausages off a tray his wife has put beside the barbecue and place them on the grill. Bill is in beige BDU pants and a dark blue shirt. He smiles, and waves Sara over with the giant barbecue tong. She stands and walks over with her beer in hand.

Bill suggests. "Let's talk work before everyone is ready to eat. What's on your mind?"

"I'm really bothered by how off-track I took the Fukadero murder case. It turned into a mess."

Bill shakes his head as he rolls the bratwurst around with his tongs. "No, it's already a mess. We just directed it. You ever notice that the civilians outnumber us a bit?

Five hundred to one or some crazy number."

Sara hears the pork fat sizzle, and nods. "I understand that, but what was my goal then? How do we gauge success?"

The Wolf's eyes glint; as he grabs his Budweiser and takes a long pull before he answers. "Okay, Tony Fukadero was dealing with drugs and stealing contractors' money. Tony had worked for us since he was a teenager getting into trouble. All we ever did was follow him and make arrests for twenty years. From his murder, we arrested a street gang's head killer, Drexel. So that's one murder solved. We have a new lead on a major drug smuggling ring in the South-Asian trucking company, Pacific to Atlantic. We have an informant building leads in the Grim Sinners for the next time we need to calm a blood-feud down. You get it yet?"

Sara nods along, but her eyes dart back and forth. She questions, "So we plan to always have informants in each crime group so that when total war breaks out, we have a chance to shut it down?"

Bill spells it out. "You're analyzing one dimension. We're aiming for arrests the whole time. We will get more during this fight between Suhki Trivedi's crew and this trucking company. The Grim Sinners are loosely bound to silence, how many quiet speed-freaks you ever talked to?" They both smirk. "Drexel's girlfriend is an example, Shelly, who took off to Alberta when we brought Rocket in to begin testifying. Shelly took a bag of coke to the strip-bar she applied to work at. Our local RCMP member utilized a local waitress informant that had her house wired from another investigation. We recorded about fifteen hours of Shelly going over every detail of the murder that Rocket is saying happened. We have our long-term informant Rocket's testimony that Drexel killed that kid at the rave, and Drexel's girlfriend's voice confirming it."

Sara adds, "I think we count her clearly saying it twenty-eight times, and another nine that she tried to whisper." They both sip on their beers, this time with their eyes gleaming. Sara asks her main thought. "What about Damon and his dad?"

Bill pauses rolling the Bratwursts, "When you spoke to him, did you get the feeling he was dangerous? Like a domestic terrorist, or child killer?"

Sara's face is neutral. "There was no reason to think that, he was at the fair with his wife and son. He lives in my neighbourhood."

Bill asks, "Okay, imagine: Drexel is still free, so is Damon. Who do you follow to try to catch a violent criminal?"

Sara answers confidently, "Drexel, he's fueled by chemical drugs and two-day parties."

"That's it right there. The truckers have a hitman of some kind, Suhki's family will most likely employ a hitman. Should we go sitting on a guy we think might be a hitman or follow actual feuding families?"

"Okay, I get it. We're in a war-zone, and going after the most violent group at any moment." Bill tips his beer towards her for a cheers; they tap bottle tops and bottom-up both their beers.

Bill's wife pops out of the kitchen quickly, "Our grand-baby is here." Bill passes the tongs to Sara, "You're on the grill, I need to see my grand-baby." Sara is genuinely surprised to see the Wolf giddy and bouncing on his toes as he runs to the house to see his prized children and grandchild.

Sara frantically rearranges the sausages.

Bill is burning this half of the grill, I thought he was cooking these, not burning them.

He only mentioned the death of my informant once, when he confirmed I was seeing the company shrink.

Bill had said, "*You know Sara, I have a regular appointment with our psychiatrist. Most senior officers do. She'll help you guide your thoughts to more positive subjects. We're the front line in this society. It's disturbing.*"

Sara is staring at the grill, the smoke billowing around her head. She has a new feeling come over her, one she never expected. Disappointment, mixed with anger. She lightly shakes her head while keeping her head in the barbecue smoke to hide her face. *Bill is broken. We can do better. We should be arresting every criminal and grabbing the new ones that fill their spots. I'll do it, I'll create a stronger team. I won't tell the shrink how I'm going to change the system or she'll tell me to take a paid leave. I'll slowly gain rank and authority and clean Surrey.*

Sara snaps back, Bill stands in front of the barbecue, holding his three-year-old granddaughter, clearly waiting for Sara to notice him. He has an understanding smile for

Sara. "Sara, come around here and hold this adorable little girl, she cheers everyone up." Sara does lighten up at the sight of the toddler in a cute white dress.

SURREY, 6:30 P.M.

The sun is low in the sky. The sky is grey with a yellow overtone, with no wind, no clouds. Tony Senior and his brother Robbie are standing on the front stoop of his late son's stone house, looking out toward the street. They have come for the slime green Lamborghini.

Tony Senior speaks in Italian, asking his younger brother the same question again. "Do you think Angelo had my boy killed for taking his daughter's flower?"

Robbie shakes his head confidently, "No Tony. I took him out duck hunting and questioned him when we were alone. He swears he's mad, but not that mad; the girl was nineteen. She's not a child. Angelo said he would do the lie detector for you."

Tony Senior brushes off the idea. "I believe him, it's over, I won't ask again." Tony Senior looks forward, his weathered face stoney as he speaks. "We will keep those Indians close. You know that maybe that big kid Suhki had Tony killed for some coke-selling territory. With Suhki dead, one of his guys might leak it. We will listen real close. Good work, brother, in getting the Polish hired to build that house in North Burnaby. We will listen real close to them too, if I had to make a solid guess I'd say the

Polaks did this. You remember that Tony had Dean put away for six years…maybe Chloe and Dean made a deal of some sort, eh?"

Robbie puts his arm around his older brother; both older men have a couple tears streaming. Robbie hugs Tony tightly. "Tony, we can't guess all night. We will always chase the killer. With all this coke to sell, everyone on the street will come to us. Someone will talk. We will handle the killer the way we always have. Death sentence."

LANGLEY, 8:00 P.M.

Damon closes the door on Benji's bedroom. As he walks down the hall Naomi lets him know, "Patch never got a walk today." The ninety-pound white boxer runs across the kitchen when he hears the word walk. Damon and Naomi laugh, as the dog's feet move fast on the tile. He's doing the Scooby-Doo cartoon run on the spot.

Damon and Patch are about five blocks from his house when Damon has a sobering thought. *By accepting the furnace job from Yakub, I'm staying involved in the mess.* Damon's all-knowing voice asks him, *Who's making you stay involved? Who's making your future?*

Damon answers out loud, "I am. I am staying close to these problems for work and supporting friends. It's so easy really."

35

Damon is in the cul-de-sac kicking a soccer ball back-and-forth with Benji. Naomi is in the house getting dinner ready. Damon would swear his kid isn't even trying to kick the soccer ball to him. Benji looks to the right of Damon as he boots the ball, and the ball flies past Damon on the left. Damon takes off full speed, laughing. *I can't even guess where he's aiming, he's definitely just making me run.* As Damon sprints, he notices Benji places his hands on his hips and smiles ear-to-ear while he watches his dad chase the ball.

A black Ford Taurus car comes around the corner, with blacked out windows and black steel rims. Damon knows right away that this is a police interceptor, an unmarked vehicle. He grabs the ball while running and hops onto the curb. He checks where Benji is standing; the boy is heading to a curb as well. The black police interceptor parks in front of the neighbour that has the F250 and never waves. Damon crosses the street and walks the sidewalk to his son. The driver steps out, " Good evening, Damon."

Damon recognizes her right away; the officer from the fair. He stops and juggles the soccer ball between his hands. Damon asks, "You working right now? Or visiting friends?"

Sara hesitates. *Not shy with the questions, is he?* "I'm always on duty, even when I'm not."

Damon smiles as he jokingly asks, "So if you're off duty and you see a car doing fifty in a thirty zone, you're going after them?"

Sara is initially angered by his comment, then remembers she told Damon she was a general duty officer, "If our helicopter is close enough and I can get a swat team to help, that guy is getting his speeding ticket."

Damon is surprised by her answer and gives a wide-eyed laugh.

The owner of the F250 open his front door, "Hi Sara, I've only got fifteen minutes, will you come in?"

Sara heads to the house, "Yes, of course."

Damon sees his chance and syncs up with Sara as she walks to the house. Sara slows her walk, "Where are you going?"

Damon keeps the pace, "I live here, this is my neighbour's house." Sara has her mouth half open when Damon gets to the front door. First, he introduces himself. "Hi, I'm Damon, I live across the road. Do you work with Sara? That's my son right over there." Damon waves to his boy, and Benji waves back.

The man reaches out and shakes Damon's hand. "I'm Russ, I'm in a different department than Sara. Do you work with her?"

Damon smiles. "No, just friends from around the neighbourhood."

Sara crosses her arms; she stares at Damon like he's a street performer and waits for his next trick.

Alice yells over to the yard the three are standing in. "Hey Damon, you said you would wash my air conditioner one day, from all the dust. Do you remember?"

Damon looks back and forth between the two officers gritting his teeth and sucking air in, and both officers smile. Damon leans over and yells, "Okay, Alice, but I'm training a new guy on hose spraying on your unit." Alice opens and closes her mouth, she swings her cane around. Damon yells, "Benji let's go, meet me over at Alice's front lawn. You're my hose spray technician today." The boy keeps an eye on Damon and bolts towards Alice's. Damon accepts the challenge; he begins his run, he calls over his shoulder, "Nice to see you, Sara. Nice to meet you, Russ."

Sara pulls her self into the house when they shake hands. "I'd need more than fifteen minutes to explain this situation; it's delicate, to say the least. It's about your neighbour..." Russ shuts the door.

Damon is at the driveway, Benji on the lawn. Damon directs his boy, "Okay, Benji, we're working, you have to walk on the path of the house when you're working so you don't make a mess of their lawn."

Benji walks over ultra-slow with his eyes on the lawn, "I'm not making a mess on the lawn." They both walk on the path to the air conditioner around the side of the house. Damon sees the light film of dust on the coils of the air conditioner, *A yard hose will wash this off.*

What's that, a car coming down the block? Oh, that's my other neighbour.

"Hey Benji, let's play a game, do you see that car?"

Benji answers, "Yes, it's right there." The boy points as it drives by.

Damon whispers, "Let's watch it like a cat, no sound." The boy crouches and growls as he watches. Damon quietly asks. "Why are you growling?

"I'm not a cat, I'm a tiger."

At that instant, Benji leaps at Damon who is crouched beside him, and they tumble onto the lawn scratching and growling at each other.

Alice comes around the corner. "I bring you hard-working guys cookies, and you're playing."

Damon knows she's kidding, but he plays along and acts serious. Benji looks back and forth between the two adults and decides they're joking, so he gently smiles.

Alice beams at Benji, "these are fresh chocolate-chip cookies, eat these and I'll give you more to take home."

They answer in unison, "Thanks, Alice."

The End

ACKNOWLEDGEMENTS

The first person I have to thank is Trish, for putting a fire under my backside to get this book out of my head. Trish was also the first reader, and introduced me to common writing guidelines. I had no idea about character arcs before I wrote this book. Thank you.

Second, thanks to my beautiful and patient wife for making the time available for me to write this book. Keeping our two kids busy during the same block of time every day for three months made writing this possible.

Also, my wife came in at a clutch moment; catching spelling errors and tense consistency. We relied on an acquaintance who had volunteered to copy edit. This arrangement dissolved after ninety days, leaving us with the first draft and three months gone. My wife jumped in and went through the manuscript line by line. She would put our two-year-old baby and our elementary age boy to bed, then edit until midnight. I followed behind with deeper edits. At the end we were glad we had the opportunity to do the work ourselves. Thank you so much, my angel!

I want to thank Sensei C for helping with the backyard fight scene. C has a lifetime of training in Judo. I asked about the scene in the backyard, and C knew right away how to describe the situation. Talking about 'real' self-defence with a professional instructor was lots of fun. Sensei is a healthy and fit woman who is very kind and caring, and I have no doubt she would smash most men, definitely me. Thank you.

I am giving a big shout-out to my father-in-law. He is a loving family man with a long successful career. But the street fight stories he graphically told over beers were a major influence in the biker beat-down story. Thanks for the front row seat at story-time.

I must thank Bob for coming up with the name iHIT. Bob and I met one day for a coffee at the Vancouver Public Library. He sat and looked me in the eye and said, ' I have a good name for your book.' I immediately thought, *Yeah right, there's no way I'm letting somebody else name the book.* He said, "iHIT." I said, "No way, that's insane!" Bob held up his hand gently and explained, "It could be spelled like the iPhone, with a small i. You know how the book is about a hitman, well, iHIT." I knew right then and there that this was the name. Bob has a history in marketing and he nailed it. Everyone loves iHIT. Thank you.

I can't forget my mom and dad. I have to thank my mom for telling me, 'you can do anything.' And my dad for teaching me to be honest and to work hard.

Generally, I need to thank every person who has given me a hand to advance my education or career. I have had so many amazing instructors over the last twenty years,

I won't name you all. Although I'm sure you remember having me as a student, taking me by the hand, and showing me your craft. I love you all.

Regardless of the challenges I face, I have been blessed with smart and good-hearted friends. Thanks to all of you.

CPSIA information can be obtained
at www.ICGtesting.com
Printed in the USA
LVHW011041110322
713034LV00002B/172

9 781525 578472